WAGER OF THE HEART

"If you are correct about me," Rockham said, "I should be made to pay for my dishonesty."

"On that we agree," Aimee said with a light laugh.

"However," James said softly, "if you are wrong, is it not only fair that you should be the one to pay?"

Aimee turned toward him instantly, snapping her fan shut. "What are you suggesting, your grace?" she questioned warily.

"A wager," James stated, his eyes gleaming.

"A wager!"

"Between you and me."

Aimee's eyes widened. "And just what would this wager entail?" she asked, not masking her curiosity very well at all.

Rockham smiled slowly. He had her now, he knew. She would agree to the wager. And if fate would just cooperate, by tomorrow . . .

"It would hinge, of course, upon the discovery of Calladorn's Fire," he told her. "I propose that if you are correct about me and no diamond is found, I will proclaim myself a fraud in all the London papers and gladly suffer the consequences."

"And if I am not correct?" Aimee queried. "If it *is* found?"

"Then you will acknowledge that I behave honorably, Miss Winthrop, and you will pay for your scurrilous accusations with your hand."

"My hand!" Aimee exclaimed. "In marriage?"

"Exactly . . ."

—from DUKE OF DIAMONDS, by Jenna Jones

ZEBRA REGENCIES
ARE
THE TALK OF THE TON!

A REFORMED RAKE   (4499, $3.99)
by Jeanne Savery

After governess Harriet Cole helped her young charge flee to France—and the designs of a despicable suitor, more trouble soon arrived in the person of a London rake. Sir Frederick Carrington insisted on providing safe escort back to England. Harriet deemed Carrington more dangerous than any band of brigands, but secretly relished matching wits with him. But after being taken in his arms for a tender kiss, she found herself wondering— *could* a lady find love with an irresistible rogue?

A SCANDALOUS PROPOSAL   (4504, $4.99)
by Teresa DesJardien

After only two weeks into the London season, Lady Pamela Premington has already received her first offer of marriage. If only it hadn't come from the *ton's* most notorious rake, Lord Marchmont. Pamela had already set her sights on the distinguished Lieutenant Penford, who had the heroism and honor that made him the ideal match. Now she had to keep from falling under the spell of the seductive Lord so she could pursue the man more worthy of her love. Or was he?

A LADY'S CHAMPION   (4535, $3.99)
by Janice Bennett

Miss Daphne, art mistress of the Selwood Academy for Young Ladies, greeted the notion of ghosts haunting the academy with skepticism. However, to avoid rumors frightening off students, she found herself turning to Mr. Adrian Carstairs, sent by her uncle to be her "protector" against the "ghosts." Although, Daphne would accept no interference in her life, she *would* accept aid in exposing any spectral spirits. What she never expected was for Adrian to expose the secret wishes of her hidden heart . . .

CHARITY'S GAMBIT   (4537, $3.99)
by Marcy Stewart

Charity Abercrombie reluctantly embarks on a London season in hopes of making a suitable match. However she cannot forget the mysterious Dominic Castille—and the kiss they shared—when he fell from a tree as she strolled through the woods. Charity does not know that the dark and dashing captain harbors a dangerous secret that will ensnare them both in its web—leaving Charity to risk certain ruin and losing the man she so passionately loves . . .

Available wherever paperbacks are sold, or order direct from the Publisher. Send cover price plus 50¢ per copy for mailing and handling to Penguin USA, P.O. Box 999, c/o Dept. 17109, Bergenfield, NJ 07621. Residents of New York and Tennessee must include sales tax. DO NOT SEND CASH.

Lords and *Ladies*

DOROTHEA DONLEY
JEAN R. EWING
PAULA TANNER GIRARD
JENNA JONES
MEG-LYNN ROBERTS
MARCY STEWART

ZEBRA BOOKS
KENSINGTON PUBLISHING CORP.

A MATTER OF HONOR
by Paula Tanner Girard

DUKE OF DIAMONDS
by Jenna Jones

FOR ALL ETERNITY
by Meg-Lynn Roberts

LADY CONSTANCE WINS
by Marcy Stewart

CONTENTS

Taste of London

Dorothea Donley

Onε

It was darkening dusk, almost night, as two gentlemen sat facing each other in deep leather armchairs beside a warm grate, with a large leather stool between them to accommodate their feet and a large black-and-white cat. Nearby a table and tray with assorted bottles and glasses waited untouched.

"What are we doing here?" asked Lord Aldford, after a long silence.

"I am keeping you company," replied the other gentleman, who had been his friend for fifteen years. They had met at Eton, where the young lord's skill with his fists had defended the smaller boy, whose aptitude for Latin benefited them both. "What you are doing I cannot say."

"One always goes to London for the Season," said his lordship without much enthusiasm, "to look over the new crop of Pretties, but every year they grow younger and sillier."

"No, no. You are getting *older.*" Mr. Radnor allowed himself a chuckle. As his host started to speak, he added hurriedly, "Not old, dear fellow—may I say wiser?"

"You may say whatever you please to me, Charles. I shall not claim *wisdom* but will admit that I find the Mamas militantly ambitious and the young girls all too anxious."

"That is because you are a catch, Lewis. Title and wealth. Title and wealth. No one is pursuing *me.*"

"Only because they do not know about your tidy estate in

Somerset. I've half a mind to bolt. If I go home to Helmsworth, will you go with me?"

Lord Aldford's question went unanswered, for at that moment his portly butler, Serle, came to announce that two ladies were calling.

"Ladies? My house? This hour?"

"Yes, my lord," said Serle with gentle emphasis, *"ladies."* He extended two cards.

Having some recollection of one name, the viscount got to his feet, smoothed down his coat of blue superfine, and commanded his friend to come along and protect his reputation. The cat also rose and transferred itself into a circle on the cushion warmed by its master.

Being both obliging and curious, Mr. Radnor at once stood, and the two followed Serle to the front of the house, where a maidservant of disapproving mien sat against the wall. They hardly noticed her, for Serle was throwing open the door to a front parlor in which he with perfect discretion had deposited the unknown ladies.

Still holding the calling cards, Lord Aldford advanced into the room and addressed the elder lady, who, without jewels or high-fashion garb, managed to convey an aura of elegance.

"Miss Milner?" Aldford said.

"No, no," she replied with a slight, courteous smile. "I am Miss Amberly." She drew a younger girl forward. "This is Miss Milner. We wished to see Lord Aldford, who is cousin to Miss Milner's mother."

"I have been Lord Aldford for some months," said his lordship heavily and turned his eyes to the girl, words leaving him as he looked upon the exquisite beauty of anxious blue eyes, trembling rosy lips, and golden curls escaping from a brown bonnet with blue ribbons. A small sound from Mr. Radnor behind him recalled him to his manners. He said, "May I present my friend Mr. Radnor?"

Charles stepped forward with a bow. "Have you ladies just

reached London?" he asked, having noticed what Lord Aldford had not—that the visitors wore traveling cloaks.

"Indeed we have," replied Miss Amberly, who seemed to
be the speaker for the two. "We had hoped Lord Aldford—the
senior lord—would direct us to a suitable hotel in a respectable part of town, for we have not visited the city before now."

As the viscount continued to contemplate the charming
vision of Miss Milner, the conversation fell to Mr. Radnor's
responsibility.

"Did you come far?" he asked.

"From just outside Oxford," said Miss Amberly. "It has
been a very long day, and London seems bewildering in the
dark. Our postboys—we came post chaise, you see—were no
help. We had thought to call upon his lordship tomorrow, but
it seemed best to come directly here for advice."

Conscious that Serle waited in the doorway, Mr. Radnor
said, "You must be chilled. Lewis, the ladies need good hot
tea. *Lewis.*"

"Er—yes," said his lordship. "Tea, please, Serle."

Serle inclined his head and was replaced by a footman who
took the ladies' cloaks. Another came in to light the parlor
fire.

"Poor Nanny—" said Miss Milner faintly. It was the first
word she had spoken, but enough to reveal a melodious voice.
Both gentlemen regarded her with favor.

Awake now to his duties as host, Lord Aldford indicated
chairs, saw the ladies comfortably seated, and sat down opposite them with Mr. Radnor.

"Serle will see to your maid," he said. "You must be disappointed not to find my father. Did you come all the way in
one day?"

"It seemed wise for us to avoid a stay in a posting house,"
Miss Amberly explained, adding with another faint smile,
"We thought it best to promise a reward for fast travel, though
it meant jolting us to jelly—but we did not regard *that.*"

This sounded reasonable to gentlemen who routinely traveled at top speed.

"Miss Milner is just out of black gloves for her father, and I thought a change of scene would benefit her," Miss Amberly continued. "We wrote to Lord Aldford at Helmsworth, and his—your secretary replied that he would send our letter on to London as he—you were in residence here."

"Letter? I received no letter," asserted his lordship.

Mr. Radnor began to laugh, his slightly melancholy face brightening. "There is a pile of unopened mail on your desk. I saw that myself. Will you wager the letter is there?"

The viscount smiled ruefully. "You are right," he admitted.

Serle entered then to say, "It is beginning to rain, my lord. Shall I have the ladies' trunks brought in?"

Miss Amberly, appearing slightly taken aback that the servant should do his master's thinking, made a deprecating sound but allowed Lord Aldford to say, "Yes, yes. Pay the fellow off. My carriage can take the ladies where they wish to go after our tea. Where *is* our tea?"

"Just coming, my lord."

Serle stood aside for a footman to enter with a silver service large enough to serve a dozen. The ladies truthfully welcomed the hot beverage, for they were chilled and somewhat oppressed by the strangeness of a large city. They scarcely noticed Serle's departure to collect Nanny Bloom and take her away to the servants' hall. Mr. Radnor and their host also accepted cups with no thought of the excellent wines left behind in Aldford's study.

Miss Milner was now revealed to have a dainty figure, modestly gowned in blue, to match her eyes. She sat beautifully erect and managed her cup gracefully with slim, pretty hands—a very young girl, and shy, but unmistakably a lady Aldford could acknowledge as kin without mortification.

"How, exactly, are we connected, Miss Milner?" he asked.

"Not very closely," she admitted in a soft voice. "Lord Aldford—I mean, your father—was a cousin to my mother's father, which would make her a cousin-once-removed to him and second cousin to you. So you and I would have only a sort of *connection,* and you must not think Kate and I mean to hang upon your sleeve!" Her cheeks had become quite pink.

Just who Miss Amberly might be was not yet explained. Her figure, in a plain amber traveling dress, was slightly fuller than her protégée's. Perhaps if her dark hair had not been drawn back into a severe knot, and if her manner had been less quietly assured, the gentlemen would not have leaped to the conclusion that she was a paid companion or a governess.

Lord Aldford and his friend began to discuss just which hotel might be best suited to the ladies' comfort. His lordship recommended the Clarendon, but Mr. Radnor, fearing that might be beyond the ladies' purse, mentioned Ibbetson's as more economical.

"Convenient to good shops, please," said Miss Amberly, with her eyes sparkling in anticipation.

"Then it had better be Grillon's or the Pulteney."

There followed some debate with nothing settled until Mr. Radnor proposed that he and Lord Aldford drive the ladies past the hotels to let them choose.

"Too dark to see much, but perhaps they can select a neighborhood that pleases them," his lordship said, as he walked to call his housekeeper with a yank of the bell cord.

Serle entered promptly to ask what was desired. "Mrs. Eaton, my lord? She is waiting in the hall to be of service." He did not add that she was consumed with curiosity.

"Ah. There you are, Mrs. Eaton," said Aldford. "My cousin and her companion will be dining with us, and they will want to go upstairs to refresh themselves after a long ride. Er—will half an hour be enough, Miss Milner? Yes? You can have dinner ready for us then, Mrs. Eaton?"

"Certainly, my lord." She curtsied to the ladies and led them from the room. Serle followed.

When the door had closed, Lord Aldford asked his friend, "What do you think, Charles?"

"About what?"

"The ladies—dinner here—a hotel."

Mr. Radnor resumed his seat. "The *girls* are charming. I say 'girls,' for if the elder one pulled the pins from that knot of brown hair she would look almost as young as your cousin. Certainly you may properly give dinner to your relative and her friend. About a hotel I am less sure—even if they have a sharp-eyed nanny in attendance."

His lordship began to pace about. "Must I invite them to stay here? What am I to do?"

"Not my problem," replied Mr. Radnor, arching his brows and affecting to look blasé.

"You can be chaperon for them as well as for me."

Charles shook his head. "Not for young females who are no relation to me and with whom I am barely acquainted. Only one thing to do, Lewis. Send for Lady Crowden."

"Aunt Cora? Good God! I just got her out of my hair and settled in Merton."

"Haven't a choice, Lewis. Mustn't set the girls loose in London—shocking lack of family feeling. But if you install them here unchaperoned, you will discredit them forever."

His lordship groaned.

"I don't say you have to dance attendance," Mr. Radnor continued. "Just let people see they have your approval and let Lady Crowden set their steps aright. She may be low on funds, but she is on terms with everyone in the *ton,* isn't she?"

The viscount confirmed this. *"Le beau monde*—yes, and his highness himself."

"There you are. Nothing simpler."

"But Aunt Cora isn't here now."

"Who's to know she isn't? Or that the young ladies *are?* Send your carriage to Merton now, and you will have Lady Crowden back first thing in the morning. Can't tell me that Serle, or any of your staff, will tattle."

"Damn well better not!"

"No. I didn't think so." Turning more serious, Mr. Radnor

warned, "It would not take the bucks long to find them in a hotel!"

His lordship acknowledged this and went off to his study to pen a note to Lady Crowden. Once it had gone to the stable, he rejoined his friend and cautioned him to say nothing to the young ladies until he had had a chance for a private word with his cousin's companion.

"I will get Miss Amberly aside after dinner. You must distract my cousin—ask her to go into the music room to play for you, or sing, or something. All young females do that sort of thing."

"But suppose she doesn't?"

"Then ask her to turn pages while *you* play. Be inventive! Suggest a duet."

On an upper floor Mrs. Eaton, recognizing Quality and thinking faster than her employer, had conducted the two girls to a suite of rooms fronting on the square. These were a whole story above his lordship's chamber and the drawing room. They were entered via an anteroom which opened to two sleeping rooms. In the anteroom stood a daybed that would do nicely for the young ladies' maid, who was waiting there for them now. Their luggage had not been brought up, but already Mrs. Eaton had been preparing for them, for a fire was crackling in each chamber and hot water waited.

"My cousin is very civil and the other gentleman easy of conversation, Nanny. Aren't they, Kate?" said Phoebe, as Nanny brushed her hair.

Kate was shifting pins in her own dark knot. "Certainly *civil,*" she agreed, "but I cannot think Lord Aldford is glad to have us appear in his parlor. If you had not dazzled him, I daresay we would have been shown the door."

"Oh, Kate, I do not know how to *dazzle,*" said Phoebe.

"No, that is what is so charming about you. Let us go down."

By the time Phoebe and Kate were seated at dinner with the two men, a traveling carriage had set out for Merton, and a servant had been sent to Mr. Radnor's valet at the Albany with instructions to bring night clothes and a change for morning.

Although the young ladies came from a modest home, they were able to recognize the elegance of furnishings around them and the delicacy of the meal.

Miss Milner became "Cousin Phoebe" to Lord Aldford, but Kate remained "Miss Amberly" to him and to Mr. Radnor, who continued very proper in his manners, although he seemed, to both girls, to be a kindly disposed gentleman. After the meal his lordship dispensed with wine so as to accompany the ladies up to the drawing room. He managed adroitly to walk beside Miss Amberly, while Mr. Radnor fell behind with Miss Milner, asking her if she enjoyed music, and suggesting they go into the music room to see what music might be upon his lordship's piano.

As the music room opened from the drawing room and the girls could remain in full view of each other, Phoebe went willingly. She found Mr. Radnor less intimidating than his lordship.

Twenty-five feet away, Lord Aldford seated himself beside the elder young lady, who seemed in no way awed by his size and grandeur.

"I wish to seize this chance to speak privately with you," he began.

Miss Amberly looked alert, but said only, "Yes?"

"I feel—and my friend, Mr. Radnor concurs—that young ladies, unescorted, have no place in a public house."

"Oh, I agree," she said promptly. "Your housekeeper has already determined the same. In fact, she has set us in a suite where the entrance can be guarded by our maid's sleeping on a couch. Perhaps she is concerned for your reputation?"

"My reputation is excellent, ma'am," he replied huffily. "It is for the reputation of two green girls that I am concerned. And so—" he continued, before she could retort "—I have sent for my aunt, Lady Crowden, who, being my father's sister, is also a cousin of Miss Phoebe's. I mean no disrespect to you, for I am sure that Miss Phoebe is fond of you and that you have cared for her well, but entering London society is a far different matter from moving in the social groups of Oxford." Failing to notice Miss Amberly's expression, which had changed from compliant to thunderous, he continued: "I have sent for Lady Crowden, to come to us. My carriage set out for Merton while we were at dinner; it should bring her to London in the morning."

As Kate for a moment only scowled, he, misinterpreting, hurried to add, "It is obvious that my cousin is fond of you, so you must feel free to continue here in her company, although Lady Crowden will be in charge."

With a swelling bosom, Kate replied, "It is fortunate that you give me permission to remain in your *splendid abode,* for under no circumstances would I consider leaving my gentle young cousin adrift among strangers who—"

"Good God!" cried his lordship. "Are *you* my cousin, too?"

"Certainly not," snapped Kate. "I choose my family connections more carefully than that. Phoebe's father was the cousin of my father. Mr. Milner welcomed me to his home when I was orphaned and my grandfather refused to recognize me."

Lord Aldford muttered, "I see."

"No, I do not think you do," she continued. "I have no designs on your home, your wealth, your title, or your exalted *circle*—"

"Oh, come, now," bleated Aldford.

But she overbore him, saying, "If your aunt is more human than you and will deal kindly with my cousin, I will be glad for *her* sake. A dearer creature never lived."

At this point, having sensed quarrelsome tones, although they had not distinguished words, Phoebe and Charles Radnor came into the drawing room to fill a conversational void.

Phoebe looked anxiously at Kate, and Charles endeavored unsuccessfully to catch his friend's eye. Then the two of them made an effort at trivial talk until Kate stood up abruptly, declared she and her *cousin* were quite exhausted, begged the gentlemen to excuse them, and swept a puzzled Phoebe from the room.

The gentlemen, who had half stood, looked at each other.

"What was that all about?" asked Charles Radnor.

His lordship grimaced. "Another cousin—oh, not mine. Phoebe's. And I insulted her by assuming her to be a governess."

Charles began to laugh. "When did I ever know you to set a foot wrong? I daresay it did you a world of good to be hauled up short."

"All I can say is that I thank God that Aunt Cora will come tomorrow," Aldford replied fervently.

"Oh, yes. Things will be different here tomorrow," Charles agreed.

"Three females underfoot, when I thought I had a comfortable bachelor establishment. Think of it!" After a pause, Lord Lewis continued glumly, "Doubtless I will be driven out by a flow of mantua-makers' bills."

"No, no, old fellow," said Charles. "They don't wear mantuas this year. Lady Cora will set matters straight. Come. Let us go back to your study for a sip of something soothing. After all, we missed our after-dinner port."

A quirk appeared at one side of his lordship's mouth, but he readily led the way to the back of the house, saying, "I think I need brandy."

Already it seemed a week, instead of two hours, since females had interrupted their comfortable time in a masculine sanctuary that smelled gently and pleasantly of cigars and wood smoke. The fire had not died out and needed only a log or two to revive it. This was done by Charles while the viscount poured drinks. Then they sank into their seats and began to feel better, the cat graciously allowing his lordship to share a chair.

Two

Upstairs in their suite with Nanny Bloom, Kate related with some heat how insufferably Lord Aldford had talked to her.

"Oh," said Phoebe, clasping her hands, "I cannot think my cousin would be rude to you."

"Well, not rude," admitted Kate, "but toplofty—as if *he* knew better how to look after you than one who loves you. Making plans without consulting us! Sending for his aunt! Saying we should not stay at a respectable hotel—"

"Perhaps he is right, Miss Kate," Nanny interjected. "We do not know much about London. I may not be suitable protection for young ladies, even if I carry an umbrella to drive off unwanted attentions."

Both girls smiled at the idea of battle between their gray-haired nursemaid and bucks of the first head.

Phoebe said, "I fear it was wrong of us to descend upon my cousin and expect his help—even in the smallest matters."

"Rubbish!" declared Kate. "You are his cousin. Why should he not make himself useful?"

"But his aunt, Lady Cora, may not want to leave her home to take charge of two green girls. Suppose she turns out to be a perfect dragon?"

"Then you will cast a spell upon her," Kate said, giving her cousin a hug. "She might take me in dislike—for I shall regularly make known my wishes for you—but she will not be able to resist a nature as sweet as yours. Let us go to bed and gather our strength for tomorrow when Lady Crowden comes."

They had made the trip to London safely and been received (if reluctantly) at Aldford House, and had some not unreasonable expectations of meeting with her ladyship's approval (for the wives of Mr. Milner's associates had regularly made them pets). So they settled with Nanny what they should wear when they met Lady Crowden the next day. As Kate promised not to quarrel with his lordship, Phoebe was able to fall asleep peacefully; Kate, meanwhile, lay awake, pondering their future. If Lady Crowden proved difficult, they could always go home, she decided.

It was barely nine o'clock when Nanny wakened them, saying Lady Crowden had come unexpectedly in the night and was waiting to interview them in her chamber.

"Come in. Come in," said a voice of no nonsense, when they had dressed hurriedly and followed a maidservant along the corridor to an open chamber door. "This is still *my* room when I am in town."

Both were flushed as they curtsied to her ladyship, who reclined upon a chaise longue in a fanciful room of white paneling with emerald bed hangings and gossamer window curtains framed with draperies and swags of emerald silk. There were pictures everywhere. Baubles of delicate crystal and china littered tables and mantel shelf; there was even a large china cat set upon a corner of the hearth.

All this they saw in a fleeting glance, for their attention was at once upon the lady.

She was small and plump, with red hair which must have been real, for there were long threads of gray running through it. A few lines scored her face, but all in all, she was quite pretty and had a lively look.

"Sit down, girls," said the lady, motioning to two chairs near her. "You must not feel bad about being the cause of my rolling up to London in the night. Those two lazy gents lolling in Lewis's study were certainly surprised to see me—coming in the blackness—but I could not wait. Why, you have done me a good turn! Who wants to rusticate in Merton when the Season is in full swing? Let me look at you. Such pretty girls! This is going to be delightful . . . of course, Lewis thought I would be a drag upon him—wanting to kick up his bachelor heels, you know—but now he thinks I will be useful, and I *will*. Now which is which?"

"I am Kate Amberly, my lady," replied the elder girl, with a twinkle of appreciation for Lady Cora's frankness. "I am a cousin of your cousin Phoebe Milner, who is the one who matters. I am sure you can see she was wasted in the scholarly circles of Oxford."

Phoebe made a murmur of denial, but Lady Cora said, "Very true. And so are you. Now, don't give Lewis a thought. He will not interfere with us. I have a lot of excellent connections and can promise you a nice whirl."

At this point Phoebe uttered a small sound.

"Yes, my dear?"

"Oh, excuse me," said Phoebe, whose eyes had wandered to the hearth, "I do think that large china cat actually seemed to blink an eye!"

Lady Cora, distracted from her social plans, said, "And why should he not? He wishes to remind me that he is waiting for a bit of my kipper." She gestured to the tray upon a small table beside her. "I am fond of Lewis's cat, and Magnanimous knows I am easily persuaded to indulge him." She selected a bit of kipper and called, "Here, Mag."

The "china" cat rose and approached gracefully, accepted the morsel, swiped its whiskers with a black paw, and sprang lightly onto Kate's lap.

"Well, I declare!" said Lady Cora. "He takes whatever treats I offer but will not sit with me."

"He senses that I like cats," Kate said, making Magnanimous blissful by scratching behind the creature's ears.

"Well, so do I—on the floor. Generally he is a well-behaved beast, but like all cats, he will leave hairs behind. Take a good look at Lewis sometime and see if Mag has been in *his* lap or chair."

The girls smiled to imagine the impeccable viscount with cat hairs upon his person.

Reading their minds, Lady Cora said, "The despair of his valet. Well, now, let us make some plans. I will take you to call upon my particular friend, Lady Pembridge, this morning. She always has many callers and will never receive them before eleven, but we will go at ten-thirty and she will see *us,* for she is an intimate of mine. Something of a tartar, of course—do not look anxious, girls, for she will want to be the first to meet Lewis's houseguests. Oh, yes, the first thing we must do is visit Lady Pembridge!"

But it was not the first thing, for Lord Aldford and Mr. Radnor came in then to wish her ladyship good morning. She stretched out her hand for each to kiss, saying, "How clever of you, Aldford, to provide me with these delightful girls."

Of course the girls had provided themselves by coming uninvited to London, but it was true that Aldford had summoned his aunt to deal with them. It had been Charles Radnor's idea, although Aldford was beginning to think it his own. He turned to greet the young ladies: "Good morning, coz . . . Miss Amberly! Why are you holding my cat?"

Kate lifted her hands. "I am not holding him—he is sitting upon *me.*"

Magnanimous merely squeezed his eyes with magnificent disinterest.

"He senses a friend," Phoebe suggested.

"Yes," agreed Mr. Radnor, "animals can do that, you know, Lewis."

His lordship acknowledged this with a slight bow. "We came to ask if you ladies have had breakfast. I see Auntie has had hers. May we escort you to the breakfast parlor, Cousin Phoebe? Miss Amberly?"

Lady Crowden answered for them, "Yes, you may, but you

must not dawdle, for we want to be at Lady Pembridge's no later than half past ten."

"That tartar? Brrr."

"You may be afraid of her," replied his aunt, "but she is a particular friend of *mine*."

"If she is, it is because everyone loves you, Auntie," said his lordship, plainly meaning every word. The young ladies noticed this with interest. Although he might send her off to live in a house he owned at Merton, he appeared truly fond of his aunt. She had not complained of Merton; perhaps a lady of graying years preferred the slower pace of a smaller town.

Magnanimous was persuaded to return to the floor, where he sat at Lady Cora's feet and wrapped his tail about himself, waiting for more kipper, of which, his nose told him, all had not been eaten.

"Ring for my abigail as you go out, Aldford," his aunt commanded, and the viscount did so before offering Phoebe his arm for the trip down a carpeted hall and two flights of highly polished stairs.

Mr. Radnor followed with Kate, saying, "Lady Cora is a very astute female, for all her half sentences and seeming indolence. It was her idea to move to a house that Lewis owns in Merton to avoid hanging upon his neck, but she is glad of a reason to come to town."

"Is there no Lord Crowden?" Kate asked.

"Fortunately, no longer. He ran through his patrimony and her inheritance before sending his horse over a wall with an unexpected ditch on the other side. You will never hear Lady Cora complain about Crowden, though he must have been a sad trial."

"So she came to live here with Lord Lewis?"

"With his father, who was viscount then. As I said, she removed to Merton out of consideration for Lewis. Their relationship has remained good, in consequence."

At the bottom of the stairs, Lord Aldford was waiting for

them with Phoebe, who was too much in awe of him to talk
as easily as Kate and Mr. Radnor had done. However, by the
time their meal was over, the breakfast room had become a
cozy place, and the manners more informal. Lord Aldford and
Mr. Radnor went off about their business, feeling that having
pretty girls in the house was not a bad thing, and the visitors
decided, between them, that gentlemen of the *ton* were very
agreeable, which Lady Cora would have qualified, if she had
read their minds.

As the morning was clear and balmy, and as Lady Pembridge lived "only a street away," it was decided that the three
from Aldford House would walk to make their call.

Aldford's "tartar" proved to be a large female with an arching nose and great piercing black eyes, although her manner
was milder than his lordship had implied. Having quickly appraised the young ladies' appearance and their delicate handling of teacups, she said Dear Cora was clever to produce
such charming relations and must certainly bring them to a
small dinner the following night.

Lady Cora, who had no idea what formal gowns the girls
might own, and whether suitable frocks could be arranged in
thirty or so hours, said with deceptive calm, "How kind of
you, dear Henriette. We are pleased to accept."

"Shall I invite Aldford, too? And his friend Mr. Radnor?
One cannot count upon getting fashionable gentlemen on
short notice. Well, I shall try." She got up, an imposing figure
in a handsome morning gown of deep plum, and went across
to a secretary where she dashed off two notes. "Radnor is at
the Albany, isn't he?"

"No, visiting my nephew—at least he was today."

"Then I will send both notes with you, if I may. Time is
short." She folded the notes and handed them to Lady Cora.

"If Charles has returned to his rooms, I will send the invitation there," Lady Cora said. "If not, I can put it in the hands
of his valet."

In a tone of approval, their hostess said, "Both gentlemen

are known to have impeccable manners. They will respond promptly."

The sounding of the knocker at Lady Pembridge's front door signaled the beginning of her morning callers. With hurried goodbyes Lady Cora led her girls away, passing in the lower hall two unknown gentlemen who bowed and eyed them with interest. Lady Cora knew her influential friend had a finger in political and artistic pies, as well as social ones; those two unknowns might not be persons her nephew would wish his cousin to meet.

As they walked homeward, Lady Cora said they must first show her their wardrobes and then they would shop for what was needed.

When their clothes had been spread before her, she pronounced them excellent. "I had not thought Oxford would offer such good choices," she said.

"Kate chose them," Phoebe said.

"Then Kate has taste. A flair. The colors and fabric are just what they should be for very young ladies.,"

Kate explained that Mr. Bethelwait, Mr. Milner's man of business, said they had funds enough for their needs, but they did not want to spend recklessly and so had chosen with care.

Lady Cora nodded. "Wise as well as cautious. Two best attributes. What you are going to need are ballgowns." She did not think, she added, that Lewis intended formal debuts for the two of them, but some *exposure* at select parties. "Actually," she concluded, "to be missing from some affairs and to be seen at important ones will make you more interesting."

That afternoon they went to sample the delights of Bond Street, reveling in beautiful silks, lawns, laces, and muslins. Some seemed shockingly transparent, and those Lady Cora ruled out.

"You do not need those to attract attention," she said firmly. *"Admiration* is what we want."

Neither girl wanted attention of a lascivious sort. They were happy to choose a white muslin sprigged with blue for Phoebe and a blush-colored muslin for Kate, whom Lady Cora decreed to need something stronger than white to set off her dark hair. Before they were finished, they had ordered two other evening frocks to be delivered, and went homeward (to Aldford House), each happily carrying a new velvet bonnet in a box.

Two new dresses at once seemed many to any girl who had never attended a true ball. "Shall we wear these to Lady Pembridge's party?" asked Phoebe, watching boxes set carefully into their carriage.

"Why, none of these. These are for *balls*. You will wear pretty dresses that you brought with you," said Lady Cora.

So they returned happily to Aldford House to turn over the boxes to Nanny, who was equally happy to get her hands on them.

For the second night in a row, the viscount and Mr. Radnor sat down to dinner with the visitors, which caused some raising of brows among the servants, who seldom saw their master at an evening meal when the Season was in session. The young ladies did not know this, of course. Tomorrow they would dine again together at Lady Pembridge's house.

Three

It was with heightened expectations that Phoebe and Kate entered Lady Pembridge's mansion, walking just behind Lady Cora and followed by Lord Lewis Aldford and his friend Charles Radnor. Candles glowed and fires crackled in all the rooms. Flowers, artfully arranged, stood everywhere. All was very festive.

But there were no interesting gentlemen, no young people at all, except for one colorless damsel whom stood half behind a lady who turned out to be her mother.

They were announced, of course, and Lady Pembridge swayed forward to greet them. She and her house were as splendid as for a ball, though her manner was less formal.

"Let me make you known to my friends," she said, kicking aside the demi-train of her violet satin gown and turning to lead the girls about the room.

"Oh, do let *me*," exclaimed Lady Cora. "I see so many dear friends. Why there is Mrs. Palmer! And dear General Pogue!"

Lady Pembridge smiled, yielded, and took the gentlemen from Aldford House aside to tell them whom to escort to the dinner table.

Although only twenty-four were gathered, the number seemed much larger to Phoebe and Kate, who smiled, curtsied, and nodded as Lady Cora presented them as her "cousins," which was only half true. They did not remember a single name and were glad when discreet glances at place cards revealed who were their companions at dinner.

Lady Pembridge sat grandly at the head of her fine table. The Earl of Somewhere-or-other was at her right hand. Lord Aldford, Kate could see from where she sat, was on the hostess's left side. The only other titled gentleman present was General Sir Rupert Pogue, who fortified the table's foot by firing off hearty guffaws from time to time.

Phoebe's dinner partner was a middle-aged man, Mr. Colliard, who seemed chiefly interested in his meal, although between courses he did tell her of his niece's debut this season. Across the table was Charles Radnor, who had drawn the colorless girl as his dinner partner and who was talking to her in his kindly manner. She could not see Kate.

But she could see—while decorations were more elaborate and the meal more lavish than those in Oxford—that the people were familiar sizes, shapes, and types. They appeared to know and like one another. Perhaps they were willing to accept her and Kate as Cousin Cora Crowden's friends.

Neither newcomer ate much, Kate because she was in a crossfire of two gentlemen who wanted her to know that the Prince was close to going *too far*. "Too far where?" she asked.

"Pounds," said one.

"Weight," said the other. "Has to be hoisted onto his horse."

They helped themselves generously to Lady Pembridge's food. Though neither was as grotesquely fat as the Regent was rumored to be, Kate thought their own appetites needed curbing. People in London, she thought, were no different from those in Oxford; in this she was not entirely correct. At any rate, since they were willing to accept *her*, she was willing to like them, at least tonight . . . until there was a reason not to.

Lady Pembridge signaled for the ladies to withdraw, and it wasn't long before the gentlemen joined them. There was a congenial gathering for half an hour during which most guests made a point of saying something cordial to Phoebe and Kate; at the same time, Lady Cora stood near them, smoothly and casually inserting names to remind them. Only one other young woman stayed aloof—or so she seemed.

When Lady Pembridge's dinner partner, Earl Whoever-he-was, said something civil to his hostess and bowed himself from the room, such was his influence that the party ended. Phoebe and Kate could go home, relieved that the ordeal was over and neither tired nor disappointed. Lord Lewis and Mr. Radnor saw them safely admitted to Aldford House, tipped their hats, and vanished into the night.

"Where are they going?" asked Kate, following her chaperon up to the drawing room.

"Never," replied the lady, "ask gentlemen *that*. They have been everything civil and attentive to us. Now they will please themselves. Some chocolate, please, Serle."

Visions of smoky rooms, clinking glasses, and exotic females (about which they knew nothing) filled the girls' heads.

"Now, do not jump to conclusions," Lady Cora admonished. "Very likely Lewis and Charles have gone to their club to relax a bit. Tell me, did you enjoy your first evening of the Season?"

"Oh, yes!" chorused the girls truthfully.

"Well, I daresay that you may have found the group rather dull. I do myself, although one cannot help but like them. You would have preferred young bucks, wouldn't you? Do not spurn the gentlemen you met tonight. Your dinner partner, Phoebe, may have seemed unexciting to you, but I can tell you that he is a very astute gentleman, very highly regarded in financial circles—could buy an abbey."

"He said his niece is making a debut this season—" began Phoebe.

"Yes, and Mrs. Colliard has graciously said she will send you an invitation to the ball they are having for the girl."

The girls' eyes sparkled at the idea of their first London ball.

"And," continued her ladyship, "others at the dinner are more important than you think. Take the earl. He has the

Prince's respect—one of the few in his highness's inner court to whom he pays attention. As for General Pogue, he may seem all noise to you, but I can tell you his opinion carries weight at the War Office."

"Oh, dear!" Kate said. "I had thought him all noise and no effect. We shall have to be more careful in judging people."

"Not careful, dear, just slower. I must warn you that some fine 'fronts' may be hollow behind. Not, of course, that you will encounter trash in the best houses—which are the only ones to which I will take you—but a few persons may be fringe society. You can trust Lewis and Charles to present only suitable gentleman to you as partners."

Phoebe protested that they had come to London simply to see the sights and shop.

"So you may, as long as you do not overspend."

"Oh, no! Mr. Bethelwait is trusting us."

The three ladies drank their chocolate and were still discussing Lady Pembridge's guests when Lord Lewis and his friend returned to report that White's was dull, assorted members dozing in their chairs.

"The girls have not visited London before now," Lady Cora said. "They want to see famous places of the town."

"Then we must take them about," Mr. Radnor said promptly. "If tomorrow is fine, Lewis, you must order out your barouche for us."

His lordship said sardonically, "Us? Are you allowing me to ride in my own carriage?"

"Oh, but we mustn't impose—" began Phoebe.

"Of course you must," declared Lady Cora. "That is, Charles has a splendid idea. If Lewis does not wish to go, *Charles* will accompany you."

The viscount did not look out of temper. He said mildly that he would go, too. "My barouche is well known. What would people think if ladies rode in it without my escort? We must distinguish our visitors as well as show them palaces and prisons."

"Yes, that is what I had in mind," returned his aunt. "Charles is only teasing you, Lewis."

The three ladies retired to bed, well pleased with that day and the one to come. The gentlemen retreated to the viscount's study.

"This evening went well, I think," said Lewis, looking about for Magnanimous before putting his feet upon the stool. "Can I pour you anything?"

Charles said, "No. My valet will have fallen asleep if I do not go up to him soon." He leaned his head back and asked in an altered tone, "They are amiable girls, are they not? Easy to please. Restful."

"I cannot call Miss Amberly *that*," his host replied.

"Why, I did not hear an abrupt word from her all evening! You began on a wrong foot that first day. She feels responsible for the younger girl, who is gentle—maybe not up to snuff."

"There cannot be more than a year or two between them," Aldford said. "Perhaps Miss Amberly sees more dangers in the big city. Aunt Cora will manage both. Do you know, I think Aunt Cora is enjoying the challenge."

"Yes, yes, but Lady Cora will need help from us. *Both* of us. You, too, Lewis."

The viscount made a strangled sound, half grunt, half sigh. "Don't you feel young to be a papa, Charles? Haven't you heard older men groan about firing off daughters . . . being sure the wrong beaux don't turn their pretty, empty heads?"

Mr. Radnor raised his eyes to scrutinize the ceiling. "Might be interesting. Daresay it would give a chap a feeling of power to turn off besotted chaps." He paused. "Lady Cora mentioned a Mr. Bethelwait to me—the girls' business adviser, I think. Better find out what the girls' resources are, don't you agree?"

"Good God!" exclaimed the viscount. "Need I do that?"

His friend smiled broadly. "The girls are going to *take*. I predict it. You will find yourself receiving offers. What will you say then?"

"The pretty little one may attract offers, but Aunt Cora will steer her away from the Wrong Sort, I am sure. As for the witch, she would not take kindly to any advice or interference from me." Lewis gnawed his lower lip. "How did I get in such a tangle? I hope you are only borrowing trouble."

Charles chuckled. "Did I use the word 'trouble'? Thought you might find the Season interesting for a change."

"Well, 'trouble' or 'interest,' you will be part of it, so you had best send your man to your rooms to fetch whatever you will need for the duration of the situation." He shook his head violently. "Let's get to bed."

Four

Alas for the barouche! Morning brought a horrid drizzle, not enough to call "rain," yet more than mist, something to dampen ladies' frocks and spirits. The tour of London's most famous sights would have to be postponed.

Charles Radnor, whose easy temperament did not allow him to mope, joined the three ladies in the library for a game of whist, while Aldford retired to his study.

The viscount was feeling the weight of his responsibilities as he penned a note to Mr. Bethelwait. His concern was reflected in the terseness of what he wrote, although he did not realize this. Once written, the letter went off to Oxford by the hand of a mounted groom who was ordered to inquire at the Royal Mail terminal in Oxford for Mr. Bethelwait's address; the viscount did not wish to ask this information from his guests.

Lewis Giles Stanley Samford had been Viscount Aldford not much beyond fourteen months. Heretofore his chief concern had been the gloss of his boots and the location of the latest boxing match. He was, however, not without sense. He had finished at Cambridge with respectable (if not stellar) marks and had not disgraced his father in the salons of Society. Duty to his name hung heavy upon him, although he did not shirk it.

He went into the library to advise the card players that the weather seemed to be clearing. It was true enough. The sky seemed lighter, and only intermittent drops were falling.

The girls clapped their hands lightly, and Lady Cora hurried off to confer with Mrs. Eaton about a quick nuncheon. What had begun as a day of disappointment would become one of exploration. Lord Lewis forgot his letter to Mr. Bethelwait. Mr. Radnor forgot to send his valet for more clothes, as the girls prattled of the famous sites they wished to see—St. Paul's Cathedral, the grim Tower of London, Carlton House, elite Almack's, Pall Mall, Hyde Park, Westminster Abbey!

Shortly before one o'clock they set out. None had thought to make a list of sights to be viewed. Lord Aldford merely directed his coachman to make a circuit of notable places. Since this coachman was a competent servant of age sixty years, forty of which he had spent driving in London, he knew better than his passengers what they must see.

Lady Cora waved them off and went upstairs to her room to read the day's mail, two parts of which she found particularly satisfactory.

Sitting with their backs to the horses, Lord Aldford and his friend were able to enjoy the pulchritude of the young ladies whom they had more or less adopted. Traffic was heavy and progress slow, yet everything (and more) that the girls had wished to view was seen, ending with Hyde Park at the most fashionable hour of the afternoon.

Just after turning into the park, the carriage passed two gentlemen leaning casually upon canes. The strangers called out, gesturing with the canes. Already the carriage had gone beyond the pair when Mr. Radnor, facing backward, saw them.

"Oh *no!*" he exclaimed. "M'brother."

"Step along, Becker," snapped the viscount over his shoulder, and the coachman signaled his team for a quick trot.

Phoebe and Kate stared in astonishment.

Some explanation must be made, but for a space their escorts did not know how to proceed. Mr. Radnor cleared his throat.

"The taller—the burlier man—is my brother, Earl of Taviton," he explained. "Not a bad fellow, certainly a gentleman, but something of a—"

Aldford supplied, "Rounder."

Awed, Phoebe asked, "Do you mean someone we must not know?"

The two men looked at each other uncertainly.

"Not exactly," Aldford said. "The other man is a well-known gossip-monger whom we would not wish to supply with information that might get twisted. Lord Taviton is a widower, very much on the—prowl. Not the best acquaintance for young ladies new to town ways." He smiled slightly to moderate his words without negating them. "My aunt is the one to explain all this to you."

The gentlemen felt this would take care of matters for the moment, little realizing that Phoebe's and Kate's curiosity was now rampant. They nodded demurely, though scarcely able to wait to return to Lady Cora.

"Take the first exit north, and turn back to Mayfair," Aldford directed his coachman in a quiet voice the girls pretended not to hear.

Mr. Radnor called their attention to some flowering laurels as the carriage swung out of the park. It was time to return to Aldford House anyway, as the sun was slipping behind clouds.

Lord Aldford was first to step down at the kerb. Before Mr. Radnor could rise, Kate had stood and accepted her host's assistance to descend. Phoebe was swift to follow, and before Mr. Radnor had reached the pavement, the girls were flying up the outer steps of the house so fast that their skirts billowed out behind them. By the time the two men had started to climb the steps, the entrance door had opened and they could hear Kate ask, "Is Lady Crowden in?"

"Yes, miss," said Serle, who was standing a few paces behind the uniformed lackey. "In her room, miss."

"Good," said Kate. "We will go right up to her."

"Do you think we *should?*" whispered Phoebe, but already Kate was hastening up the steps, so she followed.

Lady Cora, who had heard the hurried approach, was at her door to greet them. "Were you eager to see *me?* How very flattering. Was it a pleasant afternoon?"

Kate said, "Yes, yes, but near the end—in Hyde Park—we passed two fine-looking gentlemen who waved in a friendly fashion for us to stop, but Aldford wouldn't."

"It was Mr. Radnor's brother," Phoebe inserted.

"I see," said Lady Cora, establishing herself on the chaise.

"Aldford said neither man was one for us to know. He said you would explain."

"What a nodcock! Well, neither he nor Charles knows how to oversee very young ladies. They have never had such responsibility . . . come in, Lewis, Charles. I daresay you are better at pursuing damsels than in chaperoning them."

"No experience at all in chaperonage," Aldford admitted, as he and Mr. Radnor entered.

"I understand we don't want any contact with a gossip, but what is wrong with the brother of his eminent lordship's closest friend?" demanded Kate.

Lady Cora shook her head. "Now, Kate, my dear, you are reacting as hastily as these two gentlemen. We do not want to encourage attentions from unsuitable beaux. There is nothing wrong with Taviton except that he has buried two wives and is looking for a third one to care for his five children."

"Oh, poor man!" murmured Phoebe.

"He is not a poor man at all," said Lady Cora. "He is rolling in wealth. Let him look elsewhere for a suitable wife. She will not hold his interest long! Oh, you may be civil to Taviton, although we will try to shield you from dances with him, for we don't want him to scare off other more agreeable *partis* for my cousins."

Kate, who was quite touched at her sudden kinship to Lady Cora, said, "Thank you. I was too hasty. Please continue to advise me in everything. Mr. Radnor, I am sure that Lord Taviton, as he is *your* brother, must have a share of Radnor good qualities." 'She looked at Aldford. "My lord, I promise to heed your instructions . . . most of the time."

Charles Radnor laughed easily and elbowed Aldford, who said, "Good God. I will be afraid to venture an opinion about *anything.*"

"Well," said Kate, "Phoebe is biddable, and I shall try to be the same, but it is not my natural self."

"We cannot all be alike," pointed out Lady Cora calmly. "However, let me recommend that you girls be guided by us—Lewis, Charles, and me. The London social scene is somewhat like a battlefield. Strategy may be needed."

"Perhaps," said Mr. Radnor whimsically, "less effort will be needed to attract dance partners than to keep the wolves at bay."

Phoebe, who had an anxious expression, said haltingly, "We did not—truly!—expect to descend—impose upon Cousin Lewis. It was the darkness—and not knowing what hotel—"

"You did exactly right. Hotel? Pshaw!" said Lady Cora.

"But we did not expect to venture into Society, did we, Kate?"

"Well, we are glad you are here," said her ladyship stoutly.

The gentlemen did not appear *un*glad.

So Kate said, "Thank you!" and Phoebe's protestations subsided.

Lady Cora now took notes from the table beside her, saying, "Here is today's mail. Mrs. Colliard has sent an invitation to the ball on Thursday for her niece, as she promised. I assume you have already received and accepted yours, Lewis? And Charles?" The gentleman nodded. "Good. Lewis, you will have the first dance with your cousin, and Charles with Kate. The next set you will switch, and after that any number of gentleman will be asking you to present them to the unknown charmers." She shuffled her notes. "Here is another that I think you will find unusual—from Mrs. Garway—an invitation to a tea at which Miss Garway will read some of her new

poems. No need to look bored, Lewis; the invitation is for
ladies only. You met Miss Garway at Lady Pembridge's dinner,
girls."

"Do you mean the girl who had nothing to say, Cousin
Cora?" Phoebe asked. "She actually writes poems?"

"Very good ones. Good enough to find a publisher who is
willing to risk the cost of printing them, which her parents
could certainly not afford. "Now Kate, *Kate,* do not jump to
conclusions from the expression on Charles's or Lewis's face.
They very likely cannot find a rhyme for 'whale' unless it is
'ale.' In any case, *they* are not invited. Depend upon it, you
will meet some of London's most discriminating hostesses at
Miss Garway's little Reading."

Two days later, what Lady Cora said proved to be completely true. The mousy Miss Garway was a different creature
when she had a paper from which to read rather beautiful
poems. Phoebe, being a romantic, was particularly enchanted
with the young author's metered words, as she said earnestly
to Miss Garway (and thereby won a friend). Kate, who considered herself (by necessity) a realist, thought the pallid Miss
Garway was an accomplished writer who was a real surprise.

Lady Cora was right, as she seemed always to be when she
made statements concerning the *ton.* The afternoon gathering
led to more choice invitations for the visitors at Aldford
House.

Five

"Lady Cora Crowden," intoned the splendidly dressed servant at the ballroom door. "Viscount Aldford. Miss Milner. The Honorable Mr. Radnor. Miss Amberly."

Dancing had begun, so the party from Aldford House stepped aside within the ballroom to make a place for latecomers who were being announced behind them.

"It seems," said Lady Cora, "I underestimated the crush. Colliard's niece is already dancing. Lewis, see that our girls are presented to her when there is a break—or I will, depending upon who has the first chance. I will find a seat near a window, I hope." She trotted away along the fringes of the dance floor, speaking happily to friends here and there as she went.

When the set had ended, Lewis led Phoebe to join a group, introducing her easily, for he seemed to know every one. As *her* pleasure was evident in her glowing eyes and sweet smile, she was cordially received. Meanwhile, Charles had taken Kate into another square. Each girl was on her own.

As they performed the dance they had a blurred view of the Colliards' elegant ballroom, lit brightly by chandeliers suspended from a pale blue ceiling and silver wall sconces ornamented with cascades of blue and white flowers. When the viscount indicated Miss Colliard by a nod, Phoebe saw a young creature not actually pretty, but flushed with pleasure.

"She has enough wealth to make a good match," Lewis whispered.

"Oh," said Phoebe, "must that determine her future?"

"I fear it has a lot to do with the matter."

"How sad."

Lewis looked down into Phoebe's sober face. He said, "Her parents are known to be people of good judgment. We can suppose they will consider her feelings as much as possible. Please smile again."

Phoebe obeyed, if weakly.

"I suppose you champion climbing boys and emaciated stray dogs," he teased lightly.

"Yes, I do. And lame horses, and impoverished widows."

"Sometimes one can help in such cases," he suggested.

"Yes. I hope to do so."

Perceiving a more serious side to his young cousin than he had guessed, the viscount was momentarily at loss for a reply. Then the music ended, and finding Miss Colliard near at hand, Lord Aldford led Phoebe to her. Mr. Radnor was close behind them with Kate. Miss Colliard greeted them graciously, although it was doubtful that either name meant anything to her; her aunt might never have mentioned two unknowns from Oxford. After a few cordial sentences, another gentleman came to claim Miss Colliard, and Lewis changed partners with Charles, who drew Phoebe aside to meet some other friends of his.

"Look," said Kate to Lewis. "Lady Cora has a beau."

Sure enough, across the room a white-headed gentleman of serious mien was just taking a seat beside Aldford's aunt. She appeared to greet him affably and to hold his attention with flowing talk.

"Ah," said Aldford. "He is not often seen at balls."

Kate asked, "Do you know him?"

"Of course. He is Lord Chilweth. Would you care to meet him?"

Even as he spoke it was evident that Miss Amberly did not wish to do so, for she had turned her back and wore a stricken look.

"What is wrong?" Lewis asked quickly.

"Lord Chilweth," she hissed through her teeth, "is the man who cast off my mother because she married against his wishes."

"Good God," said the viscount. "Your grandfather!"

"Can we leave?" she asked.

"I am afraid not after such a short time. Might offend the Colliards. But we can slip out this door and mingle with people in the refreshment room. So many are here that Lord Chilweth is not likely to see you." He drew her through a nearby door. "Would Chilweth recognize you?"

Kate said bitterly, "How can he? He has never seen me. Suppose Lady Cora should mention me to him . . ."

"She is too canny for that."

The evasion worked well, for when Aldford settled Kate with some new acquaintances and returned to scout the ballroom, Lord Chilweth had left Lady Cora's side, and a footman told him that his lordship had called for his carriage and departed.

Thereafter Aldford took Kate again to the ballroom, introduced her to a number of admiring gentlemen, and saw her dancing happily, as though without a care. If she was as distraught to encounter her grandfather as she had let him see, he wondered if she would refuse to attend other evening parties.

Five being too many for Lord Aldford's town carriage, the ladies had come in it without escort. Lewis and Charles saw the ladies off for home and waited before the Colliards' mansion for their curricle.

"I detect an air of—well, I cannot say what it is," Charles said. "Anticlimax? Or is it—"

"Later," muttered the viscount, nodding toward other guests who were waiting near them. Then, their curricle arriving, the two men stepped into it, Lewis took the reins from his groom, who sprang up at the rear, and they left the mêlée of vehicles behind.

Upon reaching Aldford House they found Lady Cora and Phoebe removing cloaks in the hall. Already Kate was fleeing up the stairs.

"Come in here," commanded Lewis, indicating the front parlor where he and Charles had first met the young ladies. It was nearest and had a sound oaken door which he closed carefully.

"Aunt Cora, you know who Kate is," he said accusingly.

"Well, to be sure I do. I was on the town before she was born. But I think most have forgotten what an ass Chilweth made of himself when his daughter ran away. Amberly was perfectly respectable and able to support her."

"You should have told me."

"And would you have turned Kate away from this house?"

Lewis frowned. "No, I would not. But to take her where she might be humiliated—"

"Pshaw! Who would have thought her grandfather would be there? He never frequents balls."

"Please," said Phoebe. "What is the trouble? Kate seemed distressed, although I thought she danced most gaily." She was ignored by both Aldford and his aunt.

"You should have warned me," his lordship said.

"And would you have sent poor Kate home to Oxford— with or without Phoebe?" Lady Cora retorted.

"I should have made certain that Chilweth was not invited tonight."

"What? And set the gossips panting?"

Charles Radnor intervened with calming voice, "All passed off without unpleasantness."

"Ah!" said Aldford, "But did Aunt Cora tell Chilweth who our visitor is?"

"Not directly," Lady Cora replied. "When he asked who was the pretty young lady with you, Lewis, I said she was a visitor, a friend of your cousin's."

"And her name?"

"Yes, I said it, and he gave no sign of its meaning anything to him. I hope it needles his conscience—the old fool."

Round-eyed and troubled, Phoebe said, "We should never have come here."

The others, who had more or less forgotten her, were momentarily silenced.

Into the gap again stepped Mr. Radnor. "This household has been enlivened by your coming, Miss Phoebe, has it not, Lewis? I do not think Lord Chilweth will act the fool as he once did, which only caused him years of loneliness. He will see the wisdom of *not* raising old ghosts."

"But what of Kate's feelings?" persisted Phoebe.

"The same argument," said Charles to her gently, "will— after a bout of tears—hold with her. The past cannot be altered, but it must be forgotten. She will have the four of us to support her, and a number of other gentlemen, if tonight is any indication."

"I shall not be able to lay eyes on such a cruel man without thinking of diabolical punishments," she said in a mournful voice, but as her three companions already had some idea of her gentle nature, they were not unduly alarmed.

"Shall you and I go up to Kate now, Phoebe?" said Lady Cora, drawing her toward the door. "Time for caresses and reassurance."

The gentlemen, left behind, exchanged solemn glances.

"What next?" asked the viscount, feeling some discomfort in his position as host to Chilweth's estranged granddaughter.

Charles Radnor looked thoughtful. "I believe," he said slowly, "that when Chilweth admits to himself what he has missed, he will be ready—indeed, eager, to acknowledge Kate. Now that his feeble son has died, the earldom will pass to a cousin, but he is reputed to have independent means which he will want to pass to his daughter's child. Or so I see it."

Aldford said bluntly, "She would refuse it. So hot at hand!"

"Only you think that. It is obvious that Phoebe is devoted to her, so she cannot be as difficult as you seem to think."

"Oh, *Phoebe*. I daresay she would find a soft spot some-where in her heart for Napoleon Bonaparte—"

"Too English for that," Charles objected.

"Very well. Then say Dick Turpin. I suspect she would think he was largely misunderstood and did not *mean* any harm."

Aldford's friend immediately said, "Exactly! Phoebe is sure to convince Kate that her grandfather must be a poor, unhappy man who is to be pitied."

The viscount threw up his hands. "As usual, you argue in circles, or is it back and forth?" He flung himself upon a couch. "So how do we proceed?"

Charles said, "By standing still."

Meanwhile, upstairs, Lady Cora and Phoebe found Kate alone, Nanny having been abruptly sent away. She was not crying, though her pallor and restless movements revealed extreme tension.

"I have shamed you," she said, her eyes on Lady Cora.

"Not at all," said her ladyship immediately. "You did not deserve such a shock, and we think you behaved very well in a difficult situation. Chilweth is very likely wringing his hands at this moment. He is obliged to reconsider his bad temper, wrong decisions, and loneliness of twenty years."

"But Mama ran away—"

"Yes, to your father's mother."

"Grandmother?" said Kate wonderingly. She looked to Phoebe for confirmation, but Phoebe knew nothing.

"Yes. There was no scandal. Almost no one remembers. *We* are acquainted with the Kate who is a charming young lady—who has a bit of temper, perhaps? If your grandfather asks forgiveness, you must give it. You have the grace for that, I think. Phoebe, go to bed. Do you need help with buttons? No? Then goodnight, my dear. Oh yes, and say a prayer for the Earl of Chilweth, while I visit for a quiet time with Kate. Come along, Kate."

They separated, Phoebe shutting herself in her chamber

and sitting upon the bed. For heaven's sake! So much had happened. As she thought it over carefully, she realized that Kate had carried a hurt all her life, but she could not believe that poor despotic old gentleman could be as bad as they supposed—making a ruin of his life and having to face the fact. Darling Kate would forgive him; Phoebe knew she would do so sooner or later. Might he not possibly repent and be reconciled with his granddaughter? Yes, Phoebe told herself, Lord Chilweth could not be so black as to fail to make amends.

Such were her thoughts, and just so Mr. Radnor had read her nature accurately.

Six

No ladies were seen or heard when the gentlemen went down for breakfast. Both his lordship and his friend were subdued as they ate gammon and eggs to fortify themselves and then slipped out in a craven fashion to stroll toward St. James Street and Brook's club. It was too early for a game, but a variety of newspapers or uncritical friends might be found there without the emotions that had rocked Aldford House.

"I hope our ladies slept well," ventured Lord Aldford, as they entered Brook's.

"Had a good cry together, I expect," opined Mr. Radnor.

They were fortunate to find two acquaintances who were wanting to talk about the next race meet at Newmarket. However, as Aldford took more interest in hunters and Radnor bred sturdy dray horses to sell profitably, they were soon bored with the subject, which the chance-met gentlemen had not exhausted. They made excuses of needing exercise and moved on to Gentleman Jackson's, although neither was in the mood for sparring.

"If I had gone to Helmsworth I would not have had to deal with females in the house," said his lordship as they idly watched Jackson coach a young fellow, new in town, to better use of his fists.

"But you aren't dealing with them," Charles pointed out. He added, "and not half watching this. Let's move along. Maybe find a card game somewhere."

Fresh air made them more cheerful, so when they encountered a friend looking for company, they went along with him to his club and eventually joined him for a hearty meal and talk of latest scandals, which were not very shocking—and which did not include any mention of Lord Chilweth or his alienated daughter and granddaughter.

"At least," said Aldford to Charles Radnor, as they turned their steps homeward, "Kate isn't a subject of rumors so far."

"We did not really expect her to be," said Charles.

"No. Brushed through that near-contact with Chilweth well enough."

The day was fair and the breeze was fresh. Both began to feel much easier until they turned into Aldford's street and beheld several vehicles attended by grooms before Aldford House.

"Hope Auntie is not holding a tea party," said Lewis, as they climbed the steps to his front door, which a footman dutifully drew open.

"Ladies having a little party, eh?" he asked.

"Some gentleman callers, sir," the servant replied. It had been a long time since ladies had received callers to Aldford House, Lord Lewis's father having lived alone there most of the time. The staff found the change a matter of intense interest.

Lewis and Charles exchanged looks. "We had best go up," said his lordship.

That the ladies had callers should not have been a surprise, since Lady Cora had many friends who wished she did not "bury herself" at Merton, and the pretty girls had been displayed at the Colliards' ball, but somehow Lord Aldford and Mr. Radnor were not prepared for what met their eyes.

First there was Kate, sitting on a loveseat with Lord Percy Taviton (of all people). Next to her, on the arm of the sofa, was a sentinel cat, wide awake and watching the earl with critical attention. Stunned, Lord Aldford looked about for his aunt and discovered her chatting with a distinguished gray-haired gentleman who was a bit thick in the middle while still a fine figure at fifty-odd years. Phoebe was filling teacups for what seemed at least twenty nattily dressed young males, though it was actually only six.

One said, "Wondered where you were, Aldford."

Lewis and Charles advanced into the room, responding to the babble of greetings. The ladies smiled in a welcoming manner. Only Magnanimous remained at watchful attention.

"Would you like tea?" Phoebe asked Mr. Radnor, who replied that he would.

"Lewis will want sherry, I feel sure," he said. Then he went toward his brother on the loveseat with Kate. "What the devil are you doing here?"

"Getting acquainted with lovely ladies," replied Taviton, arching his eyebrows and rolling his eyes. At forty, he was still handsome in a florid way and well dressed, still able to attract the admiration of females, even though his bluff manners were somewhat overdone. Charles's disapproval of his presence was obvious, but since Lord Percy's target was Phoebe, and since Kate struck him as considerably less docile, he got lazily to his feet and gradually moved away as if he were in no hurry.

Meanwhile, Aldford had taken a glass of sherry and advanced toward his aunt and her visitor.

"Good afternoon, Sir Boscobel," he said cordially. "May I give you a glass of sherry instead of that teacup?"

"Indeed you may," responded the gentleman affably, setting aside the half-drunk cup. "I am glad you asked."

The viscount handed over the wineglass he was carrying and signaled a footman to bring another.

"I was not long in learning that Lady Cora had come for a visit," said Sir Boscobel. "It is a pleasure to welcome her and her charming cousins." He smiled at Lady Cora across the rim of the glass, implying that it was her ladyship who had drawn him to Aldford House. Lady Cora was too poised a female to blush, but she looked pleased.

Presently the assorted young gentlemen had persuaded Phoebe to play a few tunes for all to sing and drew her off to the music room. Kate and Charles rose to follow. Lady Cora benignly watched them go.

"I am aware of both young ladies' histories," said Sir Boscobel softly. "It is good of you, Aldford, to give them a happy time. With you, Lady Cora, to chaperon them, they cannot come to grief. Taviton may be a bit of a nuisance, but he is not disreputable. Pray, call upon me if I can be helpful."

Lady Cora said, "Why, thank you, sir. You comfort me, although I do not think our girls will cause us any worry. They have sound heads on their shoulders. I do not think Taviton will mislead *them*."

Perhaps she was right.

Yet when Lord Aldford and Mr. Radnor returned from a light-hearted time on the town the very next afternoon and found the same beaux—plus two more—cluttering Aldford's drawing room, they were not pleased. The posturing of the younger men could be tolerated, but the smirking and flattery of Percy Radnor, Earl of Taviton (he with five motherless cubs), was hardly to be endured. Only Kate's noticeable annoyance and Phoebe's reluctant responses provided any reassurance.

Lady Cora seemed scarcely to notice, as she was deep in conversation with Sir Boscobel, who had called a second time. When, however, Serle announced, "Lord Chilweth," Lady Cora started in surprise and after only a brief hesitation surged forward to receive him.

"Good afternoon, Chilweth," she said. "Girls, here is Lord Chilweth to visit us."

Phoebe reached for Kate's hand; they came forward together gravely to curtsy.

"Will you have tea, Chilweth? Or sherry?" asked Lady Cora. He said he thought it had best be tea. "The girls will see to it," said Lady Cora, allowing Kate and Phoebe to escape. While Kate inserted herself into a group of young men who were serenely unaware of undercurrents, it was Phoebe who carried back the cup to the earl.

Sir Boscobel joined Lady Cora in conversing with the earl, who sipped his tea nervously, endeavoring to watch Kate's movements as much as he could. Before long he had excused himself to Lady Cora and gone away.

From the corner of her eye, Kate saw him leave, and when she heard the thud of the street door's closing, she slipped from the drawing room to scamper for a breathing space in her chamber on the next floor.

But he had not gone.

He had hesitated with a hand upon the newel of the stair. The door's closing below meant something else.

"Oh, Kathryn, can you forgive me?" he asked hoarsely.

Kate hesitated, seeing unmistakably a broken man. "A bit," she whispered. "A little bit at a time."

"You are generous," he said. "Thank you, my dear." Then he went down the stairs, and Kate flew up them to find sanctuary briefly until her emotions were under control.

On the lower floor Lord Chilweth passed an anxious-looking man who had just entered the house and was requesting to see Lord Aldford. Neither man paid notice to the other. Chilweth was ushered from the house by a footman, while Serle conducted the stranger into the front parlor before going up to inform his master of a caller who did not seem to fit into the group around the ladies.

"Pardon, my lord," said Serle, for Lewis's ears only. "A Mr. Bethelwait to see you."

Surprised, his lordship asked, "Where is he?"

"In the front parlor, my lord."

"Show him into my study, please, and say I will come down to him," Lord Aldford directed. Almost on Serle's heels he went onto the landing and watched Serle descend to lead a balding man along the lower hallway. Then he went down quickly.

"Mr. Bethelwait! This is unexpected," Aldford said, going into the study and closing the door. "Do sit down."

"You know who I am?" asked the visitor, groping for a chair and sitting upon it.

"Indeed, I do. A very kind friend to my cousin Phoebe."

"Good God! Are you Lord Aldford? I expected an older man."

"Yes, so did my cousin," said Lewis, sitting also.

"But this is improper! My wife will never forgive me if I leave the girls in the household of a single—"

Lewis smiled, which did agreeable things to his face. "Yes, I am single and have been Lord Aldford for only a little more than a year, but all is most proper, let me assure you. The girls are in the care of my aunt, Lady Cora Crowden, whose respectability no one dares to question, as you will see when you meet her."

"Thank God," said Mr. Bethelwait fervently.

"Let me add that your girls are enjoying a social flutter which may result in suitable marriages for them. Why, the drawing room is overflowing with interested bachelors at this moment." He laughed and leaned back easily, which Mr. Bethelwait did also with a sigh.

Then Lord Aldford probed gently and was able to learn that both girls were better endowed than either knew or supposed, Kate with ten thousand safely in the Funds, and Phoebe with a small manor that brought respectable income by way of leases.

"The young ladies do not, of course, know the details of their finances. They are very good about staying within the allowances that I make them," the visitor said.

Mr. Bethelwait, Lewis noted, was neatly turned out, if a bit behind London styles and mussed from hasty travel. His anxious voice was cultured. In short, Lewis judged him to be a gentleman. "Come," he said. "Let us go up and give the girls the pleasure of seeing an old friend."

Indeed, Phoebe and Kate were so delighted to see a familiar

face that they did not think to wonder how Mr. Bethelwait had found them, and they eagerly presented him to Lady Cora as a special friend.

"Mrs. Bethelwait," Phoebe added, "has been so kind to us, since Papa died . . . just as you have, my lady."

Her ladyship promptly said, "They have kissed the Blarney Stone, you know."

Then Aldford continued smoothly introducing the various gentlemen whose names were a perfect blur to Mr. Bethelwait, except Mr. Radnor's, he being identified as "another houseguest." Mr. Bethelwait refused a cordial invitation to stay for dinner and went away reassured about his girls. Approval of *him* was bestowed by Magnanimous, who made a circuit of his feet and wafted a tail delicately across his leg.

Seven

Without a word being spoken between them, never again did Lord Aldford and Mr. Radnor absent themselves from afternoons at Aldford House. They accomplished any errands in the morning, returning absolutely no later than two, when the knocker might begin to sound and assorted beaux might present themselves to the ladies, the older one being an attraction just as were the young ones. Lord Aldford complained to his friend that it was shocking, the amount of his tea and sherry being consumed.

"You wanted the girls to 'take,' didn't you?" reminded Charles.

Sir Boscobel was a regular. He was acceptable, if he kept Lady Cora amused, as it seemed he did. And Lord Chilweth appeared every day or so, supposedly to watch and consider his granddaughter, although mostly he sat with Lady Cora and contributed a sentence or two to her conversation with Boscobel.

Kate was beginning to adjust to her grandfather's presence, since he stayed across the drawing room with Lady Cora and did not stare at her. Mostly her duty, assigned by herself, was to stand as a buffer between Phoebe and the heavy blandishments and boisterous humor of Percy, Earl of Taviton.

It was not Phoebe's nature to repulse anyone who was inclined to seek her company, but the best she could manage in response to Taviton's jollity and leers was a weak smile. Constant attention and compliments from young dandies did not go to Phoebe's head, for she thought of them as "friendly" and "kind." Taviton's style of address she found oppressive, but as he was the brother of Mr. Radnor (who was so understanding) she tolerated him courteously, without realizing that it only led him to further excesses from his reservoir of flattery.

More invitations arrived daily. Not from mamas of young ladies less beautiful than Phoebe and Kate, but from friends of Lady Cora and other amiable dames. Perhaps the designers of social events suspected they must include Lady Cora's protégées if they wished Viscount Aldford and the Honorable Mr. Radnor to attend.

"Chilweth must make Kate uncomfortable," Lewis complained to his aunt. "Why does he keep coming here?"

"Perhaps to see *me*," she replied coyly.

"Good God! Are you thinking of marrying *him?*"

"Certainly not," she retorted. "Old fool! . . . But it will help Kate—if she wins his approbation. I shall encourage his coming. Surely he must see what a special young lady she is."

"Yes," agreed Lewis. "Aunt Cora, what is Sir Boscobel doing here?"

Her eyes twinkled. "Well, you *might* suspect him to be my suitor. I recommend you mind your own business."

Taken aback, his lordship muttered, "This is strange. I thought what passed in my house was my business."

"Pshaw!" she returned. "You are turning into a proper noble. Your father would be proud of you. For that matter, I am proud myself." She gave him what he considered a saucy look and added, "But do not issue orders to me!"

Seeing Sir Boscobel approach, he took himself off to get some sherry, for which he felt a compelling need, and to take a new look at the people in his drawing room. None of the eager visitors did he think suitable for Phoebe—men of good lineage (he knew) and adequate income (he supposed), though scarcely sensitive enough to appreciate her gentle nature. As for Kate, standing in a noisy group, she was stronger than pretty fops might appreciate; watching her talk with animation, he noticed that neither embarrassment nor hurt showed in her face or manner.

A voice said in his ear, "Why so solemn?"

"Oh—Charles. I was thinking what a responsibility these girls are," he replied. "Who really appreciates them?"

Mr. Radnor chuckled. "It looks as though a number of gents do." He sobered and added, "M'brother seems to have set his sights on Phoebe, and a more incompatible pair I cannot imagine!"

"Well, I shall not allow *that.* She does not like him by half, anyway, as I can plainly see."

"Good match, in a worldly view," Charles said gloomily. "Title. Wealth. Position. No cares—"

"And no genuine feeling. Anyway, even if I gave approval, do you think Kate would permit such a match?"

"No, thank God. There's a strong character!"

Feeling in accord on the matter, the men separated, the viscount going to join his aunt and Sir Boscobel, to see what he could make of their relationship.

"We have an invitation from the Marchioness of March to a ball next Tuesday, Lewis," said Lady Cora, as he reached her side. "May I count on you and Charles to escort us?"

"And may I add myself to make three couples?" asked Boscobel quickly. "My town carriage will accommodate the ladies comfortably and have room for me."

As Lewis, with Charles, had followed to the first ball in Lewis's curricle, he had no objection to doing this again. By Tuesday the viscount had had enough of staying home to watch various dandies posturing for Phoebe and Kate. He was ready to see other faces at a ball.

On Tuesday evening the carriages arrived together at Lady March's magnificent abode in Berkeley Square, and together the six, having handed over cloaks, joined the throng moving slowly up a great staircase. Along the way they swept into their group young Mr. Denyer, who harbored an attachment for Phoebe after seeing her at the Colliards' ball but was too timid to approach Aldford House.

Mr. Denyer was in his first season also, a slim fellow, not much more than Phoebe's age, with unruly hair which would *not* stay brushed into the Brutus style that he wished to affect. Phoebe spoke kindly to him, leading him to hope that he might be permitted to dance with her.

Lady March received them cordially, whispering to Lady Cora that the Prince had indicated that he might come.

"I do not know whether to hope he does or does not," she confided. "Such a *coup* if he does, but one never knows how many he will bring with him or what upset it may cause."

Lady Cora murmured sympathetically and passed on to the ballroom. The dancing had not yet begun, so she went off with Sir Boscobel to greet Lady Pembridge leaving the four from Aldford House at the side of the room, Mr. Denyer hovering anxiously. Lewis was summoned by an imperative wave from Mrs. Drummond Burrell, so he stepped aside to salute this lady, who was a strict patroness of the assemblies at Almack's and who might be influential in issuing vouchers to Phoebe and Kate, though it was late in the season.

In that moment of Lewis's inattention, Lord Percy arrived at Phoebe's side with a deafening "Halloo! May I have your first dance, Miss Phoebe, my girl?"

Phoebe cast an anxious glance at Kate, who said ingenuously, "But, Phoebe, you promised Mr. Denyer."

"So—so I did," faltered Phoebe, who did not fib easily, and Mr. Denyer, who did not understand what was going on but who had the wit to seize his chance, bowed slightly, took her limp hand, and led her out onto the dance floor. The music began, and they swept across the ballroom.

"Mind your own business, chit," Taviton growled at Kate, and whirled away before his brother could hit him.

Another gentleman had come for Kate, so when Lewis returned he found only Charles, looking grim.

"I do not know whether Percy's aim is to annoy me," Charles said, "or whether he really expects to attach Phoebe."

"Well, moderate your voice," Lewis returned in a low tone. "There are ears everywhere. What happened?"

"Percy tried to get Phoebe for the first dance, and Kate gave her a quick excuse of having promised Denyer, which as near as I can tell she had not. But Denyer was sharper than I had realized. He took her onto the floor in a wink. Then—"

Charles hesitated.

"Then what?"

"Percy snarled something at Kate."

"Damn!" said the viscount. "Kate offended?"

"Not visibly. I think she reads Percy very clearly."

"Do you know how serious your brother is in this mad pursuit? There is no real need for you to worry. I shall not allow him to have Phoebe, you can be sure. Ought to pick an older female. *They* seem to tolerate him—"

"And his title," Charles added.

They were silent for a few moments, watching Phoebe dance with young Mr. Denyer.

She was wearing white again, but the skirt of her dress was caught up in six or eight places by small bunches of violets to reveal a lavender underskirt; the effect was quite lovely. Mr. Denyer, although he did not talk easily, appeared to be sure of his steps. They performed gracefully.

Kate could scarcely be seen as she was farther away.

"Have you been promised a dance with either of our girls, Charles?"

"No. Have you?"

They exchanged glum looks.

"Damn," said the viscount. "Here they come. Let us speak at once for the supper dance. Should have asked before we came to this house—even if it is not proper form!"

Phoebe, being nearest, would have reached them first, except that she saw the poetess, Miss Garway, and led Mr. Denyer across to speak to her.

"Miss Garway," said Phoebe, "I am so happy to see you. This is the first chance since I had the opportunity to hear your beautiful poems. Have you met Mr. Denyer?"

The young author, feeling the genuine warmth of her new friend, blushed faintly and said she was happy to see Miss Milner again. "How do you do, Mr. Denyer? I believe I have heard my brother speak of you."

"Ron? Ronald Garway?" managed Mr. Denyer, forgetting the stiffness of his collar. "Why, we were at Eton together years ago!" Three being "years," from his point of view.

"Walk over with us and join my cousins," Phoebe suggested.

So they strolled down the room, uniting with Lord Aldford and Mr. Radnor just as Kate arrived with several gentlemen in her wake. All three girls were soon engaged for several dances, and Nell Garway, flushed with pleasure, looked a good deal prettier and was able to speak more easily than when under her mama's eye.

Kate caught Lady Cora's approving nod from the sidelines. She was beginning to feel more relaxed herself, even with her grandfather watching from the far side of the room.

The viscount and Charles Radnor were glad for their girls to be solicited for various dances, as long as *they* had been awarded the supper dance, Lord Aldford by his cousin, and Mr. Radnor by Kate. However, only two dances were enjoyed before a stirring in the anteroom and a sudden fanfare announced the arrival of Prince George with several gentlemen who basked in his royal favor. He was received by Lady March with a deep curtsy well done for someone her age. Dancers drew back to the sides of the room, seated persons rose, and as the regent made his way along the room, a wave of bows and curtsies flowed with him. The Prince was his most affable self, greeting many warmly by name.

When His Highness reached Lord Chilweth, he said loudly enough for most to hear, "Ah, Chilweth, We are told that you have had the felicity of recently finding a beautiful grand-daughter."

"Yes, Your Royal Highness," responded Chilweth, less loudly but audible.

"Is she here?" Prinny asked.

"She is across the room, Sir," said his lordship.

"We must meet her."

With no more warning than that, Kate found people drawing back from her as His Royal Highness and her grandfather walked across to her. Then her grandfather was saying, "May I present Kathryn Amberly, sir."

She with perfect aplomb sank in the most graceful curtsy imaginable, her green skirt falling in shimmering folds upon the floor.

"Welcome to our city, Miss Amberly," said the First Gentleman of Europe cordially. Her grandfather extended a hand to help her rise.

Then Phoebe, stunned, heard His Royal Highness say, "Aldford, I believe you have another visitor that We would like to know."

The viscount, at her shoulder, nudged her forward and she sank hurriedly as he said, "May I present my cousin, Phoebe Milner, Your Royal Highness?"

Perhaps Phoebe's curtsy was less perfect than Kate's, but her glowing face and gleaming golden curls were what the Regent noticed most. He was partial to beautiful women, especially to ones fresh and youthful.

Then Lord Aldford was assisting her to her feet and His Royal Highness was moving away down the room. Lord Chilweth bowed and returned to the companions he had left.

"I would like to fan myself," whispered Kate, but she did no such thing. Aldford and Mr. Radnor were smiling at her, and Lady Cora had seized Phoebe's hand to squeeze it.

Within twenty minutes of coming, the Prince had gone. The orchestra resumed its interrupted dance melody. Additional young men gathered to beg Lady Cora to introduce them as suitable partners for her "cousins," but Lewis and Charles had their dances first, each man with both girls, and the evening would have been considered perfect by those gentlemen if Lord Percy Taviton had not secured Phoebe before the evening was over.

She conducted herself politely, although she was not happy to have him as a partner, and Lewis and Charles could discern her wan expression. His lordship was sublimely unaware, being full of enthusiasm and confident of his attractions.

But all in all, the evening was a tremendous success for which two dazzled girls prettily thanked Lady Cora and their escorts later, before almost *dancing* upstairs to their rooms and beds.

"There!" said Lady Cora with satisfaction. "See what we have accomplished in a short time? Of course, it helps that our girls are wonderfully unspoiled."

"Well, you are in a fair way to spoiling them," said Charles.

"I? Nonsense. Who is it that always wants to talk and dance with them?"

The gentlemen smiled and shook their heads but looked sheepish.

Eight

Nanny Bloom was groggy with sleep when her girls returned, but she came alive in a second when she heard they had been presented to His Royal Highness.

"Oh, my! How did he look? What did he say?" she asked eagerly. "Was he very handsome?"

"Round as a ball," said Kate.

"But very fine," amended Phoebe.

"A *red* ball," Kate insisted. "I will admit, his coat was handsome—though his waistcoat was straining at the buttons."

Phoebe looked reproachful. "I did not notice those things. His face and manner were so pleasant. And he *did* ask to meet us, Kate. Who could have expected that?"

"Certainly not the two of us. Nanny asked if he was handsome, and I suppose he must have been that at one time. Too bad that he has grown so fat. I must remember that his life has been one of long frustration."

"Aunt Cora and our cousins were so pleased," Phoebe added.

Charles had become a cousin.

"It was truly thrilling. Just think! We were received by the man who is to become King someday when his poor, mad father dies."

Sobered by this thought, the girls undressed with Nanny's help and tumbled into Kate's bed to whisper more details to one another, while Nanny went back to her couch.

"Do—you—think we are expected to make a match with a man from this group we have met?" Phoebe asked hesitantly.

Kate answered lightly, "Don't be a goose. We cannot both of us make a match with *one* man. It will take two."

Phoebe thought it was not like her cousin to quibble. "You know what I mean. When we came to London, we did not even expect to *meet* gentlemen, much less attach one—two."

"No, we didn't. And I cannot say one knows a gentleman's worth simply by drinking a cup of tea with him—or exchanging polite banter—or dancing at a ball. Perhaps we should go back to Oxford, only—"

"Only what?"

"I have been hoping, now that we are here, that you would find happiness. You are not so hard to please as I."

"Why, Kate, no one could be more warm-hearted than you!"

"You think that because you think the best of everyone. I *am* hard to please. There! Now you know my worst trait."

"But we have met such agreeable gentlemen," insisted Phoebe in a troubled voice, "and I daresay we shall encounter more. Everyone is so cordial. No one could be kinder than my cousins and the people to whom they have introduced us."

Kate said sardonically, "We are fresh faces. When our modest dowries are known, do you think we will receive as much attention?"

"Now you are being cynical," Phoebe protested. "That is not like you! We did not expect to enter Society. Should we go back to Papa's manor?"

"Not at once, perhaps," said Kate. "Your cousin's social standing is giving us entrée. Even if people discover how poor—well, *un*rich—we are, they will not drop us. There is nothing to make us hurry home. Do not let me spoil your pleasure, dearest. I am enjoying our little fling, too."

Phoebe never did reach her own bed. When Lady Cora came at midmorning the next day to wish them good morning and say she was off to an appointment with her man of business, she found them just stretching and yawning.

"You can lie abed as long as you wish, my dears. There are no special plans for today. I shall try to return in time for afternoon callers. There may be a great many knocking at the door after Prinny's distinguishing attention last night, but if you do not want to see them, send word to Serle to say you are not receiving."

"Would it not be ungracious to turn callers away when they are kind enough to come?" asked Phoebe doubtfully.

"Oh, as to that," returned Lady Cora, "it will make them come even earlier tomorrow. If you are bored, I daresay Lewis and Charles will be glad to amuse you. The sun is bright today—a good day for walking in the park—a chance to wear your new bonnets. Tell Lewis if you wish to do that or go driving."

"My cousin may have plans of his own," Phoebe said.

"Fiddle-faddle," said her ladyship. "Won't be important. Ask for what you want."

However, Phoebe and Kate were curious to see who *would* come, so they had a sort of breakfast-nuncheon on trays before going down to the drawing room with bits of sewing to keep their hands busy.

After a time Phoebe had drifted into the music room to try a few melodies and was there when Lewis entered the drawing room with a sober face.

"Where is Phoebe?" he asked Kate.

"In the next room," Kate answered. "Oh, here she is—"

Phoebe was coming back, carrying some sheets of music. "Did you ask for me, Cousin Lewis?"

"Yes, my dear," said the viscount in a odd tone of voice. "You see, I have received an offer for your hand."

Phoebe gasped and crushed the music to her bosom. "No!"

"But yes, truly. You must not think I would force you into anything," he said hurriedly and seriously. "It was sure to happen—maybe several times, for you have been much admired." He glanced at Kate, who was also staring at him with a shocked face. "You may find this *soon* to be approached, but he is quite earnest and fears others may try to win you before—"

Phoebe made a little mew of protest.

"You have only to tell me if you want to decline. I will not press you. But I *can* say in his behalf that he is a person of true character whom I have always admired." He shot a glance at Kate who was looking a little alarmed. He hurried to add, "Not rich—though well able to care for your comfort. If this would not give you some expectation of happiness, you may certainly refuse. I will not fault you for that. But I do feel that he deserves a civil answer from yourself."

"In person? Must I?"

"I think you must. It is only kindness."

"But w-who?" gasped Phoebe.

"Why—Charles, of course."

Phoebe turned from white to red. "Charles! Where is he? Where?"

"In the library—"

She dropped the music to scatter across the carpet and ran hastily from the room.

"Good God!" exclaimed his lordship. He followed to latch the door and looked back across the room toward Kate. "Does that mean she will accept Charles?"

Kate smiled. "Strange to say, she has not confided in me, but that exit can hardly mean anything else. They are perfectly suited, you know. Both have such easy temperaments."

"I am not old enough for this sort of thing," Lewis said, running fingers through his hair. "But, yes, yes, I see they are suited. Charles will cherish her. He leaves me in no doubt of that—says it was all up with him the first time he saw her, and that he wished to make his offer before other beaux—with titles and greater wealth—came up to scratch." Then he added soberly, "I thought Aunt Cora might have grander ideas for my cousin."

Kate said, "There is nothing grand about Phoebe's ideas."

They stared at each other across the room.

"I did wonder," Kate ventured in a soft voice, "if you wanted her yourself."

Jolted by astonishment, he exclaimed, "I? Want Phoebe? No-no. Dashed charming girl, but I had not given many thoughts to matrimony . . . well, perhaps a thought. Only been Viscount Aldford fourteen months. I suppose Aunt Cora will begin telling me I must think of an heir—"

"Is all you want a brood mare?" asked Kate sharply, dropping her sewing and rising to her feet, the better to fight.

"Well, it's a matter of duty, you see."

She said, "No, I don't see. Oh, of course I know your family title needs to be passed on, but it seems abominable to me to choose a wife simply to breed little viscounts. *My parents* married for love, and it lasted as long as they lived."

He all but howled, "You don't understand. Were estates and a title involved in their relationship? You must not think I am made of stone. Don't you suppose I can see what Charles's and Phoebe's relationship is? And envy it? In these circles real love-matches are rare."

Momentarily she was silenced, but frowning.

"Charles is gentle. He wants a gentle girl. I, on the other hand," Lewis said, "prefer a termagant. Come here."

"I do not take orders," Kate snapped.

He said smoothly, "Very well. Then I will come to you."

"But we disagree so often," she protested.

"Do we? I find you most *agreeable.*" So saying, he started toward her. Kate retreated behind a sofa, but it was a place of no escape. Though he moved slowly, his stride was long, and he soon had his arms around her.

"We quarrel," she gasped.

"Um-m. Splendidly," he said, kissing her temple, which was the nearest spot.

A voice by the door interrupted plaintively, "Mur-r-auw."

"No, no," replied his lordship without raising his head. "I

am too busy to open the door for cats now." He progressed to Kate's soft cheek.

"I cannot," she whispered, "—cannot always be *expected* to agree with you when we are mar—" She broke off, horrified at what she had almost said, when he had not mentioned the word "marry."

Lewis threw back his head for a hearty laugh. "Fifty percent of the time will be enough. Say 'yes,' my love."

But Kate was able to say nothing. She had had no suitors except a very inhibited son of a clergyman. Nor had she been kissed before. This—this close embrace felt strange, alarming, exciting. He reached her lips and began to kiss her tenderly, warmly, urgently, with increasing passion so that her very *will* turned to water.

Then suddenly he held her off.

"Where, in God's name," he demanded, "is Aunt Cora?"

"Gone to her man of business," Kate replied faintly.

"Left you unchaperoned? Good lord!"

He began to rock with laughter. *"There's* a true witch. Set two traps and baited them—" he looked down at Kate's flushed face "—with lovely ladies! Charles and I will have to wrack our brains to think of suitable ways to pay her back."

"I shall not let you play tricks on Aunt Cora," Kate averred, her eyes flashing.

He said, "She is the one playing tricks."

"No, no! She has been wonderful to Phoebe and me."

Lewis smiled down at her. "Disagreeing with me already, love?"

Well, she was doing exactly that . . . but she thought perhaps it was also true that she was his "love."

As he was hers.

About the Author

Dorothea Donley lives with her family in Louisville, Kentucky. She is the author of two Zebra regency romances: THE BEAUX OF BAYLEY DELL, and GENTLEMAN'S CHOICE, both available at your local bookstore. Dorothea loves hearing from her readers and you may write to her c/o Zebra Books. Please include a self-addressed stamped envelope if you wish a response.

The Notorious Lord

Jean R. Ewing

There was the remote echo of a slamming door somewhere downstairs.

"Oh, dear heavens!" The Countess of Hartwood clutched at the sheet to cover her revealing, if charming, dishabille. "It's my husband! Oh, God! James, quickly! You must leave. If he finds you here I am ruined."

"I rather think, my dear," said James Edward Harding, Viscount Beaumarais, "that you are ruined anyway."

"No, no! There's time! Oh, dear Lord! My maid can show you a back way out."

Lord Beaumarais stared idly at the ceiling. He seemed unmoved by these frantic protestations. "Alice, I am not dressed. I refuse to have your maid lead me through the corridors without my boots—or my shirt and breeches, for that matter. I am surprised you would make so indelicate a suggestion."

"For heaven's sake! How long does it take to put on a shirt? Carry your boots, James!" There was a thumping in the hall beneath the countess's delightful boudoir. "Oh, Lord! If Hartwood finds you here, there'll be a duel and you'll kill him."

Beaumarais sighed and ran his elegant hands back over his dark head. "No doubt I shall, since your poor husband suffers from weak eyes and a weaker head. Alas, what if I should put a ball into his heart and leave you a widow?"

"I don't want to be a widow." The countess flung herself from the bed and glared down at him. The sunlight from the tall window lit his profile and the long black lashes. Really, he was delectable! But the dark brown eyes were laughing up at her. "Oh, you impossible man! What on earth persuaded me to invite you here, I don't know!"

The viscount sat up and watched as she rapidly gathered the garments which lay scattered across the floor. "Now that, my dear Alice, is a lie. You know very well why you invited me into your bed—at least you seemed to know."

"Here! Your clothes! Now, please, James. Get out!"

Beaumarais pulled her into his arms and kissed her. Considering the urgency of their situation, it was an unnecessarily thorough kiss. Then he slid his lean fingers into the huddle of clothing, and a small blade appeared in his hand.

"Oh, heavens!" The countess collapsed onto the bed next to him and her eyes filled with tears. The sound of boots on the stairs was unmistakable. "You have a knife! What are you going to do?"

The brown eyes widened a little. "I think I should have a memento of our charming afternoon together, don't you?"

"Whatever are you talking about?" The heavy footsteps were coming ever closer. "You want to ruin me?"

"Only to steal a lock or two of hair."

A voice called out from the corridor. "Alice! Are you resting?"

"Oh, God! Must I beg you?" She pointed to a door on the right side of the room. "That way! There's a stair down to the stableyard. You can go out unseen."

The viscount inspected the three ringlets of blond hair which he had cut from her head, caught up the bundle of clothes, and slipped from the bed. Without regard to the fact that he was entirely naked, he crossed the room and swept up his boots before glancing down into the yard at the back of Lord Hartwood's townhouse.

"I don't think so, Countess," he said. "Lord Hartwood's brother and his wife appear to be there, admiring the horses." The footsteps in the hallway stopped outside the door. "And now they approach the house." The doorknob rattled. "I fear there is no escape through the stableyard, dear Alice." With a wink to the distraught countess, Lord Beaumarais stepped through another door on the left and disappeared.

"James, no!" hissed the countess, catching up her robe and shrugging into it. "There's no way out of there! It's my dressing room!"

But her boudoir door opened and the Earl of Hartwood stepped into the room. "Madam? Ah, you are not asleep. I have pleasant news: Joseph and Elizabeth are here. Come, Countess, you're not dressed?"

"I have the headache, Hartwood. I am resting. I have no desire to entertain your tiresome brother and his infinitely more tiresome wife. There is no time to dress."

Hartwood glowered at his pretty wife. "Nonsense! Put on that strawberry-sprigged affair you wore yesterday."

"I have torn it."

"Madam, you have a thousand dresses. Any one will do! Here, I'll get something for you."

She started up in genuine alarm. "No, Hartwood! Pray, not the dressing room!"

"And why not the dressing room, madam?"

"La!" said a fine falsetto. "Oh, you gave me such a turn, my lord!"

The Earl of Hartwood spun about and glared at the dressing room door, which had opened to reveal the startling sight of a very tall lady in a dashing blue bonnet. A red velvet cloak was draped around her wide shoulders. Beneath it peeked the frills of an elaborate afternoon dress of white muslin. The lady held a bundle of other dresses draped over one arm, the skirts of which conveniently swept the floor. In the other hand she displayed a delicate silk fan. As the earl stared, she gave an elegant flip of the wrist and opened it. A scene of winsome shepherds and shepherdesses was painted on the silk. "When her ladyship was so kind as to invite me to inspect her wardrobe for myself, I never thought to have the honor of meeting your lordship, never I did!"

"Who is this person, madam?" said the earl, turning to his

wife, but the countess seemed to have lost all capacity for
speech.

The strange lady stepped farther into the room and made
a surprisingly elegant curtsy. Deep brown eyes with remarkably long lashes smiled at the earl over the top of the fan.
"Madame Celeste, at your service, my lord. Mantua-maker
to the *haut ton*—I serve only the most select clientele, of
course. I must say her ladyship's wardrobe is sadly outdated.
All these dresses need to be ripped and resewn. Look at this
yellow sarcenet! Bows like these went out last year. The cal-
amanco trim must definitely go. And this pink taffeta! Not
her ladyship's color at all. I should know since I have the
honor to be blessed with exactly her ladyship's shade of hair."
With an expressive roll of the eyes, the mantua-maker indicated the three yellow curls that peeked beneath the rim of
her bonnet. "Now, the silver pongee is very well, my lord, just
the smallest alteration will suffice. But I think her ladyship
should very seriously consider an overdress of tiffany—silver
and gold, perhaps—to update it, you know."

"Madam," said the earl. "Another time! We have company.
You will be pleased to leave."

The lady dropped him another deep curtsy and fluttered
her eyelashes over the fan. "Oh, la! I will send to let her
ladyship know when everything is ready. Your condescension
and graciousness will always be a treasure, my lord, that I
shall store up in my heart. I never thought to have the honor
to meet your lordship in her ladyship's own bedchamber. Indeed, I didn't!"

"We are somewhat pressed for time, madam," said the earl.
She curtsied again. "Good day, Lord Hartwood, my lady."

"Not my yellow sarcenet!" cried Lady Hartwood suddenly.

"Oh, indeed, yes, my lady!" The tall woman turned to the
countess and lowered the fan for a moment to smile at her.
The bonnet shielded her face from the earl. There was the
faintest dark shadow around the sardonic mouth and firm
chin. "You must trust that I know what I'm doing, Lady Hart-

wood. La! I shouldn't be able to look myself in the face were I not to take the sarcenet. Your ladyship will be most gratified with the results. After all, you seemed in transports of delight over my skills this afternoon."

And the mantua-maker stepped into the corridor, where she leaned her bonnet against the gold-and-blue striped wallpaper and allowed herself the luxury of a moment's open laughter before striding away down the stairs and out of the front door into the London street. The butler stared after her for a moment. She had winked at him over her fan. What very fine eyes! But how had that female entered the house without his knowledge? And then he gaped in amazement. For God's sake! Beneath the muslin flounces, the woman was wearing top boots!

It was a tale that would have delighted every man at the viscount's club that evening, but of course, it wasn't told. Viscount Beaumarais had no intention of saving the countess's reputation in the afternoon only to ruin it that evening. Anyway, it probably wouldn't be necessary to see Alice again; he could send the dresses back by messenger. He leaned back and admired his brandy, however, with a certain rueful regret. To have an overdeveloped sense of humor was sometimes a definite handicap. So instead he listened with indulgent patience to Mr. Archimedes Greville, who was now foxed enough to get maudlin.

"She's an antidote, Beaumarais! From her portrait she'd seem to be as scrawny as a scarecrow. Whatever am I to do?"

"Your father insists on this match?"

Mr. Greville sighed into his glass. "He says if I don't marry her, he'll strike me from the will."

"But why, dear sir," said the viscount very deliberately, "is your estimable father so set upon your marriage to a female you've never met who does not meet your requirements for buxom beauty?"

"Oh, God," said Mr. Greville, "it's textiles, of course."

"Textiles, dear sir? You mean satin and sarcenet, silk and grosgrain?"

"That's exactly what I mean! Her father is Frederick Noll— you must have heard of Noll Brothers? He has a nice little business in merino and muslin, and my father thinks to combine that trade with his."

"And have you marry the daughter to cement the alliance? Good God! How very tiresome! Why don't you refuse?"

"Oh, heavens, Beaumarais! How could you possibly understand? I'm entirely dependent upon going into business with Father."

"But what if the lady should spurn you?"

"I don't suppose Mary Noll would dare refuse me, when her family is so set upon amalgamation with Greville and Sons."

"Then you have very little knowledge of women, sir— whether it's how to go about charming them, or getting rid of them when necessary."

"Well, it's easy for you to say! I'm sure if you wanted, you could either have her in bed in a week, or convince her you were brother to the devil so she'd die an old maid rather than wed you. But then you'll never have to work a day in your life. Your father's the Earl of Hamilton; you're a lord, for God's sake!"

"Why so I am," said James innocently. "Thus I lead a life of ease, luxury, and profligate debauchery. But then, it does have its own disadvantages, sir."

"Such as?" said Mr. Greville suspiciously.

"Such as relatives. I am unhappily supposed to journey to Scotland to visit some aged aunt of my mother's in order to insinuate myself into her will. Lord Hamilton insists upon it. Thus we both seemed to be enmeshed in the burdensome prerequisites of last testaments."

"I'd rather go to Scotland than be forced to woo some female that I'd never clapped eyes on in my life. Gallantry and flirtation is more your line than mine."

"I would have thought you'd be more keen to offer her insults and a cold shoulder."

"I couldn't!" said Mr. Greville. "I haven't your nerve. Give me an aged aunt any day."

"But she resides north of Edinburgh, dear sir. Not only will the journey be gothic, but the aged aunt is deaf and blind, which is going to make the task of insinuation a little tedious, don't you think? Besides, she lives in a castle. It will be drafty and damp."

"I'd rather go to the ends of the earth, be it never so moldering, than go to Chepstow and make sheep's eyes at a beanpole."

"Chepstow?" said Viscount Beaumarais. His eyes narrowed very slightly between the lush lashes.

"Yes, Mary Noll is going there to do sketches with some friend and her brother. My father believes I could casually appear and accomplish the courtship. God! I hate women's watercolors. But what's wrong with Chepstow?"

"Why, a great deal is right with it, sir. That's where Strongbow had his castle."

"Strongbow?"

"Yes, Earl Richard de Clare, a magnificent twelfth-century ancestor of mine. I've always rather fancied seeing the place where he lived."

Mr. Archimedes Greville took a large gulp of brandy. "Are you thinking what I'm thinking?"

Viscount Beaumarais laughed lazily over the rim of his glass. "I am, indeed, sir, but I refuse to be called Archimedes! Don't you have a second name?"

"Yes," said Archimedes Greville, "it's James."

"Oh, God!" James Edward Harding grinned widely, causing two deep creases to appear in his cheeks. "How very convenient! I believe you're about to discover how much fun it is to be a lord, while I may indulge myself in the humble pastime of wooing Miss Mary Noll on the banks of the Wye."

"Done!" said Mr. Greville. He put down his brandy and put out his hand. "You know, we're awfully foxed, James," he added as Lord Beaumarais shook it.

"I make all my best decisions drunk, James," returned the viscount. And he gave way to uproarious laughter.

Miss Mary Noll frowned at the painting she had been working on these last two hours. It was a rather clumsy rendering of the toll gate in the archway of the thirteenth-century Town Gate, where a couple of farmers in homespun smocks counted out their coin to the gatekeeper. There was a great deal of bleating from the livestock which accompanied them, since two farm dogs were keeping the sheep crowded up against the barrier and the sheep objected.

"My sheep look the same as my clouds, Miss Fraser," said Mary. "Can't you show me how to fix them?"

"A little burnt umber to the undersides of the fleeces?" asked Joan Fraser gently. "The sheep must look more solid, I believe."

Mary Noll dipped her brush into her little container of water. "No, it's no use, is it? I shall never learn, however much you try to teach me." Then she dimpled and laughed up at her companion. "Never mind, I'm so glad we have met."

"And so are my brother and I, Miss Noll."

"Yet Father will be so disappointed."

"That the lady to whom you have entrusted your tour of the Wye Valley turns out to be such an incompetent teacher?"

"That I shan't marry this Greville fellow! How could Father do anything so gothic? I had to send him my miniature, just like a prize sow. Now Father has determined to send the creature here to spoil our holiday."

"Has he? Then we may be in for some entertainment," said Joan dryly.

"Oh, Miss Fraser! You clever creature! Do you guess what I've done?"

Joan Fraser watched as the toll gate opened and the sheep began to stream through. "Since I find that the miniature portrait I did of myself last week has gone missing, I rather suspect that you sent poor Mr. Greville my likeness instead of your own."

Mary laughed. It was a very attractive, open laugh. "It will be splendid when he arrives, don't you think?"

"And he makes his sheep's eyes at me? It's no use, Mary dear, it won't wash. You are a lovely thing and I'm not. He'll fall in love with you the moment he sees you. The charade won't last two minutes."

"Why not?"

"Because I have no intention of going along with it," said Joan Fraser sternly, though her eyes betrayed her amusement. "And that's final!"

Lord Beaumarais gazed idly at the miniature as the coach rocked along the turnpike. The painting was very well done. It was a strong-boned face, with a high-bridged nose and a slightly gaunt look about the cheekbones—a face rather typical of Scotland. Miss Mary Noll would appear to have ash blond hair worn in a braid about her head. She looked forbidding. She did not look like the daughter of Frederick Noll, Draper. He could imagine that the abbess of a medieval nunnery would have had such a face. No wonder Archimedes Greville was a reluctant suitor. Yet there was something about the features which intrigued him—a hint of strong character and a wry sense of humor. He thrust the portrait back into his pocket. For he had other, far more serious, reasons for going to Chepstow than either the courting of Miss Mary Noll or

the castle of Strongbow. Chepstow, of course, was a shipbuild-
ing town.

The ferry from Bristol moved across the Severn so slowly
that James thought it might have been faster to swim, but as
it entered the mouth of the River Wye, the incoming tide lifted
the boat and carried it swiftly enough to Chepstow. There was
a splendid bustle as the passengers unloaded near the Gun-
stock Wharf and James looked about. Immediately in front
of him was a forest of masts and the huge piles of timber that
marked the shipyards. Behind them lay warehouses and offices which hid most of the town from view. But in the background, towering over it all, were the broken stone towers of
Strongbow's castle on its high limestone cliff above the river.
If he had not had other, more pressing, concerns, James would
have liked to explore it.

"Take your bags, sir?"

Lord Beaumarais turned to the fellow who stood at his
elbow with a cart. For only a moment the arrogant grace of
the movement was unguarded. "No, I shall walk," he said
absently, and pressed a coin into the man's hand.

"Thank you kindly, my lord," said the man instantly.

"No such luck, sir," grinned James, allowing himself to
slouch very slightly. "It's my birthday, felt generous, that's all.
Plain Mr. Greville, at your service."

The man's face fell. "No offense, Mr. Greville."

"None taken, sir, I assure you." Shouldering his bag, James
strode away after the other passengers up the long stretch of
Lower Church Street. Behind the neat houses with their
wrought-iron railings lay a sweep of orchards known as the
Great Hop Gardens. A few minutes' walk had taken him past
the church into St. Mary Street and finally up to the doors of
the grandest inn in the Square. He entered the lobby and
stopped short. He was face to face with the lady of the portrait.
She was tall, perhaps only four inches shorter than he was

himself, quite certainly too thin, and she had a sketchbook
under one arm.

"Good heavens!" she said.

James set down his bag, smiled, and bowed. It was a charming smile and a most correct bow. "Do I have the honor of
addressing Miss Mary Noll?" The tall lady with the coronet
of blond plaits looked extremely uncomfortable for a moment. She was frowning, which made the lines of her face
even more severe. "Mr. James Greville, at your service, Miss
Noll," said Viscount Beaumarais without hesitation.

"Mr. James Greville?" she said at last. "Are you sure?"

"Good heavens! I will even reluctantly admit to the Archimedes, if that has you confused. Archimedes James Greville, sent here by my father in order that we may pursue an
acquaintance, Miss Noll. Do I have the wrong lady? Surely
not! I have your picture here."

He pulled the miniature from his inside pocket and showed
it to her. The lady glanced at it briefly, then studied his face
again. "Very well," she said grimly. "We must welcome you
to Chepstow, Mr. Greville. Allow me to tell my friend Miss
Fraser that you are here. And, as perhaps you know, Miss
Fraser's brother accompanies us on our Wye Tour."

"I shall be delighted to meet the Frasers, of course," said
James. Good Lord! What a forbidding female! Where was
that interesting glimmer of humor that he had glimpsed in the
portrait?

"Perhaps after you are settled into your room you would
like to join us for tea?" asked Joan, and with another frown,
she turned and swept away up the stair.

Mary looked up as her friend entered the room. "What is
it?" she asked. "Has something untoward happened?"

"Untoward enough!" said Joan, and she laughed. It entirely
transformed her features. "Miss Noll, you will be amazed to
hear that I have just entered your charade, after all. There is

a gentleman downstairs who claims to be Mr. Archimedes James Greville. I told him I was you. All we have to do is get my brother to go along with the deception, and I believe we shall have a very entertaining holiday."

"You said you were me? Oh, this is capital! But why did you change your mind?"

Joan sat down at a little desk and idly picked up the quill which lay there. She dipped it into her inkwell and began to make a quick sketch of the features she had seen on the man downstairs—the classic nose and strong chin, softened only by that delightful curve of lip and those extraordinary eyelashes. "Because the gentleman downstairs is not Mr. Greville," she said.

"What?" said Mary. "None of us has ever met Archimedes Greville. How do you know?"

Joan looked up. She seemed to be torn between laughter and annoyance. "Because I just saw this gentleman's portrait not two weeks ago in the home of an elderly lady in Scotland. The lady is rather blind and could hardly see it herself, but she made a point of telling me all about the subject. He is her great-nephew."

"Oh, good heavens! Go on," said Mary, sitting on the bed and pulling her knees to her chin. "This is positively delightful. What did she tell you about him?"

"That he's a rake and a dissolute wastrel." Joan added a little shading beneath the carved nostril. "No wager too deep, no vice too outrageous, everything to excess: debauchery, gaming, and wine. He drinks like a lord because he is one, I suppose."

Mary squealed and hugged her arms around her knees. "A lord?"

Joan laughed again, then she instantly assumed the most serious of expressions, though it was not quite enough to hide the twinkle in her eye. "My dear Miss Noll," she said gravely. "Though from this moment I will call you Miss Fraser, and I shall be Miss Noll,"—she picked up her sketch and crumpled it in her hand—"the fellow downstairs who has come to court you is not Mr. Archibald James Greville at all,"—the crushed ball of paper dropped into the waste basket—"but James Edward Harding: none other than the notorious Viscount Beaumarais, and he will mistakenly begin to court me!"

It did not take long for the ladies to put together a supposition of why Lord Beaumarais should be masquerading as Mr. Greville, and one which was very close to the truth. The men were probably friends and had been drinking together. The viscount was a gambler. It was surely some kind of unprincipled wager, and poor Mary was meant to be the butt of the joke. Under the circumstances Miss Joan Fraser had no compunction whatsoever in taking part in a deception of her own, if for no other reason than to avenge her wronged sex.

"All that remains," said Mary once they had settled all this to their satisfaction, "is to convince your brother to take part. Otherwise we shall be discovered instantly."

"Oh, Douglas will agree, never fear. After all, he thinks of nothing but his beloved birds. It won't matter to him in the least if we take each other's names for a week, and since he is always wrapped up in his own pursuits, he won't be around enough to embarrass us by forgetting."

Mr. Douglas Fraser was Joan's senior by six years. He was a gentleman of comfortable means with a small estate in Scotland, but his passion in life was birds. With a spyglass and a notebook he had catalogued all the feathered species of his native woods and glens, and was happy to have his sister's companionship when he ventured further afield in pursuit of his hobby. These excursions, however, could prove a little lonely for Joan, since Douglas was out at dawn, and shut up in his room over his notes and his specimens the rest of the day—thus the inclusion of Miss Mary Noll in the party. The young ladies had met in the Pump Room at Bath and become friends. When the next ornithological expedition promised to take the Frasers to the Wye Valley, made so romantically famous by Wordsworth, it pleased everyone for Mary to be invited. A letter from Mr. Noll concerning the sending of a portrait and the imminent arrival of the unwanted suitor had created only a momentary distress, for the ladies were thoroughly enjoying themselves in Chepstow. They now determined to thoroughly enjoy themselves over tea. The notorious Lord Beaumarais might think he had them fooled, but the ladies would get their revenge! Mr. Douglas Fraser was informed of the charade, grunted affably, and pointed out that he had seen a new type of waterfowl that very morning.

"Oh, good heavens!" whispered Mary into Joan's ear as they entered the pleasant hotel dining room. "You didn't say he was so very handsome. Viscount Beaumarais! How dare he masquerade as Mr. Greville?"

James stood up as the ladies came in. The tall lady he believed to be Mary Noll led the way. The other must be Miss Fraser. She was very pretty, small, and rounded, with lovely blue eyes in a heart-shaped face. Yet his glance moved back to the slender blonde with her severe gaze and high cheekbones. He wasn't quite sure how to fulfill his obligation to Archimedes Greville. He was supposed to be here to court her, of course, yet his goal must be to make her reject him. Quite suddenly, and to his own immense surprise, he wished he had not begun the deception.

"I have taken the liberty of ordering tea," he said simply, as the ladies sat down. "Then I must say how very pleased I am to make the acquaintance of such talented ladies."

"Talented?" said Joan, raising her brows.

"Your portrait, Miss Noll, shows a very marked skill and unique depth of feeling. It is your own work, isn't it?" A very subtle blush colored her cheeks. Joan was very sensitive about her painting, for unlike most of the young ladies of her acquaintance, she took it seriously. "I see that it is," he continued. His beautiful voice conveyed nothing but sincere interest. "Yet you were rather hard on yourself. It was accurate, but it wasn't flattering at all. Such a passion for truth is a rare gift."

Joan looked at him in something very like panic. This wasn't what she had expected at all. "It's nothing," she said clumsily.

Mary gave her friend a puzzled look. Joan was never at a loss for words. "Miss Fr—" She caught herself just in time. "Miss Noll always does exquisite work, Mr. Greville. I am the one whose colors are mud, whose sheep resemble clouds, and whose clouds look like cotton. And speaking of cotton, you and Miss Noll must share a stunning knowledge of fabrics, since your families share that interest." She grinned mischievously. Perhaps she could unsettle the lord right away! "What do you think of her messaline?"

Lord Beaumarais gravely studied Joan's dress. "I hesitate to correct you, Miss Fraser," he said. "But I believe that messaline is usually silk. Miss Noll's gown is a very fine calico, I believe, and is an example of our latest imports from India."

"Of course it is," said Joan, and suddenly she laughed. The lord had made a study of fabric? He must be taking this imposture very seriously!

Tea was a most confusing affair. First because the supposed Mr. Greville continued to talk about the business of trading cloth, of which Joan knew nothing. She covered up her ignorance as best as she could, but was she the one to be caught out first? Then he seemed to lose interest in that subject, and he moved on to other things. It was subtly done, but Joan realized to her chagrin that he must have noticed her discomfort. Pray he would think it was just because she was emptyheaded, not because members of the Fraser family had never taken part in trade in their lives.

Then, although Joan was determined that the disgraceful Lord Beaumarais should be the one embarrassed by his shameful **behavior,** she found herself unwittingly becoming interested in the things he had to say. He began to talk knowledgeably about the history of the area—and history, in addition to painting, was one of her passions. Before she could plan what her strategy should be to punish him for his outrageous deceit, he had managed to enthrall her in honest talk. The notorious viscount might be a villain, but he was certainly an interesting one. While Mary frowned over the failure of her plan to expose him about the fabric trade, Miss Joan Fraser saw him leave after tea with very mixed feelings.

Mr. Douglas Fraser rose early, since the birds rose early. In fact, he was up before dawn and was served breakfast in his room by candlelight. Joan was in the habit of joining him there, for otherwise brother and sister rarely shared a meal. She would then stay in his room for an hour or so, and with her delicate watercolors, make paintings of his latest collection, before following her own interests the rest of the day. The morning following the viscount's arrival, Joan noticed that Douglas had forgotten his gloves. Seizing them from the dresser, she hurried down the stairs and caught up with him at the back door which led to the stableyard. He nodded absently and kissed her on the cheek before she watched his familiar figure go shambling off. Then she noticed another figure slipping through the shadows and disappearing toward the river. By the subtle grace of movement, she knew it was the viscount. What disreputable adventure could he possibly be up to this early? A woman? An amorous intrigue would surely send him creeping back to the hotel at dawn, not leaving it. Did the man have more secrets than just his masquerade as a clothier's son? She shrugged and went quickly up the stairs to finish her work.

She then went to her own room, where she attempted to read, but she was not able to concentrate on her book. Instead, she pulled out her portfolio and looked over her paintings.

Did they really show *a very marked skill and unique depth of feeling?* It was one area in which a lord, who must have been surrounded with the works of the great masters all his life, would have a valid opinion. But then, a lord like Viscount Beaumarais would be in the habit of flattering women, wouldn't he? And he knew enough to do it with subtlety. Joan closed the collection of paintings. What had she done by trading places with Mary?

To her surprise, she next saw him at breakfast. Hers had already been taken, of course, but she kept Mary company in the dining room every day and drank tea while her friend ate her meal. Lord Beaumarais joined them. Wherever he had been on his early morning excursion, it had not stimulated his appetite. He ate with a frugality that contrasted very seriously with Joan's preconceptions of the habits of lords, and drank only coffee. Of course, he would hardly get drunk at the breakfast table! Mary was soon done, and with a private wink at Joan, made an excuse to leave them. James watched her leave, then turned to Joan with a smile.

"Your friend is generous, isn't she?"

"What do you mean, sir?"

"Why, she leaves us alone to begin our courtship. That is why I'm here, you know, Miss Noll."

Joan assumed her most forbidding manner. "Then in that case, you might as well leave again, Mr. Greville. I have determined from this moment to remain an old maid."

"Have you? How very unfortunate! For I have just determined to pursue your hand and affection in earnest."

"In that order?" said Joan, with a lift of the brows.

He laughed. "Whether you welcome me or not, I shall haunt you with soulful looks and whimsical poesy. I must woo you, for both our fathers wish it. Thus the hand-winning part comes first. Your affection, it seems to me, would be a valuable thing for anyone to win. Yet I imagine it's not lightly given, so I can be less sure of it. Thus it comes second."

Joan knew she was out of her depth. If he had in truth been Mr. Greville, he might have intrigued her, but since she knew it was all a sham, his words meant nothing but the opening gambit of a game for which she didn't know the rules. "I don't think soulful looks and poetry will go very far to change my mind, sir," she said.

He leaned back and smiled, his eyes very slightly narrowed between the lush lashes. It made him look faintly dangerous. "But I have the very best of mawkish and simpering expressions, Miss Noll, and I should love to practice them on you. You will find my sentimental looks will go far to undermine your determination, for I'm sure that beneath your severity, you have a soft heart."

"And poetry?"

"I'll offer you *'as much love in rhyme/As would be crammed up in a sheet of paper,/Writ o' both sides the leaf, margent and all.'* Won't that do?"

"Then it will be *'A huge translation of hypocrisy,/Vilely compiled, profound simplicity','"* replied Joan instantly. "Since we quote from *Love's Labours Lost,* sir, it doesn't auger well for the success of your courtship."

"Then I shall have to kiss you," said James, leaning forward and idly pouring her more tea.

She was surprised into laughter. "If you do, I shall ask my brother to call you out."

"Your brother?" he asked.

Joan blushed suddenly, for he looked up from the teapot and straight into her eyes. Had she given herself away? Mary Noll did not have a brother—and the viscount might know it. She kept her voice light. "Unfortunately, he is only fourteen, and not really a brother, just a cousin, but he's the very devil with a slingshot."

But his glance seemed to search her heart. "I am completely serious, you know," he said.

Suddenly unsure of everything, Joan leapt to her feet. "Then you would please me a great deal to leave town this instant, sir. I don't want anything to do with your idle and empty courtship."

James watched her leave, then stirred his coffee for a moment. Why on earth had he done that? All he needed was an excuse to stay in Chepstow for a week or two without his presence being questioned. Though he was here to woo her, it wasn't at all his intention to succeed. Yet he realized he wanted very much to challenge this tall, severe lady. She had never been courted, had she? She knew nothing of that delightful game between men and women. And he would like very much to kiss her, and that made no sense at all.

Joan and Mary set out from the hotel with their sketchbooks and walked down Hocker Hill. The bulk of the castle soon rose on their left, and beneath it lay the neat rows of houses leading to the bridge. The span in Monmouthshire met the Gloucestershire half at a stone pier in the center of the River Wye. The counties had never been able to agree on upkeep and repair, with the result that Chepstow Bridge had a certain reputation. There was talk of a new bridge to be designed by John Rennie, but it hadn't happened yet. As the young ladies turned past the Bridge Inn to walk along the river, Mary stopped and caught Joan by the arm.

"Isn't that our false Mr. Greville?" she asked, pointing.

Joan had already seen him. He was leaning on the rickety parapet of the bridge, gazing downstream at the cluster of boats drawn up below. Approaching Chepstow across the bridge behind him was a small cart driven by a thin lady in a plain black bonnet, obviously a governess, because the cart carried a load of young children. The horse, a scrawny chestnut with a ewe neck, had very possibly heard reports of the Chepstow bridge, for as soon as he stepped from the English half to the Welsh, he threw up his ugly head, snorted, and stopped. The governess gave him a tentative tap with her whip and clucked at him. The horse snorted again and began to back up. The loose, uneven planking was not designed to receive horses who weren't looking where they were going.

"Oh, good heavens!" said Joan. "That silly woman will upset them all into the river."

"No, she won't," replied Mary with a laugh, "because our notorious lord will save her."

James had calmly stepped across to the frightened animal. He took it by the head and said something to the governess. She shook her head at him, but with one hand on the animal's bit, he began to lead the horse to Chepstow.

"How very splendid he is!" cried Mary. "Viscount Beaumarais stoops to act the groom without hesitation."

"Oh, nonsense!" replied Joan, laughing. "Any person would have done as much."

"Yes, but not with such charm. Look, the governess is blushing!"

Once safely on solid ground, James said something more to the lady in the black bonnet and released the horse. The governess, still a little pink, gave him a nod and rattled away up Hocker Hill. Joan and Mary waited as James came up to them.

"You are the hero of the hour, sir," said Mary. "We expected to see the children go tumbling into the water. But was it really necessary to put their poor governess to the blush?"

He grinned at her and bowed at Joan. "Very necessary," he said.

"For heaven's sake!" said Joan. "Could you not offer the lady a simple courtesy without accompanying it with unwanted gallantry?"

The brown eyes smiled into hers. "Ah, Miss Noll, you are too severe. May I not flirt with governesses in black bonnets?"

Joan felt foolish and stiff. It was none of her business if he flirted with a dowager duchess! Yet she faced him without flinching. "She did not seem to enjoy it, Mr. Greville. The poor creature looked most discomforted."

"Did she?" he said. "Excellent! Then she is **not** entirely without sensibility."

Joan smiled back, though it took a certain effort. "And are you a judge of that attribute, Mr. Greville?"

"Only in others. I have none of my own, of course. Yet don't you agree that she had no business taking that young horse onto the bridge and endangering her charges? She received a speech that was circumspect, genteel—and most subtly phrased, of course—but a tongue-lashing nevertheless. So you see, your concern for her modesty is unwarranted. I didn't flirt with her, tempted as I might have been. Instead, I berated her for her foolishness. Was I wrong?"

"A governess is usually a lady, sir. For a man of business, you certainly display a very pretty arrogance of manner!"

"Not to offer flirtation?" He looked at Joan and raised a brow. It was a gesture of such exaggerated absurdity that she found herself laughing. "I'm not sure that flirtation would have achieved my aim," he went on. "You have been the object of my dastardly attentions; you know how utterly effective they are. Don't you think the lady would have entirely lost her remaining shreds of sense? Then the horse might have plunged headlong into the abyss."

"Then I'm glad you were able to prevent it," said Joan, relaxed at last.

The sunlight cast shadows under his jaw as he smiled again. "Besides, I intend to save all my unwanted gallantry and dalliance for you."

Joan instantly lost her merriment and frowned at him. "Is it really necessary to keep up this folly, Mr. Greville?"

"Folly?" he said, as if completely surprised. " *'If thou remember'st not the slightest folly/that ever love did make thee run into,/Thou hast not loved.'* "

"As You Like It, but I do not agree," she said.

"Very well," he said. "I offer you no more foolishness. But then, you have never loved, have you, Miss Noll?"

He winked at her and left. Joan Fraser watched him as he strode away toward the shipyards. Her heart was beating a little too fast.

James saw hardly anything of what he had come to reconnoiter. Was he possessed by some evil demon? His mission did not require that he torment Miss Mary Noll. And to pursue a real courtship under the circumstances would be unforgivable. Yet there was something very fascinating about her. So he could offer her the respect of his friendship, and it wouldn't do her any harm to suffer a little of his absurdity, would it?

Joan was completely absorbed. The ramparts of Chepstow Castle rose from their white cliffs on the opposite bank of the Wye. The effect of the changing light was very subtle as clouds drifted across the sun. She wanted to catch just this sense of mutability as a contrast to the solid feeling of the ocher-and-gray castle masonry. Mary was painting the bridge, some quarter mile downstream; Joan sat alone in the woods above the river. She had included the water in the foreground of her painting. On the river she had painted two of the little boats that constantly plied up and down. The figures of the boatmen gave a sense of scale and movement to the whole piece. She worked fast and with great inner conviction. After a while she stood up and stepped back to see if she had succeeded.

A man's voice began to speak softly. "We have had enough of the bard, don't you think? For this we need something both more recent and more fitting—Wordsworth, obviously. *'Once again/do I behold these steep and lofty cliffs,/that on a wild secluded scene impress/thoughts of more deep seclusion; and connects/the landscape with the quiet of the sky.'* "

Joan whirled about. The viscount stood leaning quietly against a tree. "How long have you been there spying on me?" she asked with considerable heat.

"I pray you will believe that I did not intend to spy." He gave her a small bow. "I hoped you would be glad that I did not intrude upon your concentration, or make insincere exclamations about your work."

Joan began to rinse out her brushes. "You could have quietly left, sir."

"I could not," he said simply. "It was truly entrancing to see your painting emerge piece by piece from the white paper. It was like watching a perfect flower unfold. Yet you won't mind if I don't rhapsodize over the result? You must know yourself that your talent is quite out of the ordinary, and the comments of the ignorant have no value at all."

"But you are not ignorant of art, are you, Mr. Greville?" asked Joan pointedly.

"Not entirely, no." He walked closer and examined her watercolor at length without saying a word. "You aren't quite finished? I'm sorry. Then I will indeed do you the courtesy of leaving. I had only hoped that I might prevail upon you and Miss Fraser to accompany me to Tintern later this week. I have hired a gig for the purpose."

"A gig?" She recovered her humor instantly. A lord must be used to much fancier carriages at his disposal. "How very bold of you, Mr. Greville."

"Look," he said. "I apologize if I have given offense. I meant to tease you a little, and I was clumsy. Won't you forgive me? Our fathers wish us to become better acquainted. There can be no harm in it, surely?"

"None at all," said Joan. She had been the one to be clumsy! Surely she could cope better than this with the idle attentions of a dissolute lord. "I have been longing to go to Tintern Abbey, Mr. Greville."

"Splendid! Until later, then," he said, and left.

Joan sat down and stared at her painting. How true it was that she hated people to interrupt her with questions and comments while she worked. How had the viscount known that? And how could he guess that his simple, understated appreciation of the seriousness of her work was like music to her ears? Yet his very presence here under an assumed name was dishonorable. And to pay court to her, thinking she was Mary! Joan's only satisfaction was the thought of her revenge when she and Mary revealed that he had been wooing the wrong lady. How much money would it cost him, she wondered, to lose his wager with the real Mr. Greville?

Half an hour later she packed up her easel and brushes and made her way back through the woods to the bridge. Mary was there, splashing paint onto her third attempt to render the landscape. At her elbow stood a solid-looking gentleman in a green jacket. Soft brown hair curled above a face whose most noticeable characteristic was its open, friendly simplicity.

"Ah, Miss Noll!" said Mary with a wink, as Joan came up. "Can you guess it? This is a friend of Mr. Greville's who heard he was here and thought to join him."

"How do you do, sir?" said Joan, holding out her hand. This fellow was a friend of the real Mr. Greville? Perhaps the viscount would be exposed rather more quickly than they had planned!

"Very pleased to make your acquaintance, Miss Noll," said the gentleman with a boyish smile. "Mr. Andrew Green, at your service."

They walked back to the Beaufort Arms together, but to the ladies' disappointment, did not encounter Lord Beaumarais. Thus Mr. Green was able to make his presence known to his friend in private.

"For God's sake, Greville!" said James. "You're calling yourself Mr. Andrew Green? What the devil possessed you to come here? I thought you had gone to Scotland."

"I lost my nerve," said Archimedes Greville simply. "Even a blind old lady would know I wasn't you!"

Beaumarais ran his hand over his hair and laughed. "But why come to Chepstow, you idiot? I have everything in hand. Miss Noll isn't sure what to make of me, but she has no reason to doubt that I'm you, and is thus challengingly hostile. You won't have to worry about facing your father over it, because she'll never accept you—that is, me! I don't even have to behave badly; her mind is already made up. But it is too late to call off the masquerade. Make haste back to London, there's a good chap."

The real Mr. Greville looked a little stubborn. "I don't see why I should," he said. "Nobody knows who I am. They think I'm just Andrew Green, your friend."

"You want to stay so badly? Don't say you're interested in the antiquities of the Wye Valley?" asked the viscount. "I am incredulous! Forgive me if I slander you, dear Greville, but is your sudden desire for rustication the result of a pair of bright eyes and an enchanting smile?"

"You mean Miss Fraser?" Archimedes Greville blushed a little. "She's a damned fine girl, Beaumarais! Not a beanpole like Mary Noll, for God's sake. I don't see why I shouldn't join the party—make it easier for you to spend time alone with the draper's daughter!"

"Since you are a draper's son, sir, I am amazed that you would hold her father's occupation against her."

"Not my type, that's all," said Archimedes doggedly. "I can't stand tall, forbidding women! Miss Fraser says Miss Noll's very serious about this painting business, for God's sake. At least Miss Fraser knows that it's all nonsense, and laughs about her own lack of talent."

"Ah," said Viscount Beaumarais quietly. "Then I admire Miss Fraser's honesty. Indeed, her watercolors are enough to bring discomfort to the most hardened soul. But you see, Miss Noll, in contrast, has a quite exceptional talent. And if I hear you make clumsy remarks about it that embarrass or upset her, I shall shoot you."

"Good God, my lord!" Archimedes had turned just a little green. "Wouldn't dream of doing any such thing, I assure you!"

Lord Beaumarais gazed up at the ceiling and idly wondered at the marked perversity of Fate. For having just decided that he really shouldn't pay his attentions to Miss Noll, even in fun, Greville's presence would now force him to do so. He couldn't risk his friend's wondering why he was really in Chepstow. Nevertheless, it was going to be something of a challenge, for he didn't want to see Mary Noll hurt, a desire which caused him some surprise.

"Good, then let us plan our campaign," he said, hiding his discomfort with a ruthless grin. "We shall need a second gig for our outing to Tintern Abbey."

"Who on earth is this Mr. Andrew Green?" said Joan with a delighted laugh. She was putting away her paints and brushes in her room.

Mary looked at her friend and smiled absently. "I don't see why we should assume that he's in on the deception. Maybe he met the viscount only recently and was introduced to him as Mr. Greville. Men make friendships very casually, you know."

"Unlike us females, who agreed to travel together after only a fortnight's acquaintance in Bath! Well, you may be right, Mary. And I agree with you, he seems a harmless enough fellow."

"I think he's a very nice man," said Mary with decision, "and I've agreed to let him drive me to Tintern."

The two gigs traveled the six miles north toward Tintern Abbey at a pleasant, slow trot. Their road skirted the edge of wooded hills for most of the way. Sometimes, through a gap in the trees, Joan caught a glimpse of dramatic cliffs, for to their right ran the meandering bed of the River Wye. It was a perfect day. Joan had packed her sketchbook and supplies behind the picnic hamper which the false Mr. Greville had obtained from the Beaufort Arms. As she watched the enchanting landscape unfold, she wished several times that her charcoal was in her hand. For Joan had also been fighting the most unholy desire to draw the man sitting beside her. The portrait in Scotland had not done him justice at all, and neither had her sketch from memory when she'd first seen him. She resolutely turned her attention back to the grandeur of the scenery.

For several days, they had been constantly in each other's company. He had alternately annoyed, confused, and enchanted her. There were times when it was an effort to remember what she knew about him: that he was posing as his own friend from the most dishonorable of motives. But never could she avoid being fascinated by his mobile features. Where exactly did his glamour lie? It was in more than the line of his features or the extraordinary eyes. His face was more than just handsome—it was interesting. And that's what she hoped her pencil or brush might discover: the truth about him which otherwise her eye couldn't fathom.

"You are very quiet, Miss Noll," said James after a while.

Caught out thinking about him, Joan blurted out the truth. "Because I am uncomfortably unsure of how to treat you, sir."

He turned to her in genuine surprise. "Are you? Because our fathers wish us to marry, of course. We are to cement the alliance of Greville and Noll, Drapers. It does add a certain awkwardness, doesn't it?"

"Not to *your* manner, Mr. Greville," she said instantly. "I have yet to see you discomposed or less than sure of yourself. I have wondered at it."

"You don't think, then, that I am only certain that my father's wishes are wise?"

How could he continue this? His real father was an earl! "Oh, please, sir! We are hardly well matched, are we? It hasn't escaped my notice that you are always confident of charming people wherever you go, whereas I—" She broke off. It was not at all what she had intended to say.

"Do go on, Miss Noll."

"Well, for heaven's sake!" Her family used to call her Joan of Gaunt. It would always hurt. "I am quite accustomed to being seen as an antidote, believe me, and I wish you would drop this pretense at courtship."

That faint underwash of humor still colored his expression. "Yes," he said at last. "There is definitely a certain sparseness in your figure and a distinctly unfashionable severity of line to your face."

In spite of her resolutions, she found herself smiling. "Thank you for not responding to my outburst with silly compliments, at least."

He grinned. "Yet I find there is something about you which appeals very strongly. I am quite determined to pay suit to you, you know."

Joan blushed scarlet. "I wish you would not," she said severely.

"But you can't stop me, can you? But fear not, I will not be intrusive or demanding, and I shall quote no more poesy. Let us cry truce, Miss Noll, and start afresh. Can't courtship begin with simple friendship?"

She turned to look at him. He was smiling at her, deep dimples evident in his tanned cheeks. He seemed entirely sincere, as if he had thought about it and decided that it was monstrous to continue to tease her. No wonder the viscount had such a reputation among the *beau monde!* Joan took a deep breath. "Mr. Greville, I do not believe you have ever been interested in simple friendship with ladies before."

"Then I shall have to start now, shan't I? You can teach me."

At which she laughed aloud. "Oh, no, sir," she said. "I'm sure there is nothing I can teach you!"

Joan wasn't sure what she had expected when Tintern Abbey came into view, but she was not disappointed. They passed a huddle of cottages where the valley opened up and the road swept back toward the river, and there, in a bend of the Wye, towered the arching ruins of the medieval abbey. Wooded hills rose behind them, casting the pale stone into sharp relief. In places trees grew close up against the walls, but the space in front of the ruins was open grass. Mary and the true Mr. Greville went on ahead of them, but James pulled up the horse and their gig came to a halt.

"I have Gilpin's guidebook," he said gravely. "It offers us the principles by which we may judge the picturesque correctness of the ruins. Shall we examine them now, do you think?"

"Can one judge ruins for correctness, sir?" asked Joan.

"Certainly!" His expression was very serious. "Let me read you Gilpin's opinion. He does admit to beauty, but then he complains that *'the whole is ill-shaped.'* Ah, here we are, my favorite piece: *'a number of gable-ends hurt the eye with their regularity, and disgust it by the vulgarity of their shape. A mallet judiciously used might be of service in fracturing some of them.'* Unfortunately, I have neglected to bring a mallet, Miss Noll. We shan't be able to improve the picturesque qualities of the abbey at all, and must take it as it is."

Joan laughed aloud. "Alas, sir! I think the removal of those pigsties might do more to improve the aspect than the wanton destruction of the gables on the abbey church!"

"Indeed." James frowned at the pigsties. "And if I'm not mistaken, the pigs are sacrilegiously wallowing among stones pilfered from the holy ruins."

"Not romantic at all," said Joan. "Yet the abbey looks enchanting, sir. Shall we go and judge for ourselves?"

"**Your eye and your** judgment, Miss Noll, shall be my guide," said James simply. "And in order that we not be prejudiced by Gilpin's views, I shall bury his book in a pig sty. Meanwhile I think we should humbly approach Tintern Abbey on foot, as the monks did, no doubt, when it was built."

He jumped down and offered Joan his hand. Suddenly she was reluctant to take it. This man was a rake and a wastrel! It wasn't surprising that everything he did was charming—even the unconscious grace with which he moved. Knowing that, how could she let him so affect her senses? Then she laughed at herself. No harm surely in allowing the man to hand her from a carriage. She laid her gloved hand into his open palm and stepped down.

At which moment a gaggle of ragged beggars came running toward the visitors from the cottages by the ruins. Joan saw Mary shrink back, and Mr. Green pulled her close beside him. The beggars began to importune them, even pulling at Mary's arm and hanging onto her pelisse. The viscount tucked Joan's hand firmly into the crook of his elbow and walked straight into the rabble.

His voice was not threatening. In fact it was quite merry, but the beggars dropped back in recognition of his natural authority. "Come, lads, I need a steady hand to hold my horse and that of my friend, and several strong arms to carry a hamper. The price of the work well done is a penny now and a shilling for each of you in four hours—on condition that I don't see your faces again in the meantime."

There was a ragged laugh, then a cheer, and the entire gang ran off to take charge of the gigs. Joan looked after them with a rueful grin. There were, she supposed, some advantages to being with a lord! The party walked unmolested into Tintern Abbey.

The turf beneath the ruined walls had been leveled and was mown, but fallen blocks of masonry were piled here and there against the walls. A man was at work with a rake and a basket clearing away fallen leaves, but as they entered he began to pack up. Thick sprays of dark green ivy trailed up the massive columns and over the tops of the empty windows. Walls towered away into broken vaulting, so that the sunlight scattered and danced across the ruins. Joan felt her breath instantly swept away.

"Now we must each surrender to the sublime effect," said James. Though his tone was teasing, he grinned at Joan with a clear understanding. "Take your sketchbook and be gone. We shall picnic when you are done."

Joan looked back at him in genuine surprise. He was giving her what she most wanted: the chance to explore the ruins alone. Mary and Mr. Green had already wandered off. James bowed and, striding away toward the river, left her.

Joan spent a glorious afternoon. Her sketchbook filled with rapid drawings and notes on the effects of the light and the colors of the stone. Several times she saw Mary and Mr. Green walking about together, but she did not see the viscount again. Completely absorbed, she wasn't aware that it was getting late until she felt a chill and looked up to see the sun beginning to drop behind the hills. As she watched the muted colors deepen into shadows, sweet, low music began to echo through the ruins. Joan was enchanted. Gathering her supplies, she moved in the direction of the sound. It was coming from the arched bays at the side of the Abbey Church, where a man with a harp sat on a block of masonry. Ahead of her through the great west window, low sunlight turned the walls to subtle shades of pink and salmon. The harpist began to sing in Welsh, and she felt a shiver of pure delight run down her spine. For how many hundred years had monks chanted their liturgies on this very spot?

And then she saw James Edward Harding, Lord Beaumarais. He was sitting on the ground, his long, booted legs stretched out in front of him and his back propped against one of the pillars. His eyes were closed. The lines of his jacket seemed designed to express his strength and grace—as no doubt they were, and by a most expensive tailor. One elegant

hand lay open, palm up, against a stone; the other was behind
his dark head. His expression seemed rapt, caught up—as she
was—in the music. As she came up to him the brown eyes
opened beneath the seductive sweep of black lashes and he
smiled. It was a smile of pure, shared pleasure, without artifice or flirtation, and sensible Joan Fraser fell in love.

She was furious with herself. The man had obviously set
up the whole situation. They ate a delectable picnic of smoked
salmon and cold meats, with fresh bread and cider provided
by the Beaufort Arms, while the harpist continued to play.
Mary and Mr. Andrew Green talked together in low voices;
they seemed unable to take their eyes from each other. Joan
was happy for them. Mr. Green seemed an eminently suitable
partner for pretty Mary, and they were plainly becoming besotted. Meanwhile, here was she, tall, plain Joan of Gaunt,
falling head over heels for a handsome rake, who had hardly
put himself out to attract her. The humiliation was intense.

They were to return to Chepstow by boat. Lord Beaumarais
had arranged it. The gigs were taken back by hired grooms,
and a small pleasure boat pulled up at the little landing below
the abbey. But first they would watch the moon rise over the
ruins. Another party had come out from Chepstow. The ladies
and gentlemen walked about under the remains of the cross-
tracing and exclaimed about which were the most picturesque
and romantic views. One of the gentlemen carried a torch
which cast dramatic light and shadow over the scene.

Joan spent the time in an agony of self-reproach. Lord
Beaumarais stayed unobtrusively at her elbow. She was aware
of his every breath—his scent, his subtle movement, the shape
of his hand. He was charming, brilliant, irresistible, and here
to make fools of her and her friend Mary! During the moonlit
journey down the Wye and the return to their hotel, he offered
nothing more than the simple friendship he had promised, and
Joan hated every minute of it. She wanted him to flirt with

her and tease her, as he had been doing all that week. She even, wildly, wanted him to kiss her! What harm, when she knew who he was, and that it would mean nothing! Instead he challenged her intelligence, delighted her humor, and gave her gracious, perfect courtesy.

Joan spent a restless, uncomfortable night. She could see the shape of his face in the shadows on the wall, in the folds of the curtains at the window. How could she be so foolish? With eyes burning from lack of sleep, she was up well before dawn. Douglas had caught a cold. He determined, reluctantly, to stay in bed. Would Joan please bring him a hot drink? He didn't have the heart to bother with specimens today. She went down through the silent hotel, and there was Viscount Beaumarais, slipping from the back door. What could he be up to? Without questioning her motives, Joan Fraser ran back to her room, caught up a cloak, and went after him. He had seemed to be leaving in the direction of the river the last time, so she crept down St. Mary Street and turned onto Upper Church Street. His lithe figure was striding away past the finely decorated west doorway of the church.

Keeping to the shadows, Joan followed him all the way to the shipyards. She lost sight of him for a moment, then caught a glimpse of him slipping up to the locked and shuttered windows of one of the office buildings. He seemed to stand there for several minutes. Then suddenly the shutter swung back and without hesitation he climbed in through the window. Lord Beaumarais had just broken into the building.

Joan was at a loss. The man was a lord! He could have no financial motive for crime, could he? Unless he had been losing heavily at the tables! The thought brought an unwelcome pain. Wasn't that probably his motive in coming to Chepstow to court the supposed Mary Noll, to win a wager? If that wasn't enough to pay off his debts, would he stoop to thievery like a common criminal? Why did she want to believe good of him, when all the evidence was that he was an un-principled renegade? Sick at heart, she turned to go back to the hotel. Someone else was coming down the street.

Joan slipped into a side alley. She had no desire to be found at such an odd hour creeping about the streets of Chepstow. Behind the houses lay an orchard. She could see now that the newcomer was just some boatman, up early and going to the river, but she moved away into the trees, where she could be sure he wouldn't see her. Then she clutched her cloak to her throat and stopped. Would the man notice the open shutter on the building and raise a hue and cry? Would James Edward Harding be captured red-handed, and hanged for his crimes? With no idea how she could prevent it, she hurried back toward the river. Perhaps she could create some diversion?

The breath was snatched from her. Before she could leave the shelter of the trees, someone caught her by the shoulders, then clamped a hand over her mouth. Joan thought for a second that she would faint, before she recognized her assailant and her fear was replaced with a far more confusing emotion.

"Miss Noll?" said a subtle voice in her ear. "Pray, don't cry out! I hope I didn't startle you." The hand dropped away and she was turned to face him. "Don't be afraid," said Lord Beaumarais with a grin. "But you mustn't scream."

Her mouth had opened to do it. Instead, he kissed her. Joan knew nothing but an agony of mind. She had wanted this! How could she have been so foolish? For his kiss invaded her senses and made her helpless in his arms. Tender fingers smoothed over her hair, brushing back the hood of the cloak as he pulled her closer. His hands ran down to her waist, bending her to him. She could feel the lean length of him against her legs and belly and breasts. No man had ever held her like this; no one had ever kissed her open mouth. Her knees buckled. With Beaumarais supporting her, they sank together to the ground. He was still kissing her—an entrancing, sweet exploration—as she lay beneath the rustling leaves of the summer orchard in her plain cloak, and his lovely, lithe body pressed her into the grass.

"Oh, dear God!" he said at last, releasing her and kissing her hairline at the temple. "Miss Noll, don't hate me! I shouldn't have done it, but I can't resist you."

"Let me up," sobbed Joan. "Oh, dear heaven, let me go!"

He kept her pinned beneath him for a moment. "Hush, now. It's not so bad, is it, to be kissed?"

She gazed up at him. The faint light of dawn stole over his dark hair and cast his features into relief. There seemed to be nothing but tenderness in his expression. Joan felt as if her heart would break. Her eyes blurred with tears, then her lids closed as he began to kiss the tears away.

"I'm sorry, sweetheart," he said. He pressed one more enthralling, exquisite kiss on her yielding lips, and he rolled away. Joan sat up and pulled out her handkerchief. Beaumarais gently took it from her and wiped her cheeks. "Miss Noll," he said at last, as if it cost him some great effort. "I don't know how it's to be accomplished, but I would like to marry you. If you will have me?"

Joan stared at him. Even now, he pursued his dishonorable scheme! He must have wagered money on her answer. What would he win if she said yes? And how cruelly he had played with her heart! "You despicable rogue!" she said. It came out in a choked whisper. "If you were truly Mr. Greville, I would be glad to slap your face and forget it."

His expression changed very slightly. "*Truly* Mr. Greville?" he asked calmly.

She felt filled with rage and despair. It was the rage she allowed, for the despair she couldn't face. She pulled the handkerchief from his fingers and rubbed at her nose. "What a fine joke! To take another man's name to come down to Chepstow on some cheap wager and pass yourself off as a draper's son. To make fun of the ordinary people who didn't get a silver spoon in the cradle. The flower of the dandies, the ornament of high society, a lord with a reputation as long as—but far less noble than—his pedigree, clowning as plain Mr. James Greville at the expense of simple Mary Noll! And now you pretend to ask for marriage! It is a vile, treacherous falsehood. You see, I know who you are, Viscount Beaumarais, and I despise everything about you!"

"Oh," said James, and he dropped his head into his hands for a moment. Then he looked up at her and grinned. It didn't express humor, but it did show how deeply he could appreciate the absurd. "How very inconvenient, to be sure!"

"Inconvenient! Devil take your cool manners and your insolence! You are used to taking anything and everything you want, aren't you, my lord? Well, I'm not happy to be used as a plaything or a pawn for your idle amusement."

"Don't," he said, and he seemed suddenly to be completely serious. "It isn't idle, Miss Noll. For God's sake, I think I love you! I'm trying to plan how the hell I'm going to tell my father. He won't be amused that I shall wed a draper's daughter. That's not empty snobbery, it's plain reality. But I shall still do it." Joan struggled to her feet. He rose easily and leaned back against a tree, his arms folded across his chest as if otherwise he could not stop himself from touching her. Then he smiled. "How the devil did you know who I am?"

"Because I saw your portrait at your great-aunt's home in Scotland, my lord, and was given a most complete account of your habits and behavior."

She had the empty satisfaction of seeing pure astonishment cross his features. "In Scotland? When did the Nolls ever go to Scotland? And when, for God's sake, did they ever visit my great-aunt?"

"They didn't!" said Joan. Tears ran openly down her face. "For I am not Mary Noll, daughter of Frederick Noll, the draper. I am Miss Joan Fraser. I live with my brother, the Honorable Douglas Fraser, in his home in Scotland, but our father is Viscount Brent. Perfectly respectable company for your great-aunt!"

"Oh, dear God!" James ran his hands over his hair. "And what have you heard about me, Miss Fraser?"

"That you gamble."

He inclined his head. "Sometimes."

"And drink!"

"Of course. You would find in the clubs of St. James's that I am considered a connoisseur. But I do not drink to excess, and I am never incapacitated."

"No doubt!"

He ignored her tone and continued to gaze at her quite calmly. There was even the faintest edge of irony in the curl of his mouth. "What else has my great-aunt so generously told you about my habits? About women, perhaps?"

She blushed scarlet. "She didn't have to tell me. Do you mean to claim that you are innocent after—" She stopped, yet she faced him bravely. "You are corrupt, my lord—reprehensible, abandoned. This little charade is only a small diversion for someone of your splendid talents, isn't it, Lord Beaumarais?"

"Yet you have practiced a deception of your own, haven't you? For now I must learn to call you Miss Fraser. You knew who I was from the day of my arrival and chose not to reveal it. Then you also took your friend's name to deceive me. I'm not sure who has been made the more ridiculous."

"If you had not given me a false name with such blatant, open effrontery, I'd never have done it, and now I regret it very bitterly. Yet you would willingly offer courtship to a lady you believed so far below you in social status. Did you give no thought to the effect your practiced seduction might have had on her? Thank goodness it was I who was your object, not poor Mary. Can you give me one good reason why you came to Chepstow to pursue such a monstrous scheme?"

He looked back at her and met her gaze. "No, I cannot, Miss Fraser."

"Or why you creep about the streets at night and break into offices? To steal money isn't the usual occupation of lords. I

assume you are totally to let? That your gaming debts leave
you not a feather to fly with?"

His face was calm, but his voice seemed touched with self-
derision. "That would seem to be the most likely explanation,
wouldn't it? Yet I wish very heartily that it had not turned out
like this."

"It doesn't matter. You can leave today, can't you? It can
end here!"

"No, my dear, it cannot. I must still be known as Mr. Greville—for a little while."

Joan was clutching the handkerchief so hard that her nails
had torn the fabric. She was quite unaware of it. "What purpose could you possibly have in perpetuating the deception
further, my lord?"

"The real Mary Noll and the real Mr. Greville," he said
calmly.

The cotton square came apart in her hands. "The real Mr.
Greville? You don't mean that Mr. Green—"

"Yes, I do," he said firmly. She could tell that his calmness
was now costing him a certain effort. "It is my fault, of course.
I am everything you think me, Miss Fraser. I persuaded him
to do it, for I thought it would be amusing. But he has fallen
in love with your friend, and the alliance will secure their
future. Ironically, it's what their fathers wish for them. Perhaps
I owe more to him than to destroy his happiness, and if we
reveal the deception now, Miss Noll will feel obliged to react
as you have done, and they will break their hearts."

Joan felt her knees still shake, so she also leaned against a
tree. "I wish you had thought of that before beginning this,
Lord Beaumarais."

"So do I. But we are trapped, aren't we?" He caught at a
branch and absently stripped off some leaves. They fluttered
to the ground. "We cannot let them find out yet. The masquerade continues, dear Miss Fraser."

Joan thought for a moment. She had no doubt at all that
Mary was very genuinely in love with the supposed Mr.

Green. That he was really the very Archimedes James Greville that her father so wished Mary to marry was all to the better. If they could reach the point where their love was declared, Mary would easily forgive Mr. Greville's being forced into this deception by his powerful friend, as he would forgive her. But it mustn't happen too soon! "Very well. And though I don't forgive, I will forget everything else that just passed between us," said Joan firmly.

"No, don't!" Lord Beaumarais caught her by the arm. "Don't dismiss it, I pray you. For I meant every word I said, and everything that my lips could express. I love you very deeply, Joan Fraser."

At which Joan swung back her hand, and with as much force as she could muster, slapped him across the face.

He went livid, then the mark of her fingers shone red against the pale skin. "Good Lord," he said with an icy deliberation. "No one has ever struck me before, though I have probably deserved it countless times. Thank you for your zeal, Miss Fraser. Allow me to escort you safely back to the hotel." He held out his arm.

Joan took it, for she was shaking too hard to walk steadily by herself, and head high, she marched beside him through the silent streets without saying another word.

Lord Beaumarais went back to his room and sat at his desk. He held his head in his hands for quite some time without making a sound. Then he crossed to the washstand and bathed his face in cold water. There was a pain in his throat. He took a brandy bottle from its case and swallowed a single measure. Then he reached into his inside pocket and took out the copies he had made of the papers at the boatyard. Carefully he sealed them with wax and pressed into it the signet ring which hung on a cord around his neck. He then wrapped them in another sheet, wrote a few words, sealed it also, and addressed the

Joan took some time to be sure she had washed away all the tears. As if to match her mood, it had begun to rain. Well, she had played with fire and she'd been thoroughly burned. How foolish, to think she could match wits with an experienced, dissolute rake like Beaumarais! She went down to the hotel parlor to find Mary and the real Mr. Greville playing cards.

"Ah, Miss Noll!" said Mary. "You find us bereft!"

Joan came over to them. "Bereft? Why?"

"Our mysterious Mr. Greville has left us, just like that!"

Her heart took a sudden lurch. "Left?"

Mary dimpled up at her friend. "Pray, don't gape! He ordered a horse, put on a most dashing raincoat with a great many capes, and rode away, as bold as you please!"

"He is gone for good?" asked Joan. If only it didn't matter!

"Sent off his luggage, paid off his room, and wished us a most amiable goodbye," replied Mary.

"Surely a gentleman can leave if he wishes, can't he?" asked Archimedes.

Mary laughed, and in her merriment, blurted out the truth without thinking. "What you don't know, Mr. Green, is that our supposed Mr. Greville is, in fact, a notorious lord."

Mr. Greville turned as white as his cravat, then the color flooded back to his face. "You know who he is?" he said, almost choking. "Oh, Jupiter! What must you think of me? Miss Fraser, you *must* forgive me! And you, Miss Noll. Oh, Lord, now the worst has happened!" Yet he leaned forward and grasped Mary's hand as if he would never let go.

"Oh, dear," said Joan, looking at their embarrassed faces. She sat down, and in spite of her tumult of emotions, burst out laughing. "Now the cat is very thoroughly out of the bag!"

Mary was quite pink. "You mean you *knew* Mr. Greville

was really Viscount Beaumarais, Mr. Green? Then why didn't you expose him?"

The supposed Mr. Green seemed bereft of speech.

"Our poor Mr. Green has been the victim of the most shameful manipulation, my dear friend," said Joan. "I'm afraid he has been in on the hoax from the beginning. Yet it is all the fault of Lord Beaumarais. What else was a gentleman to do when his powerful friend put him so on the spot?"

The poor man gulped, then gently released Mary's hand. "There has been a double deception, Miss Fraser. You see, I am the real Archimedes James Greville!"

And much to Joan's relief, Mary began to giggle. "Oh, no!" she exclaimed. "Then we have played right into our father's plans for us. For you see, Mr. Greville, I am not Miss Fraser—I am the real Mary Noll!"

"And that was my fault," Joan put in quickly. And although it wasn't quite the truth, for Mary's sake she decided to take the whole blame. "It was my portrait, of course, that was sent to your father—purely my own way of making mischief. And when I recognized Lord Beaumarais, I thought we should play a trick on him to serve him for so misleading us."

"Oh, fiddlesticks!" said Mary. "It was really my idea, sir! As you must guess. And I have been in an agony over how to reveal the truth to you." Then she turned back to Joan. "You shall not try to protect me, and really, I don't think it matters. You see, Mr. Greville knows me better than that—or at least, I assume that he must, for he asked for my hand only this morning."

"In marriage?" asked Joan, astonished.

"And I had to delay an answer! What could I say? That I wasn't really Miss Fraser? I never faced such a problem in my life." She grinned at Archimedes Greville. "Thank goodness you weren't really Mr. Green!"

"And thank goodness you weren't really Miss Fraser! For I have been dreading facing my father over this. So what do you say now, Mary?" asked Mr. Greville gently. "It doesn't matter a pig's whisker to me what your name is. I still love you!"

"And I you, sir," said Mary, blushing a little. "So my answer is yes, of course. Here's to Greville and Noll, Drapers! Won't our fathers be pleased?"

Discreetly, Joan stood up and left them. In spite of her own misery she was happy for Mary, yet it was a hard-won generosity of character that enabled her to feel it.

How could he have left? Joan paced her room, then stopped and stared out at the downpour. Over and over again she rehearsed in her mind that last catastrophic meeting with him. She had struck him! James Edward Harding, Viscount Beaumarais, who had never been hit before in his life! It was something he would never forgive, and so he had gone.

And left Joan to her own desolation, and a storm that kept them all cooped up in the hotel for several days after Lord Beaumarais had ridden away. She tried to bury her misery by helping Douglas with his catalogue of specimens and in the organization of his notes.

"Do you know," he said to her one morning. "I think it might be very pretty if you would paint some of these birds in their correct habitats."

Joan had previously seen her landscapes and her accurate portrayal of the birds as two separate things, but the idea was appealing. Anything to take her mind off the memory of those seductive brown eyes and that subtle mind. Thus she tried to fill the empty days with paintings of the sad little feathered creatures that her brother brought back for his collection. She posed them in settings that she painted from memory. It went on raining. Her brush dipped into the paint and lovingly outlined a dead beak or an iridescent wing, while her mind flew free on its frantic, pointless quest. Where is he now? Does he think of me at all? Is he with another lady? Does he laugh with his cronies about kissing plain Joan of Gaunt?

The next afternoon her torment came to an abrupt halt. A carriage pulled up in front of the hotel. Joan went to the window and glanced down. The rain had stopped for a moment, so Douglas had just left the room to foray for more specimens. Joan had thought she would go out and paint the damp, washed streets. Instead she was instantly curious. It was a large, imposing carriage with a noble crest on the side panel, and several outriders in attendance. A white-haired gentleman stepped down and entered the lobby below her. Joan picked up her supplies and her folding easel and started down the stairs.

"Why, if it's not Douglas Fraser!" said a gentle, cultured voice. "Upon my word, sir, well met! We haven't had the chance to compare notes for some time. Have you seen anything unusual recently?"

She saw her brother greet the stranger and the men shook hands, then spoke together for a few minutes. "My sister, Miss Joan Fraser, my lord," said Douglas as she joined them.

"Enchanted, Miss Fraser," said the white-haired gentleman. "Your brother and I are old bird-watching friends. Lord Hamilton, at your service."

The sketchbook, easel, and box of paints slid from her fingers onto the carpet. Fortunately, the lid stayed on the box, but her handful of brushes scattered across the floor. Joan knelt and quickly tried to gather up her supplies. The white-haired gentleman dropped beside her and laid his hand over hers. "Let me, my dear," he said courteously.

The elegant shape of his hand was exactly that of his son's. Joan tried to keep her voice steady. "I can hardly think, my lord, that I should expect the Earl of Hamilton to scrabble about on the floor for my brushes, but you are very kind." And then she must stop talking, or she would burst into tears and disgrace herself. Instead, she gathered up her things, smiled, and hurried out into the damp street. When Joan finished that day, she knew that in spite of everything, she had done an excellent painting, but her satisfaction was oddly mixed with the dread of once again meeting Lord Beaumarais's father.

They were all sitting together in Douglas's private parlor. Lord Hamilton and Douglas talked quietly about their shared passion for ornithology. They also seemed to be very good friends. Of course, her brother had often gone to London without her; he had many male acquaintances of whom she knew nothing. At Douglas's request, Joan had brought out the paintings she had done of the birds, and the earl pored over them. James's father had all of his son's expert and gracefully expressed appreciation for her work. But Joan found little pleasure in the earl's praise; she was lost in a flood of painful memories. Joan put the paintings away with some relief.

The evening was drawing on. The gentlemen were comfortably enjoying a brandy in front of the flames of a small fire. Joan sipped slowly at her Madeira and was listening to them talk. At last the earl brought up the very subject that she had been dreading. He had been talking of something quite different, but suddenly he said, "And you have unknowingly made my son's acquaintance, I imagine, Miss Fraser."

He knew that James had been here? And then she was amazed almost into speechlessness as the earl casually went on. "He came here as a Mr. Greville, of course, so I don't imagine you could have made the connection?"

Joan swallowed a gulp of her wine and stared at him. "You *know* that he was here under a false name, my lord?"

Lord Hamilton laughed. "So you discovered his charade? That was unusually careless of him. How did you do it?"

"I had seen his portrait in Scotland. No one else knew, except myself and my friend, Mary Noll."

"In Scotland? Ah, yes, we sent a painting of James to my wife's aunt. I am amazed that she displayed it. She has always seen us Hamiltons as a wretched lot. But then, she's very taken with religion, as you must have realized, if you know her."

"I met her only briefly. But she did tell me quite a bit about your son when I asked about the portrait."

"And gave you a very pretty picture of his character, I'll wager. She doesn't take kindly to rakes. My son has all the natural masculine virtues and vices, you see. Ladies dote upon him." He laughed. "But he was here on a serious errand for me, my dear. The imposture was necessary. If he deceived you, it was at my own suggestion."

"At *your* suggestion?"

"Indeed, my dear." He smiled and turned casually to Douglas. "You remember, Fraser, our talk about how there'd been a problem with Scottish timber? We had the same thing here."

Joan looked at her brother. He had discussed something other than birds with the Earl of Hamilton?

Douglas nodded gravely. "Did you find out anything that would satisfy the Admiralty?"

"We found out enough to put us in a very tight spot, sir," said the earl. "The man we suspected is someone with a very high standing in society. Not something that could be publicly brought out!"

"I'm sorry," said Joan, embarrassed. She had no idea what they were talking about. The information that James's father had been privy to his masquerade was confusing enough. And the casual reference to the viscount's female conquests threatened to shatter her equilibrium entirely. "Shall I leave?"

The earl was mellow and relaxed. "No, no, my dear! It's all past history now, thanks to James! No, someone was running a very pretty scheme during the war, profiteering on timber for our ships. Unfortunately, the fellow we suspected is a member of the peerage, so it was the kind of thing that could only be taken care of behind closed doors, and of course, we needed watertight proof. Too sensitive a matter to trust to our regular chaps, so my son has been discreetly pursuing the fellow for me. Finally it was plain he must come down here to Chepstow. Yet I didn't want him associated in anyone's mind with me, so I suggested James take a commoner's name and give himself some kind of real purpose. By the way, what did he claim it was?"

"To pursue a courtship with my friend Mary Noll. Mr. Greville's father desired a bond between their families," replied Joan. Her voice sounded odd in her own ears.

"Ah, very clever. I might have guessed there'd be a woman in it. And so he came as Mr. Greville, and he found proof—papers from the shipyards, that kind of thing."

"The shipyards?" echoed Joan faintly.

"Only a little more and we can embarrass the culprit into making restitution. But I thought I'd still find James here," said the earl. "Where is the rogue?"

"Here, my lord," said a voice behind them. "I trust I find you well?"

Joan spun about. Viscount Beaumarais stood in the doorway. He was pale. Rain had darkened his hair to black and moisture shone on the shoulders of his greatcoat. He looked at Joan and colored very slightly. What she saw in the brown eyes shocked her into silence. He gave her a correct bow and offered a courteous greeting to Douglas.

"You have the remainder?" said the earl, leaping up. "Then we have business to attend to. You will excuse us, Miss Fraser?" He nodded to Douglas. "Goodnight, sir."

Going to the door, the Earl of Hamilton took his son by the arm, and the two men disappeared.

"Here is the rest of what you need," said James calmly to his father several minutes later. The earl sat at the desk in his room, while his son stood next to him. He laid down a package of papers.

"You've done very well, James," said the earl after a moment. He had opened the packet and begun to look through the contents. "This completes the case. If he doesn't blow out his brains first, we'll get full restitution and an oath that he'll never stray from the straight-and-narrow again. Well done, indeed! This is even more than I had hoped. Yet you've pursued a man you hardly know." He looked up at James. "Did you ever meet him face to face?"

James smiled. "Unfortunately I did."

The earl wrinkled his brow. "I don't want him to know you are associated with this. Did he know you?"

"No! I believe I can assure you he did not." James began to pace the room, then stopped and turned to his father. His expression showed only a mild self-derision. "Since our meeting was in his wife's bedchamber, I was forced to resort to a certain subterfuge. For as you instructed, my lord, I found out most of the truth through her. Indeed, a great deal of the proceeds from his profiteering went to buy her dresses and pay off her gaming debts. I can't say I envy our poor villain. His wife Alice, Lady Hartwood, has voracious appetites."

"Devil take you, sir!" The earl broke into peals of laughter. "It was not all dull work, was it?"

James looked down. His father would never know what crossed his features, for when he smiled up at him, his face was only amused. "Not dull, my lord, no!"

"But where the devil have you been these last few days, James? I thought to find you still here, posing as Mr. Greville."

"I was found out," said James.

"So I gathered. By clever Miss Joan Fraser, I understand. Yet if the work was done, it didn't matter, did it? Where did you go?"

"To get you those, my lord," said Lord Beaumarais, gesturing toward the rest of the package he had given his father. "Hartwood's conspiracy reached all the way to Scotland, as you suspected. And while I was there, I went to see Viscount Brent to ask permission to seek his daughter's hand in marriage."

"Good Lord! Miss Fraser? You mean to offer for her?"

James sat down on the sofa, but his gaze was fixed on the

fireplace. "If she'll have me," he said. And then, exhausted by his three days and nights of riding, he dropped his head back against the upholstered arm and fell asleep.

Joan went straight to bed and took a large sleeping draught. It was so far from her habit that she sank instantly into unconsciousness and awoke in the morning with the headache. She ignored it and walked briskly to Douglas's room to demand that they leave instantly for Monmouth. Mary and Mr. Greville could come with them. With a certain regret, Douglas finally agreed.

"Yet it will look a little ungracious to the Earl of Hamilton and his son for us to leave so precipitately," he objected. "They are still abed."

"Devil take the entire Harding tribe," said Joan firmly, and she stalked back to her room to pack.

It should have been a simple enough task. Joan had only a modest wardrobe with her, and her books and art supplies were packed neatly into a box of their own. But unfortunately her concentration was regularly interrupted by a blur of tears, forcing her to stop and wash her face again. Thus when the door opened and James walked unannounced into the room, the bed was still draped with dresses and shawls.

"I have just been informed that you go to Monmouth," he said with infuriating casualness. "Is that true?"

"How dare you come in here without knocking!" Joan sat suddenly on the bed. "Where I go is none of your concern."

"Careful, Miss Fraser, you are crushing your bombazine walking dress. Here, let me assist you." He walked up to the bed.

Joan yanked aside the offending dress and thrust it onto a pile of others. "I do not require assistance, my lord." The dresses began to slide. She grabbed at them to keep them from tumbling to the floor.

"You will tear the jaconet!" He caught the wayward clothes and set them back onto the pillows.

"Lord Beaumarais, you will please leave!"

He knelt before her on one knee. "Alas, I cannot, Joan of Gaunt. For I have asked your father's permission to marry you."

The humiliating rush of tears blurred her vision again. She dashed them away and glared at him. "You have done what? Oh, you impossible man! He will badger me to death over it. But I shall never marry you!"

"Yes, you will. I am in love with you, as you are with me. Don't try to deny it."

"I deny and repudiate it entirely, Lord Beaumarais."

To her immense annoyance, he laughed. "Ah, no! Don't, my dear! Can't you forgive my foolish behavior? *'In every thing the purpose must weigh with the folly.'* You know now that I had good reason for it."

"No purpose could outweigh your conceit, your arrogance, your—"

"Maudlin verses?" he put in quickly. "I admit to every fault, Miss Fraser, but that of uncertainty about my own feelings and yours."

"I despise you!"

"Do you?" He grinned up at her. "Then we must part, after all. But only if you will agree to let me kiss you goodbye."

Joan could not take her eyes from his face. That beautiful, deceitful, beguiling face. The face that had enchanted so many women—women more desirable, more sophisticated, more experienced, than plain Joan Fraser. She wanted never to see him again. She wanted her old, calm, ordered life back, the life she had enjoyed before she'd ever met him. "Then you promise to leave me alone?"

"I promise anything to bring you what you desire. What more can you want?"

He moved to sit beside her, thrust aside her dresses, and pulled her into his arms. Gently raising her chin, he touched her mouth with his own. Joan felt her eyes fill with tears again. She angrily blinked them away as he began to bite sweetly at her lip. "Marry me," he said against her mouth. He let his kisses move away to her cheek and chin—and to a secret place which soon began to throb and tingle on her neck. Delectably, he nibbled up the length of her throat and bit at her earlobe. She could feel the warmth of his breath and the heat of his tongue. "Marry me, Joan." The words were as soft as a caress. His mouth moved back to her lips and found a welcome.

"We have ruined your entire wardrobe," said James some time later. Joan lay against him on the bed, her head cradled against his shoulder, her body shaping itself to his. He was idly playing with a strand of her hair. "Everything you possess is crushed beyond repair. When you marry me, I shall buy you a whole new wardrobe, of course."

Joan pulled herself up and looked at him. The brown eyes were like dark pools beneath the black lashes. Yet Lord Beaumarais was still impeccable. His cravat, his jacket, his beige pantaloons, were crumpled but undisturbed. "I shall never marry you," she said.

"Damnation," said James. "Must I make you my mistress? If so, we could start now. I can't tell you how difficult it has been not to do so already."

Joan smoothed down her dress. Though her hair lay in a tangle about her shoulders, her buttons were all fastened. "I can't believe you would make so indelicate a suggestion, my lord."

"Then I must kiss you until you give in, Joan."

"No, don't," she said suddenly. "It's too hard! It's not fair!"

"Then say you will marry me!" He reached up and pulled her back into his arms. He felt warm and strong and solid beneath her. "Sweet Joan," he said. "Don't fight it. We are meant for each other. For God's sake, hasn't that just been proved? The earth moves when I kiss you."

"I don't know!" she said earnestly. "How can I know? I don't have your experience."

He stroked her hair away from her neck. "Then take my word for it."

"And I shan't match up," she said honestly, "to all those other women."

"What other women? Oh, God! This is the work of my great-aunt! Or the exaggerated boasting of my father. Dear Joan, why do you think me a rake? I told you, I don't gamble or drink to excess, and although there have been women, I don't trifle with hearts. There has never been love."

"How do you know?" said Joan.

"Because I have never before spent an hour with a lady on her bed, and only kissed her and begged her to marry me! That is not because I want it that way. I am longing to take the most outrageous liberties! And if you don't agree to marry me this instant, I shall."

"Oh, God!" said Joan, and to both his and her own amazement, she burst out laughing. "I thought—"

"You thought what?"

"That you didn't really want me like you had the others. I thought if you loved me you would want to do more than kiss me."

James groaned and turned his face into her neck. "I want you so much that I'm begging you! I want you enough to need you for a lifetime. I was only trying to show some respect for my future wife. But if you want proof that I adore your every sweet curve and crevice, I'm very happy to oblige."

He turned her so that she lay beneath him and reached for the buttons at the neck of her dress. They fell open one by one beneath his deft fingers. Each gentle touch ran melting into Joan's blood. Tentatively she reached up her hand and stroked the side of his cheek as if she painted him at last with her brushes. She reveled in the strange delight of it. Then she lifted her face to his and kissed him again.

"Good heavens, my lord!" said a voice from the doorway. "What is the meaning of this?"

James released her. Joan clutched together her gaping bodice and scrambled off the bed. "Douglas! Oh, dear heavens!"

Douglas came farther into the room. He looked puzzled. "Viscount Beaumarais? My sister? Good Lord! Shall I have to seek satisfaction?"

"Douglas, no! Pray, don't call him out!" Joan pushed back her hair. Her fumbling fingers refused to function, and her buttons seemed suddenly to have grown too large for their buttonholes. She must look like a hussy! She glanced down at the viscount. Good heavens! Her mouth must look as bruised and swollen as James's did.

James still lay on the bed, arms outstretched among the wreckage of fine wool shawls and muslin gowns. He was laughing quietly. His dark, dilated eyes met hers, inviting her to share his keen appreciation of the absurdity of it all. "You do," he said, with the sure insight that had been creeping up on them since they'd first met. "But you make a delightful hussy."

"I suppose I really must ask for satisfaction, Lord Beaumarais," repeated Douglas.

"And I advise strongly against it, Fraser," said the amused tones of Lord Hamilton. "My son will kill you, and that would create difficulties for your sister."

"But look at this, my lord!" Douglas turned with some indignation to the earl. "They were together on her bed! He has taken liberties. He laughs about it. I can hardly overlook it, can I? Will it be pistols? I'll have to buy some and practice my marksmanship."

"Oh, don't be silly, Douglas," said Joan. She sat back on the bed and took James by the hand. "Father has given his permission."

James turned her palm to his lips and kissed it. Then he reached up and gently fastened her dress. Blushing, Joan glanced back at her brother and the earl. Lord Hamilton gave her a wink.

"Lord Beaumarais has asked for my hand," said Joan of Gaunt firmly, "and I am very happy to accept him."

Author's Note

Wordsworth loved the valley of the Wye River which runs into the Severn on the border between England and Wales. His famous "Lines Composed a Few Miles above Tintern Abbey" resulted from his tour of 1798; the artist Joseph Turner was there that same year. Both poet and painter may well have carried William Gilpin's bestselling guidebook *Observations on the River Wye,* published in 1782, which Lord Beaumarais quotes to Joan. The fifth Duke of Beaufort had initially cleared the abbey ruins, but the site was later extensively "improved" by the Victorians. If you visit Tintern today you'll find bigger crowds, no ivy, and no pigs, but it's still very beautiful. The new cast-iron Chepstow Bridge was opened in 1816 with an elaborate ceremony attended by 4,000 sightseers.

This is my second short story, tucked in between my regency *Reward* novels. My first regency, *Scandal's Reward,* won the 1995 Award of Excellence for Best Regency, took third place for the HOLT Medallion, and was a nominee for *Romantic Times* Reviewers' Choice Best First Regency Award! It was followed by *Virtue's Reward,* which has just been nominated for Romantic Times 1995 Reviewer's Choice Best Regency Romance Award. My fourth regency, *Valor's Reward,* will be published by Zebra in September 1996. I love to hear from readers. If you would like to write and send a long SASE to P.O. Box 197, Ridgway, CO 81432, I'd be happy to send you a brochure with complete information about my books, past and forthcoming!

A Matter of Honor

Paula Tanner Girard

One

Great saffron clouds skidded across orange skies, silhouetting the treeless isles off the western shores of Ireland. Overhead, gannets circled their nests in the limestone cliffs, their barking *arrahs* carried on the wind.

"Inishgallan ahead!"

The Duke of Maitland's sleek new yacht, *Cadence,* rounded the maze of rocky islands and slid gracefully through the narrow tidal inlet toward the deep harbor. His appreciative gaze honed in on the ancient, five-storied, towerhouse sitting atop a hill on the largest island. In the glow of the setting sun, it appeared fairylike. The color reminded him of the citrine, the little yellow gemstone he'd had mounted onto a gold locket to present to the lady of the castle. A smile spread across his face. When would men learn that a little diplomacy did far more to smooth the ruffled feathers of a female than rough actions?

Without warning, the *shirr-shirr-shirr* of arrows sprang from the castle, shattering his peaceful state of mind. Fire seared Maitland's temple. He clamped a hand over the stinging wound and yelled, "Take cover!"

Captain Forsythe shouted directions to his crew, and as the twanging arrows plummeted into the sea around them, a frenzied scramble for shelter ensued. Another volley shot from the parapet on the opposite side of the old fortress arched high

gan a wobbly descent. Most of the arrows
e ship. A few bounced off the sails.

looked at the tiny spots of blood on his hand and
What the devil? Has the woman gone berserk?"

captain appeared at his side, and seeing that the duke's wound was no more than a scratch, said, "She may be mad, your grace, but her men seem more intent on giving us warning than doing us harm. Only one arrow has hit the deck."

The duke wasn't as easily convinced. "After it hit my head, you mean. I consider *that* serious intent. How many soldiers do you judge she has?"

"So far, we know there are at least a dozen on either side, and I saw frenetic movement along the battlements."

Four more arrows flew from the narrow window-slits lower in the corner tower. The duke cursed again. "And now we know there are men on the other floors as well. She must have an army holed up in there."

"I don't want to risk the lives of my crew," Captain Forsythe said.

"Nor I. Turn about," Maitland ordered. "We shall have to consider another way of getting onto the island tomorrow."

Atop the castle, a small group of people watched the yacht leave the channel.

Father Gregory, his long white beard the only moving thing about him, kept his hands clasped in the folds of his coarse, brown habit and fixed his young mistress with a critical stare.

Cailin O'Mullan tried to ignore the censure of the monk. Stuffing her pale yellow hair haphazardly up into an old helmet, she spoke Gaelic to the small boy in front of her. "Can't you find any more arrows, Peter?"

"No, yir majesty, we canna even find sticks that don't break in our hands."

"Then we shall have to use the slings. Thank the Good Lord now, we'll never run out of rocks to hurl at them."

Cailin studied the eleven people clustered around her, clad in old quilted, heavy tunics and two-hundred-year-old remnants of chain-armor she'd found in one of her father's storerooms. Exhaustion from running back and forth along the top of the battlements and up and down the stairwell showed in their sagging shoulders and heaving chests. On one side stood Sean O'Flaherty and his wife, the couple who maintained the castle along with their ten-year-old twin sons, Peter and Paul. Roe, her old nursemaid, two elderly servants, and four fishermen watched from her left. They were all that remained of the proud O'Mullan clan, once protected by 200 gallant warriors.

The four largest islands of Inishgallan were no longer fertile meadows and hills alive with plentiful families and sheep. Across the inlet, atop the high cliffs of the fifth, the ancient monastery of *In Aimn De,* "In God's Name," once a haven for learning and meditation for up to sixty-five holy men, now housed only one balding priest. What treasures it held, Cailin didn't know, for females were forbidden to enter. She only envisioned it through the books which the aged man had her copy for hours on end to teach her to read.

Now, in front of her, Father Gregory, who'd refused to take up a weapon, stroked his beard, a sure sign he wanted her attention. She couldn't ignore her mentor any longer. "I do not want to marry that *Sasanach,* that heathen Angle," she said defiantly.

The monk, speaking English, admonished her. "Sure and you are the O'Mullan now, and that is akin to swearing on the Holy Book itself. You promised your father on his deathbed that you would honor the pledge made by your ancestor."

Cailin stuck out her lower lip, but insisted on speaking in her native tongue. "Well, if I must, I must. But the duke will have to defeat my army first."

Father Gregory chanted a few prayers in melodious Gaelic before reprimanding her. "Faith, 'tis obstinate you are, your

majesty. Getting your loyal subjects hurt, is that what you are
wanting?"

Twenty-two pleading eyes looked her way. The wily repro-
bate knew just how to get around her. "No, of course not,"
she said, her head held high, "I will marry the duke."

An audible sigh of relief ran through the group.

Cailin raised her chin defiantly. "But for sure, I'll not be
liking it."

Once outside the ring of islands, the *Cadence* dropped an-
chor. "We will wait until the next high tide just before dawn
and go in again," Maitland said. "Do you think you can find
the channel at that hour?"

Captain Forsythe nodded. "Aye, your grace. This jewel can
turn on a sixpence. However, I doubt our arrival will be any
more welcome at that early hour than it was this evening."

"But their aim will be hindered by the dark, and, one hopes,
fog."

Maitland picked up the splintered shaft of the arrow from
the deck. It fell apart in his hand as easily as a piece of straw.
"Good Lord!" he spouted, handing the sliver to the captain.
"No wonder their arrows fell short of their mark. There isn't
even a metal tip on it."

Forsythe laughed heartily, fingering the piece of rotted
wood. "I swear, your grace, I do believe we have been duped.
If this is any indication of their weaponry, the O'Mullan army
is sadly lacking in defense. I doubt we will have much trouble
tomorrow taking the castle."

The duke feigned a confident smile until the captain walked
away, then, dropping any pretense at amusement, rubbed his
forehead and turned to glare at the tall stone structure.

Up until a month before, he, David Ashton, thirteenth Duke
of Maitland, had been pleased with his life. It had been five

years—five years of hard work—since he'd assumed the dukedom at the age of nineteen. The Ashton estates ran smoothly. His mother was content raising her three younger daughters and son at their manor house at Maitland Park, their family seat near Scadbury, just south of the city. The 1816 social Season was commencing and David and Lady Priscilla Vere, daughter of the Earl of Ransleigh, whose estate marched along the eastern border of Ashton lands, planned to announce their engagement at the end of the festivities. To add to the excitement, the duke had had his first correspondence in over two years from his adventurous brother Bennett, saying he would be returning home in August from Canada, where he'd stayed after the War of 1812. Maitland informed Priscilla that they would await Bennett's arrival to have their engagement ball. As she always did, she amicably acceded to his wishes.

Dear Pris. Both sets of parents had hoped for years that their two eldest children would join their families even closer. She was a year older than he, but Maitland had had to grow up quickly. When his father died, he found that most of the year he either had to be in London to take his seat in the House of Lords or traveling to one of his widely scattered properties. During that time, Pris proved a solace to his mother as well as a steadying influence on all the younger Ashton children. He couldn't have handled his new responsibilities without her.

The duke thought nothing could possibly upset his world. Then, *the letter* arrived.

The moment he'd returned from Exeter to his London residence in Grosvenor Square, his secretary, Emmett Binkley, had asked for an audience. The eager young man had handed him a long lambskin scroll. "It arrived several weeks ago, your grace. A letter of explanation, written by a Father Gregory, came with it," he said. "He claims it to be the last testament of one Milesius O'Mullan, high chieftain of the O'Mullan clan. The missive was posted to you upon the old king's death. Father Gregory says he has copied an agreement entered into by your forebear, the third duke of Maitland, with

Hugh O'Mullan and his wife, Queen Essa, in 1589, agreeing to give their firstborn daughter in marriage to the eldest son of the duke. In return, the islands of Inishgallan, which the old chieftain claims Queen Elizabeth unfairly confiscated from his family and gave to yours, were to remain in the hands of the O'Mullan under Breton law."

Maitland had taken the document to read before he realized it was written in a script foreign to him. "I cannot decipher this, Binkley. Is it in a secret code?"

" 'Tis Irish Gaelic, your grace. I have taken it upon myself to have it translated."

Maitland handed it back. "Binkley, you are a credit to your profession."

"Thank you, your grace. It seems that our good queen was not overly fond of your ancestor, and yet she had to show some recognition for his service to the Crown. She awarded him the barony of the Clan O'Mullan, which consisted at that time of a maze of small islands off the western coast of Ireland. His grace visited Inishgallan to see what revenue he could expect. On seeing them, he understood the full extent of the queen's snub. They were isolated miles from the mainland and mostly given over to the raising of sheep. A monastery took up one island. The duke was met with great opposition by the old chieftain, who was not in the least agreeable about giving up his kingdom. Your ancestor had so many holdings in England and far more lucrative revenues coming in on his ships from the West Indies that he decided the rewards involved, if he pursued his advantage, were not worth it. Besides, from what I gather, it was the wife of the chieftain who *turned the tide,* so to speak."

Maitland sat forward, his interest now thoroughly attached. "How so?"

"The duke was himself married at that time with a young son, but he was so overcome by Queen Essa's charm and beauty, Father Gregory says, that he made an agreement. If the chieftain pledged the hand of his firstborn daughter to the duke's son, he could retain his title and his lands during his lifetime. If the chieftain had no daughter, then the pledge would go on down to the next generation, and so forth."

Maitland mused a moment. "I don't remember being told that any of my great-grandmothers was Irish."

"As far as I could find out, none was. Father Gregory states that there hasn't been a daughter born into the O'Mullan chief's family for eleven generations, until the present princess, Cailin, arrived some nineteen years ago. By the by, your grace, I found that Cailin is Gaelic for 'girl' and is pronounced 'Kaleen.' "

The duke sat back in his chair and steepled his fingers. "Thank you for that information, Binkley. Pray proceed."

"Well, in the letter, King Milesius says he is dying and is calling up that old agreement, demanding that its provisions be kept. You are to take his daughter to wife and provide her with a life befitting her station. He leaves his kingdom: castle, lands, livestock, and his daughter to you. The letter was mailed after his death. Two original documents were written, both signed and sealed with the family crests. Father Gregory made you a replica, in case you do not have your grandfather's document. He said he was keeping his original copy, which will be shown to your representative when he comes."

"I have the distinct feeling that the man does not trust the English, Binkley."

"No, it does not seem so, your grace."

"Well, I have never seen or heard of such a document."

"I found it, your grace, behind a hidden panel in the library at the Yorkshire estate. You said you would be in Southampton on an important matter, and then planned to continue on to Devonshire. I hope I did not overstep my authority."

Maitland waved his hand. "No, no! In fact, I commend you. Lord knows whenever I inspected our Yorkshire farms, I never stayed longer than I had to in that old Gorgonian house. Your investigative abilities outshine the Bow Street runners, Binkley. What did it say?"

The duke's praise brought a flush to the secretary's face. " 'Tis an ancient scroll written in both Old English and Gaelic. I had it translated. That is why it took me so long to deliver these. It says exactly what the king claimed."

Maitland perused the monk's letter. "Certainly, no court in the land will find anything binding about such a ridiculous agreement made so many years ago. But there is, of course, the matter of my family's honor being at stake."

"Rightly so, your grace. And what about Lady O'Mullan?"

"Miss O'Mullan, Binkley? No matter what Banbury tale my ancestor fed the old chief, the Irish barons lost their sovereignty long ago. According to this letter, it was only upon the generosity of my family that the O'Mullans retained use of their lands."

"But what is to become of her now?"

Maitland pondered this for a moment. "I suppose I do have some obligation to the girl. If things are as poor as this Father Gregory claims them to be, I shall of course accept her as my ward and bring her to England." *After all, I can send her to Mother at Ashton Hall. What is one more daughter, when she has three already?* "Miss O'Mullan must have lived a very lonely life on that island, Binkley, but I am certain she will settle in nicely with my younger siblings. She is a little older than most debutantes, but later on, when she has had some education and feels more at ease with our ways, I can give her a Season and find her a husband here."

"What are your orders, your grace?"

" 'Tis a simple matter. I shall trust you to send someone over to escort Miss O'Mullan back to England."

Mr. Binkley cleared his throat. "While you were away, I took it upon myself to hire an agent, a Mr. Petersen, to investigate further. He traveled to Ireland and then hired a boat and crew to take him to Inishgallan."

Binkley amazed the duke more and more. He must remember to increase his salary. "Then all is taken care of. This Petersen can arrange for her transfer."

"A slight complication arose, your grace. Although he was able to gather a description of the property and learn of the destitute situation of the local economy on the mainland, he wasn't able to go to the islands directly."

"Why is that?"

"The boat was fired upon and the men could not land."

"Good Lord! Was anyone injured?"

"Petersen got struck by an arrow on the arm . . . nothing serious."

"Arrow? What about guns?"

"None were evident, your grace. Should I prepare the men to attack?"

"Lord, no, Binkley! We are not savages fighting some medieval battle. However hostile these people are, I don't want anyone hurt. Does everyone have to use force?"

"I'm sorry, your grace."

"Never mind, Binkley. You did your best. I'm sure it is all a misunderstanding. However, I *am* in need of a holiday. My new yacht is ready to be inspected at Southampton. It is to be a wedding present for my bride, and I'm eager to see how it navigates." *Besides,* he thought, *Priscilla is so caught up in the social goings-on in town I'll not be missed.* "I will sail around to this Inishgallan and fetch Miss O'Mullan myself."

"Perhaps 'tis best, your grace."

"I don't know how people can make such a botchery of something so elementary." Maitland caught the shattered look in the young man's eyes. "I don't mean you Binkley. You did more than was called for. That will be all for now. Inform my man Deevers that I want to see him immediately about packing my things. I shall stop off at Maitland Park on my way to Southampton to inform the duchess of my plans."

"Yes, your grace," the secretary said then, as quickly as propriety allowed, bowed out of the room.

* * *

The duke had thought it such a simple matter, but now that he'd arrived at Inishgallan, he realized collecting Miss O'Mullan wasn't to be as easy as he'd thought. These windblown, skeletal isles were at the edge of the earth, and no place for a woman of quality to be living. Tomorrow, he'd put an end to this foolishness. The young lady would do as he said and come with him to a civilized country. She'd thank him in the long run.

Two

Father Gregory stared seaward from the roof of the castle at the sleek sailing vessel growing smaller and smaller in the distance. "The duke is a powerful man, your majesty. You know as well as I do that he'll be back."

"Perhaps if we pray, the good Lord will send a storm and blow him back out to sea," Cailin said hopefully.

The monk shook his finger at her. "Shame on you, lass, for making light of your father's last wish."

Cailin snorted. Shrugging out of the unwieldy mail vest, she picked up her heavy bow and started to follow the servants down the winding staircase. As soon as everyone was on the third floor, she announced that the O'Mullan would receive the Duke of Maitland in the Great Hall the next day. "We will allow the ship to dock. Father Gregory will go down to meet the enemy."

Father Gregory had frowned at her choice of words, but early the next morning, he followed Cailin's instructions and proceeded to the shore to await the duke. The yacht was already gliding into the harbor.

Since her father's death, Cailin, as the O'Mullan, had taken over his bedchamber—the solar—which joined the great hall. Its large, hooded fireplace made it one of the warmest rooms in the castle in winter. Most mornings, she luxuriated in the huge fourposter. But this day, her mind skipped about so restlessly, she sprang up at the first hint of light. She knew she must look for a solution to her problem—how to discourage the duke.

She chose her clothes carefully for the auspicious occasion. By the time Mrs. O'Flaherty stuck her head into the room and announced that Peter and Paul had seen a ship sailing into the harbor, Cailin had been to the storage room off the kitchen and dragged a large sack back up to the third floor.

However, her old nurse wasn't in agreement with her choices. "Ye'll wear yir mither's white linen tunic," Roe said, laying out a beautifully embroidered frock on the bed.

"No!" Cailin disagreed, donning a rough homespun with a voluminous skirt which fell just above her bare ankles. Surely, it was a full twenty-two feet around the hem. Covering her head with her hands, she refused to let her old nurse dress her hair with a wreath she'd made of her mother's jewels— intertwined with blue wildflowers.

Roe stood her ground. "The blossoms match yir lovely eyes."

Ignoring the woman's protests, Cailin plaited her waist-length tresses herself then wound the braid around her head indifferently and secured it with a yellowed chicken bone.

Roe gave her a swat on the bottom, not that it hurt much through the thick fabric. "Sure and when the duke sees ye, he'll think ye're a peasant."

Cailin looked intently at the determined face, browned by the ocean winds, wrinkled with the Lord knew how many years of service to the O'Mullan clan. One would think the tiny woman was ancient, except for the shocks of brilliant orange hair sticking out every which way from under the black mantle. "Oh, do you think so, Roe? If the duke takes an aversion to how I look, perchance he'll have second thoughts about wanting to marry me. Then I can stay here and he will sail back to England.

Roe shook her head. " 'Tis a naughty lass ye are, yir majesty. Mind ye, no good comes of a mischievous mind. Faith, the way ye look, 'tis more than likely he'll dump ye into the sea to drown."

Cailin wrapped a black shawl around her shoulders and giggled. "Then I'll just swim back to Inishgallan." But the laughter stopped abruptly, and grabbing her nurse's hands, she cried, "You won't leave me, will you, Roe?"

Switching to the more soothing lilt of their native tongue, the woman put her arms around the slender girl. "Of course not, lass. Don't ye be worrying yirself about that."

Cailin nestled into the comforting arms. "I want Father Gregory to come, too."

"He is a man of God and his place is near the Lord on top of *In Aimn De*. Besides, he says, he's not quite sure Irish priests are entirely safe in England. Now, I'm not going to say that I agree with what ye insist on wearing, but that don't mean I won't always be looking out after my little princess. 'Tis about time ye take yirself into the hall. The duke will be arriving soon. Here," she said, reaching into the trunk, "at least put on yir mither's lovely embroidered slippers."

"No," Cailin said firmly.

Roe threw up her hands. "Saints alive! Ye aren't meaning to meet his grace with yir bare toes a-peeking out?"

"That I am," Cailin said, padding from the room.

She'd no sooner stepped onto the dais than Elimelech, a scarecrow of a man in an ill-fitting tunic drawn up and secured by a belt around his skinny waist, shuffled forward and announced in his wavery voice, "Father Gregory and the Duke of Maitland."

Across the room, two men entered from the corner stairwell. The windows on this floor were more generous than the narrow slits in the lower rooms, and torches burned in the iron sconces on the walls. Nevertheless, they gave Cailin little advantage in the early morning hours to see the two men clearly. Curiosity threatened to swallow her up, but she vowed not to show it. Of course, she was quite familiar with Father Gregory's rounder outline. His companion towered over him, but she could tell little else. His cape covered most of his figure. A tall hat the likes of which she'd never seen sat on his head, making her wonder if Englishmen's skulls were fashioned differently than those of the Irish. She could never tolerate a husband with a pointed head. This gave Cailin one more reason to dislike the *Sasanach*.

Father Gregory left the shadowy figure, approached the platform, and bowed to his queen. When he raised his head, she interpreted from his furrowed brow that her adviser didn't approve of her selection of apparel.

"Your majesty, I hope you know what you are doing," he rasped.

Cailin's eyes opened wide with feigned innocence. She only hoped the duke was as appalled as the priest. Then she glanced over Father Gregory's shoulder to the man waiting to be summoned into her presence. While she'd been listening to the monk, the duke had removed his hat and cloak, and she saw that his head wasn't long or pointed, after all. In fact, although she couldn't see his features clearly, he seemed well appointed all over. A shiver ran through her. Surely, 'twas the relief of knowing that his head wasn't misshapen, and nothing more.

Maitland watched the priest walk away from him toward the dark figure standing on the raised platform. Surreptitiously, he glanced about. It took a moment to accustom his eyes to the hazy interior of the castle. Seeing only a few servants peeking out from behind the stone pillars, he surmised Miss O'Mullan was keeping her soldiers out of sight. He fought to maintain an air of confidence while at the same time listening for unusual sounds, his body honed for any action against him.

Thank God there'd been no opposition to the yacht's arrival into the harbor. A cold wind, tasting slightly of salt, blew in from the north, and Maitland was glad he'd worn his cape.

Captain Forsythe insisted on accompanying him and the four crewmen who rowed him ashore in a lifeboat. They saw only a small, tarred curragh resting on the pebbly beach and a not much larger sailing vessel tied to the dilapidated dock. The solitary figure awaiting them on the shore proved to be Father Gregory, who most graciously welcomed them, *"Dia's Muire dhuit."*

Maitland frowned. "I don't understand. Speak his majesty's language."

The priest's eyebrows shot up. "I said, God and Mary be with you, your grace. Her majesty welcomes you to Inishgallan. However, she has decreed that you come to the castle alone—without weapons."

Her majesty, indeed. However, Maitland nodded agreeably before returning to the lifeboat. There, in full sight of the monk, he handed Captain Forsythe his pistol, but kept the small dagger he'd hidden inside his boot. "Go back to the yacht for reinforcements. I doubt they would dare to harm me, but if I'm not at the dock within two hours, come in." Acknowledging the captain's silent agreement Maitland turned and followed the monk.

The main entrance to the garrison on the second floor of the square structure was reached by an outside flight of stairs. Once inside the castle, the duke saw no one until Father Gregory led him up a circular flight to the great hall on the third floor.

Now, the monk was returning to him after speaking to Miss O'Mullan.

"Her majesty will receive you," he said.

It was all Maitland could do to keep from rolling his eyes upward. He held the ancient scroll in one hand and with the other took the gold locket from his vest pocket. This nonsense was taking up a demmed lot more time than he'd anticipated. He had promised Priscilla he'd be back in London to take her to the Lauder's Ball six days hence. No sooner did he start toward the dais at the other end of the room than for some inexplicable reason his heart began to pound. He slowed his pace. Surely a certain amount of curiosity about the descendant of a beautiful queen who'd captivated his ancestor so many years ago was to be expected, but he hadn't predicted the unaccountable surge of excitement which charged through him.

He reached the dais and made a deep bow, nearly choking when he spotted the bare toes sticking out from beneath the voluminous skirt. Fighting to control any outward reaction, he raised his gaze to study the woman called the O'Mullan.

Heavy black brows shaded the intense brown eyes appraising her. Cailin gasped. Such audacity! The man hadn't shown her the proper respect, and she didn't know what to do about it. But no matter how much she glared or reminded herself that this was the *English* she was determined to hate, she discovered she was failing miserably to find him offensive. His head, covered with thick brown hair, was most magnificently sculpted. Whereas all the men on Inishgallan wore beards, the duke was clean-shaven. His jaw was square, his mouth generous—though drawn in a severe, straight line.

A sickening feeling clutched Maitland's stomach. Heaven help him! This bowl of bread pudding was the young woman he'd hoped to launch into polite society. Her eyes squinted, but he thought they were blue. A bird's nest of yellow hair coiled atop her head, and her clothes appeared to have been washed in by the tide. Silently, he cursed his ancestor who'd placed this burden upon him. But duty was duty. As the thirteenth Duke of Maitland, he'd made a commitment. He only hoped his mother could accomplish the miracle of making her presentable.

For what seemed minutes, though in truth was but seconds, a deafening silence prevailed throughout the high-domed room. The girl's mute arrogance irked him. He had to put an end to this nonsense. Lord, he hoped she spoke English! He jammed the locket back into his vest pocket and said more authoritatively than he'd meant to, "You know why I am here. Be ready to sail tomorrow morning."

Cailin's reserve dissolved instantly. "Tomorrow?" All she had done to repulse him hadn't worked. He was going to carry her away, after all. She folded her arms to keep from trembling. " 'Tis impossible to have all my furniture and trunks transferred to your boat in that short time."

The duke saw that he hadn't made himself clear. "You will have no need to take any furnishings, Miss O'Mullan. And as to clothing—" His eyes scanned her. "My mother, the duchess, will see that you are fitted with a proper wardrobe." She glared. His gaze locked with hers. Demme! He expected some show of appreciation for his offer. It wasn't as if he was tearing her away from paradise. He glanced at the thimble-sized woman, her face ringed in flames, observing him from behind Miss O'Mullan. For some reason, fairy witches came to mind. Since he'd seen only one other female, a young matron with two young boys, he supposed the little black spider to be Miss O'Mullan's chaperon. "And one for your companion. 'Tis all my coach in England will handle."

Cailin looked at him incredulously. "You are telling me that I am to bring nothing but clothing? I insist on taking my father's four-poster."

Maitland stood his ground. "Impossible!"

"My mother's chair?" The voice was a little less sure.

"Definitely not. As it is, this trip has taken far longer than I'd anticipated. I would leave today, if I could." Disappointment showed in her eyes. It was hard to believe she was nineteen. She seemed no more sophisticated than his sisters, Obedience and Mirabelle, who were only sixteen and nearly seventeen years old. Suddenly, an unexpected twinge of guilt softened Maitland's response. "I'll tell you what, in addition to the three trunks, you may take anything that you are able to hold on your lap."

Her brows knit together. "Anything?" she asked.

He was glad he was able to divert her attention from removing half the castle furnishings. Now if she wanted to take some little memento of her childhood home—some toy, or a box of her mother's remembrances—it wouldn't be too cumbersome to transport from Southampton to Maitland Park. "Yes, anything. But remember, you must carry it on your lap for some distance once we arrive in England."

Cailin looked up hopefully. "I have a pet, your grace."

Maitland blinked. He hadn't been thinking of something alive. It wasn't that he was against animals. He'd just never been one who'd cared for pets, like his other siblings, especially his little brother Timothy. Animals belonged in their natural habitat, not in a house.

Cailin saw the involuntary rise of his eyebrows and spoke quickly. " 'Tis but an orphan lamb named Ezra. I mothered him from the day he was born. Sure and he'll die if I leave him." Cailin dismissed Roe's pinch from behind with a swat of her hand, never taking her wide-eyed gaze from the duke's face.

"There will be no milk on board the yacht to feed him."

"Oh, Ezra is weaned."

"Ah . . ." He contemplated a moment. If that is what it took to get her to leave peacefully, so be it. Cook could keep the animal in the hold and his farms at Maitland Park had large flocks of sheep. "I see no reason why you cannot take your pet."

For the first time, Maitland saw her smile. It was a lovely smile, and for a moment, he was lost in its brilliance. Then she turned abruptly to stare out the window. It startled him that the uppity termagant should stir such disturbing feelings in him.

The exchange hadn't escaped the notice of Father Gregory, and with a sly grin, he approached the duke.

"Your grace, you brought your copy of the agreement, did you not?"

Maitland didn't consider furniture or pets to be in his line of responsibilities. Those were trivial domestic concerns his mother took care of, and soon Priscilla would assume them. Distracted as he had been by Miss O'Mullan's unexpected impression on him, Maitland was glad to return to the business at hand. "Yes. Father. I have it here."

"You and the O'Mullan are to sign both documents. You will take King Milesius's copy and I shall keep yours. I will witness for the queen. Is there someone who can attest for you?"

Maitland pulled out his watch. The boat should have returned from the yacht. "Send a message to Captain Forsythe. He will represent me."

As soon as Elimelech left on the errand, the monk brought out a sheet of parchment and handed it to the duke. In an instant, he produced an ink pot and several quill pens, which were waiting conveniently on a sideboard.

Maitland thought he was through with legalities. "What is this?"

Father Gregory whispered. "You cannot read Old English or Latin as well as Gaelic, your grace?"

"Not very well." Maitland wished he'd brought a solicitor—or at least, an interpreter—with him to translate. Languages hadn't been his favorite subjects at university, but he wasn't going to admit to total ignorance.

The holy man shrugged, pity showing in his eyes. "Sure and I thought the English were better educated. Ah, well, I tried my best to be gracious by not writing in the Irish script."

The duke bristled. Odsbodikins! The priest had a way of twisting a phrase to make a man feel somehow lacking.

Father Gregory pointed to the parchment. " 'Tis only a formality, your grace. Your promise to take care of the poor, helpless lass."

Maitland tried to take the edge off his voice. "I had papers drawn up in London by my solicitor, proclaiming my responsibility for Miss O'Mullan."

"Then a reaffirmation in front of witnesses shouldn't bother you, should it, now?" Father Gregory said, motioning

to the two identical lads standing nearby to step onto the dais.
One held a candelabrum the other an incense burner. Then,
poking about inside the folds of his robe, the priest finally
pulled out a little book. "If it meets with your approval, your
grace, while we await the captain, I will say a prayer. I know
you are not of our faith, but I see you as a broadminded man,
and, I trust, one of discretion?"

The jackanape had him over a barrel, but Maitland admitted
that the monk had reason to show caution. After years of dodg-
ing the British priest-hunters, Irish clergymen were still wary
of the persecution which had sent many holymen to Europe
or isolated islands like Inishgallan. This retreat had obviously
flourished for centuries without the knowledge of the authori-
ties. How could he live down the *on-dit* that the Ashtons had
permitted a Catholic monastery to operate on English soil for
over 200 years?

Father Gregory spoke humbly. "Will you forbid my giving
a benediction before our mistress sets out on her new life?"

"Of course not," Maitland said defensively. Silently, he
swore that once he got to London, he'd have to take precau-
tions to keep Miss O'Mullan from revealing the follies of his
ancestors, or he'd be the laughingstock of the *ton*.

The monk turned and motioned for the old woman to bring
the girl to his side. Not until she stepped down from the dais
and stood beside him did Maitland realize how short she was.
She barely came up to his shoulder.

"Thank you. Our hearts will be warmed, knowing the dear
lass goes with God's blessing. Now, if everyone will kneel."
Father Gregory bowed to the duke. "We would be most honored if you would join us, your grace."

Maitland decided it was the least he could do. From the
corner of his eye, he saw Forsythe enter. Before lowering himself to the floor, he motioned for the captain to stay where he
was. Instead of the short prayer Maitland expected, the monk
droned on and on, first in Latin, then in Gaelic. The servants
chanted in Irish, as did Miss O'Mullan. He was expected to

say something, and he did the best he could to imitate the ancient tongue. Thank goodness, Father Gregory helped him along, but still, he felt he only made a muddle of mimicking the right inflections. Finally, the agony ended. He was able to rise and give his aching bones a respite. Miss O'Mullan seemed to suffer no ill effects from the unnatural position. Evidently, she was used to going through this routine, and her knees were accustomed to the hard floor.

The two women cried aloud and the men blew their noses. Maitland, afraid his patience was running out, signaled the captain to join him.

Meanwhile, the priest kissed Cailin on both cheeks. Then, sighing deeply, he spread several papers out on the white-clothed trestle table. "Now, for you both to show your good faith . . ."

Cailin took the quill pen from Father Gregory and wrote her name.

The old man wiped his eyes with the corner of his sleeve. "Letting my little princess go is like losing a daughter, your grace. Please sign here."

Feeling extremely uncomfortable in the presence of such freely expressed emotion, the duke turned and said gruffly, "Captain Forsythe, witness these papers, or we shall never be out of here."

Father Gregory's gloom dissolved instantly in a rich burst of laughter. "Sure and you won't go back on your pledge now, your grace?"

Maitland, his irritation growing over the continued attack on his scruples, began to tuck the documents inside his coat. "An Ashton is true to his word. Miss O'Mullan will be quite safe under my protection."

"Glad I am to hear that," the monk said, reaching over to remove the scrolls from the duke's hand. " 'Tis better by far than your countrymen have done to the Irish in the past, but I plan on giving those documents to her majesty to tend."

Maitland blinked. "Queen Charlotte?"

"You forget, your grace, Cailin is an Irish queen."

For a moment, it had slipped Maitland's mind that these islanders considered Miss O'Mullan their sovereign. Once she was in England, she'd have to get over that illusion. Now, he'd humor the old man. "I swear on my family name, the papers will be far more secure in my London safe than left in the care of a young girl."

Father Gregory released his hold on the scrolls and bowed. "Then I shall trust them to your keeping, your grace."

Maitland was glad the priest realized he really had nothing to say on the matter. Miss O'Mullan was now his ward, and until she married, she was his responsibility. Honor demanded nothing less of him.

Cailin signed her name, then taking a deep breath, stepped back. The deed was done. She was now married to the duke. But whereas she was quite shaken by that realization, the *Sasanach* seemed no more affected than if he'd only attended a Sunday mass. A sinking feeling stirred somewhere within her, and she chanced a quick look at Father Gregory. She couldn't fault the old rogue for sending her away. After all, it was she who'd promised her father to honor the agreement to marry the Duke of Maitland. Now there was nothing any of them could do to change the situation.

The holy man bowed. "Your grace will be staying the night, of course."

Three

The sudden brightness in Miss O'Mullan's eyes unsettled Maitland. He feared the monk's invitation set no more agreeably with her than it did with him. However, now that the paperwork was done, he felt far more charitable and smiled amiably. "My clothes and valet are aboard my yacht, and 'twould be cumbersome to have them brought ashore on such short notice. I'm certain Miss O'Mullan, however, will want to say her farewells this evening, alone."

Father Gregory sent a censorial glance toward Cailin before answering. "An emotional turn it has been for all of us, your grace, but I beg you at least to stay to supper. 'Twould be a great insult to refuse the castle's hospitality to join us for her majesty's last meal."

Once more, Maitland found himself backed into a corner. "Of course, I beg your forgiveness for my abysmal manners," he said, inclining his head slightly toward Cailin. "I shall be honored to dine with you. But as soon as Captain Gregory and I have eaten, we must return to the ship."

Cailin let out a loud sigh of relief.

Maitland's back stiffened. He might have been accused more than once of acting out of reach himself, but he'd never experienced rejection by a woman.

Deliberately, the priest engaged his mistress in a low conversation.

Determined to cover his pique at the chit's snub, Maitland

spoke sharply to the captain. "I'm not certain that all whom we saw in the castle are the full extent of *her majesty's* army."

Captain Forsythe glanced back and forth from Cailin to the duke and broke into a broad grin. "You may have the right of it, your grace. I feel a strange wind blowing, and from the daggers the lass has been throwing your way, I don't think she's too happy about leaving her island. You made the best choice not to sleep in the castle. Shall I have the yacht brought to the dock?"

Maitland saw nothing humorous in the situation and gave the captain a warning look. "Wisdom tells me to keep the *Cadence* anchored where it is in the middle of the harbor. We cannot be certain that Miss O'Mullan doesn't have men hiding among the rocks, now, can we? Leave four armed crewmen at the dock with a boat to be ready to load her belongings in the morning. I wish to be gone from here as quickly as possible."

"As you wish, your grace," the captain said, with great solemnity.

That evening the two men were treated to a medieval feast. Trenchers overflowed with meat and vegetables. Mead ran freely, and the duke mellowed with each tankard set before him. They ate primarily with their fingers, using the snow-white linen tablecloth to wipe their hands. Maitland thought the taste of mutton produced on his own chalkland downs couldn't be challenged, but that which the castle cook presented to them surpassed anything he'd ever tasted. After bowls of scented water were brought to wash their hands, the party rose and the two men prepared to leave.

Cailin, who'd been silent for most of the meal, excused herself. "I must pack," she announced crisply, heading for the solar.

Maitland's smile disappeared. He'd expected his acceptance of her pet to ease the strain between them, but judging by her terse tone, he was mistaken. Annoyance colored his reply. "Remember, we leave with the first tide. Anything you don't have on board by dawn will be left behind." He saw the quick set of her shoulders. At first he thought she wasn't going to acknowledge him, until she glanced at the priest.

Slowly stroking his beard, Father Gregory stood with eyes closed, lips moving silently, as if in prayer.

Maitland detected a change in Miss O'Mullan's mood. *"Ta, m'anam!"*

The monk cleared his throat.

Cailin's chin jutted out. "I said, *yes, indeed,* we shall be ready."

Her acquiescence was too glib. Suspicion ran through Maitland. He wouldn't put it past *her majesty* to try to delay their leaving.

The next morning, before a cock crowed, Deevers awakened the duke. "I'm sorry to disturb you, your grace, but you did say to wake you before first light."

Surprised that he'd slept so soundly, Maitland rubbed his eyes. "So I did, Deevers. I wonder how long will it take Miss O'Mullan to pack. I hope I'm not forced to go ashore to fetch her."

"I believe the boat is approaching the yacht now, your grace."

Maitland leaped from the bed. "Demme! How dare she be on time?" It took but a few moments to dress. He ran his hand over his rough jaw and decided to delay shaving. Taking a gulp of the hot coffee his valet offered him, Maitland threw his cape around his shoulders and went on deck.

Burning torches held by a handful of servants lining the shore silhouetted the two passengers huddled in the boat coming alongside the yacht. Maitland shuddered. With her loose-fitting bodice and enormous skirt, which she'd worn at their first meeting, he hadn't been able to discern what sort of figure Miss O'Mullan had, but now, from his vantage at the rail, she appeared larger than Mount Snowdon. Regardless of the fact that he'd assured her that there was plenty of fodder on board, was she bringing sacks of food for her lamb? Plainly, she distrusted him, but for now, he'd let the matter pass. Time was short. The tide was going out.

In the boat, Cailin hugged her cape tighter around the bundle on her lap and mumbled, "You canna do this. You canna do that."

"Now, now," cooed Roe, patting the leather bags tied to her belt. " 'Twill do no good to cry over spilt milk. The duke seems a reasonable man. For sure he's set in his ways—but that is the way of his sex. There was no more stubborn a man than yir father, but no greater heart, God rest his soul."

"Humph!"

Roe nodded toward the mound in front of her mistress. "Ye got what ye wanted, didn't ye? That demon, Ezra."

Cailin looked anxiously toward the sailor watching them, and whispered in Gaelic, "Speak Irish, old woman."

"Now why would ye be wanting me to do such a thing when we'll be living in England?" Roe hissed, switching to their native tongue.

"Last night, Father Gregory told me that the duke doesn't understand Gaelic. He said that if I want to tell you something in the duke's presence, I can do so with him no more the wiser."

Roe narrowed her eyes. "Then I'm thinking the duke doesn't know he's married, does he? Ye're a wicked lass, yir majesty. And it's sure I am that the devil behind most of yir tricks is that holy sainted father," she said, crossing herself.

With the hint of a grin, Cailin whispered, "I know, but I trust him, so you mind me just the same."

"And when do ye plan on informing his grace that he's a husband?"

"Father Gregory says to tell him when I get to know him better."

"To my way of thinking, no good will come of this. 'Twill only give ye time to plot more of yir naughty schemes. 'Tis best ye put it all on the table so the two of ye can come to terms with the consequences."

It was too late to say more, for they'd pulled alongside the yacht. She looked up at the stern man staring down at them. The morning light played on his strong features and the enormity of her situation overwhelmed her. He was no better than a pirate spiriting her away. Cailin couldn't spite the *Sasanach* by calling him bad-looking, but she wondered if he ever sang, or danced, or said amusing things. She couldn't imagine being married to such a heartless man. She shivered and her apprehension forced her to look away. She didn't want him to see how his presence affected her. Father Gregory had assured her that he was doing what was best, but that was easy for him to say. He wasn't the one having to move into the enemy camp.

"Dia le m'anam! God bless my soul," Cailin prayed. She was leaving everything she held dear. The islands were dying, her father had said, just as surely as he was. No longer did the great sailing vessels from around the world stop at Inishgallan for their fine fleece and mutton, and the young people began deserting the islands for the mainland long before Cailin was born. But it was the only home she'd known. Would she never walk the gray-pebbled beaches with their twittering sandpipers or hear the gannets call from the cliffs across the channel? Would she never get to lie in the booley, their summer dwelling atop a hilltop, and listen to the bleating of newborn lambs in the stony pasture? Fighting to hide the tears, she burrowed her face into the soft mound in front of her. She'd not look back.

Above them, Maitland studied the silver sky in the east. If the good weather continued, he could still meet schedule and be back in London in time to escort Priscilla to the ball. As the oarsmen eased the lifeboat up against the *Cadence,* he strained to see the figures in the boat. He tried to catch Miss

O'Mullan's attention, but after her first fleeting glance, she stared straight ahead, eyes wide, like those of a rabbit caught in a snare. Was he that frightening? For a second he recalled his mother's words: *You can appear quite ferocious to those who don't know you, David. It comes with being a duke, I suppose. Your father always seemed to enjoy terrorizing people and you know how amiable he could be.* Maitland never remembered his father as anything but a strict disciplinarian. Was it possible his mother had seen another side of him?

He hadn't meant to be so adamant to Miss O'Mullan, but dash it, he *did* have a schedule to keep, and this interruption had been a demmed nuisance. He'd make it a point to try to be more pleasant on their way back. Perhaps tell her about his family and give her some instruction as to how she should act in England. That should set her at ease, and Maitland felt quite confident she'd soon settle in. Maitland forced a smile. Then, disgruntled that she still refused to look his way, barked down to the men, "Bring the women up first."

The crewmen followed his directions with great fervor, but for some strange reason, avoided his gaze.

A seat was lowered, and before Roe could speak, Cailin called up, "She doesn't understand English." Thereupon, she poked her nurse, who reluctantly allowed herself to be swung aboard.

The men lowered the ropes once more, and much to Maitland's annoyance, Miss O'Mullan made no move to rise. Then she opened her cape to reveal a mountain of fleece, beady eyes, and over two feet of horn twisted into two deadly weapons. The monster had to be crushing her. The duke stared. The beast stared back.

Cailin cleared her throat and shouted, "This is Ezra."

"Unfair!" Maitland spouted.

"But you said . . ."

Maitland felt the scrutiny of the entire crew, who to a man now lined the rail. "I know what I said," he rasped. "Men, haul him up."

He was sure that if he insisted on pursuing the subject further, the girl would argue that her lap included the fullness of her skirt which cradled the beast on the bottom of the boat. His dignity already stretched to the extreme, Maitland refused to get into a discussion in front of his grinning crew on the extent of a lady's lap.

Ezra, once off his backside and hurled into space, began a coughing and hissing the likes of which Maitland had heard only between rutting rams. It didn't stop. Over Miss O'Mullan's protests, the duke ordered the beast taken below. He gave over his own larger quarters to Miss O'Mullan and her nurse, and except for her visits to Ezra's prison, as she called it, she refused to spend a minute with Maitland for the entire journey back to England. The brat even ordered Captain Forsythe to have her meals sent to her room.

For the next three days, the wind and weather cooperated. The only mishap was when Ezra broke free of his pen and made his way topside, where he cornered Deevers in the bow of the boat. Once rescued, the valet, his elegant manner in desperate danger of collapsing, walked stiffly to his room, declaring he'd not come on deck until they docked at Southampton.

The absurd picture of Deevers cornered by a 250-pound disgruntled ram released the most wicked humor in Maitland. The animal seemed to know where his mistress abided and tried to butt down the door of her cabin. It took six burly men to bring the ram to bay and drag him back to the hold.

The duke would never think of humiliating one of his servants. However, the minute Deevers disappeared, Maitland's shoulders shook with suppressed mirth. When he at last thought himself alone, he burst out laughing.

Inside the cabin, Cailin heard the scuffle and grinned smugly. She trusted Ezra to hold his own. It was after the noise had abated that the explosion of deep laughter penetrated the door and startled her. 'Twas the duke; there was no denying it. He *could* laugh, after all. The knowledge excited and frightened her at the same time.

Roe, head bent, needles flying, sat quietly in a chair. If her fingers worked diligently on her knitting, her observant eyes were on her mistress.

Maitland stared at the closed door and his merriment ended as quickly as it had begun. He made his way out onto the deck and, hands spread on the rail, stared out over the water. With both Deevers and Miss O'Mullan holed up in their rooms and Captain Forsythe busy with his duties, he was finding a lot of time to mull over his situation.

What did he know about educating young women? He'd made certain that his eight-year-old brother, Timothy, had the best tutors to prepare him for Eton. His sisters just seemed to grow. He'd paid little attention to what went into young girls' schooling before they appeared at Almacks. After all, their responsibility was to prepare to be helpmates to their husbands, good mothers, and gracious hostesses. It occurred to him that he knew little of what Priscilla had done or thought as a young student in boarding school. Agreeing to marry each other seemed to follow the natural line of events. In his eyes, the fact that she'd been willing to wait while he learned to run his vast empire, only added to her merit.

When Maitland assumed the dukedom at age nineteen, Pris had already been making her way in polite society for three years and quickly took him, and later Bennett, under her wing to guide them through the maze of the world of *le beau monde*. She seemed to do everything with such ease, and the mere thought of her brought him peace. If she had any wishes that opposed his, she never spoke of them.

No woman had bucked his every move as this Irish brat had. Her behavior went against all conventions of polite society. Maitland began to have serious doubts about his benevolent endeavor to civilize Miss O'Mullan. 'Twould be a burden off his shoulders if he could find her a husband. A bit of guilt niggled his conscience when he thought of the prickly problem he was handing his mother, but he had every confidence in the duchess's abilities.

The delay came at Southampton, and they docked later than expected. As Cailin stood between the duke and Roe, her eyes grew enormous with wonder. She never dreamed there were so many people in the world. Men, women, and children spread like sand over the quay. They ran. They jostled each other. They pushed carts or carried great burdens on their backs. All shouted; some cursed. Some sang songs advertising their wares. She clapped her hands. "I do believe all England has come to greet me, your grace."

At first, Maitland couldn't assimilate what she meant. The brat hadn't spoken a word to him for three days, and she'd never before called him *your grace*. She had to be jesting. However, it took but one look into those expressive eyes to see her sincerity. His first impulse was to laugh at her. Instead he found himself replying seriously, "Why, so they have, my lady!"

Cailin nodded regally to the mobs moving below them.

The corners of Maitland's mouth twitched; trying his best to ignore the animal she held on the leash, he escorted her from the yacht. They'd no sooner stepped ashore than Cailin screamed. Maitland, moved by the unexpected suggestion of vulnerability in this unpredictable female, pulled her against him and looked about for what had frightened her.

Cailin pointed to a pair of hair-heeled drayhorses straining to pull a heavy, barrel-loaded wagon. "Horses!"

Before Maitland could interpret that odd exclamation, she pulled away and began an animated conversation in Gaelic with her nurse. Although confused over what had scared her, he took advantage of her distraction to send a crewman to the Inn of the Seventh Dog to alert his driver and two grooms that he wanted his coach dockside within the hour. No sooner was this matter taken care of than he'd hired another messenger to ride ahead to Ashton Hall to advise the duchess that his party would arrive late that afternoon.

By now, Cailin and her large ram had attracted a crowd. On his lead, the animal was as docile as a well-trained dog, but when he approached the coach, Ezra tossed his head menacingly and began to hiss through his nose.

Cailin tugged him toward the open door held by a groom.

When Maitland saw her destination, he said emphatically, "The beast will ride in the rumble seat, where my men can control him."

Cailin stood her ground. "You change the rules to suit you, English? You said I had to carry him on my lap, and I will."

Ezra faced down the duke and snorted.

Cailin glared at Maitland triumphantly. "Ezra says he won't ride up there."

Maitland sucked in his breath. "You're creating a scene."

Cailin's nose rose another two inches into the air. "Sure and it's you who are making a fool of yourself, *your grace.*"

He could tell she wasn't very pleased with him, but Maitland forced a smile anyway for the inquisitive group of people beginning to push in around them. Speaking from the side of his mouth, he growled, "For Lord's sake, you're making us a laughingstock. Get the demmed animal into the coach."

Cailin was glad the duke was beginning to see reason. Holding Ezra's lead, she clambered up the steps, and with the help of the two grooms pushing from behind, they hefted the reluctant beast into the vehicle.

Maitland refused to look at what was happening to his newly upholstered squabs. Before he'd left for Ireland, he'd informed his mother that their ancestor the third duke had let the O'Mullan chiefs live under the illusion that they were kings. But he'd warned her he didn't want to perpetuate the myth with Milesius's daughter. Now, jumping up alongside the driver, he grabbed the reins and swore he'd drive off his anger.

Deever, who abhorred the out-of-doors, was of like mind as his master and chose to ride sandwiched between the grooms on the rumble seat, leaving the inside to the two women and the ram.

As soon as they were under way, Cailin shifted Ezra to the floor of the coach. He sank to his knees and rested his head on his mistress's shoes.

For the next several hours, Cailin sat with her nose pressed against the coach window, entranced. There were trees everywhere! She'd never seen a tree. Only a few stunted bushes, not really trees, grew on Inishgallan, their twisted branches reaching out as if trying desperately to escape the wind. Hordes of people jammed the carriageway, cows roamed the fields, and—horses! She'd never seen a horse before, either. Only the illustrations in the books from the monastery hinted to Cailin of such wonders.

"Oh, Roe," she sighed, "it *is* lovely, isn't it?"

The old woman sat across from Cailin. She'd been born on the Irish mainland, but it had been years since she'd seen small hamlets and fertile farms like the ones she viewed from her side of the coach. She patted the leather bags attached to her belt. This *Sasana* might be lovely, but not so lovely as it would be after she sprinkled it with fairy dust. The Angles thought they owned Ireland, but with God's help, Irish seed would soon be setting down roots in England.

Four

"Oh, Roe, we're here," Cailin exclaimed, as they drove through the ornate iron gates, up an avenue canopied by giant elms, and came to a halt at the end of the long circular drive.

As Maitland alighted from the high coach seat, the massive front door of Ashton manor opened and his brother Timothy, a smaller version of himself, skirted the stiff-rumped butler and barreled down the stone steps. Close behind him hurried a squealing sprite and two taller girls.

A groom opened the coach door and Maitland anxiously watched his ward alight. Why, he was even concerned about the brat he didn't know. True, Miss O'Mullan made a better appearance than the first time he'd seen her. Her hair was now braided neatly, but her full skirted gown still looked more suited to a provincial play. Thank goodness, she wore shoes. His gaze traveled to her face, now impudently toward him. A black smudge decorated the end of her nose, similar to the one Timothy always sported from pressing against the coach window. Lord! What would his mother think?

The duchess had now joined her daughters. Maitland hastily pulled out his handkerchief to wipe the dirt from Miss O'Mullan's face, but just as he was about to do so, two hundred and fifty pounds of sinew and fleece exploded from the carriage, arced high in the air, and landed stiff-legged on the gravelly carriageway. Before anyone could stop him, Ezra took off across the lawn and disappeared through the ornamental shrubbery, leaving a gaping hole.

Brown eyes sparkling, Timothy cried, "Oh, I say! That is smashing. Is he a present for me, Davy?" Without waiting for an answer, the boy gamboled across the lawn after the ram.

Maitland groaned. Why, pray tell, did he feel everything was his fault?

Cailin would have gone, too, had not Maitland firmly grasped her arm, restraining her. "The animal cannot get away," he said. "The park is enclosed. My men will catch him." The look she gave him wasn't altogether trusting, but he was glad to see she ceased her flight.

Roe, now out of the coach, wiped the spot from her mistress's nose.

The duchess came forward and hugged her eldest son. "I was going to receive you in fine fashion in the drawing room, as I know you would have preferred, but your exuberant brother and sisters wouldn't have it," she said, holding out her hands to Cailin. "Welcome to Ashton Hall, my dear."

Cailin felt her face grow warm as she observed the duke's sisters in their fine gowns. Delicate fabrics flowed freely around their youthful figures, and their beautifully coiffed hair was decorated with colorful ribbons. Roe's "I told ye so," behind her, only made Cailin hold her head higher.

Maitland watched his mother carefully. If she thought the young woman was anything out of the ordinary or wanting in manners, the ever-gracious duchess gave no outward sign. He was glad to see she followed his previous orders to give no reference to a royal title, but his sisters obviously hadn't gotten the word. Mirabelle curtsied quite prettily, while Obedience followed with a slight wobble. "We've been practicing, your majesty," Obedience said breathlessly. "We don't make our come-out 'til next year, but Mama says we need to practice before we are presented at court."

Maitland shot a disconciliatory look at his mother, but she was trying to restrain her six-year-old daughter, who wanted to see the queen.

"Stephanie!" The duchess gave Maitland an apologetic

shrug, then turned to Cailin. "You must be tired after your long journey. Let me have a maid take you and your nurse to your rooms."

"Oh, may we, Mama?" Obedience asked.

"Oh, yes, Mama, please? We can help her dress for dinner," Mirabelle echoed. "We've never had a queen visit before."

"Me, too. Me, too," Stephanie echoed.

They ignored Maitland's frown, and as he watched helplessly, his sisters bore their visitor like one of their china dolls off toward the stairs. Adding to his annoyance, the servants lined the hallway, bowing and scraping so low he was afraid their noses would be imprinted permanently in the floor.

The duke's eyebrows shot up. "What I told you before I left for Ireland was for your ears alone, madam. I don't want the girl taking on airs."

The duchess glanced at her son fondly. "Oh, dear, I know you're perturbed with me when you address me as *madam,* just as your father did. I suppose they overheard us discussing Miss O'Mullan's pending arrival when you stopped off here a fortnight ago."

"Am I to believe that you are raising a passel of eavesdroppers?"

The duchess placed a finger on her lips. "Your voice does travel a great distance when you are upset."

Maitland lowered his voice. "Then I take it the servants are of the same misapprehension about our guest?"

A blush crept up the duchess's neck and colored her face. "I don't think you should linger on it, son. It cannot hurt to give the child a little more attention. After all, she has been torn away from all those things she held dear. Perhaps you will see matters in a more relaxed light after you have rested."

"I hope you are right, Mother, but for some reason Miss O'Mullan seems to have taken an aversion to me."

"Oh, David, you didn't put on your high and mighty face for her, did you? Don't give me that look. I can see that you did. You probably frightened her half to death."

"I doubt that," Maitland said defensively.

"Well, you do get rather stuffy, dear."

"Someone has to be in charge, madam." Maitland tried once more. "Mother, do you think it wise to let the girls carry on so? Miss O'Mullan is here to be a part of the family, not rule it."

"Now, now, son," the duchess said. "From the look in the young lady's eyes, I think a little soft diplomacy is needed. Isn't that what you are always saying? Besides, I'm glad they are out of earshot, for I wish to speak to you alone. Priscilla was home last weekend and paid me a visit. She seemed quite eager to speak to you, but she had to leave yesterday for London."

"Did it have something to do with the Lauders' Ball? I told her I'd be back in time to escort her."

"Oh, I'm so glad to hear that. I do wish you would see more of each other. Your father and I had always hoped . . . well, never mind that." The duchess started for the stairs. "Priscilla didn't mention the ball. I gathered it was another matter she wished to discuss. Now, I think I should go see that our new family member has everything she needs. The children are dying to hear all about your journey at dinner. I promised the two little ones that you would permit them to dine with us. That is, if you approve, of course."

The twinkle in her eyes was catching and Maitland found his ill humor disappearing. "And if I didn't, I'm certain that halfway through the meal I'd discover the imps hiding under the table. But I doubt you will be able to persuade Miss O'Mullan to come down to dinner. She didn't eat with me once on the way back to England."

The duchess looked up the stairs. "Then I see all the more necessity for me to let her know how pleased we are to have her here."

"Once she's made it up, no one can change the termagant's mind."

"Leave that to me," she said, laying her hand gently on his arm. "Why don't you go to your apartment and rest awhile?"

Maitland glanced at the hall clock. "I must check the estate accounts with Catchpole. I'd hoped to ride over the farms with him, but there seems there will be no time for that if I am to see Priscilla before tomorrow night."

Abovestairs, in Cailin's room, the sisters were discussing their visitor with unbridled curiosity. "We must wash her hair."

"It is pretty, isn't it?" said Obedience exuberantly, catching up a loose strand from around Cailin's face and curling it around her finger.

"Girls, girls," their mother exclaimed from the doorway. "What are you thinking of? Let our guest have some peace." Her voice was full of laughter, but her words were obeyed instantly.

Perfect little ringlets encircled both girl's heart-shaped faces, and Cailin wondered how in the world they got them to stay that way. She'd always plaited her hair, and doing it any other way had never occurred to her.

The duchess shooed her daughters out, then transferred her smile to Cailin. "Would you like for me to assign you a personal maid, my dear?"

After the duke's unreasonableness, the duchess's generosity unsettled Cailin. "No, thank you. We can do very well for ourself, thank you."

"Ta ceann faoi orm. I'm ashamed of ye. Sure and I could do with some help," Roe said in Gaelic.

The duchess gave the tiny woman a questioning look.

Cailin ignored the dark glares her nurse cast her way. "Roe doesn't speak English," she said cheerfully, "but she takes care of all my needs."

"Sure, and working m'self to the bone," the nurse mumbled, as she began to untie the rope around her waist.

"I'll help, Roe. I'll dress myself," Cailin shot back in kind.

"Dia linn! God bless us. A lot of help ye've ever been."

The duchess raised her eyebrows.

Cailin smiled pleasantly. "Roe says to assure you she can manage."

At that moment a maid entered with a tray of tea and biscuits. "I thought you would like a little refreshment to tide you over until dinner."

"I do believe I shall eat in my room."

The duchess clasped her hands to her bosom. "Oh, my, everyone will be so disappointed. Cook planned a special menu for your welcome, and his grace has even given permission for the younger children to dine with us."

Cailin flushed. Did *he* think dinner with her was a special occasion?

The duchess patted her cheek. "Well, dear, if you decide otherwise, we eat at seven. The bell rings fifteen minutes before the hour."

When she was certain they were alone, Roe spoke in English. "There now, missy. How can ye think of embarrassing such a gracious lady? And herself treating ye like a queen. Do ye plan to hide up here forever? What better opportunity will ye have to show yir master what ye're made of?"

Cailin guffawed. "Master? He's only a duke. I am a queen."

"I told ye. Look like a peasant, treated like one. Ye wouldn't listen to old Roe, would ye? Now ye're wishing ye looked pretty in his grace's eyes."

Cailin stubbornly raised her chin. "I wish no such thing."

"Well, there's still time to hang up the hatchet," Roe said.

"Don't prattle on so, old woman. I shall go down to dinner."

Roe gave a knowing smile and laid out a finely woven, cream-colored tunic intertwined with gold thread and embroidered with flowers of variegated twist. Beside the gown she placed matching satin slippers.

Two hours later, Cailin wrapped a chain of rose-colored pearls around her neck, then stooped for Roe to place a jew-

eled tiara on her head. She pulled her hair back, letting it flow
freely to her waist. A sense of excitement rushed through her
as she studied herself in the cheval mirror. She thought smugly
of the look of surprise—perhaps even approval—on the
duke's face when he saw her dressed in the royal raiment of
the queen of Inishgallan.

At seven o'clock, Cailin swept into the salon. Gasps of
admiration rippled through the room, but none of them was
deep and masculine.

The duchess stepped forward to welcome her. "You look
beautiful, my dear. How sorry his grace will be to find he
missed such a lovely sight. He left for London an hour ago."

In the days that followed, Cailin concluded that the duke
had abandoned her. She'd have forgotten altogether what the
pirate looked like if it hadn't for the large painting of him
hanging over the stairs. She was drawn more and more to stop
in front of it until she had his every feature written on her
mind. She told herself she was glad she didn't have to face
those dark, disapproving eyes, that proud demeanor. The days
stretched into weeks and Cailin began to wonder if the lord
of the manor ever planned to return.

"Good riddance, Roe," she said. "I don't even think about
him."

Roe shook her finger at her mistress. "Well, ye'd better
start thinking about him. For I hear tales from the kitchen ye
wouldn't believe. Now, I won't say I go along with the she-
nanigans that old priest put in yir head, but Roe is one to give
credit where credit is due. Father Gregory was right when he
said to let them think I don't understand English. I sit in me
corner unnoticed, for who takes heed of an old woman? But
you listen to what I tell you. For all their tongue wagging,
they say the master is a good man. Oh, strict he is—and to be
obeyed—but he's fair and honest and knows his duty."

Cailin glared at Roe. "Hmph! The *Sasanach* took my lands

and plunked me down with no more thought than if I were a sack of potatoes."

Roe wagged her head. "And whose fault is that? I warned ye nothing good would come of yir tricks. They say the master must choose a wife soon. There's plenty a fine lady—and many not so fine—in Londontown, trying to catch the duke—him being so handsome, wealthy, and titled."

"Cease your prattling, old woman. I don't want to hear any more."

"Hah! I see ye looking and longing at his picture and I warn ye, lass. Ye keep baiting yir husband with bitter words and he won't take the hook."

"I don't know as I shall ever tell him he's my husband. I'll invoke the old Brehan law and divorce him. Then I can go back to Inishgallan."

"Ye were married by canon law, missy."

A sudden panic seized Cailin as she recalled something Father Gregory had told her. "What if the English won't accept a Catholic marriage, Roe?"

"Sure and I thought ye said ye weren't worrying."

"I'm not. If the duke does come back, I shan't speak to him at all."

Another week, and still no sign of the duke. Mirabelle and Obedience didn't seem the least upset by their brother's long absence. They eagerly showed Cailin their palatial house and gardens. Her only disappointment was that the girls showed no interest in going into the forest. So when they retired to their rooms on the warm afternoons to read, Cailin set off with Roe and Ezra to explore the vast wooded areas surrounding Maitland Park.

The duchess had her seamstress sew her some pretty day dresses and she took lessons with the girls in dancing and deportment.

Timothy thought Cailin a jolly playmate and happily drove

her about in his pony cart. But when it came to getting on a horse, she refused. He looked at her as if it were an unbelievable absurdity. "You cannot be afraid of a horse, your majesty. Davy says I'm to have my own fast trotter when I am ten," he said, with pride and affection, not fear, at the mention of his brother.

As yet, Cailin couldn't picture the duke as a "Davy."

When Maitland arrived at Grosvenor Square, he'd called for his secretary. "I have two documents I want placed in the safe, Binkley. One is the ancient agreement you saw before. The other is a pledge Father Gregory insisted I sign attesting to my guardianship of Miss O'Mullan."

The young man was aghast. "He didn't take your word that you'd had papers already drawn up here in England, your grace?"

The duke sat down at his desk and drew out a sheet of paper. "I'm afraid not, and I didn't have time to argue. The Irish are a very stubborn race, Binkley. I fear we haven't heard the end of them. But now I'd like you to have a message delivered to Lady Priscilla."

Not long after that, Maitland found Priscilla wished to talk about their engagement party. "Most of the *ton* will have escaped from the city by August, David, and I discovered Mother plans to give a small country party at Ransleigh then." She looked at him anxiously. "Would it be all right with you if we waited and announced it there?"

David took her hand and tried to hide the relief he felt. "Of course, Pris. If that is what pleases you, that is the way it shall be."

"Oh, thank you. You are so patient with me." Priscilla lowered her gaze. "There is one more thing: I don't want a long engagement, David."

He felt her hand shake. "Nor I, my dear. There seems no point in it, does there? It is what was expected."

She looked up quickly. "Do you think everyone will guess? I did *so* want it to be a surprise."

"Then it shall be," he said, giving her hand a reassuring squeeze. "Oftentimes that which is most expected is the most surprising when it happens." He was glad to see her smile return.

"Have you heard anything from Bennett?" she asked.

"Not after his letter saying he'd be home at the end of the summer."

"I know you wish him to be here, but what if he isn't back by then?"

"We shall go ahead and make the announcement and hope he's home by the time we are to be wed."

Priscilla gave a little laugh. "It is becoming more and more difficult to keep it a secret. This way Mother will be doing all the preparing for our engagement fête and she won't know it."

"If we can keep our mothers from becoming suspicious, that will be the *on-dit* of the year, my dear."

Priscilla was warming to the game. "We must be very circumspect, David. From now on, you must show me no undo attention."

So it was decided. They'd appear to be only the best of friends. Now that Maitland wasn't escorting Priscilla about town, boredom became his constant companion. She'd given him a reason for going someplace or being somewhere. The more boring London became, the more he thought of Maitland Park. The days passed and still he hesitated to return.

Priscilla settled the matter. She sent a note telling him she'd visited Ransleigh for a few days and asked him to call early the next morning.

Maitland was sure she'd chosen that unfashionable hour so they could be alone. He found her waiting for him with only her lady's maid, at the far end of the room. Their conspiracy seemed to put a new sparkle in Pris's eyes, and that surprised him. He'd never thought of her as adventurous.

Priscilla looked at him, a hint of amusement in her eyes. "I visited Ashton Hall and met your new family member."

Since he'd dropped off Miss O'Mullan, Maitland hadn't heard one word from his usually loquacious mother, a circumstance which made him question whether he'd be welcomed back to Ashton Hall any time in the near future. He hated to admit cowardice, but curiosity won out. "How is everyone?"

Priscilla looked suspiciously innocent. "Why everyone is fine as far as I could see. She asked about you."

"Mother always asks about me."

"I meant your ward. I saw her looking at your portrait."

He didn't know why that should please him. "You did?"

"I did," Priscilla said, the corners of her eyes crinkling in amusement. "Though *scowling* may be a more appropriate word."

Maitland's humor took a quick turn. "What did you think of her?"

"I thought her quite an original. Oh, yes, her majesty asked when you would be returning."

Her majesty? Warning bells rang in Maitland's head. "You too, Pris?"

"That I called her *your majesty?* I saw no harm in it, if it makes her feel more comfortable."

Maitland interrupted. "Don't you see what you are all doing by perpetuating the fable? She'll be laughed to scorn by the *ton.*"

Priscilla looked contrite. "You are right, as always, David. I'd not thought of it quite in that light. We should have listened to you. I *do* want her to come to our ball."

Maitland wondered if she'd taken leave of her senses.

"Her deportment is quite acceptable," Priscilla hurried to assure him. "But I couldn't believe it when your mother told me you have not been home since you came back to England."

Maitland stood up and walked to the fireplace. "I have

estates to run. I cannot be trotting home to play nursemaid to a little provincial. Is it not enough that I have taken responsibility for her livelihood?"

"Then 'tis true." Disbelief edged Lady Priscilla's voice. "David! You mean that after snatching the child from the only home she's ever known, you just left her among strangers and departed? How *could* you?"

Priscilla had never questioned his actions before. Snatching, indeed. Made him sound like a regular bandit. "She is a grown woman of nineteen. That is the age when I took on the liabilities as head of the family."

Priscilla's voice wavered. "I didn't mean to upset you, David. I know you have never shirked your duty. Forgive me?"

Maitland came back and sat down across from Priscilla. "We have never quarreled, Pris. Let us not start now." He was glad to see her smile.

The remainder of the visit they talked of inconsequential matters and parted half an hour later.

Back at his townhouse, Maitland pored over the four letters he'd received from his steward saying he needed to see him. In three of them, Mr. Catchpole mentioned her majesty's ram. Nothing specific, only that some of his tenants had talked to him about the animal. Maitland wadded the paper in his fist. *Her majesty?* There it was again. No telling what havoc the little Irish had caused in his absence.

That evening, as Deevers straightened his master's wardrobe, he discovered the gold locket. "I found it in your vest lining, your grace."

Maitland held the trinket up to the light. The last time he remembered seeing it was in the castle on Inishgallan. Perhaps it would still serve its original purpose to help gain the trust of Miss O'Mullan before she hoodwinked his servants and turned his sisters into jackanapes. "Wrap it in a cloth, Deevers, and box it with my accessories. We are returning to Ashton Hall."

Five

The duchess sat across from her son in the yellow salon and said apprehensively, "Now, don't fly into the boughs, David, but I must warn you. The children insist on addressing Cailin as *your majesty*. They adore her. She plays tag with Timothy and the girls dress up in each other's clothes."

"Madam! How can you permit such childish behavior?"

"Oh, for goodness' sakes, David! Girls have so little freedom after they are declared grown up." Her heart fell as she watched those dark expressive brows turn downward. "Allow them what you didn't get to have."

"Madam you are evading the subject. I left implicit orders that Miss O'Mullan was not to be coddled."

The duchess sighed. "I didn't see you around to enforce those dicta."

Maitland believed there was a conspiracy against him. "Well, I'm here now, and I shall demand that all of you put an end to this farce."

The duchess studied her nails. "You will have to include the servants as well. They all curtsy and bow before they address her."

Maitland shook his head. He refused to be defeated. "I shall speak to them. How can she be presented if she expects everyone to curtsy to her?"

"I think you underestimate your Miss O'Mullan."

The reference to her as *your Miss O'Mullan* further irritated him. He sat back and steepled his fingers. "Eating with her fingers at Lady Collingham's stately dinners? That would really raise a hum, now, wouldn't it?"

The duchess reached over and rapped him on the arm with her fan.

Maitland had the charity to turn red. "I suppose I was a trifle remiss in not telling you that before I left for London."

His mother's good humor returned. "Yes, that was a bit naughty of you, David—but it is easily remedied. Cailin had just never seen such an array of cutlery before. Her etiquette was quite appropriate for another century, but she watched me and learned quickly."

"I'm relieved to find that my ward is no nimwit, but mimicking your good manners won't carry her through a Season."

The duchess leaned forward her eyes communicating her concern. "She doesn't belong in London David."

"If I don't present her to polite society, how, pray tell, am I to find her a suitable match?"

The duchess's eyes twinkled. "I'm sure some young man will find her attractive—and interesting."

Maitland snorted.

"Just you wait, David. You know, she reads and speaks Greek and Latin quite well. Randolph Vere was quite taken with her."

"Priscilla's brother was here?" Though the viscount was good-looking enough and of an age to marry, Maitland thought it a wonder that the young man would take his nose out of a book long enough to look at a girl.

"The Veres came to dinner, and you know Randy *will* bend anyone's ear who is willing to listen to those populates and angels he likes to talk about."

"*Postulates* and *angles,* Mother," Maitland corrected, trying to keep a straight face. "And what sort of reply did our little Irish give?"

The duchess placed a finger on her chin and concentrated a moment. "I do recall her mentioning Euclid. I remember that because of Euclid Mesmer—that nice young man you knew at Oxford who you said helped you with your numbers. But she couldn't have known him, could she? She also mentioned someone named Pithy-something, I believe."

Maitland didn't believe what he was hearing. "Pythagoras?"

"Why yes. How clever of you, David. You did know him, then?"

"Vaguely." Maitland was having a hard time assimilating what his mother was saying. The young lady his mother described bore no resemblance to the one he'd brought to England. Curiosity got the better of him. "Where did you say I could find Miss O'Mullan?"

"I didn't. But I suggest you look in the vicinity of Stovall's Folly."

Maitland envisioned the gigantic ancient oak which one of his Ashton ancestors had tried to preserve by making a room out of it. "I thought you said she went for a stroll. That is a good three miles from here. Surely you don't let her go that far alone."

"Her nurse accompanies her."

"An old woman is no protection."

"I'm not so sure," the duchess said. "Seldom does one see Roe. She always appears when one least expects it—as if she's a spirit. The servants say she puts forth no effort to learn English. Cook gave her space in the herb garden and she seems content cultivating seeds she brought from Ireland." She paused. "Of course, Cailin always takes her lamb with her."

The beast was another matter Maitland meant to tend to later.

"If it makes you feel better, dear, I gave your stablemaster Dibbs instructions to have Cailin followed discretely."

"Thank you, Mother. I shouldn't have questioned your wisdom, but why don't they take horses?"

"Didn't you know? Cailin never saw a horse before. She'll

get into a carriage, but I'm afraid nothing can persuade her to mount a horse."

"Never seen a horse?" Maitland gave a bark of laughter. So that was what had startled the little Irish at Southampton.

"Trees fascinate her. I do think that is where you will find her."

Half an hour later, the duke spotted a stable hand sitting on a stump at the foot of the path which ran up an incline into the forest.

Maitland climbed all the way to the clearing at the top of a knoll without seeing anyone. Lord! How many years had it been since he'd been up here? The old folly stood before him. The absurdly shaped trunk of the pollarded oak still sported the dead branches, which reached out their ghostly arms to catch scared little boys. The eccentric Stovall had shored up the tree with stones and completely plastered the inside of the hollowed trunk with inlaid shells and colorful stones. The doorway was a bit lopsided, but not much else had changed from what he remembered. He took out his handkerchief to wipe the perspiration from his forehead and listened. A woodpecker pounded somewhere in the forest, and he thought he identified the shivery trill of a warbler. Maitland was about to leave when from the interior of the tree floated the strains of an Irish ditty, sweet and clear but terribly off-key. A grin spread across this face. The brat couldn't even carry a tune! He patted his pocket to make certain his peace offering—the locket—was still there.

Maitland didn't want to startle her, and he was debating whether or not to call out when the song ended abruptly and the female voice queried, "Ho, tree! Do you have a riddle for me?" There followed a brief conversation which led Maitland to believe her nurse was with her, until he heard snorts and coughs which definitely were not of human origin.

He should have known that a brat who talked freely to animals would converse with trees as well. Then, remembering his resolve to make peace with her, he called out, "I have a gift to present to a special lady."

A breathtaking silence followed. Then half a face and one wide blue eye peered cautiously around the opening.

A triumphant smile spread across Maitland's face.

"Oh, it's you." The head withdrew.

That wasn't exactly the response he'd expected. "May I speak with you?" The voice echoed back from the tree a bit timidly, it seemed to him.

"What do you want?" Inside the plastered room, Cailin was struggling with her resolve to have nothing to do with the duke. He'd shown no interest whatsoever in her for weeks. She'd studied his portrait so many times, she knew every line, every feature of his face. She hated him. Now she had only to see his smile and her knees were ready to buckle. What was his reason for bringing her a present? Was he tiring of all his lady friends in Londontown? Whatever his motive, curiosity pushed her through the portal.

As Maitland watched, a tiny angel in a filmy pink dress emerged from the tree. If he could have swallowed his tongue, he would have. Instead, his mouth fell open and his blood raced. A pink bow drew up the fabric just under the rounded curves of her breasts, and for a moment he couldn't take his eyes away. No bonnet obscured or imprisoned the long blond hair, which flowed freely down her back to her waist. A wreath of feathers and wildflowers crowned her head. Her feet were bare. Instead of being repelled, Maitland felt a strange compulsion to kneel down and kiss them. However, common sense prevailed. He had to stop this farce. With exaggerated elegancy he fell to one knee. *"Your majesty."*

She looked down gratuitously. "Rise, English."

Maitland stared unbelieving. Good Lord! The brat had taken him seriously. What devils had he raised? He was grappling with the need to give her a setdown when she shattered him with a smile that would wake the gods.

Cailin clapped her hands. "What do you have for me?"

Her childlike eagerness further unglued Maitland, and he scrambled to withdraw the locket from his pocket. He placed it in the palm of her hand. "I had this made especially for you." Buried as she was on that godforsaken island all her life, he was certain she'd never seen anything so lovely.

Cailin turned it this way and that. "How pretty," she said.

Pretty? Was that all she had to say? He'd paid a *pretty penny* for that locket. But how could he expect the little provincial to know the value of a well-cut gem? Then she blushed and he grinned with satisfaction.

Cailin regard him with suspicion. "You wanted something else?"

"Why do you come up here, when there are woods nearer the hall?"

She found it difficult to be mad at him. "Because of the booley."

Maitland blinked. She was pointing to Stovall's folly. "The booley?"

"The island chieftains built simple dwellings out among the pastures where their families spend the hot summer months tending their flocks or fishing. 'Tis a plain life away from the castle, and quite pleasant."

"Ahh," he said. "I take it you've never seen such a huge tree before."

Cailin looked up in awe. "There are *no* trees on Inishgallan."

It took a moment for Maitland to assimilate that. *There are no trees. She never saw a horse before, David. How would you feel if you were taken from the only home you knew and plunked down among strangers?* Suddenly the enormity of what he'd done to Cailin crashed down on him. What injury had he done her? At that moment, Ezra emerged from inside the tree. Cailin took hold of the ram's leash. Warily, Maitland stepped back. "Would you like to know what the trees are called?"

"Oh, yes," she cried, reaching out to touch his hand. "I recognize some of the birds and flowers, but I'm sure you name them differently here."

At her touch, a gentle truce settled between them and Maitland spent the rest of the afternoon trying to identify all the trees, plants, birds, and insects he could recall. But to his annoyance, she appeared to have far deeper knowledge of herbs and flowers than he. More often than not, he didn't even remember the common name, and he couldn't very well fake a scientific one; because, *demmit,* the little Irish knew Latin. However, Truth was the more honorable path, so he nobly admitted he didn't know.

Her eyes laughed. "You don't know much, do you, *Sasanach?*"

Still not sure if *Sasanach* was an endearment or an insult, Maitland chose to let that pass; but he'd at least expected some praise for his honesty.

By the time they returned to the hall, the dinner hour had approached, and for some reason which he attributed to the fresh air, the duke felt more alive than he had in a long time. The fairy child enchanted him, and an hour later he found himself impatiently awaiting her arrival in the drawing room.

Cailin chose the same cream-colored tunic she'd worn her first evening at Ashton Hall. Roe gave her mistress's hair one last brush, and even though no one else was about; whispered, "I tell ye there's something afoot. Rumors are running through the house like a creeper vine. One of the Ransleigh groomsmen is courting an Ashton Hall chambermaid, who passes on the gossip to the Cook, who tells every soul belowstairs. Lady Ransleigh is planning a big party and quite a few young ladies are invited. The help are all betting on which one is going to catch the eye of the duke."

Cailin settled her tiara on her head. "You are just imagining things, old woman. The duke is already married to me."

"Ye know that and I know that, but he doesn't; does he? Ye don't fool me, princess. I see the way ye stand staring at his picture."

Cailin felt her body grow warm. " 'Tis too early to know how I feel."

"Once a husband jumps out of the net, 'tis hard to pull him back in. 'Specially if he don't know he's in it in the first place." She eyed her charge suspiciously. "No tricks now. Be yir own sweet self and he'll notice ye."

"Hand me mother's ruby and diamond necklaces."

"Ye already have on the pearls."

"You said I had to make the duke notice me." Cailin held out both wrists. "Put on the matching bracelets, too."

Maitland took notice. When Cailin walked into the drawing room, he wondered who had been the pirate in the O'Mullan clan. His little gold locket must have looked like a mere bauble to her. He'd rather she had laughed in his face outright than to humiliate him with such an ostentatious display. However, at that moment, the butler announced dinner and Maitland had no more time to speculate on Miss O'Mullan's sudden riches. His mother took his arm and they proceeded to the dining room.

At first Maitland wondered why his family ignored him, until the thought struck him that they weren't used to having him with them. To his surprise, he found himself joining in the banter. Then and there, he pledged that once he and Priscilla were married, he'd spend more time at home.

The next morning, Maitland stood facing his mother in her private sitting room. "The jewels. Mother. You knew about them, didn't you?"

"They are beautiful, aren't they? We've seen a few of them,

but never such a display as last night. I do think Cailin was trying to impress you."

He looked at her unbelieving. "You mean she has more?"

"As the last O'Mullan, Cailin inherited all the treasures of her clan."

"I'm amazed they weren't confiscated by all the conquerors who attacked Ireland over the centuries."

"Cailin said she only brought a few things of her mother's and her father's signet ring and sword." The duchess looked at him accusingly. "She said you forbade her anything that didn't fit into two trunks."

Maitland obliged her by turning red. Good Lord! He'd had her trunks thrown carelessly atop the coach. "What about her clothes?"

"With those restrictions, no woman could bring much, now, could she? She brought a few lovely robes and tunics that had belonged to the queens of Inishgallan. She wore one last night. I'm certain you noticed."

Maitland wasn't going to admit how well he'd noticed. "What about that pink dress she had on yesterday afternoon?"

"I had my seamstress commence immediately after you left here to sew several day dresses, and she is working on a more extensive wardrobe."

He nodded. "Something else puzzles me: I found out today that Miss O'Mullan had never seen a tree."

"She was never off those islands," the duchess said.

"But why? Is it that her father kept her a prisoner?"

"I doubt that, David. She has spoken only with love and respect for her parents. Perhaps he did so to protect her—or because he was afraid of losing her. She was all he had left, you know. The Irish fought the Vikings and Turkish pirates. Then the dukes of Maitland were given everything Cailin's family owned—even his daughter. Only the threat of death made Milesius O'Mullan surrender her to you in hopes that you would protect her."

"And I pledge on my honor to do that, Mother."

He was reassured by her smile that his next admonition would be received as well. "I have advised the children and staff that from now on, anyone referring to Miss O'Mullan as *your majesty* will be reprimanded."

The duchess watched her eldest son exit the room and sighed.

Roe placed the pot of hot cocoa back on the tray beside the bed. "Well, missy, I hope ye feel proud of yirself."

Cailin sat up and yawned. "I made the duke notice me."

"Sure and ye got his attention so good that he stayed only one day. Word belowstairs is he left for Londontown as soon as he saw his mama."

Cailin wasn't going to admit that the duke hadn't spoken more than a few polite words to her all through dinner. He'd only stared. Evidently, her fine dress and jewelry weren't nice enough for him to be impressed. She could have worn more, but as it was her neck was sore by the time Roe undressed her for bed. Cailin didn't know what to make of the duke. The truth was, she'd never known many men. She'd loved her parent and Father Gregory. She loved Peter and Paul. She'd held them in her arms the day they were born and watched them grow up. The mischievous Timothy had already stolen her heart. They were all males, but their presence meant peace, and safety and companionship. They didn't make her body burn or her hands tremble. But no matter how much the duke disturbed her, Cailin found herself listening eagerly for any news of when he was to return.

The following week, instead of going to his clubs, Maitland found himself at Hatchard's bookstore, searching for references on the flora and fauna native to south London. He also came to the conclusion that there were several matters which needed his personal attention at home. At the time of his revelation, he couldn't recall exactly what those things were, but he was certain he'd remember the minute he set foot inside Maitland Park.

The duke arrived home soon after the noon meal and though he was disappointed that Miss O'Mullan was nowhere to be seen, it was with a sense of self-satisfaction that he realized he'd not heard one reference to *your majesty.*

He chose first to tackle the matter of Ezra. To his surprise, his steward only asked "Have you felt his coat, your grace?"

"Ezra and I aren't on the best of terms, Catchpole."

"The folds in his skin and thick silky fleece show Spanish merino, but the black face is a mystery. Did you see the other sheep or note the turf?"

"I wasn't thinking *sheep* at the time I visited Inishgallan." But he did remember the succulent meat. In Tudor times, the excellent flavor of mutton on these chalk downs was attributed to the quality of the turf. Now the pile was thin and full of weeds choking out the good herbage.

The steward scratched his head. "I think the ram is only half grown."

"Good Lord, Catchpole, he's as big as a bull now."

"Ezra could be your chance to upgrade your flocks, your grace."

"If I see Miss O'Mullan, I'll ask if she knows his origin."

An hour later, Maitland found Miss O'Mullan at Stovall's folly.

"Of course I know," she said, "God made the sheep from seafoam." Cailin sensed his skepticism, but then, the *Sasanach* didn't know much, anyway. "Many years ago, great storms came and the people of Inishgallan sought refuge in the monastery. When the rains stopped, the lands lay bare and most of their flocks of black-faced sheep had been washed out to sea. The good people prayed for a miracle and in the morning, when they arose, they found the islands covered with hundreds of thousands of birds, but by nightfall the birds had flown away. They prayed some more, and the waves covered the beaches with layers of foam which were really great white sheep. When the sun began to shine, lush new grasses sprang up all over the islands. Sure and it was a miracle." Cailin sat back with a satisfied look on her face.

Maitland didn't know what to say. The Spanish Armada had wrecked off the western coast of Ireland, and that could explain the big sheep. Migrating birds were known to be blown off course during great storms, and they could have dropped the seeds.

"If you don't believe me, Roe will show you her bags of seeds. She says Ezras must have his white clover, trefoil, thyme—things like that."

Maitland felt like shouting. *Cook gave her space in the herb garden.*

He took Cailin's right hand in his and she didn't know what to do.

"Do you think Ezra would like to live with my sheep?"

Cailin hoped he didn't feel her shaking. "He would like that, I think."

Still holding her hand, Maitland pointed to a bird rising from the downs. It's distinct *kikiwick* carrying up to them. "Oh, I say, there's a stone curlew," he said, casually. One of her eyebrows shot up, and he grinned.

Over the next few days, Maitland saw a definite softening in Miss O'Mullan's attitude, but she still refused to mount a horse. He felt a twinge of jealousy as he watched Timothy ride her around in his pony cart.

However, on his second trip home, Maitland coaxed Cailin up on a pretty little mare, but not before she told him, "I must talk to her first."

He didn't know if he was becoming addlepated, but he found himself accepting her statement as if it was the most sensible way to go about it.

In the meantime, the Ransleigh country party had begun. The duchess went each day for tea and to see old friends. Maitland waited until the third day to ride over. He paid his respects to Lord and Lady Ransleigh and met the other guests. He greeted Priscilla cordially, proceeded to join in watching a group playing a game of bowls on the lawn, and engaged in light-hearted banter with Lord Finley. Two hours passed before he and Priscilla had a chance to speak alone in the flower garden.

Priscilla gazed at him fondly. "Everything is going according to plan," she said. "I am sure no one suspects a thing—not even my mother."

Maitland was happy for her. "See? Your worries were all for naught."

"Oh, I do hope so, David. We've waited such a long time for this."

"You wait and see. Our announcement will be a great surprise."

"The Watts sisters and Miss Hugsby haven't hidden their hopes of snaring you," she teased. "They say they plan to be here the whole two weeks."

"Then I definitely will go back to London tomorrow."

Priscilla rapped his arm. "Coward. But then, if we are to pull off this ruse, it may be best if you stay in town. Then there will be no question of why you aren't coming over every day with your mother. Are your sisters and Miss O'Mullan looking forward to their first ball?"

"Quite ecstatically, if I can judge by their whispers and giggles."

Voices signaled the approach of guests and Maitland rose. "I shall see you at the ball, Lady Priscilla," he said loudly and departed.

After three lonely days in his townhouse in Grosvenor Square, Maitland wondered why he thought he needed an excuse to go home. He *was* lord of the manor, wasn't he? His appointment with his man of business was three days off and he could travel to Maitland Park and back by then.

Four hours later, Maitland arrived at Ashton Hall. The minute he'd changed into country attire, he had a horse saddled and was riding toward the south hills. He wanted to find out if Cailin had seen the curlew again.

Maitland found her where he knew she'd be, sitting on one of the sprawling roots of her booley. He sat down beside her.

She faced him boldly, hands on hips. "You told them I wasn't a queen?"

Maitland sensed she wasn't too happy to see him, and what he planned to ask her caught on his tongue. He laid his hand on hers. She withdrew it. Not a good sign. Diplomacy was needed. "I only meant here in England."

She clasped her hands in her lap and glared at him.

He tried to reconnoiter. "In a few days, you will be going to your first ball. Don't you want to be received favorably?"

She nodded. An encouraging sign.

He didn't touch her again, but he noticed her fingers uncurled and she gave his hand a sideways glance. "On Inishgallan you are the O'Mullan, but England has a queen, so it isn't proper for you to be addressed as *your majesty* here. It would embarrass my mother," he added for credibility.

"Oh, I would never do anything to embarrass the duchess."

He tried to keep a straight face. "So, now—how will you be addressed?"

She clapped her hands in that exuberant way of hers. "Cailin!"

It was going so well he wouldn't argue. "Well, yes, in the immediate family, but to anyone else, you will be addressed as *Miss* O'Mullan."

Understanding lit her eyes. "Then I have to call you David."

He couldn't have her calling him by his Christian name in polite society. "When we are in public, I shall address you as Miss O'Mullan and you will refer to me as . . . Maitland, or Duke." He thought he'd better leave out the *your grace,* for that might bring up the subject of *your majesty* again.

Maitland waited patiently while she mulled that over. He was happy when she smiled and nodded. "All right, David."

His name rolled off her tongue like honey, and it took a moment for him to collect himself. He didn't dare take her hand again. "I'm glad you agree."

Cailin's gaze took in all of him, from his polished boots to his tousled hair. *Soon,* she thought, *soon, I'll tell him."*

Maitland made one more trip to London. Now, as he tooled through the entrance gates of Maitland Park, his thoughts were running to the ball at Ransleigh that evening, when suddenly Timothy appeared, riding his pony neck or nothing toward the coach. "Davy! Bennett is home!" he shouted, reining up just as the duke was bracing himself for a head-on collision.

"Is he, now?" Maitland said, giving a bark of laughter.

"He's taller than you. Davy—and he's got a beard. He looks quite fierce. He's rich, too. He's brought us all presents."

Maitland's prayers were answered. His brother was home— home in time to share one of the most important occasions in his life.

The family was gathered in the salon. As he entered on Timothy's heels, happiness shone in his mother's eyes. Maitland grasped Bennett to him.

Timothy added gleefully. "See, I told you, Davy, he's bigger than you."

Bennett fisted Maitland on the arm. "I've been told I'm just in time for a party tonight. And I hear we've added another member to our family."

Maitland was suspicious of that laugh and looked around him. There was no sight of Cailin.

"Well!" Bennett thundered. "Where is her majesty?"

Six

Bennett could always be counted on to upset the applecart. Maitland directed an agitated look toward his mother. However, the duchess was making a great show of adjusting her sleeves and unfortunately didn't see it.

"By the by, everyone has agreed to keep my arrival a secret," Bennett said. "I'll make my grand entrance at the ball later tonight."

"I'll go fetch Cailin," Maitland said. "I think I know where she'll be."

Maitland found her atop the nearby knoll not far from the folly. His heart stopped the moment he saw her gazing out over the vast meadows below. She seemed to sense his presence, for she turned before he said anything. Did he see her eyes light up when she saw him? For some reason, that thought bedeviled him, and he spoke more impatiently than he meant. "Why were you not at the hall resting for this evening's ball?"

"Gah! I don't need to rest, David, and it was such a lovely afternoon."

The familiarity of his given name jolted him as it always did. "My brother Bennett has returned from Canada. I have come to fetch you home."

Cailin clapped her hands. "He's here?"

Now that she had turned fully toward him, Maitland saw that her dress was coated with leaves and grass. She'd obviously been sleeping in the folly again. Totally unacceptable. "Look at your frock, Cailin. 'Twill not do. I thought we'd talked about deportment. Tonight you will be making your entry into Society." The nymph evidently didn't seem to grasp the importance of what he was saying, for she merely shrugged and turned to study the grassy hill descending into the meadow, her head cocking one way, then another. An uneasy feeling took hold of Maitland.

"Did you never roll down a hill when you were young?"

The implication that he was so ancient ruffled him. "Aye—and that was not so many years ago as you may think."

"Really?" she said, raising her eyebrows.

He didn't like that look.

"Like this?" Cailin coiled into a ball and went tumbling through the high grasses her bell-like laughter growing fainter and fainter.

"You little fool!" Maitland shouted, too late to stop her. The instant his hand reached out, two hundred and fifty pounds of horn and muscle hit him from behind. His knees buckled and he was catapulted down the hill after her. Arms and legs entangling, they rolled into a heap at the bottom.

Maitland rose onto one elbow, ready to give a lordly scold. Cailin sprawled beneath him, her hair full of grass, spread like a yellow veil around her. Dear God, she was beautiful!

He kissed her. Surprise and something else played in the depths of her eyes. For a second, his thoughts lost themselves in their promise.

Cailin giggled. "You have a daisy petal on the tip of your nose," she said, going into gales of laughter which brought tears to her eyes.

Maitland laughed, too. Flinging his arms wide, he fell back upon the earth and filled his lungs with the clean, fresh summer air. For an instant—just for an instant—he'd escaped. He became that carefree young man he'd almost forgotten had ever existed. He loved her. He'd never experienced the emotion before—not like this—so how was he to have known? Not for Priscilla—not with the pretty little Cyprian he'd kept for two years.

Cailin rolled over and cupped his face with her hands . . . his strong, dear face. By now, she'd memorized every part. *It is time to tell him,* she thought. Yes, she'd tell him they were already husband and wife and what they felt for each other *had* to be all right. But before the words could escape her lips, a shadow passed over his eyes.

Maitland rose quickly and brushed off his clothes. The realization of what he'd done tore all the warmth from him. "My apologies, *Miss O'Mullan.* It will never happen again." He extended his hand to help her up, but she refused it. For a second, he thought he saw disappointment in her eyes, and the temptation to take her in his arms nearly overpowered him. He tried to think of Priscilla and couldn't even picture what she looked like.

Ezra, atop the ridge, wasn't the only one observing the young people below. Roe stood, arms folded across her chest, a satisfied smile on her face.

Cailin watched him retrace his steps over the hill, then returned with Roe and Ezra to Ashton Hall. What had caused David's strange behavior? He seemed happy to see her—then fussed about a few blades of grass on her skirt. He'd kissed her and laughed—then said he'd never do it again. And she did *so* want him to do it again. Her head was aching when they arrived at the manor. She hurried to her room to change clothes before going down to meet Bennett.

The big man monopolized the room. "So *this* is our queen from Ireland," Bennett said. He bent to kiss her hand, but his gaze didn't leave her face. "Ah, such sad eyes. That will *never* do," he said, and whispered in her ear, *"Is maith lion prátaí."*

Cailin gasped, then broke into laughter. "Oh, yes, indeed, Bennett. I do, too."

Maitland cast a dark look first at his brother, then at Cailin.

"You speak Gaelic," Cailin said, the mischief back in her eyes.

"The Irish are flooding Canada, your majesty. Can't help but pick up a helpful phrase here or there." Bennett took her arm and walked her over to where his sisters stood. Much to Maitland's annoyance, the two conversed in a lively discussion until the duchess rose and started for the door.

"Come, children," she said. " 'Tis time to prepare for the dinner party."

Bennett gallantly raised Cailin's fingers to his lips and winked. "I'll put in my claim now for a dance at the ball this evening. Maybe two?"

The duchess whispered in Maitland's ear as she passed him. "Perhaps you won't have to look far afield after all to find Cailin a husband."

"Don't be ridiculous, madam."

His mother's innocent smile only made Maitland more irritable, and he caught his brother's arm. "What did you say to Cailin in Gaelic?"

Bennett gave him a maddening grin. "Don't tell me you have run out of pretties to say to the ladies, Davy." His boisterous laughter followed Maitland all the way up the stairs.

Cailin stood in front of the clothespress, noting the contrast between her mother's ancient tunic and the lace sarcenet gown the duchess's seamstress had made. She had no clue to the meaning of any of the emotions she'd gone through in the last two hours. She hesitated a moment. " 'Tis lovely, isn't it?"

"Aye, 'tis that."

"I am a queen, aren't I, Roe?"

"That ye are, and don't let anyone tell ye differently, yir majesty."

"The duke said you aren't to call me that."

"I'll call ye as I see fit. Now, get into yir pretty things and remember it isn't what ye wear that makes ye a fine lady."

Cailin began to dress. "I'm glad you're coming to Ransleigh with us."

"Sure and the duchess said she'd have no peace if she had to be watching after three beautiful girls all at the same time." But Roe would have gone whether she'd been asked or not. Something was amiss; she felt it in her bones.

An hour later, her hair combed and shining, Cailin contemplated her jewelry, then made her selection. Roe nodded her approval. Cailin no sooner finished her toilette than a servant knocked and said the coaches were waiting.

Roe stood back to assess her mistress. "Faith, it's a pretty sight ye are, yir majesty. If yir husband don't notice ye this night, he's blind. Now, put on yir cape and off we go."

By the time Maitland saw his mother and her companion into the family coach, Bennett had already assisted his sisters and Cailin into theirs.

The duchess observed the furrowed brows. "David, don't look so Friday-faced. The girls will look lovely in their new gowns."

"I'm certain you have them attired quite properly, Mother."

"Don't fudge with me. It isn't your sisters that bother you, is it? It's Bennett. He'll be leaving us, David. I've made peace with that fact. He can no longer be confined to our stuffy English society, with all its rules and regulations—and neither can Cailin. That is why I enjoyed watching them together. He makes her laugh, and she needs that."

But I need her laughter, too, Maitland thought. Life at Ashton Hall would be empty without her. Lord! It was Cailin he wanted, not Priscilla. When had he switched their images in his mind? This afternoon in the meadow was not the first time he'd wanted her. He'd known for some time, but he'd refused to acknowledge it. Now it was too late. Pris was waiting.

Lord and Lady Ransleigh's dinner guests assembled in the drawing room. The duchess tugged on Maitland's sleeve and gasped, "Oh, my goodness! *That's* not the gown I had made for Cailin."

Everyone's attention focused on the three young ladies entering. His two sisters, taller and darker-haired, were perfect foils for Cailin's fragile beauty. She wore a long, exquisitely embroidered white tunic. Her hair, unrestrained by either comb or ribbon, fell around her shoulders. She was every bit a queen, and Maitland thought her more desirable than any of the fashionably dressed women in the room. Then his gaze fell upon her one piece of jewelry, the delicate chain and gold locket. Of all the rubies and emeralds she could have worn to her first ball, she'd chosen his insignificant gift. Maitland dared not look into her eyes for fear of what he'd see there. He'd had no right to kiss her. His mother was right: Cailin didn't belong with them. She belonged in fairyland. Without reasoning why, he started toward her. But the viscount, Randolph Vere, had already elbowed his way to her side, past several other eager young men. No one laughed, and Maitland didn't know why that disconcerted him more than if Cailin had been made fun of. It was then that Priscilla caught his eye and Maitland was obliged to turn away.

"The duke has danced with every other young lady in the room. What did ye say to him that he hasn't come near ye all evening?"

Cailin stood on the terrace outside the ballroom, trying to think of an excuse to give Roe. "I didn't say anything, and I'm going to the retiring room. My feet are tired from dancing and trying to escape the viscount's attentions."

"Well, ye'd better do something. The butler is taking bets belowstairs as to which one the duke'll choose. I'll be in the garden if ye need me."

Before she could call her a silly old woman, Roe slipped back into the shadows. To avoid being seen by the viscount, who was hunting diligently for her, Cailin had pulled back into the hedge, when a tall figure grabbed her. If he'd been shot from a cannon, Bennett Ashton couldn't have startled her more.

"Ah, your majesty," he whispered, pointing through the window. "I wish to play a joke on one of my old playmates. See Lady Priscilla going up the stairs? Would you give her this note? Tell her a servant gave it to you."

Cailin's eyes twinkled. " 'Tis a rascal you are, Bennett Ashton."

He chuckled. "I knew you'd make a good conspirator."

He was gone before she knew it, and Cailin hurried after Priscilla.

From her hiding place, Roe frowned. Her mistress had enough tricks up her sleeve. She didn't need a partner filling her head with more mischief.

The soft light of the three-quarter moon illuminated the path to the rose garden. Roe had no sooner leaned over to smell a blossom than her keen ears heard the hushed voices of two people coming toward her. She recognized Lord Ashton's deep tone. He stopped speaking when he saw her.

"It's Cailin's nurse," Priscilla said. "She doesn't understand English."

Roe dipped a curtsy as they continued toward the summerhouse.

"Why did you stay away so long, Bennett?"

"You know why. While David was struggling to keep the estates going, I fell in love with you. Everyone called it calf-love. I was only seventeen when Father died—and you were twenty. You'd already had your come-out and half the young bucks in London were seeking your hand."

"Why do you think I turned them down?"

"I thought you loved David."

"Oh, Bennett, it was *you* I loved. I thought myself foolish to feel for you what I did. And when you left and didn't come back, I believed I'd deceived myself into thinking you cared for me."

Bennett laughed uproariously. "My God, Pris—how wrong we both were! Now you can imagine my elation this afternoon when Mother told me that you weren't married yet. That's why I had to see you before I let your guests know I was home—to let you know how I felt. No—don't say anything yet, my darling. I want to tell you about Canada. It's a rich country, and I'm a rich man. The land to the west is wild and beautiful. My trading company is doing well. Furs and skins are in great demand here and in Europe. I've bought property outside Toronto and have started building a fine house."

Priscilla began to sob. "Then you're going back?"

"Pris—please don't, Pris. I can't *stand* to see you cry. Don't you understand, darling? I want you to come with me . . . I want you to be my wife."

"Oh, Bennett . . ."

The sentence was cut off abruptly and Roe smiled. If she could get Cailin to see how happy Lord Ashton and Lady Priscilla were when they confessed their love, perhaps she'd tell the duke that they were married.

At that instant, the sound of chimes floated out from the manor house. At the count of six, Priscilla pleaded, "Please, Bennett, I must leave. David is going to announce our engagement at midnight. I cannot go back on my word. It would break his heart. Come. David waited for you to be here."

"Nay, I'll stay out here 'til the deed is done. Go, now."

Roe fell back into the shadows as Lady Priscilla ran down the path.

The big man stood at the edge of the summerhouse and repeated her name tenderly, "Pris . . . Oh, my Pris." Then, groaning, he went back inside.

"Tricks, tricks," Roe harrumphed. Her mind a whirlwind, she picked up her skirts and scurried toward the terrace. She had to find *hir majesty*.

* * *

The duke raised his hands to stop the music. Priscilla stood beside him on the dais poised and beautiful as always. Yes, she would make a lovely bride, and a wonderful mother to his children. His eyes scanned the room to make certain their parents were there. Maitland was surprised he hadn't seen or heard from Bennett, but surely he'd arrived. The scalawag never missed a party, if he could help it. "Are you ready, duchess-to-be?" Maitland whispered looking down at her. Tears glistened in her eyes. She'd waited so long for this, he couldn't cry off now.

"I'm ready, *your grace,*" she said softly.

Maitland felt her hand tremble as he placed it over his arm. He gave her a reassuring smile before turning to the crowd. "Good friends and neighbors, I wish to announce that Lady Priscilla Vere has made me the happiest of men. She has consented to be my wife."

The shouts of congratulations rose to such a pitch in the ballroom that no one noticed Roe pull Cailin out onto the terrace. Her breath came out in a *whoosh.* "He cannot do that! He already has one wife, and I'm sure even in England he cannot have two."

"Only if yir royalty," Roe rasped. "I hear talk that the Prince Regent took a good Catholic woman to wife, and the Parliament said he had to marry another. If their future king can marry two women, a duke may not think twice on it either."

"Oh, Roe, what am I going to do? I don't want him to have two wives."

"He don't even know he has *one.*"

"Do something, Roe."

"Oh, and now it's yir old nurse that has to get ye out of the pot, is it?"

"Don't just stand there, old woman—think of something."

"Will ye do as Roe says?" She got a nod. "I need paper and pen."

"Whatever for?"

"Never ye mind. For once in yir life, do as ye're told."

"In the library—this way," Cailin said. "No one should be there now."

Finding what she needed, Roe quickly scribbled a few words and folded the note. "Now," she said, "ye have to act quickly. There is a bower arch at the end of the rose garden that leads to a gazebo. After ye see Lady Priscilla leave, follow her, but stop at the archway . . . and wait."

"For what?"

"Don't argue, missy. Just do as I say. Now, hide behind the bushes and wait until ye see her ladyship come out." As soon as Cailin did as she was told, Roe went back inside. When she saw Lady Priscilla turn away from the duke for a second, Roe skittered over and handed her the note.

Priscilla blanched when she read it.

Maitland was at her side instantly. "What is it, my dear? You're pale."

She laughed a bit shakily. "Nothing really, David. The excitement, I suppose. A few moments in my chambers will be sufficient, I think."

"Of course. Shall I call your maid?"

"Please don't fuss," she said, hurrying away from him. But instead of going upstairs, Priscilla, looking this way and that, sped across the terrace.

As soon as Roe saw Lady Priscilla leave, she made her way through the press to the duke's side. She curtsied and looked up with what she hoped was a worried expression. "Yir grace," she whispered, "I must speak to ye."

Maitland's eyes narrowed. The little black spider looked terrified, but something didn't ring true, and he couldn't quite put his finger on what it was.

Roe wrung her hands. " 'Tis me mistress. I fear she is planning to run away to Gretna Green with Lord Ashton. Ye must stop her, yir grace."

"What?" spouted Maitland, then lowered his voice. "I

knew I couldn't trust that Gaelic-speaking jackanapes brother of mine. Where are they?"

"I heard her say that she'd meet him in the bower at the end of the rose garden." Roe watched as the duke excused himself to those around him and hurried toward the doors. She followed close behind. "Don't let her hear ye coming, yir grace, or ye'll frighten her away."

Maitland took the steps two at a time and was halfway across the lawn before it suddenly occurred to him that the black spider didn't speak English. A lot more was going on here than was evident, and he swore to get to the bottom of it as soon as he'd caught up with the little Irish and his wayward brother. He ran silently along the grassy strip bordering the gravel path. There she was, the termagant. He'd recognize her silhouette anywhere. He was just about to make his presence known when he heard a scream and saw another woman running toward the summerhouse. At her cry, a man came out of the shadows and caught her in his arms.

"Oh, darling," she sobbed, "don't do it."

"You mean you've come back to me, Pris?"

"You know I would if I could, my sweet, but 'tis impossible. David has already announced our engagement."

"Then why did you come out here?"

My God! It was Pris—throwing herself into his brother's arms. Maitland was now only a few feet from Cailin, and fearing she'd call out, he put his hand over her mouth and pulled her back against his body.

Cailin struggled. Without being aware that he still held Cailin's wrist firmly in his hand, Maitland stepped away from the arch, pulling her behind him. "You scoundrel," he called out. "You worsted-stocking knave."

Priscilla waved a piece of paper at Maitland. "He was going to kill himself and it would have been all my fault."

Bennett grinned and hugged Priscilla. He wasn't going to ask her why she thought he was going to do away with himself.

Maitland scowled. "All I know is that my brother has been home only one day and already has connived to run away with the woman I love—and attempted to *compromise* my fiancée, as well."

Bennett's grin grew wider. "What did you just say, big brother?"

"I said—"

Bennett pointed his finger at him. "You said I was planning to run off with *the woman you love*—and you weren't speaking of Pris, were you?"

Maitland realized what he'd admitted. "Oh, Lord, Pris, I'm sorry."

Priscilla put her arms around Bennett's neck. "Don't be. Bennett and I fell in love years ago. We didn't want to break *your* heart."

Maitland looked down at Cailin who was being unusually quiet. He wasn't sure he could trust her to stay put, so he encircled her waist with his arm.

Cailin gave him a quick glance through her lashes. The realization of what he'd meant made her shiver, and instinctively she moved closer to him.

That was all the answer Maitland needed. "I believe I have something to ask the young lady, so if you and Pris will excuse us—?"

Bennett obliged him by taking Priscilla's hand to help her down from the gazebo. "What shall we tell our parents and the guests?"

Maitland hadn't thought of that ticklish problem. "Do you suppose if we make it a double wedding, they will forget my previous announcement?"

Cailin pulled on his sleeve. "David, I have something to tell you."

Maitland placed his fingertip on her lips, his spirits rising by the minute. "Not now, Irish, I have something more important to ask *you*. That is, after I kiss you first," he said, enfolding her in his arms.

When he released her, Cailin sighed.

Maitland led her into the summerhouse. After seating her

on a bench, he took her hand. "I love you, Cailin, and want you to be my wife. Will you marry me?"

Cailin fidgeted uneasily.

"What is it? Was I wrong in thinking you had come to care for me?" She couldn't stand hearing the anguish in his voice, and she blurted out, "Oh David, we are already married."

The silence was deadening.

"I meant to tell you before this—only Father Gregory—" She looked at him apologetically and shrugged.

Maitlan exploded. "What nonsense is this?"

Cailin clasped her hands in her lap. "Father Gregory married us in the castle. You signed your name and Captain Forsythe witnessed it."

Good Lord! No wonder that wily monk had made Maitland pledge to keep the papers safe! His wedding certificate—if that is what it was—sat in his office in London. Of course, he wouldn't believe anything Cailin told him—not until he checked it out. If she lied to him about being married, would she lie to him about other things? Would she be unfaithful? Lord! He'd been jealous of Randy Vere. He'd been jealous of Timothy when she'd preferred to ride in the pony cart with him. He even saw red when that beady-eyed Ezra looked at Cailin. But, demme! He wanted her! "I was furious when I thought you were running away with Bennett."

"Whyever would I do such a thing, David, when I've already got one husband? And I'm beginning to think that that is enough for me."

"Is there anything else you haven't told me?" he said, running his hand up and down her back.

Cailin closed her eyes and hunched her shoulders. "That feels good." Her eyes popped open. "That's all right for me to say, isn't it, David?"

"Perfectly all right," he said, slipping his arm around her and settling her head against his chest. "We're an old married couple, remember?" He swore he heard her purr, which for some reason didn't surprise him. "But I want you to promise me that from now on, no more secrets."

"You have my word, David. I'll never ever keep a secret from you."

Her questionable sincerity brought out the wicked humor that had lain dormant in him for so long. "There is something I must know. What did my brother say to you in Gaelic when he first met you?"

She gave him a sideways glance. "Oh, you don't want to know David."

Maitland frowned. That wasn't the answer he wanted. Questions began to form which he didn't like. "I am your husband and you will answer me. You told him that you *did too*. I want to know what you *did too*."

The tone of his voice sounded quite dangerous, but Cailin was no coward. "Sure and you won't be angry when I tell you?"

"I guarantee nothing," he said menacingly.

Cailin looked at his lips and studied the situation. "I will tell you only if you call me *your majesty.*"

Thick brows shadowed his eyes, hiding his expression from her. "And I'll agree to call you *your grace,*" she said, a little hesitantly.

Maitland tapped the end of her nose with his finger, then kissed the spot. "Fair enough, my little fairy queen. Now, will *your majesty* tell me what that rapscallion said to you?"

Cailin pulled back, laughing. "He said, *'Is maith lion prátaí.'*" She wasn't ready for his lips searing a path down her neck or the hand that encircled her waist, pressing her to him. She gasped. "What are you doing, David?"

"I want to know what my brother whispered to you—in English."

She gave a squeal. "Bennett said, *'I like potatoes.'* "

As Maitland clasp her to him, Cailin felt his laughter against her body. "Your grace?" she said, with concern in her voice.

Those were the last words she spoke until the sun came up.

About the Author

Paula Tanner Girard lives with her family in Maitland, Florida. She is the author of two Zebra regency romances: LORD WAKEFORD'S GOLD WATCH, and CHARADE OF HEARTS, both of which are available at your local bookstore. Paula is currently working on her next Zebra regency romance, *A Father for Christmas,* which will be published in December 1996. She loves hearing from her readers and you may write to her at: P.O. Box 941982 Maitland, FL 32794-1982. Please include a self-addressed stamped envelope if you wish a response.

Duke of Diamonds

Jenna Jones

James Richmond, Duke of Rockham, leaned one velvet-clad shoulder of his large frame against the warm stone arch of his drawing room's substantial inglenook and let his gaze wander at will across the expanse of the room, lazily swirling sherry in the narrow bowl of his Flemish crystal as he did so. The room seemed filled with women . . . oppressively so, he thought, as his jaw tightened . . . yet there really were not so many. Perhaps it was just that these particular women disgusted him so. They were the *crème de la crème* of London society, carefully chosen by him to be in attendance at this house party, yet at the moment, he could easily wish each of them to perdition.

For the nonce, however, and thank God, he conceded with slight charity, they seemed to have settled into a watchful, predatory stillness, quite unlike the torrent of gushing and fawning they had subjected him to earlier that afternoon upon their arrival. His lips whispered a smile. Most in the *ton* would count their mood extremely odd, given the fact that each of the ladies present had long been acquainted. He, however, did not. He knew exactly what filled their thoughts as they meandered about the elegant room awaiting his butler's announcement of dinner, trying to make their purposeful movements seem idle. He had, after all, been the one who had extended the invitations that had brought them with such eager expectancy to The Crags, his palatial estate in the wilds of Northumberland. He had been the one to issue the challenge that had put each one of those thoughts into their conniving feminine heads.

"Well, James, are we ever to know what this rather extraordinary gathering is all about?" asked Stanley Prescott, Viscount Moreland, as he arose from the captured warmth of one of the settles bracketing the huge fireplace recessed within the inglenook, then stepped through the arch into the elegant room. A friend of the duke's since their days at Eton, the viscount enjoyed aping the Beau on such occasions in a cutaway of immaculate blue velvet, black evening slippers, and white silk inexpressibles. He carefully smoothed his *coiffure à la Brutus* as he came to stand beside Rockham.

"I shall tell you now, if you like," the duke answered, observing the countess of Cawthon with dry amusement.

Across the room, quite ignorant of his notice, the countess surreptitiously slid her gloved fingers along the underside of one of the buhl tables placed near a conversational arrangement of several immaculate Hepplewhite chairs, afterward glancing about to see if her action had been noted by any of the others. Deciding that it had not, she again wove herself into the strange choreography being performed by the rest of the women as they, too, moved about the room, touching surfaces, lifting cushion corners, slightly shaking the room's assorted figurines and vases.

"And about time," added Edward Littleton, Marquess of Ashford, as he, too, rose with a slight stretch from the opposite settle and joined them.

The duke's smile widened somewhat, though mirthlessly. "It is quite simple, really," he told them, seizing a nearby decanter and tipping more sherry into their glasses. "I have had enough. I am about to exact my revenge."

"The deuce, you say!" Moreland laughed, sputtering slightly on his last sip. "On whom, James? . . . Not these gentle ladies! What a very odd concept."

There is nothing odd about it," Rockham stated coldly. "These *gentle ladies,* as *you* call them, I name as grasping, calculating wasps who haven't an honorable impulse among them."

"Lud, James, coming it a bit too brown, don't you think?" Ashford chided with a grin.

"Easy for you to say," the duke countered warmly. "You have not had to put up with their antics. Take, for instance, Miss Trixie Stanhope," he offered as an example, gesturing with his glass toward the young beauty fidgeting near the drawing room door.

"Gladly!" asserted the marquess, delight blossoming across his face.

". . . And her mother, the Countess of Cawthon," the duke added quellingly, "whom you will note has now begun using Miss Stanhope as a shield while she palpates the lining of my bell pull."

"Jove, so she is!" breathed Moreland, peering across the room nearsightedly.

As the gentlemen watched, exactly as the duke had indicated, from behind Miss Stanhope's *coiffure à la Sappho,* the countess's arm suddenly snaked upward like a hungry shipworm to grope the heavy brocade with such vigor that the hem of her pomona green sarcenet rose indecently far above her thick ankles.

"I say . . ." the viscount added in wonder. And then he lapsed into silence.

"Well, let's have it, man," Ashford demanded, taking up the conversational slack with an eager smile. "What about them, James . . . ? Aside from the fact that the countess would look much more the thing in a pair of Wellingtons."

Again the duke cast his friend a chiding glance. "Simply this," he told them. "Every day since the beginning of the Season, Lady Cawthon has accompanied Miss Stanhope to my town home . . . in her crested carriage, no less . . . solely for the purpose of hand delivering rumpled love poems to me which the young lady has written in my honor. The countess, as both of you are well aware, is reputed to be one of the *ton's* highest sticklers. Yet pattern card or no, not only has our *gentle* countess scandalously abetted her daughter in breaking one of society's most rigid rules for its unmarried women, but she has the whole of London bruiting it about that I welcome the chit's advances!

"And over there," he continued, gesturing with his sherry glass, "the beauteous Miss Effie Fotheringale . . . a young woman our own Prince Florizel only days ago commended as the perfect picture of proper comportment, yet who is even now running her hands under my sofa cushions while her mother, Countess Rutherford, squeezes my pillows."

"Ah, I know what you would complain of her," Ashford stated, his grin widening. "Five times last Season the chit tried to bring you up to scratch by putting an announcement in the *Morning Post* telling the *ton* of your nonexistent engagement."

"She did," the duke responded, biting out each word in remembered anger.

"As I recall, the situation was deuced difficult for you to get out of."

"Not difficult at all," Rockham ground out. "I merely had to become a jilt in the eyes of every person of consequence in England . . . five times over! And then, of course, we must not forget the lovely Miss Adelaide Cox and her mother, the Marchioness of Foxborough," he continued, gesturing with his chin toward a diamond of the first water who, after tugging an aquamarine glove from her delicate fingers, glanced warily about and then plunged her hand into one of the duke's matched Sèvres vases.

"Egad!" gasped Moreland, finally finding voice enough to add that tidbit to the conversation.

"Don't stop now, James, I beg you," chortled the marquess. "What has Miss Cox done, aside from taking a vast interest in your crockery?"

The duke took a large swallow of his sherry, then raked long fingers through his tawny blond hair. "Actually, it was her action that precipitated this house party," he told them.

"Ah, the last straw," nodded Ashford.

"Just so," Rockham agreed. "It happened two weeks ago, as I was on my way home from Rundell and Bridge with my newest acquisition. Miss Cox fairly flew into the street at me as I was driving by, then enacted a fit of the vapors that would have put Mrs. Siddons to shame. Deuce take it, Eddie, the jade threw herself down in front of my curricle. I might have killed her! I was barely able to keep my bloods in hand! It was then that I decided I would bear no more of these plots. Gentlemen, I *will* be left alone by these predators to choose my own bride!"

"Here, here!" cried Ashford, drawing the ladies' scowls. In a cocky response, he cast them a roguish grin, lifting his glass to the room at large before granting them a very pretty leg.

"You have yet to explain Lady Braxton, James," Moreland said, noticing for the first time the woman dressed in jet-draped black brocade standing in a dimly lit corner of the room, casually running her fingers over the edges of a section of silk wall covering. "Why have you invited her?"

"Because she is the worst of the lot," the duke ground out. "Not a day has gone by in recent memory when she has not pursued me into shops, the opera, inside the very columns of Tattersall's . . . all to bore me with drivel about her daughter. The lady has even had the effrontery to accost me outside my club. I tell you, it is not to be borne!"

"I was not aware that the countess had a daughter," the viscount commented.

"Miss Aimee Winthrop," Rockham stated dispassionately. "No doubt she has been delayed upstairs, measuring my mother's old apartments for new carpeting."

Moreland erupted into a low chuckle.

"Curious none of us has met her," Ashford offered.

"She is quite new to Town, I understand. Country bred . . . brought up by her father at his Shropshire estate and allowed to molder on the shelf without ever having a Season. She is four-and-twenty, Lady Braxton tells me with great apology."

Ah, yes, now I recall it," Moreland added. "Braxton and

his lady have lived separately for most of their marriage, have they not? As I remember, the *on-dit* was that Braxton wanted his wife to have no influence over his daughter's rearing. He would not even allow visitations. What does the girl look like, James?"

"I have yet to meet her," he responded. "I did get a glimpse of dark curls wedged behind Lady Foxborough and Miss Fotheringale as they enveloped me upon their arrival, but immediately after, Lady Cawthon and the others joined them and soon had me completely surrounded. Miss Winthrop most likely found her own thrust neatly parried and decided to retreat to her room to regroup. But what's bred in the bone will come out in the roast, gentlemen. I misdoubt Lady Braxton has already had ample time to remake her daughter into the pattern card of a nagging, eyelash-batting conniver. I am persuaded that Miss Winthrop will put whatever scheme was thwarted this afternoon into full play tonight. She will be disappointed, however. I have had enough, gentlemen. I will tolerate no more."

"Again, here, here!" cried Ashford, raising his glass. "Another stalwart soul who shall go to his grave free of leg shackles."

"On the contrary," Rockham countered. "I have every intention of marrying. In fact, I shall make you this promise. Show me one woman, Eddie . . . just one who is without guile, who will cease her endless female fawning and accept me, not because I am a duke, but for the man that I am . . . and I shall snatch her up before you can drain that glass of sherry. One thing you can be sure of, however," he concluded dryly. "That woman is not to be found among the occupants of this room."

"Give over, James," the viscount drawled, adjusted the costly white silk of his waistcoat before drawing in a small sip of his sherry. "You are arguably the richest man in all of England, one of the highest titled, and not a shriveled old man into the bargain, but a mere thirty and two. Devil take it, man,

your face and physique have sent more than twelve Seasons'
worth of Society's darlings over the boughs! What do you
expect, my friend?"

"What does any of that signify?" Rockham argued into his
glass.

"A great deal, if one happens to be standing in your
shadow!" the viscount teased. "And, of course, there is the
rather insignificant fact that you possess a collection of rare
and priceless diamonds whose smaller specimens alone I misdoubt could finance the war against Napoleon to its conclusion without having even to touch the larger items. You *are*
known about Town as the Duke of Diamonds, you know. Egad,
James, that title alone seals your fate with the ladies!"

Unconsciously, the duke glanced down at the thumb-sized
yellow brilliant nestled amid the soft folds of his immaculate
cravat *en cascade*. After a moment, his gaze again rose.

"And therein lies my whole point," Rockham declared
softly. "My fate, Stanley, is *my* fate . . ."

Suddenly Miss Fotheringale appeared nearby, arresting the
duke's response. Aware of the gentlemen's stares, the lady
blushed prettily. Then, quite amazingly, she wiggled the toe
of one soft kid slipper beneath the edge of the room's patterned
Aubusson carpet and began to shuffle forward, sliding her
foot along under the carpet edge until she had awkwardly
passed them by. Upon reaching the corner, she made a neat
turn and continued on, soon disappearing behind a large
screen masking the gaming table.

"Devil a bit, James!" Ashford hissed as soon as she was
out of hearing. "I can stand it no longer! Just what the deuce
is going on here?"

Rockham chuckled softly, then buried several of his fingers
in the pocket of his white silk waistcoat. Soon he drew forth
a small drawstring bag made of dark green velvet.

"The ladies are searching," he murmured, loosening the
ties and pouring the bag's contents into his palm, ". . . for
this."

A moment of immobility followed.

"The deuce!" Stanley finally whispered, his gaze riveted upon a huge, heart-shaped diamond glittering against Rockham's hand, watching as captured firelight writhed and pulsed within each facet, appearing to make it throb.

"Incredible!" breathed the marquess, setting aside his sherry glass to look more closely.

"My newest acquisition, gentlemen," the duke said softly. "The rarest diamond ever found in India. A pink of nineteen carats so singular in shape, clarity, and color that there is no other like it in existence. My friends, I give you Calladorn's Fire."

"Dear God . . . beautiful!" whispered Moreland. Then he peered questioningly into the duke's eyes. "But, James . . . why the deuce are the ladies looking for it?"

"Because I have invited them to," Rockham said rather casually, and then he scowled slightly. "Rather pointless at the moment, though, since I still have the stone in my possession. They were not to begin searching until after breaking their fast tomorrow, but, of course, they are already bending the rules."

"You invited them to?" reiterated Ashford, drawing the duke back to his previous statement.

"I did indeed," Rockham agreed. "It is all a part of my plan."

"For revenge," stated Moreland.

"Exactly so. It is my intention to allow these four most eligible, most beautiful . . . most aggravating, obnoxious, manipulative young females in the *haut ton* to compete in a search for this stone."

"But . . . to what end?" asked Moreland, his eyes now quite round.

"To provide a clear demonstration for *le haut monde* of just how loathsome its ladies' excesses have come to be," he replied through clenched teeth. "It is my intention, gentlemen, to make fools of them. I can think of no better way to end their constant scheming."

"You cannot be serious!" hissed Moreland in response.

"I am," Rockham disagreed.

"But what lady of Society would lower herself to participate in such a crass activity? Why, they should all be insulted at the mere suggestion!"

Rockham laughed slightly. "Look around you, Stan. They are here, are they not? And already searching."

"But . . but these are the Incomparables!" the viscount sputtered, looking about him in disbelief. "Every Pink in Town is at their feet . . . with the exception of you, of course. Why, the very concept must be beneath them."

"And so it should be," the duke countered calmly. "Yet here they are. Telling, is it not?"

"But . . . how? Why?"

"Probably because I have added a bit of incentive," the duke confessed.

"Which is . . . ?" Ashford eagerly asked, leaning slightly forward.

"I have told them that whoever finds the diamond might also become my wife."

"The deuce!" Moreland gasped as both he and the marquess turned to stare. "But you vowed none of these would become your wife. How . . . ?"

Rockham's response was a sly smile and a shrug. He sipped more sherry.

He glanced up, then, into a large, oval Adams mirror hanging above a small settee placed against the adjoining wall. The mirror, because of its angle, allowed him to view a part of the huge hall which he could not see through the drawing room door. By chance, just as his gaze rested upon the glass, a young woman suddenly dashed through the corridor entrance into the Hall and fairly skidded to a halt within the mirror's oval reflection.

The duke started, straightening slightly, his brow elevating as his gaze locked upon the image. The reflection in the mirror was the face of a breathless, blushing country girl . . . completely without artifice . . . entirely beautiful. Rockham swallowed thickly and stared. He could not have looked away had Prinny himself commanded it.

Within the oval frame, the lady paused, looking cautiously about as she placed a hand to her décolleté for a moment as if to steady her breathing. Satisfied that she was unobserved, she glanced down at her gown. A lock of dark brown hair fell free from its binding of sapphire ribbons to tumble captivatingly down upon her forehead.

A moue of vexation flickered across her lips. With the back of her hand, she absently brushed the lock aside, then began banishing her gown's wayward folds, removing tidbits of lint, straightening the broad sapphire bow which drew the costly fabric snugly beneath her shapely breasts, completely unaware of how fetchingly she was smoothing the skirt's goldshot muslin around her slim form. Rockham noted it all, and his reaction rivered through him.

She looked up, then, and rolled her eyes. Again Rockham started, the corner of his mouth twitching with amusement. As he watched, the lady once more looked to see if she was alone, then suddenly thrust her fingers quite deeply into her bodice, seizing the gown's low décolleté in both hands while she tugged upward on the soft fabric and wriggled within its confines.

Still she was not satisfied. She frowned, then cupped her breasts and wriggled again. Her décolleté remained embarrassingly low. She pursed her lips in vexation, then puffed the fallen lock of hair back in the direction of her Grecian style. Forced to concede the battle to her neckline, she threw up her hands.

Rockham barely conquered his compulsion to laugh. He was charmed. By a country spinster named Miss Aimee Winthrop, he concluded with a slight nod. Oh, yes, it had to be her. The lady of the dark brown curls. And not a scheming shrew at all, it seemed, but a rare diamond still in the raw, unblemished by even a whit of Town polish. The combination was heady. He sipped more sherry, smiling at the irony. In the midst of his scheme to discredit the females of Society, had he found his lady at last?

"By God, what a bold stroke!" the marquess interjected into his thoughts, restoring a particle of his attention to the conversation. "Brilliant, James . . . absolutely brilliant. Trapping the ladies by their own greed. Deuce take it, given the prizes you've offered, I shouldn't be at all surprised if the chits scratch each other's eyes out!"

"Which, of course, is exactly the point of the exercise," Rockham agreed, smiling at the image in the mirror, not the accolade.

Out in the hall the lady pinched her cheeks slightly, then began to practice the several Attitudes that were a part of each debutante's repertoire. Rockham bit his inner cheek. As he regarded her, she quickly discarded "Diana at the Hunt" and "Nymph Pursued by Satyr." When she struck the pose "Venus Arising from the Sea," though, the corners of his eyes noticeably crinkled.

"You *wish* to embarrass them, James?" Moreland gasped as his gentleman's honor bruised. "But they must be protected. You know as well as I that when word reaches the tabbies of their impropriety, all London shall know of it within hours. The *ton* shall cut them utterly!"

"Oh, I think not," the duke countered easily, thoroughly entertained by the sight of Miss Winthrop inflating her tired cheeks several times into muscle-relaxing pillows after deciding that her Venus, too, was unsatisfactory. Within moments, however, she was again posturing "Helen Receiving Troy's Adulation." Rockham squeezed the corners of his mouth. A wide grin threatened.

"The ladies shall be embarrassed by the whole scandal broth, certainly," he managed to continue, "and perhaps experience the withdrawal of a few social invitations, but as you yourself pointed out, Stanley, these four are the *crème de la crème* . . . the Incomparables. It shall not be long before the *ton* extends its forgiveness and the Tulips are again blooming in their path."

"They, however, will never again bloom around you," Ashford concluded with a wide grin of sheer admiration.

"Not if everything goes according to plan," he agreed, watching as the lady in the mirror again released her Attitude, her shoulders heaving with frustration. She placed a finger to her lips, then, obviously considering her next experiment. At last she assumed an attitude Rockham knew was called "Juno Regarding the Lesser Goddesses." It was an expression he could only name as "arrogant unapproachability." At last she seemed satisfied.

The duke's eyes gleamed. She was not the only one who was satisfied. A slight nod acknowledged it.

"How long shall the search last?" Ashford asked.

"Only tomorrow," Rockham told them. "The contest will end at the conclusion of a small, intimate ball I have planned for tomorrow evening. I have invited several of the local gentry to fill out our numbers. It should prove to be an interesting event."

"Absolutely brilliant," reiterated the marquess.

"Well, I for one think it astoundingly callous," Stanley muttered, turning to face the inglenook. "You forget I know you, James. You have some trick up your sleeve, do you not? . . . some escape planned to prevent your marrying . . ."

In the mirror, the lady's chin rose to a level of haughtiness that finally unbalanced her. Toppling backward, she quickly caught hold of the edge of a large nearby table, then glanced nervously about, coloring prettily. The duke's throat clenched with his effort to control a bark of laughter. He could not remember having ever been so entertained.

And then all traces of Miss Winthrop's manufactured expression fell instantly from her flawless face. As Rockham watched, she stilled and stared straight ahead, gaping like a child on her first trip to the Mechanical Museum. Her eyes widened into lovely ovals. Her lips parted enchantingly with unadulterated awe. She had discovered that which countless travelers had come to The Crags for centuries to view, he knew. She had spotted the fireplace.

Pride thrummed in the duke's veins.

"Calm yourself, Stanley," chuckled the marquess, extending his glass for a refill. "Can you doubt that James knows exactly what he is doing?"

"That is not the point!" the viscount responded, turning back to face them. "Nothing in this speaks to honor!"

Within the oval, Miss Winthrop's fingers rose to touch lightly against her chin. Rockham knew that she was studying the massive mantel, carved six generations ago by a master Italian stone cutter commissioned by one of his ancestors. The mantel had been formed into a sculpted composition of the Fates, daughters of Zeus, each of them spinning a different part of the destiny awaiting mankind. An intricately sculpted rope draped gracefully between them, symbolizing life. On the left, Clotho spun life's thread. Lachesis, in the center, measured its length; while Atropos, on the right, cut the cord at life's end.

"What would you have me do, Stan?" Rockham questioned, watching Miss Winthrop's gaze begin to rise.

Above the mantel, over fifty painted panels reposed, depicting life and death in nature through scenes of animals posed gracefully in natural settings. Above this display, the panels developed into floral designs rising up the two stories of the hall until they melded with stonework which also was carved with animal and insect themes. From his place by the inglenook, the duke watched as the lady absorbed each scene, enjoying each of her honest, unschooled reactions as her head tipped almost fully backward, exposing the quite delicious arch of her slim neck to his slow perusal. His body tensed, yet grew languorous at the same time.

"I have tried everything I know to do, Stan," he continued

quietly, "yet still they come after me, trying every scheme to catch me alone and unawares. They have even secreted themselves in my bed in their efforts to compromise me. If I must be callous, even a bit cruel, in order to put a period to it, can you blame me?"

In the mirror, Miss Winthrop's eyes widened slightly. Rockham knew that she had spotted the delicate carvings of the thousands of marble butterflies studding the ceiling vault's ribs. His shoulders lightened.

"You know I cannot, James, but . . ."

The lady's gaze rose again, finally viewing the vault itself, ingeniously portrayed as a starry sky populated by flocks of rare species of birds. He watched as Miss Winthrop's jaw fell completely open . . . watched as her shoulders sagged slightly on an astounded sigh. His heart kicked against his ribs.

". . . Yes, I know. It is not the act of a gentleman," he finally completed, as Miss Winthrop's gaze at last dropped to her folded hands.

"No, it is not!" Stanley cried hotly.

"And you would not be wrong," Rockham agreed. In the hall, Miss Winthrop gathered herself and finally stepped from the mirror's sight, leaving the duke feeling strangely deserted. Mentally, he shook himself. "Yet I am certain the *ton's* notice of the ladies' impropriety shall merely be a nine days' wonder, as is every other sip of scandal broth. And I have taken steps to soothe their ruffled feminine feathers, Stan. I have already had made four parures of diamonds, each one interspersed with a different precious stone so as to be unlike any of the others. They shall each receive one."

Moreland stiffened, his gaze firming. "Why four, James, if one of the ladies is to gain the Fire?" he asked tersely.

The duke's answering smile held no mirth. "You have the right of it, of course. It was never my intention that any of them find the Fire," he confessed evenly.

"Deuce take it, James . . . !"

"Lud, Stanley, do but think for a moment!" ordered Ashford. "If the whole point of the house party is to free James from female machinations, why would he turn right around and snap his own leg into a shackle?"

"But how shall you honorably prevent it?" Stanley cried again, looking toward the duke.

Rockham gave him a soft grin.

And then Miss Aimee Winthrop entered the drawing room as "Juno Addressing the Lesser Goddesses" with an extraordinary elevation of her nose, stumbled over the edge of the Aubusson carpet disturbed earlier by Miss Fotheringale's investigation, then tipped and twirled for several yards 'til she landed quite conveniently, so the duke thought, in the midst of his steadying arms.

James stared down into Miss Winthrop's warm, astounded eyes. Two thoughts swept all others from his mind: first, would that very moment be too soon to kiss his future wife; and second, how the deuce was he going to get the Fire into her lovely hands?

"My goodness, your grace, I do beg your pardon!" Aimee breathed, staring back into the most handsome face she had ever seen. Not that she had never seen the face before, of course. She had seen this particular face not two weeks past, but it had been at a comfortable distance. Now, so close she could see the flecks of silver in his eyes, even her teeth were curling.

"Aimee!" gasped Lady Braxton, reaching out to grasp the top of her evening glove and yanking it backward. "Release his grace at once!"

"I did so, Mama . . ." Aimee replied, at the moment quite enthralled by the tip of Rockham's nose, "several moments ago."

The duke scanned her curls and grinned.

Then why are you not standing here beside me?" the countess asked in a whisper loud enough to be heard in the servant's quarters on the fourth floor.

"Because his grace has not as yet released me," Aimee whispered back while carefully studying the slight indentation bisecting the duke's chin. "You really should, my lord," she then whispered to him.

"I know," was all Rockham said.

"But how am I to present you in such a posture?" the countess hissed, again tugging upon Aimee's long glove. "How shall you curtsy to his grace?"

"On suspended knee?" Aimee suggested with a soft laugh.

Beneath her hands, Rockham's shoulders began shaking suspiciously.

Aimee bit her lip, blushing furiously at her own temerity. What could she have been thinking? Was it not enough that she had not yet managed to extricate herself from such an improper situation? Did she also have to jest about it? A soft sigh escaped from her lips. When would she learn to guard her tongue? she wondered, toying with Rockham's crisp lapels.

And then she brightened somewhat. What did it matter, after all? She had already disgraced herself beyond redemption and had plans to do so again shortly. Besides, the whole situation really was quite ludicrous. Looking up into the duke's dancing eyes, she again softly laughed.

"Oh, that my efforts should have come to this . . ." breathed the countess from behind her, raising a wrist to her brow, ". . . my salts, dearest . . . I feel quite faint . . ."

"There now, Mama," Aimee soothed with a smile, finally managing to extract herself from the duke's embrace to place a supporting arm about her parent. "See? I am standing on my own two feet again. You may now present me with at least the remnants of propriety. But I warn you, nothing has changed. My mind is quite settled on the matter."

"What hasn't changed?" the duke asked, still vastly amused.

"Unnatural child!" the countess hissed under her breath, this time low enough for only those in the drawing room to hear. "Why, oh why, did your stubborn fool of a father insist upon keeping you from me? Just look at you! You are already on the shelf. You have no Town polish, and now you are set upon rejecting everything your poor mother has tried, in your absence, to do for you. Why must you wound me so? You know I have worked tirelessly all these years with only your welfare at heart!"

"For which I am very grateful," Aimee said, gently squeezing her mother's frail shoulders. "But on this point I cannot bend, Mama. I will not . . ."

". . . Silence! We are within hearing of the duke," her mother replied in a whisper that gave the pot boys and scullery maids in the kitchen pause. "We shall discuss all that later. But for now, I believe it best if we act as if this latest faux pas never occurred. Just follow my lead."

Turning, the countess immediately sank into a deep curtsy before Rockham. "Ah, your grace," she cooed. "Here she is at last! May I present to you my daughter, Miss Aimee Winthrop. Aimee, my lamb," she continued upon rising, "make your curtsy to the duke. Oh, Rockham, is she not as lovely as I have always told you?"

"More so," murmured the duke, meeting Aimee's forthright gaze.

"Good evening, your grace," Aimee said evenly, at last sweeping into a proper curtsy, her eyes laughing into his. "How gracious of you to receive me!"

In truth, Aimee felt quite ridiculous perpetuating her mother's charade, but the absurdity of the situation overwhelmed her sense of embarrassment. Her cheeks colored attractively as she fought laughter and concentrated upon holding her unpracticed position. Naturally, in keeping with the moment, one calf suddenly began to cramp.

"Oh!" she gasped as her supporting foot wobbled and her derrière slipped dangerously close to the floor.

Instantly she was pulled back up into Rockham's arms. To her astonishment, she found that her body was now actually touching his. Even more astonishing, she rather liked it. As he easily recaptured her startled stare, an odd thrill skipped down the length of her spine, completely sweeping her breath away. She trembled slightly, groping for the composure she knew was necessary. It was not to be found.

"A distinct pleasure, Miss Winthrop," James murmured to her, keeping her scandalously close while his gleaming eyes roved over her form and face. "How nice of you to drop in."

Aimee's eyes blinked and then widened. Was Rockham teasing her? Her head tipped to the side as she assessed his face.

A slight smile caught at the edge of the duke's mouth.

Good heavens, he was! She was being teased by the Duke of Diamonds! Aimee's heart stumbled into its rhythm again. A light laugh escaped her and she relaxed with relief.

"Is it indeed?" she finally questioned as she again freed herself and stepped back to a seemly distance, her warm smile revealing one small dimple on her cheek. ". . . A pleasure, I mean."

"Absolutely," James answered, absorbed by the tiny imperfection.

"But why, sir?" she again questioned, her head once more tipping prettily to one side. "Because I might, by tomorrow's end, be your fiancée?"

"Most assuredly." The duke grinned as he again took her elbow into his hand.

"Ah," Aimee commented, once more gently extricating her arm as her enchanting smile returned. "That means, of course, that you must be equally pleased to have the acquaintance of the other contestants."

Rockham's smile faded somewhat. "I . . . suppose that I am," he finally concurred.

"Then it is as I thought," Miss Winthrop concluded with a

tiny sigh. "You, sir, can be neither an honest nor an honorable man."

Beside the duke, Moreland and Ashford stiffened. Assorted gasps came from those around them.

"What?" Rockham questioned at last, completely taken aback.

Lady Braxton clutched at her bosom behind a wafting chicken-skin fan. "Oh, lud . . . my salts . . . !" she gasped in an emoting that surely startled the sleeping stable hands.

Miss Winthrop was not swayed. "It is a logical conclusion, your grace," she stated brightly. "You cannot be pleased to have made the acquaintance of each of the contestants equally, yet at the same time, name the pleasure of my acquaintance as distinct. That is a prevarication, sir . . . a plumper, as I have heard the Town Birds say."

"What . . . ?" the duke echoed helplessly.

"It is of no moment, however," the lady continued with a dismissive gesture. "As I shall not win your contest and therefore cannot become your wife, I have no concern over the flaws in your character. The others, however, should be warned," she continued, again briefly curtsying before beginning to turn away. "It is my duty as a fellow female, you see."

"Why do you say you shan't win, madam?" James asked, masking a surge of desperation. "You have as good a chance as any here."

"Oh, I hardly think so," Aimee told him. And then she again smiled. "You see, I have no intention of participating." She then took firm hold of her vaporous parent, most improperly turned her back upon Rockham, and walked away.

The duke stared after her, speechless.

"I say, James, you didn't even introduce me," Ashford commented dryly, his hand covering his wayward grin.

"Lud, the chit's a beauty!" Stanley offered, struggling with his own smile. "As unsullied as a country daisy. Got spirit, too, James. By Jove," he teased, "as long as she ain't in the contest any longer, I believe I shall have a go at her."

"Think again," the duke stated quietly, his gaze still clinging to Aimee. "No matter what the lady says, she still belongs to me."

"Ah, but only if she finds the Fire," the marquess countered.

"She'll find it," James vowed, his hands fisted at his sides.

"How? She won't even be looking," Stanley chuckled. "And if you put the Fire where Miss Winthrop can find it, you run the risk that the others will be able to find it, too. You've put yourself in a nice, neat box, James, have you not? I knew you would regret all this."

Slowly Rockham's gaze left Aimee to settle upon his friend. "I am crushed, Stanley," he replied with a very predatory smile, downing the last of his sherry. "Your faith in my powers of persuasion leaves much to be desired. The lady will find the Fire, gentlemen."

"Mmm, I don't know, James," Ashford countered, resting a wrist on the duke's shoulder. "Given the look Miss Winthrop gave you when she walked away, even if she does find the stone, I shouldn't be surprised if the lady turns right around and gives the deuced thing to someone else."

At that moment, to everyone's relief, Blair, the butler, entered the room to announce dinner.

It was not long after breaking his fast the following morning that Rockham again crossed swords with Aimee . . . not long, too, after the hunt for Calladorn's Fire got fully under way.

The search had begun, much to the duke's chagrin, even before he had savored the last bite of his deviled kidney deliciously topped by a bit of boiled egg. A series of telltale thumps had sounded, followed by a sort of arrhythmic growling which had emanated from somewhere within the vast corridors of the upstairs and begun to reverberate through the ancient stones; a scraping protestation that had sounded as if long-coddled furniture was being forced to remove from places where it had rightfully stood in dignity and decorum for years. The duke had lifted his head, listened, his fork suspended in mid-air, and then winced as a costly sounding crash had occurred, followed by a tearful spate of muffled feminine excuses.

He had made the decision quite quickly as his forehead had sunk into the heel of his hand. Not at all anxious to witness the destruction of his hearth and home, he had fled the table with alacrity, donned riding buckskins, a bottle-green superfine cutaway, and mirror-toed Hessians, and had quit the premises for the solace of a long, sanity-sustaining ride.

To his pleasure, he discovered that Miss Winthrop had been of the same mind.

"Miss Winthrop!" he exclaimed, as he entered the stables and found a groom helping her to mount Cloud, a gentle dappled gray. "I thought you would be with the others prying sharp, heavy objects under my wainscoting. Jem!" he called to his head groom. "Saddle Bachelor for me, if you please."

Aimee could not stop her bright laugh. "I told you I would not," she chuckled. After a pause in which she stroked Cloud's pewter mane, she asked, "Is it quite awful?"

"Mmm, let me see," the duke replied, thoughtfully rubbing his jaw. "At the time I made my escape, Lady Cawthon and Miss Stanhope were emptying all the drawers in the blue, gold, and Chinese bedrooms, Lady Foxborough and Miss Cox had commandeered seven of my footmen to remove all my downstairs furniture to the front lawn, Lady Rutherford and Miss Fotheringale had decided that there was no better hiding place for the Fire than in the bottle of French Armagnac I keep in the library, and your mother was quite seriously thinking of draining the midden. Yes, Miss Winthrop, I believe 'awful' describes it quite well."

"Oh, dear!" she cried, again bursting into light laughter. "I do apologize . . . for Mama, at least. She was under my strictest orders not to participate."

The duke eyed her consideringly. "Care to tell me why?" he asked softly, as Jem walked Bachelor to his side.

"I suppose there is no reason not to," Aimee replied, picking at a piece of straw that had settled on the aquamarine kerseymere of her riding skirt.

"Then let us ride a ways where you may speak openly," the duke suggested, mounting lithely. "You have obviously taken me in great disfavor. I should like to know your reason." Giving Aimee a second perusal that penetrated to her toes, he touched his whip to Bachelor's shoulder, then took the lead down a well-worn bridle path.

The two rode in relative silence away from The Crags' main grounds, through cool copses of oak and linden, across meadows splashed with wildflowers, for the better part of an hour. When Aimee began to wonder if the duke had forgotten the reason for their ride in his obvious delight in being away from his guests, he at last drew to a halt beside a narrow stream, where he gave his mount enough lead to taste a bit of the water. Turning, he invited Aimee to do likewise.

"You called me dishonest last evening," he said bluntly, as Aimee came to a halt beside him.

Aimee's gaze lifted to his. "Yes."

"It made me angry," he told her, his jaw bulging slightly.

"I would imagine so," she responded quietly. "Although I did not say it to anger you."

"I am aware of that. You engaged in your little game of semantics to level the ground between us, so that I would be less the duke and you more than the ingenue."

"Perceptive," she commented, acknowledging the kernel of admiration that sprang to life inside her, though not welcoming it.

Rockham smiled not only at the compliment he knew she begrudged, but at her honesty. No one had ever dared speak to him as she did.

"Do you truly think that of me?" he asked, his posture seemingly relaxed, yet every muscle tensed.

"I have no reason not to," Aimee responded, crossing her wrists over the saddle horn.

"I must ask you to explain," James said, his voice calm.

"Very well," Aimee responded, looking directly at him.

In the light of day, he saw that her eyes were hazel, gold-dappled. The duke approved.

"I was present in Ludgate Hill when the incident between you and Miss Cox occurred," she told him. "I had just visited the drapers. To my everlasting dismay, I witnessed the whole thing."

Then you would have seen the lady quite foolishly put herself in grave danger by throwing herself in front of my curricle," Rockham replied, his voice taking on an edge.

"Worse," Aimee stated grimly. "I saw her mother push her from behind."

A small silence ensued while the duke digested that information. "I had not realized that," he said, shaking his head slightly in disgust. At last he looked up. "I also cannot see the connection. How does the incident with Miss Cox make me dishonest?"

Aimee's returning smile was genuine. "I saw more than the accident, your grace," she told him. "I also saw your face after you had gotten your horses back under control, and while you waited for your tiger to help Miss Cox up from the street. I have never before seen such coldness . . . such dislike."

"Can you blame me?" he asked, with a softness that let Aimee know the depth of the control he was employing.

She shivered slightly, knowing that to speak in such a manner to a duke was very bad *ton,* knowing full well what the repercussions to her family might be.

"No," she again responded with a tentative smile, deciding that she may as well continue as the damage had probably already been done. "The actions of both mother and daughter were beyond anything. But I do question why, not one day after you looked with such repugnance upon Miss Cox, you then gave her the opportunity to become your wife."

Rockham inhaled deeply.

"I wondered, too, what might have motivated you to extend the same invitation to others of us . . . to me," Aimee continued, drawing Cloud's head back from the stream. "Logic would have me conclude, of course, that for some reason you must look upon each of us in the same way."

James shifted slightly in his saddle, but could not force words past the breath he was holding. He gestured for her to continue.

"I confess that I suspected, but was not sure of, your reason until I entered the drawing room last evening," she stated, her voice softening with sympathy. "Just before I entered, I watched you for a moment as you regarded the other ladies in the room. I noticed the very same coldness in your expression that I had seen in Ludgate Hill. I knew then of a certainty what you were about, sir."

"Did you indeed?" James finally managed to murmur.

"I am quite convinced of it," Aimee told him confidently. "You have invited us to participate in this hunt because in some way we have all taxed you beyond bearing, is that not correct?"

Rockham flushed slightly. Having his motives so baldly, and so easily, revealed by Miss Winthrop shook him. In tandem, and aggravatingly, another part of his mind could not help but appreciate her intuitiveness.

"You have no intention of marrying any of us, have you?" she continued, still regarding him with sympathy. "As a matter of fact, your grace, you have only one intention where we are concerned, do you not? You wish to make complete gulls of us."

"Miss Winthrop . . ." the duke husked.

Aimee held up a silencing hand.

"I must tell you that I doubted my own suspicions at first," she interrupted. "I could not understand why I had received one of your invitations. I had never even met you, after all. How could I have offended you to such a degree? But having spent these few days since coming to Town in Mama's company," she continued, suddenly breaking into a soft chuckle, "I believe I finally have the solution. How difficult it must have been for you, your grace! I imagine Mama has trailed after you like the brush on a fox for a good part of my childhood."

Trapped by the truth, Rockham could only shrug his broad shoulders and smile ruefully.

"I thought as much." Aimee nodded, her lovely mouth spread with a playful grin. "And I have to admit, you know, that it is a very good plan. What better set down could there be for a woman of *le haut monde* than complete and utter embarrassment before all of Society? Why, I can think of nothing more effective. But it is not at all honorable, you know," she told him, her chin lifting slightly. "Understandable . . . but not at all the thing."

Rockham drew in another deep breath. "Miss Winthrop, I must tell you . . ."

". . . I assure you, your grace, there is no need," she informed him. "I merely wished you to understand why, though Mama will not allow me to return to Town until the contest's end and chides me unmercifully for my lack of gratitude, I shall still not participate in your little scheme. I am quite capable of making a fool of myself, you see." She grinned as she turned Cloud's head. "I simply have no need of help from you. Now, if you will excuse me, I have promised Miss Fotheringale that I would help her search the nests in the dovecote. I must be away." Nodding her farewell, Miss Winthrop touched her whip to Cloud's heavy flanks and started at a trot back toward The Crags.

"Miss Winthrop . . . wait!" Rockham commanded, dragging Bachelor's head up from the water.

Aimee brought her mount to a reluctant halt. Turning, she answered, "Yes, your grace?"

"Very well, you have uncovered my purpose for the contest," he admitted, after he had cantered up beside her.

"There," he added, smiling warmly. "I have confessed. I acknowledge that I can be a bit of a scoundrel when pushed to the edge. But will you now at least call me an honest one?"

Aimee shook her head.

Again Rockham's jaw flexed. "But why?" he asked, perplexed.

"Because, knowing your sentiments toward us, your grace, I cannot see that you would risk a leg shackle, nor can I believe that you would take a chance on losing Calladorn's Fire, even though you could probably quite easily absorb the loss, as you are as rich as Golden Ball. No," she concluded, again shaking her head, "I am persuaded that it has never been your intention to risk anything at all."

Rockham remained motionless. "And how am I to have accomplished that, Miss Winthrop, considering that my house is even now being shredded by my guests?"

"Quite easily," Aimee stated with a pleasant smile. "You have not hidden the diamond, sir."

After a last lengthy look, the lady turned again and continued at a brisk trot back toward the stables.

"Well, how goes it?" Ashford asked, as Rockham stepped into the dining room for a bite to eat after changing out of his riding clothes into yellow nankeen pantaloons and a deep blue superfine cutaway.

"I believe the house speaks for itself," the duke replied dryly, gesturing toward their surroundings as he stepped over a broken chamberpot that had once been stored on the lower shelf of the massive Louis XV sideboard. Sighing lightly, he picked up a plate and began filling it with cold roast beef, ham, and pickled salmon, followed by tidbits of river trout, potatoes, poultry filets *à la maréchale,* and assorted vegetables. He topped the tower with two hardboiled eggs.

The sound of raised voices drew his and the marquess' attention toward the dining room entrance.

". . . No, I tell you, Rockham has discussed nothing with me!" they heard Stanley cry. Immediately the harassed viscount appeared in the doorway, backing into the room with Miss Cox hanging on to his lapels. "I have no idea where the diamond is hidden," Moreland vowed, tearing her hands free. "Wouldn't tell you if I did. There is such a thing as a gentleman's honor, don't you know! Now, take yourself off and do your own looking!" Spinning the lady around, he quite forcefully nudged her back out into the hall.

Ashford burst into laughter.

"Deuce take it, James!" Stanley cried, stalking toward them. "How have you borne it all these years? It is enough to make me grateful for thin calves and a prominent nose. I've a mind to leave for Town this very day."

"No, you will not," Rockham told him. "I shall need you two till the contest ends after the ball tonight."

"Oh? Why?" Ashford asked, brushing aside crumbs of plaster and a tattered sheet of wallpaper in order to seat himself at the huge, claw-footed dining room table.

"That is precisely what I would like to know," Moreland said, helping himself to the nuncheon spread. "We know why you invited the ladies, James, but why the devil are we here?"

"Because of all this," Rockham responded, again gesturing toward the destruction in the room around them.

From the hall, the sounds of the Ladies Rutherford and Cawthon heatedly squabbling over something unintelligible assaulted them. A shriek, followed by the sound of ripping cloth, caused even the thousands of butterflies clinging to the vault to tremble. To a man, the occupants of the dining room cringed.

"And because of that," the duke added dully, nodding toward the hall. "You, gentlemen, are my witnesses. It shall be your duty to testify truthfully in Town to what you have seen here today."

Ashford tucked a corner of his cravat tied in the Irish style back under the rolled collar of his buff cutaway and grinned.

"What's the point in waiting?" he asked, spearing a piece of salmon. "I, for one, have seen quite enough. If we leave for Town now, we shall be able to set the tabbies to tattling even before the rest of you return."

"No, I want you here 'til after the ball tonight," Rockham ordered. Suddenly, through the dining room window he caught sight of Aimee stepping out onto the terrace, her flounced umbrella twirling above a simple gown of peach mull. "I shall also need your brute strength to keep the ladies from drawing each others' blood. Besides," he added, eyeing his friends with amusement before setting down his plate and starting toward the door, "a ball implies dancing, does it not? Someone has to offer his toes up in sacrifice."

"Of course," Moreland moaned. "What are a man's friends for?"

Aimee had nearly strolled the length of the raised grass-covered terrace that looked out over the rear gardens by the time the duke again spotted her. He hurried to catch up with her, watching as she studied the terrace's well-trimmed plantings, occasionally stopping to lightly touch a particularly appealing blossom adorning one of the potted rose trees standing at attention at intervals along the balustrade, or bending to stroke one of The Crags' numerous lethargic sun-soaked mousers. Once, just before he drew near, she lowered her umbrella to turn her face toward the sun. James paused a moment when she did so to watch her breathe in the perfume of the country afternoon. A smile touched his lips as he again started forward, ridiculously pleased by her delight in his home.

"How very fetching you look, Miss Winthrop," he said, as he came up behind her, his gaze appreciating the matching spencer hugging her torso.

Startled, Aimee spun around to face him, her heart stuttering oddly. "Thank you," she breathed, turning quickly away to continue her walk alone.

The duke dogged her heels. "Ah, so I am still *de trop*," he sighed, woefully shaking his head.

"Nothing of the sort," Aimee asserted when he attained her side. "It is merely that I cannot imagine either of us has anything left to say to the other."

"I disagree," Rockham countered firmly, clasping his hands behind his back. "You, madam, have maligned me utterly."

A small smile escaped to flit across Aimee's mouth. "Have I?" she replied, mocking him with a coy flutter of her fan before her cheeks.

"Utterly," the duke repeated. "You have proclaimed me a dishonorable bounder and a dishonest fraud, madam."

"I have, haven't I?" Aimee agreed, nodding with vast seriousness.

"You have. But what if you are wrong?"

"Wrong?" Aimee echoed, fingering one of the frogs securing her spencer.

"Just so," James replied. "What if I am as honorable as an archbishop and you have completely misjudged me?"

"Then you will have gained yourself a bride and we can all go along our merry way," Aimee answered with a laugh.

"With no consequence to yourself for having so abused me?" he asked, taking her elbow to halt their progress.

For a moment, Aimee stared. "I don't know what you mean," she said at last.

"Simply that if you are correct about me," Rockham responded, "I should be made to pay for my dishonesty."

"On that we agree," Aimee said with another light laugh.

"However," James said softly, "if you are wrong, is it not only fair that you should be the one to pay?"

Aimee turned toward him instantly, snapping her fan shut. "What are you suggesting, your grace?" she questioned warily.

"A wager," James stated, his eyes gleaming.

"A wager!"

"Between you and me."

Aimee's eyes widened, their gold flecks dancing with possibilities. "I am not a gambler, sir," she said stiffly, although her breathing had become curiously shallow. And then she chewed her inner cheek, eyeing him thoughtfully. "Just what would this wager entail?" she asked, not masking her curiosity very well at all.

Rockham smiled slowly. He had her now, he knew. She would agree to the wager. And if fate would just cooperate, by tomorrow . . .

"It would hinge, of course, upon the discovery of Calladorn's Fire," he told her. "I propose that if you are correct about me and no diamond is found, I will proclaim myself a fraud in all the London papers and gladly suffer the consequences, both social and legal."

"And if I am not correct?" Aimee queried. "If it is found?"

"Then you will acknowledge that I behaved honorably, Miss Winthrop, and you will pay for your scurrilous accusations with your hand."

"My hand!" Aimee exclaimed. *"In marriage?"*

"Exactly."

"What nonsense!" she cried. "It was never your intention to marry any of us. We have completely cut up your peace."

"So you have," the duke calmly replied. "But I am willing to overlook it in your case. After all, it was the countess, not you, who nearly drove me daft."

It occurred to Aimee, then, why the duke was so willing to make this wager. Her eyes grew huge.

"You scoundrel!" she suddenly cried, planting her fists upon her hips. "You jackanapes!"

Rockham stiffened at the unexpected attack. "Calm yourself, Miss Winthrop," he soothed. "Whatever . . . ?"

"Do you think me so ignorant that I cannot see through your scheme?" she asked, backing him toward the terrace bal-

ustrade, scattering kittens in their wake. "You are promised
to the finder of the Fire. You can make all the wagers with me
you wish and still be safe. Have you forgotten? I am not participating! You cannot lose in a wager of marriage to me!"

"Unless you join in the search," Rockham suggested with
a gentle grin.

"I have no intention of taking part in that spurious endeavor," Aimee said cuttingly.

"That is up to you, of course," Rockham replied, his eyes
twinkling with challenge. "But the wager still stands. If I have
no honor, what does it matter *what* I promise to *whom?* I am
sure to be exposed, and you will win. You are quite certain of
what I am, are you not? Take the wager, Miss Winthrop," he
coaxed. "This is your chance. Come now, what say you? Am
I a man of honor? Have I indeed hidden the stone?"

"You are not," Aimee stated with a tiny frown, "and have
not, sir."

"Then take the wager, Miss Winthrop," Rockham urged.
"Make me pay."

"You have so little honor you will not even notify the papers
when you lose," Aimee softly declared.

"On the contrary," the duke replied, grinning. "I have never
welshed on a gaming debt. Ask any of my friends. Take the
wager, Miss Winthrop. Deal me what I so richly deserve."

"But how can you even make the wager?" she protested
softly. "You have not hidden the stone!"

"I say that I have," the duke countered, his eyes glittering
as he stepped close enough for Aimee to feel his body's heat,
"that my honor, if not my comportment, is intact, and that I
will fulfill all my obligations to my guests. Miss Winthrop,
will you gamble that what I have said is false?"

Aimee's heart began to beat quite wildly.

"I do not gamble . . ." she protested, fluttering her ivory
fan.

". . . Of course, you do," Rockham gently interrupted, stepping even closer. "You live. And all life is a gamble, Miss

Winthrop. Chances must sometimes be taken. Opportunities must be seized."

"But you have not even hidden the stone," Aimee objected once more in a faint whisper. "Your words mean nothing."

"There is a simple enough way to find out," Rockham murmured, his voice resonant against Aimee's taut nerves. "Take the wager, Miss Winthrop."

For long moments Aimee hesitated, standing quietly, searching the duke's open gaze. At last she straightened and again backed away from him, once more restoring a proper distance between them.

Slowly, her chin elevated. "Very well," she told him, amazed by what she was saying and very much aware that she could not possibly be in her right mind at all. "I shall accept your wager. But I warn you, sir. I shall not give you the opportunity to secrete the stone now that I have agreed. From this moment on I shall not leave your side."

"A condition I accept with pleasure, Miss Winthrop," Rockham responded with gleaming eyes and a courtly nod.

Aimee pursed her lips. "I must tell you, though, I cannot conceive of how you shall prove your innocence," she told him tartly.

"Ah, well, as to that," the duke told her, his gaze never leaving her face as he dropped a kiss upon the backs of her fingers, "like everything else in life, it lies in the hands of the Fates."

Aimee was as good as her word. For the remainder of the afternoon, she tenaciously inserted herself into Rockham's round of activities, following him to his meeting with the house steward in his medallioned, barrel-vaulted study, to a game of billiards with Lords Ashford and Moreland, and for a bit of pheasant shooting in the southeast park. By the time she found herself being readied by her maid to accompany the duke on a visit to one of his tenants, she could say with all honesty that her host had made no attempt to escape her company, nor had he, by some sleight of hand, managed to hide the diamond. She could also say with all honesty that she had never had such an enjoyable time.

"Your shako, milady," her maid, Mary, said, coming up behind her just as she finished binding up a reluctant curl. "Hurry now. It won't do to leave his lordship alone too long."

"He isn't alone," Aimee said with a soft laugh, accepting the aquamarine, military-style hat. "His friends Moreland and Ashford are with him. I have set them to guarding the duke for me while I change. *Their* honor, at least, I can trust."

"Well, just the same, a great deal is at stake, milady," Mary replied, scooping up another curl just before Aimee set the hat rakishly upon her head.

"You have the right of that," Aimee agreed, setting pins to her hat and hair. "You haven't told my mother of the wager, Mary, have you?"

"Goodness, no! Haven't had the chance to, anyway, milady. Her ladyship's been picking the hems out of the household bedding for the better part of the day. I've barely seen her."

"Oh, dear!" Aimee breathed, her gaze growing horrified. And then she shook her head. "Well, it is his lordship's own fault, after all."

"Oh, he don't mind," Mary commented.

"No?"

"Oh, no. Why, Fenn, the duke's man, told me not an hour ago that after today his lordship figured he'd have to completely redecorate anyway," Mary informed her, "what with him getting a wife and all."

"What a bouncer!" Aimee responded with a merry laugh. "This Fenn is obviously the duke's accomplice. His grace cannot be getting a wife, Mary. I tell you, he has not hidden the diamond. Well, I must be off," she finished, tugging on her riding gloves before rising and walking briskly toward the door. "Lay out my yellow gauze for the ball, Mary, will you?

Oh, and while you are about it you might try to steal her ladyship's scissors."

Even before Mary's hearty laughter could reverberate throughout the room, Miss Winthrop had dashed like a country hoyden more than halfway down the stairs.

To her chagrin, the gentlemen were awaiting her in the large vestibule leading toward the stables. Aimee arrested her headlong flight at the first sight of them, but she knew that it was too late. She had been well and truly caught. Color blossomed across her cheeks. Deciding that she had no choice but to beard the lions, she squared her shoulders into a semblance of decorum, righted her shako, and then bit at her lower lip. As she completed her descent, she hadn't the least idea of how lovely she had become.

"A vision," uttered Moreland, as she gained the floor and joined them.

"The fairest of roses," murmured Ashford, seizing her hand and raising it to his lips.

Rockham laughed heartily. "A hoydenish spinster who just ran down the stairs," he corrected as he proprietarily retrieved Aimee's hand from Ashford's tight grasp and tapped her upon her nose. Drawing the captive hand through his arm, he then turned her and started toward the door.

Aimee blushed scarlet. "Really, your grace, you could have left me with at least a shred of my imagined dignity," she scolded. "Are you gentlemen not coming with us?"

"Alas, no," Moreland answered with a bow. "We have been charged to stay in the house. We are to be . . ."

Lady Cawthon suddenly burst wild-eyed into the room, her hair unsure of its confinement, her gown covered with dark streaks of filth. Aimee quickly conquered a gasp. The lady was one of Society's highest sticklers, yet it seemed that the contest for duke and diamond had made her forget every propriety. The same woman who had once snubbed Queen

Caroline at one of her drawing rooms now looked for all the world like a chimney boy with a flame to his feet.

"Ashes," Lady Cawthon explained distractedly, coming to a halt before them. "It is in the ashes, of course. It is all that is logical. From coal comes diamonds, you see. But I could not find it in the coal bin . . . therefore it is, of course, in the ashes," she concluded with a nod, turning back the way she had come. "I suppose it is just as well the others do not credit my opinion," she added, as she reached the frame of the door. "After all, diamonds and husbands are not items one can readily share, are they?" Giving them another nod, she then disappeared back into the corridor.

" . . To be witnesses?" Aimee offered when she was gone, ruefully completing Moreland's interrupted explanation.

Ashford sighed. "Just so."

Rockham squeezed Aimee's arm against his side, looked at the expression on her face, and began to laugh uproariously. Following him from the house into the brilliant afternoon sunshine, she jabbed him with her elbow.

The air along the garden path leading toward the stables was warm and somnolent, filled with the resonance of insects and the sweetness of peach blossoms and pine. For a time, Aimee walked silently beside the duke, conscious only of the crunch of their footsteps and his presence. Her conscience chided her simple enjoyment of his company.

It was the height of foolishness, she knew, for her to allow any feelings whatsoever, even friendship, for a man who could plan what he had for the ladies. However, she realized with more than a little discomfiture, feelings did exist.

Yet there was no doubt about it. The man was a scoundrel. Definitely.

A slight frown marred her brow. He was, wasn't he?

"Will you really go through with your plan?" she finally, and rather hopefully, asked as they rounded a small planting of cherry trees and started down the path bordering a huge vegetable garden.

"My plan to marry the finder of the Fire?" Rockham asked, tucking her hand more firmly into the crook of his elbow.

"No, of course not," Aimee replied, noticing a stooped, ancient man crouched several yards beyond the garden fence painstakingly weeding between the rows of cabbages. "You and I both know that is merely a sham. No, I meant your plan to vilify your guests."

"Vilify? What a monster you must think me, Miss Winthrop," the duke chuckled. "I merely intend to teach them, and others, a much needed lesson."

"But you cannot mean to destroy their reputations," Aimee exclaimed.

The man in the garden caught sight of them and slowly, achingly, unfolded his length. As they approached he stood watching, stabbing the duke with a hard gaze of pure challenge under thick white brows, his jaw firmly obstinate.

"Far from it," Rockham agreed, turning from her to acknowledge the gardener. "I only mean to tarnish them a bit. Have they not done the same to me?"

And then his countenance grew unaccountably stony; all his attention was given over to the wizened man.

Aimee peeked up from beneath her umbrella, watching the duke in curiosity. As he scanned the garden, the same coldness crept into his gaze that she had seen after the accident in Ludgate Hill. Curiosity veered toward alarm.

"Jocko," Rockham pronounced, after a long moment in which the two glared at each other.

"Yer grace," the gardener replied with equal gruffness, though with a proper doffing of his wide-brimmed hat.

"Those cabbages are half the size they should be for this time of year. What is your excuse this time?"

Beside him, Aimee gasped, bristling at the duke's caustic attack upon his retainer. She stared at Rockham, her eyes wide with appalled indignation.

"Don't need one," the gardener replied, his chin lifting arrogantly. "They be the same size as Squire Peckman's and twice't as big as Lord Campbell's."

"They are full of worm holes," the duke countered. "I can see them clearly from here."

"Ain't a one!" the gardener vowed, pulling himself up even straighter along the length of his hoe. "Come on over that fence, you young scamp! I'll show you holes . . . !"

". . . Unfortunately," the duke interrupted in bored tones, "the lady and I are expected elsewhere. Besides, my valet has just polished my boots."

"Ain't no worm holes," the gardener again declared. "Not in Jocko's garden."

"There had better not be," Rockham threatened mildly. "You know how I detest having my palate dismayed." Having said that, the duke again appropriated Aimee's arm and turned her once again toward the stables.

She followed, completely ignorant of the crinkles that suddenly formed at the corners of Jocko's eyes.

"Having his palate dismayed?" the old man repeated, shaking his head. Again he bent to his work, but only after several minutes of laughing wheezily.

Aimee, however, was not amused. "How utterly contemptible!" she exclaimed when they had gone beyond the gardener's hearing, jerking her arm away.

"I beg your pardon?" the duke responded, his brows lifting into a question.

"Your treatment of that man!" she cried. "It was beyond anything. Why, anyone could see there was nothing wrong with those cabbages!"

"I am aware of that," James replied with a grin.

"You are incorrigible!" Aimee uttered in soft astonishment. ". . . But . . ."

"But, what, Miss Winthrop?" the duke questioned softly. "Egad, madam, never say that you have jumped to a conclusion! You, who is always so temperate in her judgments?

Madam, I am quite stunned. Could it be that there are more to my actions than it might seem?"

"You are mocking me, sir," Aimee stated rather stiffly.

James squeezed her hand and grinned. "A bit," he confessed. "But as it happens, you deserve it."

"Do I?" she asked, looking him in the eye. "Then perhaps you would be so good as to explain why."

"If you wish it, of course," the duke responded with a warm smile. "Ten years ago Jocko was my head groom, until a riding accident left him more dead than alive and too crippled to work the bloods again. Ah, you should have seen him in his prime, Aimee," James breathed, forgetting propriety as his gaze grew distant and he spoke her given name. "I have never seen a man who could handle a horse as he could. Understandably, the accident was quite devastating to him. It was a long time before I hit upon something that he could not only do, but do well enough to again take pride in."

"Gardening," Aimee concluded softly.

"Yes. The old hedgehog really loves it."

"Most in the peerage would have cut him off when he could no longer do his work," Aimee said thoughtfully.

"Some, perhaps. But I could never have done that," James replied as the stable came into sight. "Jocko has been with my family since before I was born. He was more of a father to me than my own."

"But . . . the way you spoke to him . . ." Aimee began as they reached the stableyard and their mounts were brought forward.

We always speak that way to one another," James revealed with a laugh. "It is a game we play. I ruffle Jocko's fur so that he will be forced to defend his new and rather more demeaning occupation, and he, of course, knows exactly what I am doing. Once in a while we get together for a bumper of small beer at the Blue Badger in the village and ride each other unmercifully about it."

"I see . . ." Aimee said, much more subdued. Taking the

duke's hand to stand upon the block, she then mounted Cloud. "There can be no question, then. I have done you a disservice, your grace. I owe you an apology . . ."

"Not at all," James responded with a ready grin, lithely mounting Bachelor beside her and leading the way at a gentle canter toward a wide expanse of lush, grassy park land. "Whether it is to my peers who think that I should have turned him off years ago, or to ladies such as yourself who have not yet quite figured out the strange morass of the male mind, I seem to be always having to explain Jocko's presence at The Crags to someone."

"Still, I made an incorrect assumption," Aimee stated.

"More than one," the duke commented, his eyes teasing.

"Only one," Aimee vowed with a laugh. "You forget. I have it from your own lips that you are a scoundrel of the worst kind."

"Because I take my revenge upon helpless ladies?" James offered helpfully. In the distance, nestled near an outcropping of rocks in a small, verdant valley, the first of the tenant's cottages came into sight.

"Precisely," Aimee grinned.

"And because I am a prodigious prevaricator of plumpers?" Rockham ventured, waggling his brows at her.

Aimee giggled happily. "Exactly so," she chortled in reply.

"And possibly because, solely in your view, of course, I possess neither honor nor honesty?" the duke suggested finally.

"Absolutely," the lady told him, her eyes still holding a smile. "But none of that signifies."

"Egad, Miss Winthrop, what else is there?" James asked, feigning exasperation.

"Only a true blackguard, sir, would hold a contest and then set about eliminating all the contestants."

"I have done that?" the duke laughed as they drew near the cottage.

"You have," Aimee stated. "Had you even once entered

your residence today instead of hiding yourself away and leaving the running of the competition to your friends, you would have seen the results of your negligence."

"What results?" James asked, his smile waning.

"Lady Cawthon has taken to her bed to nurse the numerous bruises she obtained when a shelf of simples in the still room collapsed upon her," Aimee informed him tartly.

"The deuce!" James murmured, sobering with concern.

"Oh, yes. And not only that, but the poor dear can hardly find a soul to serve her. Of course, she does have quite the most remarkable odor . . ." Aimee bit the inside of her cheek to control her laughter. Finally gaining control, she added, "Lady Rutherford and Miss Fotheringale, however, fared even worse."

"Indeed?" James commented, his eyes now sparkling as he caught on to her game.

"Oh, yes," she exclaimed. "Why, they could not even get to their beds! Several of your footmen had to be called away from clearing the attics to carry them there."

All mirth fled from the duke's countenance. "Clearing the attics!" he bellowed.

Aimee had to turn away. "For shame, your grace," she said in as chiding a tone as she could muster. "Are you more concerned for your priceless family antiques than the welfare of your guests?"

"Of course not!" James vowed warmly, and then he caught sight of Aimee's smile and relaxed. Laughter again welled within him. "Very well, then, Miss Winthrop, why could the ladies not get themselves to their beds?"

"Because they were completely boskey!" Aimee burbled. "And it is your fault, of course. Did you think they would be able to see whether or not the diamond lay at the bottom of the Armagnac without emptying the bottles?"

"Bottles! Good Lord!" the duke barked, quickly calculating the cost of his hoard of the precious, smuggled brew. "I thought they meant to search only the open one. How many did they broach?"

"Only three before they began a rather good duet of 'Slow Gently, Fweet Afton,' I believe," Aimee replied, now pressing her lower lip between her teeth. "One more had them attempting to tickle Blair. I believe that is when the footmen were called in."

"And to think," James stated, struggling against a threatening outburst of laughter, "I missed it all."

"You are a scoundrel of the worst kind," Aimee restated, a new bubble of laughter now riding the back of her throat.

"Given the evidence, what can I do but agree?" James shrugged, his inner cheeks bitten, his head, too, turned away.

At last he ventured to meet her gaze. Even as he did it, he knew it was a mistake. The two rode into the cottage clearing chortling quite uncontrollably.

"Afternoon, yer grace," called a solidly muscular man, dressed in a farmer's smock, breeches, black stockings, and boots, from the cottage doorway as they came to a rather ungainly halt in front of his house. Smiling broadly, the man stepped from the low frame into the bright sunshine and began to walk toward them. Like a cork wiggled out of a port bottle, as soon as he had stepped aside, several children were released to spill out after him. They soon raced ahead to cluster around Cloud and Bachelor.

"How goes it, Tom?" James asked, his smile warm and wide.

"Well enough," the farmer answered as he reached them. "Most of the ewes have lambed now," he continued, bowing politely. "Only lost three of 'em, praise God. Here now, Henry," he scolded, as he again straightened. "Let go of that stallion's tail! Ye'll get what sense ye got kicked out of ye." Stretching out a ham-sized hand, he seized one of his boys by the collar and tucked him against his side. "How do, milady," he finally added, bowing again.

Aimee knew that the man was making his obeisance to her and must be politely acknowledged, but she could not take her horrified eyes from the cottage long enough to do so. The house lay in ruins, its roof completely gone, its plaster buckled and scorched. Stretching beyond the dwelling, the remains of a forest rode the valley for several miles until the river of black char rounded a hill and disappeared from sight. Yet behind the house, several acres of crops, miraculously spared by the fire, thrived; where the meadows climbed the rugged mountains all the way to the top, sheep dotted the slopes like an outbreak of the pox, grazing contentedly.

"Sir, what has happened here?" she asked, her earlier merriment a mere memory.

"Oh that, milady," Tom replied dismissively. "Fire come down the valley there during the drought last autumn. Took out most all the tenants' homes."

"Last autumn! But that was months ago!" Aimee stated indignantly, suddenly turning toward James. "You, sir," she continued warmly. "How is it that this man still has no roof? Do you mean to tell me that he and his children spent the winter here without protection from the cold?"

"Miss Winthrop . . ." James began in objection.

"It is the outside of enough!" she continued to scold.

"Miss Winthrop . . ." the duke tried again with a sigh.

"Sir, where is the children's mother?" Aimee demanded to know.

"She's took sick, milady," Tom responded quickly, glancing worriedly toward the duke. "She's abed inside."

"Abed! You see?" she cried, again rounding on Rockham. "How could you allow such conditions to exist for such a long time? Sir, you *are* a scoundrel of the worst kind!"

"I have not allowed it, Miss Winthrop," James said patiently, shaking his head over a smile, "and you are jumping to yet another conclusion."

"Beggin' yer pardon, milady, but his lordship's right. It ain't the way you think at all," Tom asserted.

Aimee hesitated, a bit startled by the man's ready defense of the duke when this was obviously his chance to force Rockham into setting things right.

"It's not?" she asked. Suddenly she was quite unsure of herself. The indignation flowed out of her.

"No, milady. His grace had all of us up to The Crags to spend the winter," Tom told her. "We just come down here a sennight past to get started on the repairs. Couldn't do 'em during the winter, y'know. It were too cold. And besides, the ground freezes in the winter this far north."

"Oh," Aimee said softly. "I had thought perhaps you might be displaced . . ."

"Like the Scots? Why, bless you, no, milady. His lordship wouldn't do that."

"But your wife . . ."

"Come down with the quinsy two days ago, milady," he said with a smile. "Her throat's swelled up some and she's got the fever, but that's all."

Aimee slowly straightened in her saddle. "Oh, dear," she said, finally realizing how deeply she had again erred. She drew in a steadying breath instead of daring to look at the duke.

"Had school for my brood, too," Tom offered, trying to ease the awkwardness, yet succeeding only in making it worse.

"Oh, dear . . ."

"Come now, Miss Winthrop," teased Rockham as he grinned at her discomfiture. "Hang on to those convictions. Don't give up, now. I am a proven scoundrel, remember . . . a vengeful desecrator of helpless female reputations. Pray, don't start actually finding something to admire in me! I might fly over the boughs."

A smile fluttered at the corners of Aimee's mouth. "I apologize," she murmured, finally looking at him.

"Accepted," he replied, just as softly.

His hand rose then, slowly. Aimee watched as his warm fingers neared, then lightly touched her cheek. She blinked twice in amazement. For some inexplicable reason, her whole body came suddenly, tinglingly alive.

"But still, you have not hidden the stone," she whispered through a tremble.

"That's it, Miss Winthrop," James whispered, his fingers stroking the curve beneath her soft chin. "By all means, keep that unimpeachable fact at the forefront of your most appealing mind." Trailing his fingers up to run across the seam of her lips, he then slowly, reluctantly, released her to straighten in his saddle, gently breaking her thrall.

Tom," he continued, again smiling toward his tenant, "my purpose in coming today is to tell you that the building materials should arrive in three or four days. I shall have them brought to the valley by wagon. But for now, I am rather anxious to return to The Crags to see what has become of my other guests. If I might ask you to pass the word on to the others, Miss Winthrop and I shall be on our way."

"I'll do it, sir," Tom replied.

"Very well, then," Rockham responded, wheeling Bachelor about. "I shall see you on the day. Come along, Miss Winthrop," he called, spurring his mount into a ground-eating pace. "We've a ball to dress for, and, I think, a great deal of coffee to pour into Lady Rutherford and Miss Fotheringale."

Still pulsating with lingering tingles, Aimee shakily followed.

With the onset of night, and the rising of a bright, full moon, the promised ball began. Aimee accepted the invitation of Viscount Moreland to dance the first set, but performed the steps distractedly. Her thoughts tossed like an unsettled sea. It was almost over. It would not be long before all London would know what the duke had schemed. Why was she so troubled? She should be glad, shouldn't she?

"Which is it that is not to your liking, Miss Winthrop," asked Moreland, interrupting her thoughts as the precisely patterned dance again brought them side-by-side, "the minuet, or the man?"

Startled back from her inattention, Aimee smiled and flushed prettily, self-consciously fluttering her yellow silk fan. "Do forgive me, sir," she pleaded softly. "It is neither. I fear my mind is on other things."

As if to emphasize her point, her gaze again wandered over the expanse of the great hall, now filled with the duke's houseguests and a selection of local society, each dressed in the ultimate of their finery. She easily located the others of her party. Miss Cox and Lady Foxborough were slowly moving about the perimeter of the room, pausing to speak to several of the others as they came within their sphere, but, oddly, refusing all offers to dance. Lady Cawthon and Miss Stanhope were huddled in conversation as she drew near.

"Mama, it simply did not occur to me to search the instruments!" she heard Miss Stanhope hiss as she swept by.

The instruments? Aimee felt her gaze rise. She smiled and shook her head slightly. From the minstrel balcony high along the wall opposite the now tattered hall's spectacular fireplace, a small orchestra swathed the huge room in Mozart, in its own way as pleasing and sensuous a canopy as the star-specked sky gracing the ceiling vaults. Hundreds of candles bloomed just below the balcony and around the room in the dozens of polished sconces hanging from the walls, looking like the playful newborn of the huge, sinuous mother fire writhing nearby in the ancient hearth.

Well, do so at once!" Lady Cawthon commanded. "Can you imagine that Estelle Cox will not perceive the same thing momentarily? Just look at them," she sneered, "sidling about the room like the veriest cut-purses! I tell you, Trixie, Estelle has not yet given up the search. Look there! Did you see dearest Adelaide run her finger around in that sconce's wax guard just then?"

Aimee looked, too . . . just in time to see Miss Cox stare hard at her finger and then wipe the offending wax off into her wadded handkerchief.

"I am more concerned about dearest Effie," Miss Stanhope uttered snidely, as Aimee dipped and twirled nearby. "She likes for everyone to think her sweet and biddable," she continued, her eyes narrowing with malice, "but she schemes just as much as the rest of us. Her plots, though, are more insidious."

"There is no question about it, dearest!" the countess agreed warmly. "Putting announcements of engagement to the duke in the paper . . . wretched child!"

Aimee's gaze flickered toward the entrance where she knew she would find the countess of Rutherford and Miss Fotheringale. As she watched, the countess was approached by a green silk-clad squire who bobbed down before her, scrubbing at the perspiration on his forehead with his handkerchief before rising to ask for a dance. As an answer, the countess wafted a fan of denial in the poor man's face, an attempt to disperse both him and his cloying fragrance before she clutched at her stomach and sagged against her equally pale, flaccid daughter. Reluctantly, the squire bowed himself away.

Aimee smothered a grin. Aided by Armagnac, Miss Stanhope obviously had no need for concern in that quarter. The musicians, however, were a different matter. She wondered if she should send a message of warning to them. It seemed only fair. The duke would likely be just the tiniest bit displeased if the instruments proved unusable after only the first of the orchestra's periods of rest.

It was not her intention to do so, but at the thought of the duke, without volition her gaze searched out and came to rest upon him as he stood just outside the entrance to the great hall, still engaged in his duty as host to receive his guests. She had passed through that same reception line earlier herself, of course, and had again been reduced to those most annoying tingles merely by the dratted man's proximity. Even now, as she watched him shake hands with another of the local landowners and the movement drew his black evening coat even more snugly across his shoulders, she felt her body's reaction to the sight sweep through her again. White muslin frothed at his throat. He was exquisitely handsome. Aimee's flesh tightened, and then pebbled. Irritatingly, her heart accelerated.

"His mind is on you as well," Moreland said quietly, escorting her into another dainty turn.

Again caught in inattention, Aimee started and then laughed with the viscount. "Surely not," she replied *sotto voce.* "He is toying with us all."

"Is he?" the viscount asked.

"You are his friend," she stated with a smile. And then she bit her lip, her eyes again darting toward the duke. "You know that he is. I admit that he does have his good points, of course, but still, he is quite the consummate scoundrel."

"Because he is intent upon exacting his revenge?" Moreland questioned, raising their arms as the steps brought them together.

Aimee smiled at the suggestion. "In truth, after what I have witnessed today, sir, I can hardly fault him for that any longer. No, my objection is to the ruse of the contest. He made a promise to these ladies which he made certain he would not have to keep."

"By not hiding Calladorn's Fire," the viscount finished.

"Exactly so," Aimee agreed.

"Can you guarantee that Rockham has not?" Moreland asked gently.

Aimee's eyes widened. "You know very well, sir, that I have been with him every moment since he made that wager with me. I will swear that at no time did he hide anything even remotely like it. No, I am quite sure of my conclusion. The diamond has never been available for the ladies to find."

"Unless, of course, the stone was hidden before you made

your bargain with him," Moreland offered with a subdued smile.

Aimee was forced to pause. "Oh, no, he couldn't . . ." she finally began. And then she tipped her head to one side. "But he couldn't have . . . But, of course, he did not! He would open himself up to losing the contest. Besides, sir, the diamond has not been found!"

"Which might only mean, my dear, that no one has found it yet," Moreland suggested, his smile widening as the music drew to a close. He made her a pretty leg, then, stretching out a black dancing slipper toward her as he kissed her gloved hand.

"He has not hidden it," Aimee repeated, her voice unnecessarily firm.

"Perhaps. In any event, we shall soon see, shall we not? Come," he gently commanded, taking her elbow. "I am persuaded that you have a few things yet to consider. Let me get you a glass of negus and then I shall leave you to your thoughts," he continued, leading her from the floor. "Assuming, of course, that somewhere among this debris I can ferret out an unbroken glass."

Aimee soon had her refreshment and her solitude, the viscount having taken his leave to seek another partner for the country dance that was forming in the center of the vast hall, and her mother having decided with last minute inspiration to take a knife to the stucco frieze in the library.

She had done so quite dramatically, much to Aimee's chagrin. The notion had suddenly come to her as she bit into a bit of apple-shaped marzipan that Rockham must of course have imbedded the diamond within one of the apples or pomegranates figuratively dangling within the room's panoramic scene of a Babylonian garden. With a great flurry of excitement, Lady Braxton had seized the first sharp instrument she could lay her hands on and fled the hall. Miss Fotheringale and Lady Rutherford had tried to struggle after, but unfortunately had made it, so word later reached her, only as far as the nearest chamberpot.

For her part, Aimee merely drew in a deep breath. It was much better to take the viscount's advice, she thought, and she did so, slowly wandering the room's perimeter, occasionally sipping negus, for the most part worrying . . . wondering.

Was it possible that she had completely misread the duke? Had he hidden the stone? Aimee allowed that perhaps she had. She did have a penchant for jumping to conclusions, after all. She acknowledged, too, that she had often been wrong. But was she this time? It would appear so, at least as far as the old gardener and the tenant, Tom, were concerned. In those instances his actions had exhibited nothing but the proper care of a lord for his people . . . not only that, but a great deal of unexpected kindness as well. Still, he had put into play an unconscionable scheme, though Aimee had come to understand the why of it. He had been pushed beyond his endurance to a point that had overwhelmed his inbred manners and good sense, and he had acted rashly. On the other hand, there was no indication that he regretted it. So which was the real Rockham? Was he a saint? Hardly, Aimee thought as she chuckled softly. But was he, as it certainly seemed likely, a scoundrel? Aimee did not know.

And what of the diamond? she thought, as she found herself standing before the great, magnificently carved marble fireplace, her free hand extended toward its warmth. Why would he risk losing it? It made no sense to her. Risking it was not the act of a sane man, and the duke was no candidate for Bedlam. It was only logical, therefore, that he could not have hidden it. It was the only solution that added up. Aimee straightened then, letting her gaze rest upon Lachesis at the center of the mantel, her conclusion drawn. Yes, she was certain of it. She no longer had any doubts. He had forsaken his honor both in the pledge he had made to the other ladies and in the wager he had made with her. He was indeed a scoundrel.

She sighed softly, then, hating her conclusion, yet knowing

it to be correct. She turned toward the room again, willing herself to keep her eyes averted. It did not work. Her gaze found him as easily as a heart finds home.

He was free of his duties as host now and stood within a cluster of people. Aimee watched as Miss Cox slapped her fan flirtatiously against his chest, her arm linked solidly through his. She heard the green silk squire drown out the delicate strains of Schubert with loud guffaws at something the duke must have said; saw Countess Cawthon pressing her torso against his other arm in an attempt to draw his attention away from any notice of Miss Stanhope's presence in the minstrel balcony; counted several others . . . yet he was staring across the wide expanse at her.

Aimee's lips separated. Her eyes touched his. His look grew wistful, tender, full of promise. He raised his flute of champagne to her and smiled. Aimee responded against her will. Fighting her impulse to go to him, she turned back toward the fire.

His face was there in the flames, the way she had seen it at different times during the hours they had spent in each other's company. She saw his laughter, remembered the teasing that had brought it about. Yet he had sobered instantly when he thought that some of his guests had come to harm.

She recalled his arrogance as he deftly maneuvered her into accepting his wager, blushed all over again at the thought that, even in jest, he had spoken to her of marriage. He had had quite the oddest look in his eyes, she remembered, recalling their conversation on the terrace earlier that afternoon. He had looked at her so piercingly before he had kissed her hand and left all in the hands of the Fates.

She would not be honest, she thought with a rueful nod, if she did not admit that she had enjoyed his company. She had relished this one day more than any of the days she had spent since she had convinced her father to allow her to spend some time with the countess in London so that she might have the chance to know her mother. Too, she allowed, though she knew it was quite out of character, Rockham had spoken to her the entire day in quite the most forthright manner. Why, if it were not for what she knew of his character, she might have ended their acquaintance thinking him the most candid of men.

It was all very confusing. She concluded that she was quite glad there was no way for her to lose the wager, though her heart reacted quite oddly . . . wrenchingly, in fact . . . when the thought came to her. It would take a woman of strong character to live as wife to the Duke of Rockham. Of a certainty, he was a very complex man.

It lies in the hands of the Fates . . .

He had said so. Was it true? Logically, it could not be. Human beings were creatures with a free will, were they not? Yet, if that were true, why did she feel that strange, compelling pull . . .

It lies in the hands of the Fates . . .

No, that must be wrong. It could not be.

. . . In the hands of the Fates . . .

Suddenly Aimee paused, slowing the maelstrom within her mind.

In the hands of the Fates? she repeated to herself. Why had Rockham said it in precisely that way? It was not the usual phrasing. One normally said that one would leave things in the hands of fate, yet he had specifically said *the Fates*. Why?

And then she knew. Her eyes rounded. Slowly she lifted her gaze from the slumbering fire to the carved mantelpiece before her, its marble relief thrown into demoniacal half-shadow by the licking flames. She straightened into rigidity as her eyes began to trail along the mantel's length, along the figures of the Fates and the carved rope which joined them . . . from Atropos . . . to Lachesis . . . to Clotho, still eternally spinning the thread of life.

She looked closer. As she watched, a slight draft caused the flames in the great fireplace to stutter. Something flickered within the delicate marble fingers of Clotho's hand. Aimee started, then leaned closer still. A smile touched her lips. It was the diamond, there for anyone at all to see. Again the firelight touched, then snagged upon a facet of Calladorn's Fire. Unconcerned, Clotho continued to spin. Was the Fate spinning her life, Aimee wondered, feeling unaccountably happy? Her life . . . and, perhaps, his?

She did not need to look up to know that he was beside her. She felt his presence as surely as she stood staring at the Fate's hand, her daft grin still quite firmly in place, as if he were a part of her and had always belonged there. She shifted slightly toward him, marveling. How odd that it felt quite the most natural of things to move closer to his side.

"The Fire," she stated softly, her gaze still mesmerized by the play of the firelight within what she could see of the huge diamond.

"Yes," Rockham replied, so softly and so close to her ear that his simple response rumbled against each nerve ending.

"It has been here all the time, has it not?" she questioned, absorbed by the pink brilliance radiating from the diamond's depths.

"Yes."

"For anyone to find," she continued.

"Yes."

"At any time."

"Yes, Aimee," Rockham said.

She looked at him then, turning her body to face him squarely. His eyes were deep and dark in the firelight, their silver flecks glittering like sparks from a Roman candle against a midnight sky.

"And I have lost our wager," she concluded, her gaze locked with his, trying very hard to force the broad grin that refused to desert her lips to override the beginning bite of tears.

"Yes, you have," James responded with a teasing smile.

"Why did you make it?" she dared to breathe.

The duke laughed softly, the sound so appealing that Aimee had to catch herself before she leaned into him. "I saw your

'Venus Arising from the Sea.' " He chuckled. "From that moment I wanted you."

Aimee's face grew radiant. "You saw?"

"In a mirror whose reflection encompassed the hall," the duke told her.

Aimee thought for a moment, her tongue riding the length of her full upper lip as she looked at him. At last she nodded slowly. "I owe you yet another an apology, it seems. You devised a scurrilous scheme to discredit the highest sticklers of the female *ton,* yet you did so honorably."

"I did but try," the duke murmured, placing a hand to his chest and bowing his head in humility.

Aimee's smile widened. "What would you have done if one of the others had found this diamond?" she said through a laugh.

"I would have wed her, of course," James responded.

"But you despise us!"

"Not you, Aimee," James told her softly. "In you I delight."

"I . . ." Aimee began, thoroughly flustered. "But . . . but still you might have been made to marry one of the others if they had found the Fire, and yet you made the wager with me!"

"Yes."

"*That* makes you a scoundrel, sir," Aimee concluded warmly, "of the very worst kind."

"Not at all," James countered, setting his glass upon the mantel so that he might fold his arms across his chest and lean against Clotho.

"No? Why not?" Aimee asked with equal heat.

"Because there was scant chance that the others would find this hiding place, and every chance that you would."

"Why?" Aimee asked again.

"Because this fireplace is a treasure known even on the Continent, my dear," James stated. "Everyone in the *ton* recognizes that fact. I knew this was the one place on the entire estate I could be sure would not be molested by those female termites."

"And you knew that I would find it . . ." Aimee began.

". . . Because I watched your reflection last night when you discovered it," James concluded. "I knew that you would be drawn to study it again and again. I did take the chance, of course, that you still might not notice where the Fire had been hidden."

"What a bouncer!" Aimee pronounced warmly, her hands rising to rest upon her hips. "You had every reason to believe that I would find it, your grace. You gave me a clue!"

"Yes," the duke responded as his eyes glowed mischievously. "I did."

"You are still a scoundrel, sir," Aimee groused.

"Sometimes," Rockham allowed.

"I could inform the others," she told him softly. "I could leave the Fire right where it is and go this very moment to tell them of how you tried to influence the contest by giving me a clue."

"You could," the duke conceded with a smile.

"I could bring them back to this very spot and show them where it is hidden, without even touching the diamond myself."

"You could do that, too," James agreed. "Or you could understand that love comes to a man unexpectedly, Aimee. He is never ready for it, and sometimes, as now, it comes under the most daft of circumstances, but when it happens, he knows to do only one thing: to reach, and with what power is at his disposal, to take what his very soul needs. That is why I made the wager with you, my dear," he stated, his gaze amused but tender, "the wager you lost, if you recall."

The duke pushed away from the mantel, then, straightening to his full height. The Fire again became visible in Clotho's frozen hand. "So tell me," he said, almost coldly, one eyebrow elevating in question, "are you, too, a scoundrel, Miss Winthrop? Do you intend to honor your vowels? Will you marry me?"

For long moments Aimee held her silence, tearing her gaze away from the duke's to move over the room slowly as she considered her choice. And she did have a choice, she realized. In the midst of this room full of schemes upon plots upon maneuverings, she alone had a choice. And Rockham, of all people, had given it to her.

Suddenly the orchestra began one of the new Strauss waltzes, sounding a great deal like the school-aged daughters of Mrs. Hannah Helmsley at their last musicale. Aimee winced but still let her gaze rove.

A bit farther on, near the negus bowl, Lady Cawthon began pulling Lady Foxborough's hair. As Aimee watched, Lord Ashford rushed over to officiate, but was quickly, and in quite the most unsportsmanlike fashion, clipped in the jaw. For her part, Lady Foxborough, unused to having to fend off such aggression, began to rival the cello with her unearthly howls.

Across the room, Lady Rutherford and Miss Fotheringale lay stretched out and moaning along several of the chairs while the green silk squire scurried between them, helpfully wafting his handkerchief over one pasty-faced lady for a time, and then rushing to do the same for the other.

And standing close beside her, the Duke of Diamonds, that scoundrel, was asking her to marry him.

And, heaven help her, she was top over tails in love.

"When we go up to Town again after the ceremony," she informed him, as she finally turned toward him again, "neither you nor either of your friends will say a word."

"Agreed," Rockham said.

Aimee's fingers rose, then, to close around the diamond. Carefully she took it from Clotho's hand and settled it upon her own, watching, together with the duke, as the firelight fractured into pink dancers upon the planes of her palm.

"And my mother shall be allowed to visit us as often as she

wishes," Aimee stated, her face alive with challenge as her fingers closed around the Fire.

Rockham rolled his eyes. "Agreed," he finally responded on a rather pitiful sigh.

Aimee gave him a gentle smile. "And you, James, shall never stop being just a bit of a scoundrel," she murmured, meaning it and thoroughly surprised by the fact.

James sighed again, this time with quiet contentment. "Agreed," he whispered in reply.

"Good," Aimee commented, seizing the duke's hand, dropping the Fire into it, and then closing his fingers protectively around its cold hardness. "You have a special license, I suppose."

Rockham grinned and replied, "Of course."

"And does your village have a vicar?"

"A curate. He can be here in half an hour."

Then send for him," Aimee commanded. "I am most anxious to do the deed."

"Indeed!" Rockham stated, brightening considerably. Reaching for her, he murmured, "Are you truly in such a hurry to marry me?"

"Absolutely," she told him dancing away from his grasp, her eyes brilliant with suppressed mischief. "The sooner, the better, your grace. I suggest you make the announcement right away," she continued, backing toward the door. "You might yet be able to save a bit of your Babylonian frieze. Do send for me when you are ready for the ceremony."

"Aimee, wait!" Rockham called just before she reached the corridor. "You don't intend to stay here with me?"

"Gracious, no," she said, her eyes still filled with an impish gleam. "Have you taken a good look around you, your grace? I have a great deal to do. As your wife, it is my sworn duty to make your home comfortable for you as soon as can be. Why, I am persuaded that I shall be swamped with work for days and days . . . perhaps even weeks . . . no, months, I am certain. Months and months, I think."

"With no time for your husband, I suppose," the duke concluded with narrowed eyes.

His suspicions were confirmed by her answering smile.

"Alas, I hardly think so," she sighed, slipping past the door frame. "Now, if you will excuse me, I shall begin immediately. There is no time like the present, is there? When you are ready, do send for me. I shall be upstairs measuring your mother's old apartments for new carpeting." Grinning wickedly, she then turned and disappeared from view.

The duke settled back against Clotho, shaking his head around a dry chuckle as he again opened his palm to gaze at Calladorn's Fire. So the lady thought she could wrest control over their marriage from him this easily, he thought, mentally embracing the thrown gauntlet . . . that she had the upper hand. He knew better, of course . . . and she would, too, a matter of mere hours from now. Oh, yes, he reiterated, his body already warming in anticipation. The lady was in for a big surprise.

"You are a scoundrel, Miss Winthrop!" he called out after her.

"Of the worst kind!" came Aimee's echoing response.

And then she laughed, and the laughter filled the great Hall and was undeniably happy.

The Duke of Diamonds grinned.

About the Author

Jenna Jones lives with her family in Phoenix, Arizona. Her first Zebra regency romance, A MERRY ESCAPADE, is currently available at your local bookstore. Jenna's second Zebra regency romance, A DELICATE DECEPTION, will be published in July 1996. Jenna loves hearing from her readers and you may write to her c/o Zebra Books. Please include a self-addressed stamped envelope if you wish a response.

For All Eternity

Meg-Lynn Roberts

Devil take it, *she* would be there tonight!

Justin Westbridge, Viscount Fulbrooke, stood at the window in the ground-floor reception room of his Brook Street townhouse and gazed out into the fashionable London thoroughfare. He ran a long finger back and forth over his full lower lip while his other hand played absently over the soft crimson velvet of the floor-to-ceiling drapes.

Lost as he was in painful memories, he did not see the activity in the street passing before his eyes. The dustman's cart rattling by, a smart rider clip-clopping along on a well-set-up chestnut hack, the two maids with straw baskets on their arms, chatting animatedly as they went off to do some shopping, made no impression on his conscious mind.

Christina. He would see Christina tonight for the first time in almost ten years. Would she even recognize him after all this time? he wondered with a painful contraction of his heart. What would he say to her if she did?

Christina. He had loved her once. So deeply, he would gladly have died for her.

He had thought he *would* die when she'd married Sir Geoffrey Elliott, poor, deceived youth that he had been. He had been heartsick, feverish for weeks afterward, unable to eat, unable to sleep, unable to think of anything useful to do with his life. It had taken him more than a year to recover the will to go on with that life. He had stayed away from London, with all its reminders of their encounters there, for three years after that, even though she had gone to the country with her husband and had remained there permanently, for all he knew.

Certainly since his father had finally convinced him to return to London to take up a junior appointment in the Treasury some seven years ago, Christina had made no appearance in the metropolis.

Until this year.

What would she be like now, the beautiful, young girl he had once known? Would she be changed out of all recognition?

His lips twisted. Certainly she would be changed. She had been a wife for almost eight years, a widow for two, and she was the mother of two young sons now.

The memory of her as he had first seen her gripped him. A slight, sylphlike girl, only just turned eighteen, with dark, lustrous hair, warm, sherry-colored eyes, and a wide, friendly smile, she had been the most enchanting girl he had ever seen. He had been irresistibly drawn to her warmth and beauty, her grace, and her fresh, vivacious charm.

He had been a callow youth of only one-and-twenty, just down from university. He had not really stood a chance.

No chance at all.

But it was too late when he learned that. Far too late for his trusting, young heart not to have been captured, then broken.

Since he had become a man he had learned to control his emotions, to maintain a cool, unreadable facade. That lesson would stand him in good stead now. He hardened his heart against his maudlin memories. He would face Christina again tonight, face her and remain unmoved. He *would* not let her affect him. Would not let her destroy the peace that had taken him so long to acquire.

"Ahem, my lord?" His butler coughed, interrupting his distracted thoughts. "Sir Philip is here to see you."

"What?" Justin started and turned toward his servant, a vacant look in his eyes.

Morris, his butler, repeated his announcement.

"Ah, of course. Show him in, Morris."

Before the words were out of his mouth, Sir Philip Baines was strolling into the room, dressed for riding, his hand extended in greeting.

Justin strode across the room with lithe grace to take the outstretched hand of his friend.

"Justin. Did you forget our appointment to ride this morning?" Philip asked, a quizzical look on his open, square-jawed face. "I waited for you in the park for upwards of half an hour before I decided you were not coming and went on with my ride. It was too fine a morning to postpone the exercise."

As he released Philip's hand, a faint tinge of red rose up from under Justin's neckcloth to stain the strong column of his neck and his lean cheeks. He shook his head, shrugging off his embarrassment. "Forgive me, my friend." He grinned ruefully. "I have had things on my mind. Treasury matters and such." He waved a hand toward his study across the hallway. "Something I had to look into rather urgently for the Chancellor."

"You are not telling me you are about to back out of attending the Saltrams' entertainment this evening, are you, old chap? You have been to only one or two events since the season started three weeks ago, after promising your mother faithfully that you would look around you for a bride this year. At long last!" Philip looked at him with a glint in his eyes that bespoke determination to have his friend attend the ball.

"Since when have you been the enforcer of my mother's whims, Phil?" Justin flashed a grin at his friend.

Philip smiled back and admitted a trifle sheepishly, "I would hardly call the matter of your marriage a whim, Justin . . . you, ah, must have noticed that Lady Fulbrooke and I have been as thick as thieves these past weeks. She has confided her hopes to me regarding your future."

"Indeed, I have been surprised to see you in Portman Square the last two or three times I have called on my mother. Couldn't have anything to do with my sister MaryLiz, now, could it?" Justin quizzed wickedly.

Clearing his throat, Philip confessed, "As a matter of fact, yes. And my visits to your mother . . . well, just trying to get my feet under the table, so to speak, my boy."

Justin whistled through his teeth. "Sits the wind in that direction, then? I must warn you, Phil, MaryLiz is a handful. As willful as she can hold together. Sure you want to court the little hoyden?"

Philip grinned crookedly. "She's as beautiful as she can hold together, too." He sighed. "As for courting her . . . shouldn't think there's much chance for me, with this phiz." He ran a hand over his rather plain, open face. "She has got Carleton hanging around her already, and a score of others, too."

"What, the duke? I did not know that. Mother said nothing to me about Carleton the last time I spoke with her."

"I understand Lady Fulbrooke has other worries where you are concerned, Justin. Since your father died three years ago, she has been trying to persuade you that you need to wed. In order to secure the succession, among other things. And this year, I thought she had convinced you to look around you. Especially since you will be moving about in society more with your sister making her come-out. You will be taking her around and about, escorting her and your mother to *ton* events."

Justin broke eye contact and moved away from his friend, rubbing a long-fingered hand against the back of his head, tousling his valet's careful arrangement of his thick honey brown hair. "Yes, well, I have been trying to convince Mother that the succession is secure. There is no need for me to marry. Cousin George stands heir to the viscountcy and he has three sons already, with the promise of more to come, I hear."

"Justin, you know Lady Fulbrooke is concerned for your future. For your happiness."

Justin turned to look at his friend, his head a little on one side. "And that necessitates taking a wife, does it?"

"Well, the *ton* would say so," Philip replied, rendered a

trifle uncomfortable by the keen look in his friend's eyes. Ordinarily he would have been the last person to meddle in such matters.

"Indeed, the female denizens would certainly insist that such is the case," Justin admitted with a wry grimace.

Philip fixed him with a determined look. "Nevertheless, you have promised to escort your mother and sister to the Saltrams' ball tonight, have you not? You will not allow your work to prevent you from keeping that engagement, will you? . . . Or anything else, for that matter?"

"Such as?" Justin queried, raising his brows and glancing at his friend with a blank look.

"The widow Fordham holds certain attractions for you, or so you have admitted to me in the past," Philip returned readily, not mincing words.

Justin waved this away. "Did I? I must confess, I do not recall the lady's charms. Lady Fordham is nothing to me. I fully intend to accompany mother and MaryLiz to the Saltrams' this evening. You need have no worry on that score, Phil."

Philip breathed a sigh of relief. "Good. I shall look forward to seeing you there, then. And I trust you will not be too fashionably late."

"What! Are you *that* eager to see MaryLiz? You *are* in a bad way, my friend." Justin laughed at him, his mood lifted by the light-hearted teasing of his friend.

Was it Christina, or was it not? Justin wondered, as he gazed across the crowded ballroom at the back of a dark-haired woman clad in an emerald green gown. A patterned silk shawl shot through with gold thread rested elegantly over her elbows, and a single white rosebud anchored the severe chignon at her neck. She was with a large group of people, among them the Duke of Carleton, one of his sister's suitors.

He debated whether or not to cross the room and satisfy

his curiosity, his need to know, but there was an odd feeling about his heart and his breath constricted at just the thought of looking into her impossibly wide, dark-fringed hazel eyes once more. He would bring himself under control, as he had learned to do in the past, before he satisfied that burning curiosity.

He did not move, but continued to gaze across at the woman assessingly, one hand toying with his dangling quizzing glass. His hand clenched into a fist at his side and his jaw firmed as he attempted to master his emotions. He would not allow Christina Granford—Christina *Elliott*—to hurt him again. He would see her, and by God, he would speak to her, too. But he would remain unmoved.

He vowed it.

The woman he watched did not appear to be speaking much. Something about the way she stood so quietly and held her head so rigidly and her back so straight was not quite like the Christina he remembered. His Christina had been a vivacious girl, too animated to stand so still.

No. It could not be Christina. His breathing slowed when he had convinced himself of this. He turned when he felt a touch on his arm to find that Lady Saltram had come up to greet him.

"Why, Fulbrooke! How pleased I am to see you here this evening at my little entertainment. You do not often come among us, naughty boy!" Lady Saltram addressed him in a teasing vein, the long feathery plumes in her turban waving busily above her head as she spoke.

"No, I am afraid my work for the Treasury keeps me quite busy. You understand, Lady Saltram, I cannot often neglect my duties for frivolity, enjoyable though it is," he added appeasingly, as he saw her poker up.

"Do they keep your nose to the grindstone, indeed? Humph. They should not work you so hard. You should enjoy yourself more, a handsome young man like you. Saltram will have a word with the Chancellor. I shall see to it." The plumes positively danced at this determined speech.

"Ah, do not exert yourself on my behalf, dear Lady Saltram. There is really no need, I assure you. I greatly enjoy my work, time-consuming and tiring though it is on occasion." He smiled coolly at her disbelieving look.

"*Enjoy* your work? All those money matters? I find that hard to credit. So many confusing numbers and figures. Does it not make your head ache just to *look* at a sheet full of figures? Dear, dear, dear! How do you ever make sense of 'em?" Her skeptical look spoke volumes.

"Ah, but you see, my dear lady, the Treasury is the center of political power. What we do has an effect on the entire country. I find it challenging to balance an account, to try to convince the various governmental departments that they must live within their budgets."

"And do you try to convince our dear spendthrift Prinny to live within a budget?"

"Alas, that task is beyond my meager powers of persuasion, I fear."

She shook her head, her plumes dipping ponderously. "I am sure it must be bad for one's digestion to see so many debts. All that money the government must pay out just to keep Prinny out of dun territory . . . well, better you than me, dear boy."

After a moment, Justin could not refrain from asking the question that teased at his thoughts. "Perhaps you can satisfy my curiosity, Lady Saltram. I thought I glimpsed an old acquaintance earlier. Is it possible Lady Elliott is here tonight?"

"Christina Elliott? Why, yes. She has finally decided to leave off her mourning and has come to London for the season. And about time, too! It's more than two years since poor Sir Geoffrey was carried off by an inflammation of the lungs . . . I saw her not a moment ago." Lady Saltram raised her jeweled lorgnette to her eyes and scanned the room.

Justin looked around, too. The group he had been watching had dispersed and the lady who bore some resemblance to Christina was nowhere to be seen.

"Now where is she, I wonder?" Lady Saltram asked, then turned to Justin with a perceptive look. "Do you have some particular interest in Christina Elliott, Fulbrooke?"

"Ah, I knew her many years ago. I heard she would be in town this spring and promised myself that I would look her up. If she is here tonight, it is only polite that I pay her my respects," he said, trying for an off-hand manner.

"Ah, I see." Lady Saltram fixed him with a knowing smile. "Ready to set up a flirtation with a young widow, are you, Fulbrooke? Naughty boy!" She rapped him on the wrist with her furled fan, her plumes bobbing above her turbaned head. "I would advise you to turn your attention to some of the eligible young gels here tonight, instead, dear boy. It is high time you were married—as I am sure dear Lady Fulbrooke has been urging since your poor father died."

"How kind of you to take an interest, Lady Saltram," Justin said, his lips twisting sardonically. He bowed over her hand and moved off, cursing his impatient tongue. He did not wish the world to know his secrets, and he was very much afraid that they would do after his indiscreet question to Lady Saltram. Most particularly, he did not wish his mother to learn that he was still interested in Christina, and Lady Saltram was a bosom bow of hers.

Damnation! Stop acting like a green schoolboy, he chided himself.

He moved about the ballroom, speaking to an acquaintance here, nodding to a friend there, keeping an eagle eye out for Christina. The press of people in the Saltrams' ballroom restricted his movements and narrowed his field of view. Lord and Lady Saltram had not neglected to invite a single soul among the upper ten thousand, he decided with heavy irony. Half the *ton* seemed to be in attendance this evening.

He was edgy, hoping, dreading to see Christina at any moment. But the crowd of people made it impossible to see more than the persons in one's immediate vicinity. He let out a breath with something like relief. Perhaps he would not have to confront Christina and his painful memories tonight, after all.

Though he did not spy his mother, he glimpsed his sister, MaryLiz, standing not too far away with Sir Philip Baines at her elbow. Good. Lizzy was in capable hands for now. He would escape to the balcony for a breath of air.

He made his way to the French windows that opened onto the balcony and put his hand on the latch to open them when a lady tumbled against his arm, thrust there by a corpulent gentleman who was shoving his way through the crowd shouting "Air, I must have air!"

Justin caught the lady just in time to prevent her from falling.

"Are you all right, ma'am?" he asked, at the same time as she straightened in his arms and exclaimed, "Oh, dear! How rude of that gentleman to push me that way! And how gallant of you, sir, to come to the rescue." Her hand grabbed for the rose that had been dislodged in the collision, sending loosened strands of her hair tumbling down about her cheeks.

"Christina!" Justin uttered in a rough whisper. Releasing his tight hold on her, he stepped back. And froze.

"Oh!" she said, looking up into his intense gray-green eyes. *"Justin!* I never expected—"

Their eyes met and locked.

Justin gripped his lips together in a frown as he struggled to master his emotions. Words leapt to his mind—words of accusation, of her heartless betrayal. He wanted to beg her to tell him why she had spurned his love. Why she had broken his heart. With an effort, he controlled the urge to confront her, to tell her of the almost unbearable pain she had caused him. He would abhor creating such a scene here in front of half the *ton*. He would abhor baring his heart to her.

He did not speak, did not move. But continued to stare down at her, his face grim and unsmiling.

"Justin! I—I mean, Lord Fulbrooke. I did not expect to see you here." Christina uttered the first thing that came into her mind, then chided herself for the inanity of her comment. She felt a tightness in her chest and had difficulty catching her breath as she looked up at him, looked up into the green flame burning behind his eyes.

His eyes, those compelling gray-green eyes that had mirrored his soul, that had once held only the light of gladness when he beheld her, now bore down into hers reproachfully.

He looked older, of course, and quite stern and forbidding. And quite impossibly attractive.

He had been very well looking as a boy, with honey brown hair streaked with gold and his intense, changeable eyes that had looked so often and so tenderly into hers. But now—now his face had thinned out and hardened. And he had a man's frame. He was no longer sporting a boy's tall, lanky form; his shoulders had widened and firmed; and if he was not actually taller, he was certainly more imposing. She swallowed with difficulty and struggled for something light to say.

"I trust you took no hurt, Lady Elliott?" he asked in a cold voice before she could speak.

"No, Justin, I . . . no, I am quite unharmed, thanks to you." She tried to smile, but her lips would not obey.

Attempting to step back from him, she found her way blocked by the crowd.

Before she could escape, Justin reached out and took her by the elbow. "You are looking quite pale, Christina. Perhaps a breath of air—?"

"Oh, I should not, my lord!" she murmured, as his strong fingers closed about her arm.

He took no notice of her mild protest, but propelled her through the French windows, giving her no choice but to accompany him to the deserted balcony beyond. They stepped across the narrow balcony to lean against the stone balustrade that overlooked the darkened garden below.

He stood close beside her, so close she could feel his breath stirring the tendrils of her hair against her forehead.

"I do not think this wise," she said through stiff lips, trying to read his expression in the little light that penetrated to the balcony from the ballroom.

"Why not? It is insufferably crowded in there. Why should you not come out for a breath of air? . . . Or is it that you are afraid of me?" he asked, tightening his grip on her elbow and looking down into her wide eyes intently.

His fingers burned where they gripped her flesh.

"Oh, no. Of course, not. But I—I really am quite unharmed, you know. And I must find my friends. They will be wondering what has become of me." The touch of his hand was like fire along her skin through the thin silk of her ballgown.

"Ah, you are afraid." He let her go, his hand dropping to his side. "Do not worry. I am not about to attack you. You will come to no harm from me." He turned away to stare out into the velvety night, its softness lit by a low-hanging moon.

"No, indeed, I am not afraid," Christina protested in a stronger voice. She had got herself in hand now after the first jolt of surprise at his sudden appearance, at finding herself in his arms again. Afraid of Justin, the beautiful boy whom she had been unable to put from her mind after all these years? "How could I ever be afraid of you, Justin?" she asked softly, her words echoing the thought in her mind.

"There was a time when you wanted no part of me."

He sounded angry. She looked up at him uneasily, her wide eyes sorrowful. "Please do not be angry after all this time, Justin. I was so sorry—that is, I did not mean to hurt you. There—there was no help for it."

Her words seemed to have layers of meaning. He heard her voice speaking to him across the years. "Please do not look like that. Do not be angry, please," she had said, after she had told him of her engagement to Sir Geoffrey Elliott.

After she had broken his heart.

Had he felt anger? He couldn't recall it now. He rather thought he had been too blinded by hurt to leave room for any other emotion.

He took a deep breath. "I am sorry, Christina. I had no

right to drag you out here against your will. We have nothing to say to one another now, do we?"

"I was just a girl, quite a foolish one when I first came to London and met you. I have never forgotten that season, and—"

He put up a staying hand, his long, slender fingers outlined in the shadowy night by the light coming through the French windows. "It was all a long time ago. We are both quite different people now. There is no need to dig up old—" He had been going to say "hurts," but he stopped himself. "Disagreements."

"But we never disagreed," she whispered.

He stared out into the night, his hands clenched into fists rested on top of the hard, cold balustrade. The smell of roses from the crushed bud she still held in her hand teased at his nostrils.

She had always smelled of roses.

"Christina, you no longer know me. I no longer know you. I regret my impulsive action in bringing you out here against your will. I thought you were about to faint. You seemed to need a breath of air. Any gentleman would have done the same."

"But . . . you are not 'any gentleman' to me," she replied softly.

Gritting his teeth, he hardened his heart protectively against the wistful note in her voice. "Our acquaintance was a passing one all those years ago, after all. We were young, as you said. Neither of us knew the world. How long did we know one another? A few weeks at most. A few weeks out of a lifetime . . . It does not matter now."

Does not matter? Christina thought bleakly. The dearest memories of her heart did not matter?

"We should be able to meet one another now without letting the past interfere," he continued. He was still staring out into the darkness, avoiding her gaze.

She half lifted her hand toward him but drew back, instead

adjusting one edge of her shawl that had slipped off her elbow. She bit her lip and lifted her hands to pin up the loosened strands of hair that brushed her cheeks. The crushed rose fell unnoticed from her fingers. "I really must go in, Justin. Susan will be wondering what has become of me."

"Susan?" he asked, a quizzical brow lifted as he turned to look her fully in the eyes once more. His emotions were on a tight rein now.

"My—my sister-in-law. Susan Henshaw, Geoffrey's sister." She winced as she pronounced her husband's name. "I do not believe you ever met her."

"No."

"She virtually dragged me to London this year, kicking and screaming all the way. I—I am used to a quiet country life, you see . . . I am staying with her and her husband in Jermyn Street. They have a quite delightful house. Perhaps you would—ah, that is, perhaps you did not know that I have two sons?"

"Yes, I did know it," he answered quietly.

"Oh! Well, they are with me here in London. I could not leave them behind with just their nurse to look after them, though everyone thought I should. They are seven and five now, and quite the delight of my life." Christina heard herself babbling, but was powerless to stop. There was so much tension between them, she could feel the very air vibrating with it. It was as though she had told him of her engagement only yesterday.

Oh, why did she feel as though he were protesting his undying love and accusing her of ruining his life all over again? He had done no such thing, but had said instead that they should forget the past, implying that he scarcely recollected it.

Justin made a move toward the French windows, silently inviting her to precede him back into Lady Saltram's ballroom.

Justin clasped his hands behind his back as he followed

Christina into the room. It had been a mistake to touch her before. Just touching her had stirred powerful emotions in his soul, emotions he was determined to conquer. And she was a delicate thing, more so than he remembered. He had gripped her arm so hard, he must have left bruises. He winced at his gaucheness.

"There you are, Justin," MaryLiz piped, squeezing between two portly dowagers to link her arm through her brother's. "Mama bade me discover where you had disappeared to. It is time for supper, and you are to accompany us."

"You are willing to make do with a mere brother as a supper partner? Do not expect me to believe you have not had several gentlemen clamoring for your company," he teased lightly, looking down at his sister with a half smile on his lips and patting her hand where it rested on his sleeve.

"Of course not, silly!" MaryLiz gave his arm a playful shake. "Sir Philip Baines is to take me in, though the Duke of Carleton asked for that privilege as well," she announced smugly. "But he was too late. He shall just have to learn to ask sooner next time."

MaryLiz stared curiously at the woman standing quietly at her brother's side. She saw the woman smile at her tentatively.

"Justin," MaryLiz hissed, tugging his arm and tilting her head toward Christina.

Assuming a rather bored manner, Justin made the introductions. He introduced Christina not only to MaryLiz, but also to Sir Philip, who had determinedly forced his way through the throng to join them.

"Let us all go in to supper together," Philip said, smiling at them all as he claimed MaryLiz's arm.

The situation was awkward in the extreme. Justin cast a tentative, apologetic look at Christina. "Would you care to join us, Lady Elliott? Or may we see you to your party in the supper room?"

Christina looked up at him and nodded. "Thank you. It

would be very kind if you could help me find my friends."
She raised her chin a notch.

Justin smiled slightly, his lashes coming down to veil his
eyes. "Certainly." She looked very unhappy about being
forced to accept his escort.

He extended his arm rather stiffly. They followed a chattering MaryLiz and Sir Philip through the crowd.

Christina was quiet. He had to look down to assure himself
that she was really there beside him, for he could not feel her
touch through the cloth of his sleeve. Seeing her delicate
white-gloved hand resting lightly against the blue superfine
of his jacketsleeve, he could not help the quiver that shook
him.

The pressure of her hold on his arm increased slightly as
they made their way through the crowded ballroom. Pulling
her protectively to his side, he caught a whiff of her perfume.

He breathed in the scent of her. Roses.

Reality receded. He felt transported back in time. She had
always used to smell sweetly of roses.

She still did.

He moved as one in a dream. To have Christina on his arm
again was the most exquisite pleasure, the most exquisite torture he could conceive. He steeled himself against the on-
slaught of longing that threatened to overcome him.

There was an awkward little pause at the door to the supper
room when she looked around for her friends among the press
of people.

"Oh, there is Susan," she breathed with obvious relief when
she spotted a woman, presumably her sister-in-law, not far
away. She turned to go.

When she took a step away from him, Justin relinquished
her with great reluctance—and great relief. He did not know
how he would have been able to conduct himself with anything
like his usual cool imperturbability if she had been at his side
throughout supper. There was too much unspoken between
them, too many undercurrents of emotion, too much recrimi-

nation on his part, to have made it anything but an awkward, tense affair for all concerned.

She turned back and looked at him, holding her shawl tightly, her two hands crossed over her waist.

She met his gaze, her wide eyes shadowed. "Thank you, Lord Fulbrooke, for your escort," she said, gathering her dignity about her as tightly as she held the shawl.

"Not at all, ma'am," he replied coolly, still feeling as though he were floating in a dream, that the woman before him were some phantasm.

Something flickered in her eyes at his tone. "I am glad you have nothing to reproach yourself with from our past acquaintance, as—as I do. But I trust you have forgiven me, or—or forgotten about—well, as you said, we are both quite different people now. Good evening, Lord Fulbrooke."

She was swallowed up by the crowd, leaving him to stare after her in stunned silence.

God! He had behaved like a prize idiot, Justin castigated himself, as he sat in the town carriage on the way to Portman Square, while a voluble MaryLiz regaled him and his mother with all her conquests of the evening. Where was his prized sangfroid? Why had all his practiced aloofness deserted him when he needed it most? He had wanted to behave with perfect equanimity toward Christina. To show her he was a gentleman in perfect control of himself, that he no longer had any feelings for her whatsoever. Instead, he had been by turns cold, brutal, resentful, and angry.

His mask had slipped, control had almost completely deserted him. What a precious fool he had made of himself!

And her parting speech of apology! What was he to make of that? The words had spilled out, beyond her control to stop. He had been staggered. He had wanted to reach out and seize her and ask her why she'd refused him and married Elliott.

MaryLiz and his mother chattered on.

"I beg your pardon, Lizzy, I was not perfectly attending," Justin said, only half hearing some remark directed his way.

"I was asking how long you have known Lady Elliott, Justin?" MaryLiz repeated, curiosity making her eyes bright in the dimly-lit carriage.

"Elliott? Not *Christina* Elliott, Justin?" his mother asked in alarm, leaning forward on her seat to peer at him across the gloomy interior.

"Yes, Mama, it was Christina Elliott. And to answer your question, Lizzy, I knew the lady some years ago. We were merely exchanging social pleasantries when you joined us," he drawled, seeking to calm his mother and assuage his sister's interest with an off-hand comment.

He leaned back at his ease against the squabs and crossed one elegantly-clad leg over the other, trying to appear nonchalant and hoping his inquisitive relatives would not delve further. His thoughts might be obsessed with her, but he had no wish to discuss her with anyone else.

"She seemed a pleasant woman, if a little on the quiet side, not to mention somewhat old for you," MaryLiz continued, probing him.

"There is no question of her being 'too old' for me. She is an acquaintance merely," he insisted, his hands beginning to clench where they were folded across his chest.

"Was she his old flame, Mama?" MaryLiz asked.

"No!" he barked.

"Well, I believe he did have a *tendre* for her at one time," Lady Fulbrooke said carefully, not wanting to stir up painful memories for her only son. "But he was very young at the time."

"I beg you to put that idea from your mind, Mama. The matter was exaggerated out of all proportion," he iterated in more measured tones, seeking to quell the painful discussion.

"As you say, dearest," his mother placated.

MaryLiz was regarding him with her head a little on one side.

"She must have been more attractive when she was younger, if you had an interest in her years ago, Justin, for she's nothing special to look at now."

"I really do not recall," he said dismissively, putting an end to her quizzing by turning his head to gaze out into the badly lit streets they were traversing.

Seeing that her son had turned taciturn on the subject, Lady Fulbrooke found that her curiosity prompted her to ask her daughter. "What is Lady Elliott like now, my dear?"

"Oh, she's well enough, I suppose, for a matron past her first bloom. Not at all dashing, you know. Her dark hair was rather unfashionably dressed. Confined too tightly to her head, with nary a curl for softness. And of course, she's a widow; perhaps that accounts for the dark green gown she wore. Though it was not unflattering, considering her coloring. She seemed subdued. Quiet."

"She does not sound like the same person," Lady Fulbrooke murmured, peering across at her unresponsive son. "Little Christina Granford was a lively thing, always dressed in white or bright colors with her hair flying about, coming out of its pins. Not in an unattractive way, you understand. And always surrounded by all the young men. Always chattering away merrily to them. Perhaps her widowhood has subdued her."

Justin sat perfectly still, his chin resting on his fisted hand as he gazed out into the street and heard MaryLiz term Christina rather unremarkable—quiet and subdued.

She had changed over the years. Of course, she had changed, he reminded himself. Her beauty remained, but it was quieter, more mature. Once, she had been as lively and full of high spirits as MaryLiz. But she was no longer the laughing, vivacious girl he had known.

Her eyes were still the same delicious warm sherry color, but their warmth had dimmed and her smile was not quite so bright, so assured, as it once had been.

There was an air of fragility, of vulnerability, about her that was new. She was less self-assured than she had been as a girl new come to town. Wariness showed in her expression. Her spontaneous smile was a little tentative now. And there had been a certain bruised look about her eyes that had tugged at his heartstrings.

Despite the loss of her girlish charms, and despite his vow to remain unmoved, he had been as powerfully affected by her as ever.

More so, perhaps.

His hand strayed to his pocket, where he fingered the sadly crushed remains of a single white rosebud.

Her new air of vulnerability had made him want to reach out and take her in his arms, to hold her, to protect her against all the woes of the world. She had implied that he had much to forgive her for, touching him deeply. He had had great difficulty in maintaining his composure at her words.

But he would not act on his reignited desires. To do so would be to invite disaster, for he would lose himself again. He doubted that he could recover from a second wound.

He stifled a sigh. It seemed his vow to remain unaffected could not be kept. He resolved to stay away from her instead.

Shedding his jacket for a dressing gown, Justin wandered downstairs and poured himself a glass of brandy. His chest hurt and he was exhausted. He had seen his mother and sister home, then returned to Brook Street feeling as though he had just run a ten-mile race. He had held himself stiffly all evening—physically and emotionally. And now a tiredness invaded his limbs that he usually experienced only after heavy exercise.

He walked into his study and absently lit a brace of candles on his desk. He sat in his chair and picked up the report he was working on, staring at it unseeingly. One hand slipped into the pocket of his dressing gown and played with the crushed rose petals that had so lately touched her hair. He had been unable to prevent himself from going back to the balcony to retrieve the forgotten bloom.

The first time he had seen Christina Granford, he had been utterly entranced. There had been a sparkle, a vitality, about her, as well as a delicate feminine beauty, that had captured his heart. He had stood stock still and stared at her for a full five minutes before he was capable of movement again. He had immediately joined the press of men around her. And then, when she had turned her friendly smile on him and agreed to dance with him, he had fallen head over heels in love with her.

As the weeks wore on, she had seemed to favor him over her other, more distinguished beaux. She had been lovely and desirable, of course, but sweet, warm, and fun, too. They had talked and laughed and danced. They had shared the same ideas, the same humor, and, it seemed to him, a deep contentment in one another's company. He had fallen more deeply in love with her with each passing day. He had been delirious with joy, filled with hope, fired with the determination to win her for himself.

And there had been physical attraction, too.

Yes. They had been powerfully attracted to one another.

Every time he had touched her, his body had ignited with desire. She had been physically affected by him, too; he had had no doubts about that. He had read it in the way she clung tightly to his hand when they danced and secretly laced her fingers with his whenever they sat at table together, in the way she had looked into his eyes with a light in her own, in the way the breath had seemed to catch in her throat whenever he kissed her hand.

And one magical night under the stars, she had allowed him to kiss her lips. It had been his first kiss and he had assumed it had been hers, also. It had been unbearably sweet, leaving him shaken to his very soul.

It had begun as a mere touching of his lips to hers, but somehow, despite his lack of expertise at the time, it had become something more. Without conscious volition, his arms had wrapped round her waist and back and he had pulled her against himself while he increased the pressure of his mouth on hers.

And she—she had wound her arms round his neck and he had felt her fingers threading themselves through his hair over and over as she clung to him. He had felt the wild fluttering of her heart against his own. He lost all sense of time and place and continued that kiss for untold minutes. Somehow, his mouth had opened over hers and hers under his, and he had deepened the kiss to a level he had only guessed at before. She had responded by grasping him even more tightly, holding onto him for dear life. And when she had moaned low in her throat, he had thought he would die of pure happiness. He was overcome with desire, with love.

"I will love you for all eternity," he had whispered in her ear.

Voices floating out into the garden from the ballroom of the house where they had met to honor the engagement of one of Christina's friends had finally roused them to a sense of where they were, and they had sprung apart. Her breath coming in short gasps, Christina had cried, "I must go!"

He had grabbed her hand and planted an impassioned kiss on her wrist before he'd let her go, rasping urgently, "We must talk soon, my dearest love. Tomorrow."

"Yes! No! Oh, Justin, what can I say? I must go!" And with that, she had broken from his hold and fled back through the garden to the house. When he had gone in, after several moments of deep, steadying breaths to compose himself, Christina had been nowhere in sight.

Filled with love, fired with enthusiasm, and determined to settle the matter as soon as possible, he had called at her house the following morning as early as good manners permitted. He had been nonplussed when the butler had told him Miss Granford was indisposed.

The pattern repeated itself for the next several days. He

called at her house and tried to see her, but was denied, her father's butler telling him each time that Miss Granford was not seeing callers. After the fourth day, when he tried to send up a note to her and the butler refused to take it, he feared her parents had forbidden him the house.

It could not be *Christina* who'd denied him!

It had eventually dawned on him then that her parents had some objection to him as a suitor for their only daughter's hand. He could only surmise that they were aiming for bigger game.

The viscountcy that would be his one day was not a wealthy one, but he would have a respectable income. His father was a careful man and had talked to Justin about supplementing the income from their small estate with a position in a governmental ministry. He planned to follow that advice.

Surely his love for Christina, and hers for him, would overcome any objection her parents might pose. With all the confidence and naïveté of youth, he had thought that he could not fail to win her. He knew that his love was strong enough to overcome all obstacles.

Desperate to see her again, a week after their earth-shattering kiss, he had stooped to bribing one of her father's footmen and had learned that she was to attend a garden party outside London that afternoon.

He had arrived late at the house near Richmond where the party was already in progress. He had not been invited, but no one stopped him. The hostess looked puzzled when she saw him, but gave him a welcoming smile nonetheless.

Christina had been standing almost at the end of the neatly clipped green lawn that ran down to the edge of the River Thames, chatting with a group of young people. She had looked breathtakingly lovely in a yellow-and-white muslin tea gown, with a frivolous white lace parasol held open over the chip straw hat covering her dark curls. He had thought he would burst with pride. The loveliest girl of the season would soon be his.

She had looked startled to see him at first. A smile had trembled on her lips as he'd separated her from her friends and walked away with her into a little copse of rhododendrons and azaleas in riotous bloom.

A rich palette of exuberant color, frilly pinks, gorgeous purples, flaming reds, and pure whites all contrasting with the deep green of the leaves had surrounded them, making the place a veritable Eden. He had proposed to her with all the ardor an inexperienced boy of one-and-twenty could command.

Her eyes had filled with tears and her lips had trembled when she'd laid her gloved hand lightly on his arm and looked into his eyes. "Oh, Justin, I cannot. You—you see, I am already betrothed," she had whispered, "to—to Sir Geoffrey Elliott, my father's cousin."

He had not comprehended her at once. It seemed that all the blood had drained from his head, then a swift, hot pain, like a searing brand, had pierced his heart.

"No!" he had cried, putting out his arms to her. "Christina, no!"

She had bit down hard on her lip, hesitated for a moment, then said in a shaking voice, "I am so sorry, Justin. Oh, please do not look like that! Do not be angry, please."

"I love you, Christina. I will love you for all eternity!" he had cried hoarsely. "And you love me, too—I *know* you do. Please do not do this. I cannot bear it."

Glistening tears had gathered in her eyes and begun to fall silently down her cheeks, dripping onto her quivering lips and down her chin. He had reached out for her with shaking hands, his own lips trembling, his heart breaking, but she had stepped back from his arms.

"Oh, dear God, this is so hard! Oh, Justin, I am sorry, but I have no choice! . . . I cannot stay. Goodbye, dearest Justin."

Then she had picked up her skirts and fled, leaving him there alone. Alone among the lavishly flowering plants. In hell. For all eternity.

Justin's arm jerked out and swept all the papers off his
desk. Erupting from his chair, he swore viciously. "God damn
it all to bloody hell! What kind of a fool would risk pain like
that again?" he muttered, running a hand through his hair as
he paced to the window. "I will not see her again!"

After a restless, largely sleepless night, Justin decided that
the matter he was working on for the Treasury would simply
have to wait. He needed to be out in the fresh air, taking some
exercise, blowing away the blue devils that fogged his tired
brain. He ordered his sorrel hack saddled and headed for open
land, intending to let his mount have his head, if the park
wasn't too crowded at that early hour.

He entered the park at the Grosvenor Gate and cantered
along the tan toward the Uxbridge Road end. He was relieved
to see that there was relatively little carriage traffic and few
pedestrians or other riders about. He urged the sorrel to a trot,
then dropped the reins and bent low over the horse's neck as
he allowed the powerful animal under him to stretch out into
a full-out gallop.

After half-an-hour's vigorous exercise, he walked his hack
back down through the center of the park toward the winding
little river. The pale gray mist of the morning had vanished
along with his foul mood. The sun had burned away the remnants of an overnight rime covering the grass and the Serpentine gleamed pale blue under the now cloudless sky. Justin
closed his eyes and breathed in the scents of early spring and
felt himself regaining some measure of peace.

As he neared the river he became aware of a contretemps
somewhere to his right. A child was crying and a woman's
voice was raised in indignation. He nudged his mount in that
direction with his knee and a light pull on the reins.

From a distance he saw a woman and two small children
confronting a large man who was shouting at them and making
threatening gestures toward the water. Something about the

woman's rigid back caught his complete attention. His eyes narrowed, even as he spurred his mount to speed.

He arrived on the scene to see one small boy clinging to the arm of a heavy, roughly-dressed man.

"You have no right to that boat," the youngster cried indignantly. "My brother and I made it. It is ours. Give it back! Now, if you please."

"Ger off wit ye, ye little scruff!" the bully returned, trying to shake the boy from a tenacious hold on his arm.

Justin sprang off his horse and strode forward, letting his voice precede him. "I would advise you to do as the boy says, my man." His words rang with authority and the bully's head jerked round in his direction, his mouth hanging open, then snapping shut with a snarl.

"And who be ye, ye dandified fop, to stick up for this little thief 'ere?" the bully asked brashly. "Ow!" he exclaimed, as the boy bit his hand, causing him to drop the little wooden boat. The other child darted in and whisked the boat safely away.

Justin advanced menacingly, a ferocious frown on his face, brandishing his crop.

The bully retreated, holding his hands out in front of him, his gap-toothed mouth split in an unpleasant grin. "Ahh, h'I didn't mean nothin', gov'ner," he blustered.

"Do not let me ever see your bloody face again, or I'll have your cobbler's awls! Do you understand me?" Justin slapped his crop against his thigh for emphasis.

"Naw, ye won't never, gov'ner." The man lost his swagger and showed them a dirty pair of heels, disappearing among the trees to the north of the river.

Justin stared after the scoundrel, half tempted to ride after him and teach him a well-deserved lesson. A hand on his arm stayed him.

"Thank you, Justin." Christina's warm voice forced him to turn and face her, something he had wanted to postpone for as long as possible, once he realized it was she and her children who stood in need of his aid. Now he looked down into her wide hazel eyes glowing with gratitude.

"I do not know what we would have done, if you had not arrived when you did. I was so afraid that villain would lash out at Stephen with his fists at any moment and do him serious injury. My heart was in my throat," she admitted shakily, putting her other hand to her throat and giving a small laugh as her fear dissipated.

"I am thankful that I heard the boys' cries," he replied, reaching to cover her hand with his where it rested on his sleeve. "Though it looked as though your sons had devised a plan to deal with the brute, even without my help." He smiled fully, right into her eyes.

"I tried to convince the boys to let the man take the boat. They could always build another. But I'm afraid my sons have inherited a stubborn streak from one of their ancestors. They will never give up. Why the villain wanted their toy in the first place is a mystery to me."

"Doubtless he would sell it for a few pennies in order to buy his next pint of blue ruin."

"Oh! You are probably right." Christina released Justin's arm. She turned and gathered her wriggling sons close in her arms, hugging them to her, and planting a kiss on each curly head.

Justin looked on, a tightness in his throat that he was at a loss to explain. The taller of the two broke from his mother's hold and came toward him.

"Thank you, sir, for coming to the rescue," the boy Christina referred to as Stephen said in a high young voice, coming up to Justin and extending his hand.

Justin placed his hand in the boy's and gave it a firm shake. "You are quite welcome. You are a stout fellow for standing up to that bully the way you did."

"I *couldn't* let that man take Sebastian's boat, you know. It took him *weeks* to make it."

A smile twitched at the corners of Justin's mouth at the

seriousness with which this was uttered. "Of course you could not. You are the gentleman of the family now, I believe."

"Yes, sir, I am that," Stephen allowed, putting his hands behind his back and surveying the fashionable gentleman who stood before him. "I am Stephen Elliott, and that is my brother, Sebastian. We are having a holiday from our lessons, you know, because it rained last week and we could not go out. Oh, and this is my mother, Lady Elliott."

"I am acquainted with your mother already, Stephen. You are a lucky boy. I am Justin Westbridge."

"Mr. Westbridge, very pleased to meet you," Stephen said seriously.

"Oh, Stephen, dear," Christina hurried into speech, "Mr. Westbridge is also Viscount Fulbrooke. You must call him Lord Fulbrooke."

"I am sorry, sir. Lord Fulbrooke, then." Stephen faltered, clearly embarrassed at his unintentional faux pas.

"Do you know, I believe I would prefer to be called something less formal, say, just Westbridge. That is what I was called at school, you see." Stephen and Justin smiled at one another in perfect understanding.

"Westbridge, then, sir. I am to be called Elliott Major when I go to school, you know, and Sebastian will be Elliott Minor, when he joins me."

"Do you want to see this boat sail across the ocean, Westbridge?" Sebastian asked, in a piping young voice.

"Oh, Sebastian, dear, I do not really think Lord Fulbrooke has the time to watch you launch your boat." Christina looked apologetically at Justin. "You must not let them importune you, my lord. I am sure you are quite busy."

Justin smiled at Sebastian, then raised his eyes to Christina and winked. "I can spare a few minutes . . . is this her maiden voyage?" he asked the children, dropping down on his haunches beside Sebastian to examine the little vessel the boy proudly extended to him. "This is a fine piece of work, lad. Do you know, I believe I would like to see her sail."

"Oh, famous!" the boys chorused, then led the adults down to the water's edge.

They all spent a happy half hour beside the gleaming Serpentine. The boys sent the little boat bravely sailing out across the water, then ran up and down the bank, pulling it along the river with the string they had wisely attached to its stern. The sun shimmered off the surface of the river, sending a shower of sparks playing across the water like starbursts in the little boat's wake.

Christina and Justin stood shoulder to shoulder in companionable silence, watching the boys playing with the boat. Though they spoke little, Justin felt himself relax in her company. Her heavy brown cloak was not remarkable, and the plain brown bonnet she wore was more serviceable than fashionable. But to him she looked lovely, standing there in the sunlight, especially when she tipped back her head and smiled, her bright, warm gaze meeting his own wide grin when one of the boys began flapping his arms about and turning in wide circles, pretending to be a seagull.

The sun warmed her and released the scent of roses to tantalize his senses.

Their shoulders were almost touching. He shifted his weight a few inches, wanting to touch her. Wanting to take her hand and hold it in his and lace their fingers together as they always had done. He flexed his fingers and turned to her.

"I say, Westbridge—would you like a turn?" Stephen called, offering to give up one of his own turns to Justin.

Justin was oddly moved and accepted without hesitation. Removing his hat and jacket, he rolled up the sleeves of his shirt, then knelt down near the edge of the river to haul in the boat.

"Oh, Jus—Lord Fulbrooke, you will get dirty down there." Christina laughed the same musical laugh she'd had as a girl. His stomach lurched and he was flooded with memories.

"Now, you know, ma'am, we sailors do not mind a little dirt when we are about our work, preparing to sail a mighty vessel like this one out over the vast ocean," he called back, and watched her eyes crinkle and her lips curve up in a delicious smile again. The sun was behind her, producing a halo effect. Oh, but he wanted to see her always like that, warm and lovely and full of joy—and smiling at him.

He was teaching the boys a rather boisterous song about sailing ships and pirates and their adventures when a strident voice interrupted them.

"Why, Lord Fulbrooke, is that you down there with those children? In your shirtsleeves, playing with a toy boat?" A woman's derisive laughter broke into their happy idyll, disturbing the fragile new understanding that had been building between Justin and Christina. "When I tell them, no one will believe this!"

Justin looked up to see Olivia, Lady Fordham, leaning back in her sidesaddle and gazing down at them with a patronizing smile pasted across her haughty face. His lips firmed into a hard line.

"Good morning, Lady Fordham," he replied formally, ignoring her deprecating remarks and her marked curiosity. "I trust you are enjoying your morning ride."

"Indeed I am. I have not seen much of you lately, Justin. Why do not we ride together some morning soon, as we used to do, and catch up on all the news? We used to enjoy that, among other things."

"Alas, my work keeps me from enjoying morning rides as often as I would like," he replied repressively. He recalled with distaste the one morning ride he had taken many months ago with Lady Fordham. She had virtually issued him an open invitation to become her lover. He had not been interested.

Lady Fordham took his answer as encouragement. Casting a dismissive glance at Christina, she smiled triumphantly. Throwing a seductive look at Justin over her shoulder, she rode away.

Glancing at Christina after Lady Fordham departed, Justin saw that she had turned away from him and was watching her children as they played down by the river. Her back was very rigid.

The incident seemed to have cast a pall over her spirits and over the outing.

He frowned, realizing that half the morning had flown by. He wondered how he had allowed himself to be captivated by a pair of charming halflings for such a time when he had sworn to stay away from their mother. He should have seen the bully off, then ridden away with a polite "Good morning."

He sighed. "Should haves" had rarely governed his behavior where Christina was concerned.

"I must go," he said reluctantly, pushing his rolled-up shirt-sleeves down over his strong forearms and pulling on his jacket. "A pile of papers on my desk urgently awaits attention."

"Yes. We must return home now, too. It must be almost time for the boys' luncheon."

Christina did not look at him as she spoke, Justin saw, but began to gather up the children's jackets, which had been spread on the grass. He glanced at the river. The boys were still there, happily bent over the boat.

"Christina—" He hesitated. "I have enjoyed this morning. I could almost thank that blackguard for disturbing you, for it gave me an excuse to stop. I like your sons. They are fine boys."

"Thank you, Justin. Your good opinion means a great deal to me," she said, her eyes warming at his speech and gleaming with the golden lights that had always awakened desire in him.

Their gazes met and locked for a long moment. A soft breeze stirred the air between them, and Christina put up her hand to capture a curl of hair that escaped from under her bonnet to blow over her mouth.

Justin's eyes followed her hand, lingering on her lips. He had tasted the sweetness there once. His breath quickened and he reached out to catch her arm, but she looked away from him and stepped back before he could touch her.

His hand fell to his side and he closed his eyes briefly. He must not allow himself to become entangled with her again. Did someone who had been badly burned once deliberately put his hand into the fire again?

He would not do so.

The boys realized their new friend was leaving and came pelting up, trying to convince him to stay. Their combined efforts were unsuccessful, but Stephen did have one last bright idea. "Oh, sir, you must come to tea tomorrow, mustn't he, Mama?"

"Stephen, my dear." Christina tried to hush her son. "I do not know that Lord Fulbrooke has the time. He is a very busy man, and we must not expect him to wait on our pleasure."

Before he could stop to think—before Christina could revoke her son's invitation—the words were out of Justin's mouth. "I would be delighted to come to tea with you, Stephen. Will it be just for the three of us fellows, or do you think your mama could be persuaded to join us?"

Stephen crowed with triumph. "You see, Mama? He's a great gun. He wants to come to tea with us!"

Seeing all his resolutions to stay away from Christina slipping away, Justin bade them adieu. He swung onto his mount, tethered nearby, touched his crop to his hat in farewell, and kicked his horse into motion.

"And, sir, you will not be sorry you've agreed to come," Stephen called after him. "They serve a bang-up tea at my Aunt Susan's! The best in all of London!"

Sitting at his desk later that afternoon, trying to concentrate on the sheet of numbers he held before him, Justin wondered what had come over him that morning. To be beguiled by a beautiful woman was one thing, but to be captivated by a pair of dark-haired urchins was something else again.

He felt a strange gladness take possession of his heart. He had expected to hate her children, but he didn't. He had not been around children much before, but he rather liked Christina's boys.

A pleased grin spread over his face and he leaned back in his chair, stretching his arms, then clasping his hands behind his neck. He began to anticipate his nursery tea on the following afternoon with something like eagerness. Christina had been wary of him at first that morning, but after he began to play with her sons, she relaxed and became completely easy in his company, calling him Justin, smiling at him with that wide, warm smile of hers. Yes, and laughing like a girl again, and at one point even singing the slightly expurgated sea-chantey he'd taught her boys.

Leaning back in his chair, he lifted his legs to his desktop, crossing them at the ankles, and closed his eyes, picturing Christina as she had stood in the sunlight that morning. It was good to hear her laughter once more and to see a bright smile light up her face.

But the hesitancy in her manner he had noticed last night was there again. Her girlish vivaciousness had dimmed since he'd known her last, and there was an air of diffidence about her that had not been there when she was a girl, full of gig and high spirits, filled with all the confidence of youth. She was not quite so quick to speak or laugh as she had been and seemed to weigh her words more carefully. But in place of those girlish attributes was a new womanly maturity, a delicate femininity that attracted him as much as had her youthful charms.

Pensively, he realized that he would no longer be attracted to such a young girl as she had been. That was the problem with all the eligible misses his mother had pushed at him these last few years. They were too youthful. He was a man now and he wanted a woman of some maturity to share his life with.

Oh, but she was an enchanting creature, never mind the passage of years. There had always been a special glow about

Christina and she had glowed for him that morning. Until Lady Fordham had interrupted them, anyway.

He could not deny that he was in love with her. Was *still* in love with her, after all these years, and after the devastating hurt he had suffered.

Was it possible that his love would be enough? Would she accept him now that she was a widow, were he to offer again?

Dear God! Did such a sweet heaven await him after all?

He closed his eyes and sighed. It was too soon. He must not hope for too much. Perhaps nothing would come of their renewed acquaintance. Perhaps there was already another man in the picture, he reminded himself grimly.

Well, he would move cautiously. He would see how she behaved toward him at tea on the morrow. 'Til then, he would not allow himself to hope, to dream of the future. And perhaps he'd better purchase a pair of fireproof gloves before he ventured forth, he thought with self-deprecating humor, for he most certainly was going to put his hand into the fire once again.

"Well, Phil, you dark horse, looks like you have the inside track with Lizzy. Every time I see her, she's with you. Are we soon to be related?" Justin quizzed his friend as they stood near the door to his box at Drury Lane Theatre that evening. His mother had requested his escort to see the latest play everyone was talking about, a mocking pastiche of a Restoration comedy called *Lovers' Vows,* reputed to have been penned by a lady of delicate sensibilities who wished her identity to remain secret, and he had been glad to oblige. He had been surprised and pleased when he'd learned that Philip was to be MaryLiz's escort.

"No," Philip answered gloomily, his eyes on the back of MaryLiz's head where she sat chatting to one of the gentlemen who had dropped by the box to pay her their compliments during the interval. He and Justin had decided to stretch their legs after sitting through the first two scenes, and if they hadn't decided to vacate their seats voluntarily, they'd have been forced to do so because the box had been inundated with callers. "She sees me as a friend. A convenient sort of escort, when she cannot make up her mind which suitor to favor with her company."

Justin raised his brows. "Is Lizzy that much of a coquette?"

Philip frowned, stroking his square chin with strong fingers. "Oh, I would not say that. She's just a young girl, making her come-out. She is enjoying herself." He sighed. "It's just that she does not see *me* as one of her admirers."

Philip's words struck a chord with Justin. He was forcibly put in mind of Christina as she had been during her first Season. He put a friendly hand on Philip's shoulder. "A word of caution, Phil. Do not allow your heart to become too deeply involved. I love my sister, but I have no idea what sort of gentleman would find favor with her, or who will eventually win her hand. I would not like to see you hurt, as I—as I have seen some of my friends disappointed by hopeless *tendres.*"

Philip smiled crookedly "Well, I thank you for that sage advice, Grandfather, but I'm a grown man now, and I will just have to chance disappointment, should it come to that. Better to have loved and lost, and all that, you know."

The Duke of Carleton appeared at the door to the box. He greeted Justin and Philip absently, his eyes on MaryLiz. "Who do you think wrote this dashed play?" Carleton asked, by way of making conversation.

"Devil if I know," Justin answered. "Said to be a reclusive lady, an eccentric of some sort. But I wonder if someone is not just having us on."

"To me, makes no matter who wrote it. It's dashed entertaining," Philip said.

MaryLiz turned when she became aware of the duke's presence and smiled dazzlingly. Encouraged by such a welcome, Carleton hastened to her side, ousting another gentleman from the chair next to her.

Philip frowned and Justin gave him a sympathetic glance. "Women! They put us through hoops, do they not?" Justin commented lightly.

"Oh, I'm a good athlete. I will jump through as many hoops as are put in my path for as long as necessary. Perhaps I will prove the better jumper and can outlast the other contestants and win the prize." Philip grinned good-naturedly at Justin, not at all disheartened by such a prospect.

When Justin was ushered into the back parlor of the Henshaws' Jermyn Street townhouse the following afternoon, he was met by two boys hurling themselves at him and nearly knocking him off his pins. "Hello, Westbridge," shouted Stephen.

"You came, you came!" cried Sebastian. "Mama said we must not be too disappointed if you could not make it, after all. But you came!"

"Well, how could I stay away? I have been toiling away all day over a budget sheet, looking at numbers until my eyes are ready to cross, and I have worked up quite an appetite. You promised me a bang-up tea, did you not?"

The boys eagerly agreed that they had, explaining that they were to have a tasty variety of small meat paste sandwiches, fresh, hot scones thick with butter and jam, as well as plum cake, apricot tarts, and a special fruit jelly.

"Umm. Apricot tarts! My favorites. My mouth is watering already." Justin responded to this list of ambrosial treats with a boyish grin.

While he detached himself from the boys, who had been dancing round him, Christina came forward with such a bright, welcoming smile curving her mouth and lighting up her eyes that she looked like a girl again. He was dazzled.

"Just—I mean, Lord Fulbrooke, I was half expecting you to send your excuses," Christina said, giving him her hand in greeting.

He saw the light of gladness that lit her eyes as he took her small, cold hand and held it tightly, warming it with his own. "Not come to tea? I must confess, I have been looking forward to it all day. I was even spurred on to finish my report and deliver it to the Chancellor's office before I came so that my superior could not claim I was slacking off." He flashed a grin at her and was pleased to see that she blushed and laughed cheerfully at his light remark.

She drew him into the comfortably furnished room and gestured for him to seat himself on the gold-and-brown-striped scrolled-end sofa. He was pleased to see there was no sign of her sister-in-law, Susan Henshaw, or any other members of the household. It was to be a private tea, then. Good, he thought allowing himself to relax. He caught Christina's eye and smiled fully at her, allowing the last of the defenses he had built up against her to slip away.

He admired the jonquil-colored gown she was wearing for the way it emphasized the glow in her hazel eyes and softly enhanced her womanly curves. Her dark hair looked lovely, too, almost girlish. It was arranged in a looser style today, so that a few dusky curls escaped the tight confines of the knot she had arranged on her head and softly caressed her cheek and neck.

Had she brightened her appearance for his sake? he wondered, with a stab of hope.

"Try this, Westbridge," Stephen advised, piling the plate Justin balanced on his knee high with plum cake. "It is delicious."

"And this. And this." Sebastian followed his brother and slipped two sticky tarts and a handful of rather mashed sandwiches onto Justin's overflowing plate. "Do you like jelly? It's my favorite," the boy declared, handing Justin a bowl of it.

Justin was not particularly fond of jelly, but he would not disappoint the eager boys by letting them know that he found it not to his taste. He ate everything on his plate with a good grace and some genuine enjoyment, and accepted three cups of tea from Christina with which to wash it all down. The boys plied him with questions as well as food, and he was occupied between bites with telling them all about his work and about the horses he owned. He enjoyed their bright faces and eager, interested questions, but wished he might have a little time to chat to their mother as well.

From her post behind the china teapot, Christina watched Justin laughing with her boys while they pressed him to try the sticky cakes and all manner of hearty treats and dainty morsels, all their favorite tea-time refreshments, that had been served up.

A smile trembled on her mouth. Their meeting at the Saltrams' ball and in the park had been accidental. He had been unable to avoid speaking to her. But now he had accepted the invitation to tea with her and her children and seemed perfectly happy to be there. He did not mean to shun her company, after all, as she had feared. Was it possible that he would forgive her after all these years? Did she dare allow herself to hope?

She knew she had hurt him badly all those years ago, during her come-out season. What he could not know was that she had hurt herself, too, allowing herself to fall all the way in love with him when all the while she had known she was promised to Geoffrey.

Her mother had wanted her to have some experience of London before she retired to the country to become a wife and mother. So Mrs. Granford had convinced her husband and Sir Geoffrey that Christina should have a Season before the engagement was announced. Geoffrey had had no use for London and had not accompanied her, judging her parents were chaperon enough.

Oh, but London had been a glorious fairy-tale place to a country-bred girl, filled with fashionable people and beautiful clothes and wonderful parties. She was only just eighteen, and so she had allowed herself to forget that she was engaged.

She had been so enjoying herself, delighting in all the male attention lavished on her, that she had laughed and danced and flirted and allowed several men to pay court to her. But all the while it had been a game, an exciting game. She had not seriously encouraged any of them.

When young Justin Westbridge had joined her court, she treated him with friendly warmth, as she did the others she liked. But there was something different about the intensity of Justin's admiration for her, something different about *him,* and she had responded to it.

He had been so young, so vulnerable. And so very attractive. She had not been able to bear seeing him unhappy, and he was unhappy each time she had turned down his escort, or even a dance. Every time she had gone off on the arm of another man, she had seen his expressive eyes cloud over with disappointment and had felt a pain about her own heart at wounding him.

And then the night had come when Justin had kissed her. At the faint brush of his lips against hers, she had shut her eyes and seen a starburst of color behind her tightly closed lids. Her whole body had quivered, and it had seemed as though she could not catch her breath. She had wanted more than that light touch and had shamelessly leaned into his body and reached up her arms round his neck so that she could press herself against him. So that she could hold him. Her own passionate response to their kiss had surprised and frightened her.

She had wanted him, wanted him in every way that a woman could want a man. She had wanted his body, his company, his teasing laughter, his life united to hers. She had wanted to be able to look into those melting eyes of his and to see his full, firm lips parted in the special smile he frequently directed her way, every day for the rest of her life.

She had united her soul to his for all eternity during those few timeless, earth-shattering minutes.

Then she knew—knew for certain—what she had suspected for weeks. She was in love with him. So wildly, deeply in love, she wanted to break off the longstanding engagement with Geoffrey and be with Justin.

She had kept to the house for days after their kiss, trying to find the courage to tell her parents that she could not marry Geoffrey, but she saw no way to do it that would not bring dishonor to her and her loving family and to kind-hearted Geoffrey.

From the depths of her young soul she had somehow summoned up the courage to take the honorable course. And so she had told Justin she was engaged . . . and had seen the heartbreak in his eyes and heard the anguish in his voice. She had suffered with him. It had been all she could do not to throw her arms around his neck and beg him to elope with her that very afternoon.

But she had not done that. No. She had acted honorably—for the best, she thought.

Had it been for the best? She had broken Justin's heart—and her own. She had grieved for him for years afterward, crying bitterly each year on the anniversary of their kiss. She had gone on with life as best she could, trying to be a dutiful wife. Geoffrey had been a pleasant, attentive companion, and a good father, but she had only ever been able to feel affection for him, not love.

And now, here she was in London again. And here was Justin, seated not two feet away, having tea with her sons, making them laugh, setting her pulses racing just by sitting there looking as he did.

If he had been irresistibly attractive as a boy, he was ten times more handsome, now that he was grown into a man. With his trim, muscular frame, his thick, overlong honey-colored hair grazing his collar, and his wonderful eyes full of laughter again, he was . . . devastating.

And when he smiled at her, as he had been doing all afternoon, with his full lips quirking up on one side and curving into that absolutely heartstopping smile of his, she was left feeling as though her stomach had lurched up into her throat, then plummeted to her shoes.

And, oh, but she couldn't help but hope. Hope that there would be a second chance for them.

"A penny for them," Justin said, setting down his teacup and smiling again at Christina. He wanted to take her hand where it rested in her lap and hold it warmly in his clasp, but he restrained himself. He must not touch her, he told himself, or he would indeed be lost.

She shook her head. "They are not worth it. I have only been woolgathering."

"Gammon! You have been lost in thought for the past half hour. Do not tell me there was not something very interesting going on in there," he teased, leaning forward to tap her forehead lightly, then, unable to resist, running the back of one finger gently down her soft cheek.

Christina felt her cheeks heat with color. His gesture was intimate and the fire she saw kindling at the back of his eyes awakened all her senses. She was overcome with the powerful urge to lean her face into his hand and kiss his wrist just where his shirt cuff exposed the golden hairs of his arm. She bit her lip instead, and dropped her eyes from his.

When she looked up, he was still leaning toward her and gazing at her with a warm light in his eyes. She swallowed against the construction in her throat. Desperate for something to say, she asked awkwardly, "I was wondering if you were going to the Hammonds' assembly tomorrow night," then gulped at her own daring.

Justin raised his brows in mock astonishment, smiling a little at her confusion. "The Hammonds'? How did you guess? Have you become a mind reader, Christina? That is indeed the very party I plan to attend." His eyes twinkled at her.

Christina's cheeks suffused with color again, to his delight. He felt light-hearted and almost light-headed at this new playful flirtation they had embarked on.

She laughed. "Oh, you are funning me, Justin. You were not going there at all, were you?" She gave him a mock serious frown and shook her head at him, loosening some of the curls from her topknot.

" 'S'truth, madam, I was." He raised his hand palm up. "And if you would honor me with your hand for the first waltz, I will make sure that I do not forget. Lamentably, at my age, you know, these things are liable to slip one's memory."

"At one-and-thirty?" she scoffed, pleasing Justin inordinately by naming his exact age. "Surely, Lord Fulbrooke, a man of your accomplishments, with your estate to run and your exacting work in the Treasury to perform—I doubt not your memory is prodigiously good. Better than mine, I daresay."

The flirtatious smile vanished from Justin's face and he gave her a look of naked longing. Was her memory short and selective? he wondered. Did she not recall the days and weeks when they had known each other ten years ago as perfectly as he did? Did not the time they had shared during their first season, every look, every touch of the hand, stand as crystal-clear in her memory as it did in his?

Had she forgotten the passionate kiss they'd shared? The kiss that for him had been the most earth-shattering moment of his life? Had she put from her mind his ardent proposal, when he had poured out all the love and longing in his soul, only to be rejected?

"Christina . . ." he whispered in a strangled voice, reaching out to take her hand, wanting to ask her if she had forgotten him, had forgotten their time together that had meant so much to him, but Stephen and Sebastian interrupted, demanding their attention, asking them to settle a squabble as to who could have the last scone.

His chance to explore more serious topics with Christina vanished. Their private conversation was at an end.

After he thanked the boys for the tea and prepared to take his leave, he was encouraged to see that Christina intended to accompany him to the door. He longed for a few more words with her in private.

"Lord Fulbrooke, it was so good of you to come to humor my boys," she said formally, after he had collected his hat and cape. Her hazel eyes glowed up at him, filled with gratitude.

"It was my pleasure. They are a lively, entertaining pair."

"But I do thank you. If there were some way to repay you for yesterday . . ." her voice trailed off.

He smiled down enigmatically into her wide eyes that were fixed on his. "First, call me 'Justin,' as you were always used to do, Christina. And the waltz tomorrow night at the Hammonds' . . . for a start," he replied in a low, vibrant voice.

"But I do not waltz, Justin."

"Not waltz! How can that be?"

"I left London before the dance was approved and I—I never learned in the country."

"Then I shall teach you."

"Will you?" she asked, bemused, meeting the heated gaze that turned his eyes to liquid green fire, drawn into that smoldering heat almost against her will.

They continued to gaze at one another, neither one looking away. The very air shimmered between them, simmering like an invisible heat wave over banked fires.

Wanting to touch her, Justin stepped closer and reached for her hand, raising it unresisting to his lips. Allowing his mouth to linger on her bare fingers, he made sure his eyes never left hers, watching her response over the tops of her fingers. 'Til tomorrow night at the Hammonds', then," he murmured in a husky voice, still holding to her hand, stroking the delicate skin with the pad of his thumb.

"Yes," she answered breathlessly. "Until tomorrow night."

"Well, will you look at that, Justin!" MaryLiz grabbed her brother's arm, causing him to jerk on the reins of his curricle.

"Watch what you are about, will you, Lizzy? You are like

to spook the horses in all this traffic, if you jostle my arm that way," Justin rebuked.

He was driving his sister in the park the following afternoon during the fashionable hour because the gentleman who had begged for the favor of driving MaryLiz had cried off at the last minute. It seemed he had met with some unspecified, quite unfortunate accident in Bond Street that morning.

Justin's lips had twitched when he'd heard the story, for he knew that the particular gentleman in question had been engaged in a bout of fisticuffs at a certain boxing salon that very morning, namely Gentleman Jackson's Rooms, that had left him with a very bruised cheek and swollen eye. Unaware of the cause of her swain's "accident," MaryLiz had sent for Justin posthaste, determined not to miss the fashionable jaunt, even if it meant driving with a mere brother.

Steadying his team of grays first, Justin obediently turned his eyes in the direction his sister indicated.

"Look! Lady Elliott, of all people, seems to have stolen my most exalted beau. See! There she is driving with Carleton. Who would have thought the duke would have been taken with a middle-aged widow with two children!"

"Dear God!" Justin exclaimed in a low voice, his lips white. He felt a buzzing in his ears and all the blood seemed to drain from his head in a rush. He swayed forward. Taking slow and steadying breaths through his nostrils, and calling on hidden resources he didn't know he possessed, he managed to maintain his grip on the reins and hold his team in check.

MaryLiz's eyes remained on the other couple and she did not notice the sudden pallor of her brother's face. "I waved, but they are not looking our way. Just look at them," she continued her observations. "She is resting her hand on his arm and whispering to him. Carleton is smiling at her with great familiarity! Humph! I do believe they must be taken with one another. Heigh ho, so much for my chances of becoming a duchess!"

The first emotion that attacked him, surprisingly, was anger. Yes, he felt a red-hot **anger** that he had allowed **himself** to be duped again. He gave a crack of bitter laughter, startling MaryLiz so that her head whipped round toward him. "Justin? What is it?"

"Nothing, Lizzy. Nothing at all," he said through clenched teeth. All his old hurt, mistrust, and disillusion resurfaced. He swallowed against the ache in his throat. All his hopes that had risen so high after the intimate family tea they had shared the previous afternoon were cruelly dashed down, evaporating like so much dew in the morning sun.

Did she think to play with him in such a calculating way? he wondered furiously, deliberately feeding his anger to keep the hurt at bay. She would find out her mistake. He was no longer a boy to put up with such tricks. He was a man now, and his man's anger prompted him to punish Christina for the way she had deceived him. He wished to hurt her the way she had hurt him.

At least two hundred candles burned in the Adam-style ballroom of Sir Henry and Lady Hammond that evening, casting flickering light on the refined plasterwork of classical motifs that decorated the ceiling, chimneypieces, and doorcases. It was the first *ton* party the Hammonds had ever given, and no expense had been spared. Everything was done on a lavish scale.

One of the guests waggishly exclaimed that he hoped the servants were standing by with buckets of water lest something, or some*one,* catch fire. Another guest looking around at such an extravagance of beeswax quoted appreciatively, " 'Nothing succeeds like excess.' " Everyone in the vicinity tittered.

Justin heard the comments but did not join in the general laughter. He stood apart, silently waiting for Christina's arrival. He had spared no effort in dressing for the occasion. His hair had been brushed until it shone like burnished gold. He had allowed his valet to garb him in a dark green evening jacket with gilt buttons, black pantaloons, and dazzling white shirt covered by a white silk waistcoat embroidered with gold, silver, and green leaves. Silk stockings covered his well-formed calves and black kid evening slippers sporting small gold buckles on his feet completed his modish ensemble. However, his elegant evening attire was at odds with the scowl on his face.

"By Jove, Justin! Is that cravat tied in the mathematical?" Sir Philip Baines teased his friend as he came up to greet him. Receiving an abstracted nod, Philip continued, "I must say, I have rarely seen you so magnificently rigged out, my friend. Are you finally on the hunt for that elusive bride?"

On receiving nothing but a grunt in reply, Philip asked, "Whatever is the matter, Justin? You look like an unleashed tiger."

"Oh? And how is that?" Justin parried, almost snarling.

"Ferocious," Philip answered with an exaggerated shudder. "I pray you, go and dunk your head in a bucket of water to cool your temper. I fear if I stand next to you much longer, I shall be burned—or bitten."

Justin did not answer, but continued his vigilant stare at the door.

"On the hunt, indeed," Philip murmured, seeing the veiled purpose in his friend's eyes. He was trying to tease Justin out of his bad mood, but his good-humored banter seemed to be having little effect. He was afraid Justin had not even heard him, for his eyes were trained on the door with unwavering intensity.

"Who are you waiting for?" he dared to ask. "Your dinner?"

"Waiting for? No one," Justin responded curtly.

"No one? I pity poor 'no one' when he, or perhaps *she*, arrives. The way you look, the hapless person might well provide the main course for your next meal . . . perhaps I had best see to your sister and mother's comfort, for it is evident you have other things on your mind tonight."

"What? Mother and Lizzy? Oh yes, look after them for me, Phil," Justin said abstractedly, then walked away to disappear out into the hallway that gave onto the gracefully curving front staircase.

Philip looked after him, shaking his head with worry. Deciding it was none of his affair, he went off to seek MaryLiz and Lady Fulbrooke.

"You are looking *très elegant ce soir, mon cher,*" Olivia, Lady Fordham, greeted Justin in French when she spied him coming through the ballroom doors. Openly admiring the way his exquisitely cut evening jacket hugged his wide shoulders and the way his form-fitting silk pantaloons caressed his lean, masculine thighs, she boldly stepped up and linked arms with him.

"Lady Fordham," Justin replied with a distant look. He didn't need the distraction of her chattering tongue at this moment. Intending to shake her off with a cool set-down, he glanced into the vestibule below and saw Christina just mounting the stairs with her companions, presumably the Henshaws. She was dressed in a lustrous ivory silk gown and carried a multicolored shawl shot through with gold threads over her elbows. She wore the pale yellow-edged rosebuds he had sent her threaded through her glossy dark curls.

As though Christina felt his eyes on her, she looked up. Her face brightened into a dazzling smile and she raised her hand to wave to him. He did not return her greeting. She dropped her hand and her smile faded to a puzzled look when she saw the frown on his face and the woman on his arm.

Good, Justin thought grimly, when he saw the dismay on her face as her smile faded. Let her know what it feels like to see me with another woman, the way I saw her with another man this afternoon.

Unable to help himself, he continued to stare down at her coldly, while Olivia chattered away at his side, clinging possessively to his arm. He watched as Christina stood motionless at the bottom of the stairs, her gloved hand gripping the railing. She was looking up at him as though she were lost. His hand tightened into a fist.

Eventually Christina's companions urged her on up the stairs. Justin turned away and strolled back into the ballroom with Lady Fordham, his thoughts and his heart frozen.

The music was playing and couples were forming into groups for a country dance. "Shall we join them, Justin?" Olivia asked.

"As you wish," he said, leading her onto the floor with cool courtesy.

Despite the movements of the dance and Lady Fordham's attempts to flirt with him when speech was possible, he kept his eye on Christina when she entered the room, aware of her whereabouts every moment. He thought she glanced at him out of the corner of her eye at one point, but he was not at all sure.

"Will you think me overbold, if I ask why you have not called on me lately, Justin?" Olivia inquired, when the dance had ended and she and Justin had strolled to the side of the room.

"You are always surrounded by admirers, my lady. With your undoubted popularity, I feel sure you cannot remark the lack of my poor presence in your drawing room. I cannot compete with all your other swains." Answering his companion in a polite but distant manner, Justin deliberately walked toward Christina with Lady Fordham still clinging to his arm. Seeing the Duke of Carleton approach Christina, he tightened his lips, his stomach clenching with anger.

Olivia was not satisfied with his off-putting answer, despite the compliment on her popularity. Redoubling her efforts to reignite the brief interest he had shown some months previously, she put her hand on his arm and nodded toward the musicians, who had begun to tune their instruments for a waltz. "Justin, shall we be daring and dance again?"

"You must excuse me. I have already solicited another lady's hand for this dance." With that, he bowed curtly and walked away from Lady Fordham, never seeing the ugly pout of displeasure his response provoked.

"Our dance, I believe, Lady Elliott," Justin drawled, approaching Christina and extending his arm just as the Duke of Carleton placed her hand on his own sleeve.

Justin's free hand clenched into a fist. It was all he could do to maintain a polite stance when he wanted to snatch Christina away from the duke and snarl at the man that he was to keep away from her in future.

"Oh, Lord Fulbrooke," Christina replied in confusion, meeting the steely look in Justin's eyes with something like fear. "I—I did not think you would care to claim—that is, you must excuse me, Bertram," she said in a stronger tone. "I have promised this dance to Lord Fulbrooke."

"Well, if that's the case, Tina, my dear, I shall see you later, then," the duke said, relinquishing her to Justin with a pleasant smile and turning to look about him for another partner.

With a delicate blush tinging her cheeks, Christina put her hand on Justin's sleeve and looked up at him with wary eyes and raised chin. He did not relieve her anxiety, but led her into the dance without a word.

"Oh, Justin, please!" she pleaded. "Please! I—I do not know what to do—and you are so strange tonight."

Recollecting that she had told him she had never danced the waltz before, he unbent slightly. With an effort, he instructed, "Put your hand in mine, so, and your arm on my shoulder." She did as he'd directed. "Yes, that is right. I will guide you. Have no fear. You are naturally graceful. Just respond to the pressure of my arm on your waist and you shall master it."

Doing as he said, she bit her lip and allowed him to guide her. "Oh, Justin, please tell me what is the matter," she implored, looking up at him after they had done one complete

circle of the room and she had caught the rhythm of the dance
and her breath somewhat.

"I do not know what you mean," he answered perversely.
"You are doing well. Just continue to follow my lead." Her
eyes turned away from him and he heard her sigh audibly.

Her hand trembled in his and he clamped down on the
almost irresistible urge to comfort her. He swallowed against
the tightness in his throat.

Torture. It was almost torture to hold her like this in his
arms. He had thought this dance would be pure heaven, a
prelude to his second proposal of marriage. But instead, it
was proving to be a purgatory. He wanted to punish her, to
make her suffer for the agony she had caused him that afternoon. But if she was suffering, so was he.

She stumbled and he pulled her against him with strong
arms to prevent her from falling. He caught the scent of the
roses in her hair and his heart turned over. A glance showed
him they were near the doors. "Come with me," he commanded, dancing her through the doors and out into a darkened vestibule. He stopped dancing and pulled her along to
a small, unoccupied room that gave off the vestibule.

"Justin, where are we going?"

"We must talk." Dragging her inside the room that was lit
sparingly in contrast to the dazzling ballroom, he shut the
door, then swung her around to face him.

She leaned back as far as she could against the door, her
hands at her side pressing against the raised wooden panels.
He was hovering over her, near enough to touch her. But they
were not touching. She licked dry lips. "We should not be
here."

He laughed mirthlessly. "It is far too late for such protestations."

Reaching forward, he gripped her shoulders. Without another word, he pulled her roughly into his arms and brought
his mouth down to hers fiercely.

He wanted to punish her with his kiss. But he was lost

before he even began to exact his revenge. Lost in the desire to swamp her senses as she was doing his. He wanted to taste all the secrets of her body, all the secrets of her soul. He wanted to possess her with his kiss, marking her as his for all eternity.

Her hands came up between them and she pushed against him. Pinned against his chest with the door at her back, she struggled helplessly against his strength.

The scent of roses was strong in his nostrils.

Feeling her fright, he groaned. He did not want to hurt Christina. He loved her. He *loved* her. Slowing his breathing and controlling his passion with an effort, he loosened his grip on her shoulders and let his hands run down her arms to settle around her waist. His eyes tightly closed, he gathered her to him, gentling her with his hands, then wrapped her into himself, settling her light weight against his strength.

His lips softened over hers, and when he felt her hands move from where they had been, pushing against his chest to slide up his shoulders and around his neck to feather in his hair, he deepened the kiss.

Ah, Christina, I love you, you see, he wanted to tell her—he tried to tell her with all the expertise at his command.

"Ah, Christina!"

He worshipped her with his lips, his mouth, his hands, his body as he kissed her eyelids, her soft cheek, her chin, the shell of her ear, her neck. Missing the mingling of their breaths, he moved back up to her lips, whispering little kisses over her mouth from one side to the other, before the pressure of her hand behind his neck forced his mouth to join with hers once again.

"Justin, oh, Justin," she murmured. "It has been so long."

It *had* been so long. Harsh reality returned.

Yes, she had condemned him to ten long years of loneliness and heartache. Breathing hard, he thrust her away from him, saying in a low, shaking voice, "How could you, Christina? How could you?"

Thoroughly frightened by his manner, the cold fury in his voice and the tight rein he seemed to be exercising over his temper, Christina gripped his arm tightly. "How could I *what*, Justin?" she asked, her lips trembling. "I do not understand why you are acting this way. First, you are cold to me, then you bring me in here and k-kiss me, and then you accuse me of I know not what. Why are you so angry with me?"

He gazed at her with a fierce light in his eyes, his anger and his desire for her unquenched. Her lips were swollen, the delicate skin around her lips red where he had grazed her with his mouth, marking her with the fierceness of his kiss. He clenched his hands at his sides to prevent himself from reaching out to her again.

"Angry at you? Why should I be angry at you? Just because you have played me for a fool a second time? It is entirely my own fault. I should have learned after the first," he grated in a whisper. His own voice was too unsteady to allow him to speak aloud.

"Played you for a fool? What on earth are you talking about?" There was genuine puzzlement in her tone. She stepped nearer and looked up into his shadowed face, trying to read what was behind his eyes.

He could not bear to look down into those wide, warm hazel eyes and see puzzlement and hurt there. He could not bear to be this close to her and not hold her. He turned and put a shaking hand on the doorhandle.

"Please, please do not turn away from me, Justin. No! Do not leave." She clung to his arm with both hands to prevent him from stalking off. "Let me know why you are so upset, my dear. Because, I assure you, you have no reason to be."

"Do not lie to me, Christina!" he answered, his voice choked with emotion. "I saw you driving in the park this afternoon, you know. You are angling for the duke, are you not? After you allowed me to think there might be a chance for me after all these years? You must think me the greatest fool in Christendom!"

"The duke? Do you mean Bertram?" He heard genuine surprise in her voice. "But there was no harm in that! Bertie is an old friend."

"Devil take it, woman, do not play with me!"

She shook his arm lightly. "Oh, Justin! Is that what this is all about?" Taking a deep breath, she explained, "My dear, I was driving with Bertie because he is Geoffrey's cousin and the boys' trustee. Surely you knew that." She laughed a little. "It was a simple courtesy drive. He is looking about him for a bride this year and was confiding to me the difficulties he is having in settling on anyone . . . You thought he was my suitor? Oh, dear, I suppose I should be flattered by this storm of jealousy, but it is so absurd. Good heavens, I must be a year or two Bertie's senior. He has no interest in me, nor I in him."

"Is this the truth? Please, Christina, do not lie to me. I could not stand it." Justin's voice shook with the power of the emotions roiling through his breast.

"Justin . . . do you not *know?* Do you not feel what I feel?" She gave him another little shake, impatient with his male density. "I love you to distraction. And I always have. Do you not *know* that, my dearest?"

His hand covered hers tightly where it clung to his sleeve and his eyes bore down into hers. "Truly, Christina? *Please.* Do you speak truly?"

She nodded, meeting his intense gaze unwaveringly. "Oh, Justin, I felt I would die when I had to leave you to marry Geoffrey. How could I not, when what had grown between us was something beyond what I had ever imagined love could be . . . something purely magical. But you see, my parents had arranged the engagement to Geoffrey when I was only sixteen. He was my father's distant cousin, and a kind, steady man. I—I came to London because my mother insisted I have a Season so that I could acquire some *ton* bronze before I was married. The engagement was known at home, but my parents saw no particular reason to announce it in London. I was to be here for such a short while. They and I had no thought of attracting suitors for my hand."

Her eyes shimmering with tears, she continued in a whisper, "Then when I met you and fell in love with you it was so totally unexpected that I did not know what to do. I—I did not mean to lead you on."

Cupping her face with his hands, he let his thumbs gently wipe away the tears that trickled down her cheeks. "Shh. I love you." Bending his head, he whispered little kisses along her trembling lips.

She pulled back slightly. "Oh, forgive me, my love! Please! I was so confused. I never meant to hurt you. I did not know what to do for the best. I should have been braver. For you. But I was afraid to risk the dishonor that might have befallen my family and Geoffrey if I had broken my betrothal."

He put a finger to her lips. "Hush, my darling. You were a brave girl for one so young. Braver than I ever knew." He lifted her hand to kiss it, then laced his fingers tightly with hers.

"I was a foolish girl! Oh, Justin, I have loved you each day since I met you! Loved you and longed for you. Even knowing you were lost to me forever, I feared to read of your marriage. Feared the hurt of it would destroy what was left of my heart." She gave a watery sniff. "Only my children sustained me. I thank the dear Lord each day for Stephen and Sebastian. You . . . you do not mind about them?"

"Mind? I thank God for your boys, too! They led me back to you. Without them, I do not think we would be here together tonight."

Resting her hands against his chest, she looked up into his eyes and admitted, "When I came to London, I wanted most desperately to see you again, but I feared that you would not want to see me. I was sure you must hate me and could never forgive me."

Stopping her mouth with a brief kiss, Justin leaned his forehead against hers and closed his eyes. "Christina, my love, I will forgive you—on one condition."

"Truly, you will forgive me? Oh, Justin!" she breathed, moving her head back so that she could look up into his eyes. The love she saw shining out at her convinced her. "What is the condition?"

"That you will marry me as soon as I can procure a special license. I have waited ten lonely years already, and I do not propose to wait a day longer than necessary now." A rumble of laughter bubbled up in his throat at the glowing look of wonder that leapt into her eyes at his words.

"Justin! Oh, my dear, of course I will marry you! As soon as you can contrive it . . . can you really, really find it in your heart to forgive me? Can you still love me after all this time? Are you to exact no punishment for the suffering I caused you?"

"Kiss me, Christina, and show me how much you love me, and then you will see what kind of punishment I have in store for you." He was smiling with his heart in his eyes.

He watched her hesitate as he made no move toward her. He was waiting for her to touch him first, waiting with thundering heart and trembling hands, trembling with the effort it took not to reach for her. But he wanted her to come to him, to give herself to him now and affirm her love.

After a few tense moments, Christina moved forward. Never taking her eyes from his, she reached up her hands to clasp his neck.

When she leaned across the last few inches separating them and pressed her lips lightly to his, Justin closed his eyes and felt a tremor shake him. This was the taste of love. He felt eternity in the touch of their two mouths.

He allowed her to embrace him, to press her breasts to his chest and tighten her arms about his neck before he reached for her. Finally, his hands tightened on her waist, then he pulled her against him, sending the blood rushing through his veins and desire pulsing through his body.

As she increased the pressure of her lips against his and opened her mouth over his, he felt an intense longing shake his soul. When at last he allowed his tongue to invade her mouth to tangle with hers, to allow his soul to join with hers, he could no more stop himself from entrusting his heart into her keeping for all time than he could stop breathing.

"Oh, Justin," she whispered huskily, "I shall love you for all eternity."

"And I you, my darling. And I you."

About the Author

Meg-Lynn Roberts lives with her family in Connecticut. Her newest Zebra regency romance, LORD DIABLO'S DEMISE, will be published in June 1996. Meg-Lynn loves hearing from her readers and you may write to her c/o Zebra Books. Please include a self-addressed stamped envelope if you wish a response.

Lady Constance Wins

Marcy Stewart

Although her heart pounded in outrage, Lady Constance Cowald exited the ballroom displaying unruffled goodwill. No sign of irritation creased her brow as she nodded past lavishly dressed ladies and gentlemen in the earl's grand marbled hall; nary a glimmer of anxiety flashed in her eyes as she requested the butler to convey her gratitude for a lovely evening to her host.

Her host, of course, was far too busy to accept her pleasantries himself. As long as the orchestra continued, Lord Vincent Oakwood appeared unable to cease waltzing with Anne Wells or Marguerite Devereaux or any of the other debutantes with whom he'd amused himself all evening. Constance had no need to step back a few paces to see him at it; his image had seared itself into her brain: Vincent's bored eyes brightening as he twirled one girl after another around the ballroom; his rare smiles thrilling his partners; his discriminating charm flowing freely.

Constance held her head a little higher, walked regally down the red-carpeted steps of the earl's townhouse, and entered her coach, wherein her family awaited. She could not, however, meet her cousins' eyes. When the carriage jerked forward, she wished the wheels rattling over the cobblestones might deaden her thoughts:

I should never have subjected myself and my cousins to this humiliation again. Better to stay in the country and rot.

In the darkness of the carriage—Beulah Cowald had requested the lamps remain unlit so she could doze—a pair of faded eyes opened and focused upon Constance.

"He could have asked you for *one* dance, at least," said the wrinkled mouth that accompanied the eyes. "They are calling you *Lady Constant,* you know."

"Hush, Beulah," exclaimed Winifred Pemberton, the woman at her side, whose black bonnet, black dress, and dark eyes almost caused her to be invisible in the shadows. "Have you no heart?"

"No, she don't," trumpeted Hermine Cowald, the stout lady sitting beside Constance. "Never did have, and too late to get one now."

"You are no sister of mine," Beulah hissed.

"That has always been *my* wish," retorted Hermine.

"Girls," chided Winifred. "Don't spat, now. It is Constant—oh, dear!—Constance whom we must cheer. And sweet child," she added, leaning forward to pat the young lady's knee, *"do not* let that skirt-chaser put you in the dismals. He's not worth one of your eyelashes. Let him waltz all he wants with those empty-brained beauties. Let him laugh at their silly patter, let him fall prey to their charms and fortunes. Let him—let him wed one of them and let *her* get fat and lazy breeding his brats, while you live your life independently and happily, pursuing your own dreams as *we* have all these years. There are"—here the elderly woman's voice faltered—"there are far worse fates than being alone, and I could name several were I not so tired."

"Very cheering, Winifred," remarked Hermine dryly. " 'Twill surprise me if Connie don't throw herself into the Thames this very night."

"No, no," Constance said, knowing her elderly cousin meant well. Despite her fondness for them all, it did sometimes seem unfair that the three surviving members of her father's family had traveled to his funeral several years ago and never departed. The three sisters were the daughters of his brother, who had served as earl before Constance's father inherited the title. The threesome felt they must chaperon her to every function, and their eccentric personalities and proclivity for wearing mourning caused many a whisper among the *ton* and more than one allusion to Macbeth's witches and bubbling caldrons.

But like all trouble in families, there was nothing to be done about it. Sighing, Constance turned her face toward the window. She felt hot. The scent of her cousins' ratafia-flavored breaths was making her dizzy. Perhaps they would not object too much if she opened the window.

"The night air will poison us!" Beulah squawked, when the glass was lowered.

"Let the child do as she pleases, for once," Hermine said. "It's enough she has to survive Vinnie's treacheries without having to please three old crones."

"You may be an old crone, but I am not," Winifred declared. "I'm a good deal younger than you both, I must remind."

"What's a year or two among so many?" Hermine queried. "Once again, Constance, I apologize that our family's so long-lived."

"Yes," Winifred added. "If your father hadn't waited so long to marry, we would all be your young cousins."

"Idiot," Hermine huffed into her double chin. "We wouldn't be young; Constance would be old."

"He doesn't like being called Vinnie," Constance broke in, harking back to an earlier conversational thread as she often had to do with her relatives. "And I don't suppose it's fair to say he was *treacherous* this evening. After all, he has not made a formal offer."

"No, but everyone knows he will," Winifred encouraged.

"But if he don't, he wouldn't be the first to dash a young girl's hopes," said Beulah with her usual dour version of comfort. "Just because your father and his were such famous friends don't mean Lord Vincent has to do what they wished when they were alive, earldoms or no. Wealth don't mean what it used to, not to the young."

Constance squirmed uncomfortably. Everyone in Society knew of the pledge, half in jest and half in earnest, between

her sire and Vincent's: that one day the two children would
unite their families and fortunes. Her plight had become a
never-ending source of amusement, and wagers, in Society.
The humiliation pained her like a festering wound.

Constance smoothed a wrinkle from her gown. Silver lamé,
it was; she'd spent a small fortune on it and half a day at her
toilette, and all for naught. Having experienced one hopeful
Season and now enduring a second, more grim one, she was
beginning to believe that no wiles or entrapments known to
the feminine tradition could bestir the young earl to declare
himself.

"With you in town, Beulah, London has no need of funereal
bells," Hermine said. She patted Constance's hand. "I do think
it's time that our girl set her sights on another, though. Vinnie's
played fast and loose with her long enough."

Winifred stirred. "You're forgetting something, aren't you,
Hermine?" When her older sister remained silent, she added
loftily, "But of course, you've never known what it is to love."

"Neither have you," Beulah snapped. "Pemberton was an
old bag of wind. 'Twas fortunate marrying you sucked the
last breath from him before he bored us all into our graves.'

While Winifred protested, Hermine inquired loudly, "You
don't love Vinnie, do you, girl?"

The cousins fell silent while Constance gathered her
thoughts. She had asked herself that question many times and
still did not know the answer. Finally, she said, "We haven'
spent much time together; only family holidays. He is well-
looking and can be a good companion . . ."

"You need to see other fellows," Hermine said. "Give you
someone to compare him with."

"But that's impossible," Constance said. "No one ap
proaches me except . . ."

"The dregs," finished Beulah, nodding glumly. "I've seen
'em. Blah!"

"The good ones are afraid," Winifred said. "The earl's

friends know he'd shoot their eyes out did they pursue Constance."

"Yes, 'tis unfortunate Vinnie's accounted one of the best shots in town," mused Hermine. "Though I must say I've always admired a man who can aim a pistol."

Constance heaved a great breath. "But it leaves me . . ."

"Twisting in the wind," Hermine confirmed. She thought for a moment. "Why won't one of those puffed-up stuffies make a declaration for our girl? They want to, you can see it in their eyes. And why not? She's a beauty, ain't she?" Hermine paused while her sisters agreed, making Constance smile and shake her head. "But none of them have one ounce of courage. If Vinnie had competition, he could be made to toe. the mark, I'm certain—"

Hermine stopped as Constance urgently waved her into quiet.

"Did you hear that?" whispered the younger lady.

An attentive silence filled the carriage. Constance leaned toward the window, hearing again the sounds of thumps, muffled groans, and boots scuffing along pavement. As she peered outward, she saw only shopfronts illuminated by streetlamps. And then, in the alley between two large buildings, sinister shadows took form and became three men overpowering a fourth.

"There!" she cried.

Hermine jerked Constance aside, leaned heavily across her, and jutted her own head out the window. Immediately she straightened and pounded her walking stick on the ceiling of their carriage.

"Stop, Eanes!" Hermine shouted. "Footpads up to no good!"

"Footpads!" screamed Beulah. "Why are we stopping, then?"

Constance had only a second to wonder the same thing when Hermine pulled a pistol from one of her voluminous pockets and pointed it from the window. In her deepest voice she called, "Stop, or I'll shoot!"

The three ruffians froze. Suspended between the rough hold of two of them, their victim slumped to his knees. Outside the carriage, Eanes could be heard muttering curses. Inside, Constance held her breath; Winifred whispered prayers; and Beulah smacked Hermine's thigh with her fist.

The moment extended, expanded, became eternity.

"I mean what I say!" Hermine blustered, her pistol shaking a little. "Run or die!"

When the criminals still did not move, Constance closed her eyes momentarily. Surely her bays could outrun three men on foot, but what if the villains had pistols as well?

The two holding the man exchanged glances. Moving with sudden decisiveness, they released their captive and ran. Constance tasted relief for only an instant, for the third ruffian thumbed his nose at Hermine's weapon, bent over the victim, and began turning out his pockets.

In the next moment, a shot rang out, piercing the night like a cannon. Four feminine screams rent the air. A shop window shattered to the sidewalk. The footpad's mouth rounded. He grabbed something from the victim's pocket and fled.

In the shadows of the carriage, Winifred's eyes shone like twin moons. "Why did you shoot the shop, Hermine? Now Constance will have to pay for the glass. And what are you doing with Father's pistol?"

The weapon clattered to the road. Hermine, her voice shaking, said, "I declare to you, I never fired! Don't even know how to load the thing."

Eane's angry voice drifted through the window. " 'Twas my blunderbuss what saved you ladies from your folly, and I hope never to see a greater lack of sense!"

Heartened by this knowledge, Hermine burst out, "Hah! Thought you knew everything about me, didn't you? Fact is I've carried this pistol for years. A female can't be too careful."

"Your face is the only weapon you need," Beulah commented.

Unwilling to listen to further arguments, Constance opened the door and jumped to the street. A carriage traveling in the opposite direction crept past, then burst into speed. She sniffed at their cowardice and crossed the road.

"What are you doing?" cried Hermine, half-tumbling from the coach, as the others declared worriedly behind.

"We can't abandon the poor soul now, not after rescuing him," Constance called over her shoulder.

"Well—wait, then!" Hermine puffed toward her, then turned back irritably. "Come, Eanes, assist us!"

"Those footpads could still be about!" screeched Winifred. "Get back here, ridiculous girls; you've done enough for one night!"

Ignoring them all, Constance knelt beside the victim. He lay as he had fallen, half-curled as a child sleeps, one side of his face pressed to the cobblestones, the other exposed to the faint light of moon and streetlamps. Dark hair hid his features, and, half-afraid he might be dead, she knelt to brush it aside. The skin beneath the hair was warm, however, warm and lightly bronzed, as if he were accustomed to working outside. Yet he could not be a laborer, for his clothing was finely textured and expensive-looking, if not of the latest cut. Aside from a bruise darkening his cheek, his features—perfect features, she couldn't help noticing with the little flutter that beauty always stirred in her—were clear.

He was young, not much older than herself. Perhaps that explained why he wandered foolishly alone down London streets at night. Mimicking the actions of the footpads earlier, she searched his pockets. The thieves had done their task well; she found no identifying information.

Whispering assurances into his ear, she tried to rouse him, but he did not respond. Compassion rushed through her. She stood and saw Hermine, hands on hips, watching and pursing her lips. Behind her cousin trailed Beulah and Winifred, with Eanes stationed half way between the carriage and themselves.

"Best get him to hospital," said Hermine.

"I don't trust hospitals," Constance stated. "We'll take him home and call the surgeon."

"Take home a complete stranger?" exclaimed Winifred. "How do we know he's not dangerous? He could murder us in our beds!"

"There's no room in the carriage," Beulah added.

Constance returned her gaze to the motionless figure on the pavement. She could not say how she knew, but she was certain the man posed no threat.

"Even if he *is* a murderer, he's too injured to endanger us at present," she said. "And we can carry him across our laps."

"Suppose it *is* our Christian duty," Hermine mumbled.

Winifred began to shred her handkerchief. "Oh, dear."

Constance said impatiently, "I'll need all of you to help me. You don't think Eanes and I are strong enough to carry him, do you?" She stared at the motionless figure again, finding it difficult to look away. "He's rather tall and appears to be, er, strongly built."

"I—I have never carried a man before," Winifred worried.

"Perhaps in a lifetime," Hermine intoned, bending to seize one of the stranger's legs, "there will be time to experience everything before one is through."

Beulah's lips tightened. "You may wish until you die, but some things will never happen. Not to you, anyway."

Some hours later, Joshua Turner opened his eyes for the second or third time since being brought into the chamber he'd begun to fear might be the anteroom to hell. Although only a single candle sputtered on the bedside table, he squinted as he tried to raise his head. Through blurred vision, he saw an expensively furnished room and someone dozing on a chaise longue near the fire.

Immediately, an ax began splitting logs inside his temples. His ribs flamed like branding irons, and his stomach ached and lurched so he thought he might be sick. He relaxed into the pillow.

He mustn't be ill. One of his nurses would fly to him again, and he didn't want to shame himself, especially not in front of the pretty one, the one who wore an angel's face. And he *surely* didn't wish to bring another of those sour-breathed hags to him, for it was their countenances he feared most. No heavenly being could look like them, which left him only one thing to think.

In spite of himself, he groaned. When he heard the rustling of skirts approaching, he tightened his muscles and waited.

"Are you awake again?" asked a silken voice. Thank God, it was the young one. He relaxed and tried to sort out her words. "Do you remember what happened? Can you tell me your name?"

Even though she lowered her voice to a whisper, her speech resonated through his head like falling rocks. Unable to keep irritability from his tone, he said, "I'm Joshua Turner, and naturally I remember what happened. I went for a walk and was robbed."

He winced at the memory. Had Luke been attacked, he would have pounded all three—and more besides—into the dust. But not him. Maybe his older brother had been right. Joshua should have stayed home.

But he wasn't being fair to himself; he had enough judgment left to know that, even if his head swelled to the size of a hot air balloon and floated through the roof—wherever this roof was. Three months he'd been away, and nothing had happened to him until this night, one of the last he'd planned to spend in London.

But none of it was the angel's fault. In a gentler voice he said, "I don't know what happened after I was attacked. Where am I, and how did I get here? And who are you?"

The young woman's eyes had widened inexplicably as he

spoke. She told him her name, and he rolled it silently across his tongue—*Constance Cowald*—liking the strong, sturdy taste of it, yet wondering if it suited this delicate wisp of a girl. But she was still talking, telling him modestly of his rescue. He struggled to concentrate.

"So you're my Good Samaritan," he said when she'd finished, his voice cracking dryly.

A pitcher of water sat upon the table beside the candle, and Constance poured a small amount into a glass and offered it to him. He tried to raise his head. Swiftly she assisted, her fingers cool and strong beneath his neck. He took a few sips and lay back, feeling ridiculously sorry when her hand returned to her lap. He felt relief to see no ring upon her fingers, then scolded himself for a fool.

"You took a terrible risk, ma'am. I don't like to think what might've happened if those rowdies had returned."

"Eanes would have protected us. And it was my cousin Hermine who truly rescued you."

Joshua wondered briefly which one of the old women he'd seen in his dream-state had challenged his attackers with an unloaded weapon. He hoped it wasn't the one with hairs on her chin. He'd rather think it was Constance who risked all for him. Smiling at his own idiocy, he said, "Still, I'm very grateful. You saved my life."

She did not respond but continued to stare at him with an expression wavering between wonder and delight.

"I don't know how I'll ever be able to repay you," he added uncertainly, then blurted, "Why are you looking at me like that?"

The pink in her cheeks deepened. "It—it's your accent. Where are you from, sir?"

Joshua narrowed his eyes, trying to focus. *She* was the one with an accent—they all were. But her hair, worn loose for bed, shone like honey in the firelight, and he forgave her.

"I'm from Georgia, ma'am."

"Georgia? In America?"

"Well . . yes, ma'am. That's the one."

"It's as I thought, then. You're an *American southerner.*"

He had experienced all kinds of reactions to his nationality during his sojourn here, many of them unpleasant, since memories of the latest war between their countries were fresh, but never had anyone seemed so pleased. His headache faded as he contemplated her.

"You sound glad. Do you . . . like southerners?" The thought warmed him suddenly. It would be nice to feel the affection of a young lady again. He hadn't had time for that in the past few months. Neither the time nor the inclination.

As if sensing his deeper meaning, her smile dimmed. "I've never known a real southerner, but my father fought against your country's rebellion. He came home with an appreciation of America and her citizens."

"A redcoat, was he?" He cleared his throat, hating the weakness he heard in his voice. "And what about our more recent disagreement; what did he think of that?"

"My father died before the war broke out, but he saw it coming. He didn't speak of his feelings openly, although in the privacy of our home he often said our leadership was unjust to search your vessels and press your sailors into English service."

"He sounds a reasonable man," Joshua said, mildly amused in spite of the ache in his bones. She looked serious, like an ambassador intent on being diplomatic. "I wish I could have met your father. I'm sorry you lost him."

"He lived a long, full life," she said, almost primly, then leaned toward him, making his heart lurch, making him think for one mad instant she meant to kiss him. But she was only getting a closer look at his face. His face! Was it all bloodied and bruised and cut, and was she seeing him that way? His hands flew from the covers to wander over forehead, cheeks, nose, and chin. Everything seemed to be in place, though devilish tender.

She watched him as he searched, an odd look coming into

her eyes. "Pray, don't be concerned," she said. "You are still han—in one piece. The surgeon said you are not severely hurt, though you will be sore a few days and should not exert yourself."

He couldn't repress a grin. So she thought him handsome, did she? That could only be to the good. Then more serious thoughts intruded.

"I've just realized: not only have you inconvenienced yourselves to save me, but now I'm imposing upon your hospitality. I'm feeling better." He made a noble attempt to rise. "I should be getting back to my hotel, ma'am."

She pressed her hand to his chest, and he returned meekly to the pillow. He hadn't the strength to fight her, and besides, he'd just noticed he was wearing someone's nightshirt—her father's, no doubt, and, judging from the snugness across his chest and the feel of a hem ending above his knees, Papa must have been a little man—and Joshua had no intention of parading himself in front of her in such attire.

"First of all, you needn't keep calling me *ma'am*," she said. "I am an unmarried lady." Joshua couldn't help being struck by the pensive look which crossed her face at this announcement. Had she been hurt, too? Surely not a pretty girl like her. "And don't consider moving for the next few days," she continued. "You don't inconvenience us, for beside myself and my cousins, there are maids aplenty to care for you. You must think of your health."

The prospect of remaining under Miss Cowald's roof sounded appealing, but he had obligations to meet. As Joshua opened his mouth to protest, the words died on his lips. The door was opening. One of the elderly relatives—the stout one, he saw—hesitated, gobbled them both with her eyes, then bustled to the bed.

"You've come to your senses, then?" she asked. It was less a question than a demand.

"Yes, ma'am," Joshua answered. Now that he saw the old woman with lucidity, he wondered why he'd feared her earlier.

He should have recognized the lady sprang from the same brusque mold as his Great-Aunt Grace. "I was telling Miss Cowald how grateful I am, and that I hope to remove myself as soon as possible—no later than morning."

The elderly woman studied him so intently that the skin along his legs began to crawl. "American . . ." she muttered to herself, "but well-spoken anyway." Before he had time to become offended, she said more loudly, "I'm Hermine. *Lady* Constance's cousin."

"Lady . . ." He received her correction with surprise and a little dismay. Although he'd never fought in a war, he had a patriot's distrust of titles.

"She's an earl's daughter," Hermine explained further. "And why do you want to leave us so quickly?"

"Well . . ." He glanced at the earl's daughter, then at Hermine. This new information had jumbled his thoughts again, though he couldn't understand why. "I don't want to impose on your hospitality, ma'am."

"Never mind that. Where do you reside in town, young man?"

"Ibbetson's," he mumbled, looking at the earl's daughter again. He'd never been this close to nobility before. Aside from being especially lovely, she looked like any other girl to him.

"Ibbetson's," Hermine repeated. "Abode of clergymen and students. Not so posh as the Clarendon or Stephen's, but decent. How are you set for funds?"

Joshua's eyes flew to Hermine in shock. On the edge of his vision, he saw Constance cover her face with her hands.

"I beg pardon?" he asked huffily.

"Money. Did the footpads take all you have?"

"Oh. No, ma'am—er, lady?"

When she nodded and explained they were all addressed as lady, as each of them were earl's daughters, he finished blearily, "I'm afraid I'll slip. I've been taught from the cradle to call every grown woman *ma'am*—married, maiden, lady

or not." Upon receiving assurances that such slips would not
offend them, he added, "And to answer your question, *lady,*
I have sufficient funds in the hotel safe."

Hermine's plump eyebrows rose slightly, but she said only,
"Good, good. Now, Mister"—Joshua quickly supplied his
name—"Mr. Turner. What is it you do for a living?"

Constance pushed her cousin toward the door. "Cannot you
see how tired our guest is?" she pled. "I think it will be safe
to leave him alone until morning. He must rest." And, excusing
herself as graciously as she could while stuffing Hermine into
the hall, she exited, closing the door behind.

Joshua stared at the door until its panels swam. He felt
weak and confused in the wake of this sudden, unexplained
grilling. But before he fell into dreams, he smiled. *Lady Constance.* And then, still smiling though a wrinkle appeared between his brows, *Lady Hermine.* She was the cousin who
leveled the pistol, he remembered. And yes, she *was* the one
with the whiskers.

"And how is the gentleman?" asked Winifred the next
morning, as she waited for her plate to be served by the maid.
The ladies had gathered for a late breakfast in the dining al-
cove off the study, eschewing the large, chilly-in-all-seasons
dining room, as they often did. "He's well, I hope, and ready
to be off, for I don't like strangers in the house."

"He's much better," Constance said, spreading marmalade
on a piece of toast. "He was up and dressed when I stopped
in a while ago. I'm certain we have nothing to fear from him,
but rest easy, Winifred. He's eager to leave." She saw no need
to mention how much his eagerness piqued her, for her feeling
was irrational and silly.

Hermine slammed the apple she was peeling onto her plate.
"He's staying if I have to poison him."

"Hermine!" squeaked Winifred.

Beulah continued spooning porridge into her mouth. "I

knew you'd come to this one day, Hermine. That's why I grow roses; to cheer your cell at the madhouse."

"Listen to me," Hermine snapped. "Don't you see what golden opportunity has fallen into our laps? We've got the means of twisting Vinnie's nose to the altar, right beneath our roof." She reclaimed the apple and waved it expansively. "Is not God good?"

Constance felt blackness pushing at the edge of her vision. "If you mean what I think you do, cousin, then say no more."

"But he's perfect, Connie. A *fine*-looking lad, and well-mannered. Moreover, he's staying at a decent hotel and has money. Such a young man *must* be from a good family, even if he is a colonial. Vincent will turn green as a frog with jealousy! When have you had a suitor so presentable as this American?"

"When has she had any suitor at all?" Beulah contributed.

Constance dropped her toast and covered her ears. "I'm not listening!"

Hermine reached across the table and pushed Constance's hands aside. "Don't you see, Connie? Our American won't be worried about Vinnie's prowess with the pistol, because he don't need to know."

"Oh, very fine," Constance retorted. "Then you are saying we've rescued Mr. Turner simply in order for Vincent to shoot him."

"Snit, snit," Hermine said. "You don't *really* think Vinnie would call out his competition, do you?"

"Probably wouldn't even notice he had any, or care if he did," stated Beulah.

"Well, aren't we cross today?" said Winifred, staring reproachfully at her sister.

Beulah shuddered, swallowed a mouthful of porridge, then gave Constance a rare look of apology.

"M'gums feel like I've been chewing prune pits," she explained.

"That's all right," Constance said, squeezing her hand. "I've not heard anything since I sat down at table."

Anderson, the maid, paused in refilling Winifred's cup of tea. "I can tell you anything you missed," she said helpfully.

"Why does *that* fail to surprise me? Let me remind you, good servants have no ears," Hermine reproached, and Anderson turned away, rolling her eyes. "Now, Connie. Think about what I've said. It could be your last chance."

"I'd rather die than use subterfuge. And besides," Constance continued, feeling ridiculously close to tears, "what makes you think Mr. Turner would participate in such a scheme?"

"Participate in what?" asked a masculine voice behind them.

Inhaling quickly, Constance turned and saw their visitor standing in the study, leaning an arm against a chair back for support. He looked from one the other of them, his eyes finally resting upon her. While she felt the blood drain from her head, he smiled uncertainly and walked forward.

"In summation," Hermine said some twenty minutes later, "you could serve us in the way no one else can. Once Vinnie understands Connie has a presentable suitor, he'll offer for her. He's not fool enough to let our girl slip through his fingers."

"Let's see if I understand you ma'am, um, *my lady,*" said Joshua evenly, stretching his aching legs beneath the table, then jerking them back when Winifred jumped and squealed. "Lady Constance loves this man?"

It was necessary to ask the cousins this question, for Constance had long since fled the room. He awaited the answer with an odd feeling of suspension. Recalling the scarlet cheeks flaming beneath Constance's hands as she ran through the study, he felt a flare of pity add to his tension. Should a similar thing happen to his sister—had anyone asked a stranger to pose as *her* suitor—he knew how she would react. But such a thing would never happen. None of the females in *his* family spun webs to ensnare men like these old spiders.

He ceased breathing for a moment. Memories played through his mind, memories of inexplicable scenes in genteel drawing rooms. Had feminine machinations been behind them all? It would explain much.

He was learning more in England than he'd intended. So caught was he in sudden revelation, he failed to hear Hermine's response and asked her to repeat it.

"I hate it when people pose questions and don't listen to the answer," she scolded. "Winifred does it all the time. Anyway, Connie's not sure she loves him, but what has that to do with anything? Everyone knows Vinnie's going to offer; it's just a matter of *when*. And while he plays and dawdles, Connie dangles. You can see how hard it is for her."

"People are beginning to laugh," Winifred added.

"So . . . it's a matter of pride, then?" he asked, a weight settling in his chest. This was what he expected of the English, particularly the nobility: pride, arrogance, haughtiness. He recalled Constance's tender eyes and could not reconcile the images. She must be a closet actress.

"No one likes being made a fool," Beulah said. "Do you?"

While Anderson moved around the table, removing plates and refilling teacups, Hermine appraised him. "Hope you're not one of those sentimental fellows that thinks love is the only reason to wed. Love seldom outlasts the wedding trip—"

"Oh, behold the voice of authority," intoned Winifred.

"—but family fortunes magnify for generations," finished Hermine, her eyes firing upon her sister.

"Then it's a matter of money." His impression of Constance grew lower by the moment. She was either prideful or avaricious or both. The realization pained him, made his ribs burn even more.

But why did he think she'd be different? Just because she

helped rescue him? That was probably a whim on her part, a craving for adventure. The sooner he left this household, the better. "I'm sorry, ladies; I can't help you. Thank you for all you've done." He scraped back his chair and rose painfully. "I'll just be getting back to my hotel now and cause you no further trouble."

Looking dismayed, Hermine stood. She breathed heavily and stretched one hand toward him in appeal, then cast a desperate glance at her sisters.

Winifred rose gracefully but spoiled the effect by brushing a snowfall of crumbs from her lap to the floor. "Perhaps we're not being fair to Mr. Turner, Hermine. We've not asked him if his feelings are otherwise engaged."

"Oh, no, ma'am, it's not that," Joshua assured her, fighting away an image of golden hair and laughing eyes. "No."

"Well, what then?" demanded Hermine. "Surely it can't be you don't like our Connie?"

He *had* liked her, that was the problem. Joshua stared down at the plump old lady and searched for suitable excuses.

"Make it worth his while," Beulah pronounced. "Give 'im some money."

Now they were making him angry. He straightened his shoulders. "Begging your pardon, my ladies, but I have no need of—"

" 'Course you don't!" cried Hermine. "Beulah, where's your tact?"

"She never had any, and you know it," Winifred said. Pressing her hands to the tabletop, she leaned toward him, an almost flirtatious look gleaming in her eye. "Now, Mr. Turner, don't be shy. Tell us why you cannot participate. Although," she added consideringly, the coquettish light fading to caution, "I'm not as certain as my older sister Hermine that this plan will work. I'm not even convinced we should try, especially since we know so little about you. The fact is, we know nothing at all." She collapsed into the chair, adding querously, "Hermine?"

Three pairs of suspicious, rheumy eyes impaled him. He could see the youngest one judging him a killer or worse. Well, it was about time they considered the possibility. Only a household of women could so foolishly trust a stranger.

Lady Constance dwelt with this trio at her own peril. But that was no concern of his.

"Allow me to put your minds at ease, my ladies," he said stiffly. "My blood may not run as blue as yours, but my people come from good stock." Except for his great-grandfather, the bloodiest pirate in the Gulf of Mexico, but that was ancient history and had no bearing here. "And to answer your question, Lady Winifred, I don't have time to, uh . . ."

"Act the part of a mouse in a snare?" offered Beulah.

He paused. "Yes, ma'am." More decisively, he added, "I have business to attend."

Hermine's nose wrinkled. "Business? What kind?"

"Steam engines," he said proudly. "I've been learning about Arthur Woolf's latest inventions in Cornwall and only came to London for a few days' resting up. My family would scalp me if I missed the usual landmarks—Buckingham Palace and all. Now I'm intending to return to Cornwall to study Richard Trevithick's developments."

"Whatever for?" asked Beulah.

He looked surprised. "Well, ma'am, it's because I believe the steam engine will soon become a part of every industrial, and perhaps even agricultural, enterprise." Although he knotted his fists behind his back, he could not prevent the wave of excitement that swept over him. "Do you realize Trevithick's Cornish boiler is supplied with 40 pounds of pressure and is powerful efficient for pumping? It costs next to nothing to maintain, too. Why, his invention's more cost effective than an air-eating mule and a whole lot better-tempered!"

Coming to himself, he saw they watched him with varying expressions of confusion, incomprehension, and boredom— in short, the same expressions he'd grown to expect on the faces of his family.

"That's why I have to leave London," he concluded.

Hermine marched to within a few feet of him. Plainly her brief fear had vanished. Hoping he wouldn't hurt her feelings, he edged back to avoid her strong, killing exhalations of apple, bacon, and molasses.

"This is all our rescue means to you, then?" she asked, her voice quivering. "Constance risks her life for you, and you can't do this one little thing for her?"

She was piping the right notes. *Pay what you owe,* his father had drummed into him. But this? How could he become part of such a farce? He didn't like it.

"Cornwall won't fall into the ocean," Winifred added winningly. "It'll still be there after Constance is betrothed."

"Or so we hope," Beulah remarked.

At that moment, Constance reentered the study, and they all turned to watch her. Joshua noted her red-rimmed eyes, but he saw no other signs of distress in her demeanor. His sister would have cried for days. This, he supposed, was the coolness of the aristocracy. His heart hardened.

"I've been in the drawing room and heard every word," she said without looking at him, a thing which did not further endear her to him. "Mr. Turner will think I'm a rotten one indeed to cause such eagerness to be rid of me."

"Oh, no," cried Hermine, her sisters echoing. "We only try to ensure your happiness."

"Our guest has no claims upon *that,*" she said, looking at Hermine as if she were the only person in the room. "I have no wish to impose upon him, and besides, this plan is foolish and doomed to failure."

"Why do you say that, ma'am?" he asked, more to see if she would acknowledge his presence than any true desire to know.

Constance did glance at him then, but looked quickly away. "Well, I don't wish to seem brutal . . ."

"I'm sure you could never be that," he said, for his mother had taught him to be gallant. Still, his smile felt forced.

The young lady clasped her hands together. "It's only that I don't believe Vincent would take you seriously. You are unknown to Society and an American, after all."

"Is there something wrong with being American, ma'am?" he asked carefully.

"Heavens, no!" Hermine declared. "Really, Constance."

"And even if he did consider you a rival," Constance continued, "what my cousins have not told you is that Vincent's skill with the pistols is well known. I could not countenance putting you in danger."

Joshua stared. "Do you imagine for a minute that one of your beak-nosed Englishmen could scare me?"

"Mr. Turner," Constance chided, "you will have my cousins thinking you mean to try their idea. But I cannot consider it. Can you imagine my embarrassment, should anyone discover the truth?"

He could not believe it. First his patriotism, then his courage, and now his discretion were being called into question.

"Surely you don't think *I'd* be so lump-headed as to tell anyone?" He heard himself with astonishment.

"You'll do it then?" shouted Hermine. "You will?"

He hesitated, then said irritably, "Yes, ma'am, I will. I want to repay what I owe."

"You owe me nothing," Constance said.

"I'll do it just to see if it can be done, then," he pronounced.

"Oh, very well, if it pleases you," she said, and left the room. Her cousins followed, chattering excitedly, leaving him alone to wonder what happened.

The next week passed in frantic, sometimes angry, activity. Constance flowed into the stream of events with a feeling of increasing buoyancy.

On the evening of Mr. Turner's first outing in Society, Constance sat at her dressing table, readying herself and reflecting upon the past few days. She could not say precisely when

she'd come to view Hermine's plan favorably. Perhaps it was
overhearing her cousin's attempts to persuade Mr. Turner on
that terrible morning while she sat trembling with shame in
the withdrawing room. More likely it was while listening to
their guest's feeble excuses at every juncture of Hermine's
arguments. Obviously *he* didn't think anything would make
her appealing—to Vincent or to anyone. Otherwise, why protest so much?

Steam engines, indeed.

At any rate, sometime during that dreadful conversation,
Constance decided Mr. Turner should be given the opportunity to see she was not, after all, a faded wallflower with no
social consequence. And if Vincent could be made to step
lively by the endeavor, why, so much the better.

She smiled at her reflection and patted rice powder on her
cheeks. For an intelligent man, Mr. Turner had been easily led
to change his mind. Perhaps observing her cousins' manipu-
lations over the past few years gave her unfair advantage.

A surge of anticipation rose in her breast. Tonight they were
to attend a ball at Lord and Lady Eustace Hollingsworth's,
one of the first families in London. Certainly Vincent would
be there. And if anyone could be used to make him jealous,
Joshua Turner was the man. She knew of no gentleman who
was better-looking, and in recent days she'd discovered his
charm, even while he was healing and in pain, waxed formi-
dable; he had a way of looking at a lady when she spoke that
made her think she was the only person in the world. Even
her cousins were susceptible to it, fluttering about him like
schoolgirls, giggling at his every *yes, ma'am* (or when he
remembered, *my lady*), and blushing at his seemingly sincere
but impossible compliments, all spoken in a soft-voiced drawl
that smoothed past the ear like honey. Such manners were far
different than those of other gentlemen she knew, and farther
still from Vincent's chilly ways. One must always earn Vincent's favor, as if every encounter were a test.

She dusted powder across her shoulders and neck, taking

care not to soil the low neckline of her ivory satin. As she did, a little frown crept across her brow.

Although Mr. Turner could charm the sconces off the wall, he was not always so kind to her. Something about her irritated him, for he frequently reacted to her simplest actions by igniting into what she could only think were *fits*.

The day they sent for his belongings, for example. When it became apparent his clothing was of fine quality but unfashionable, Constance had summoned a Bond Street tailor, prompting predictable and loud protests from her visitor.

"That waistcoat came from New York," he had said, when she'd thrown the drab object onto the rejected pile. "It was good enough for Georgia society, and it's good enough for London's."

"No, it is not," she'd answered. "Not if you're accompanying me."

His eyes narrowed. "My apologies, *Lady* Constance." He turned to the tailor, a tall, balding man who watched them with avid eyes. "I forgot for a minute that the blood of kings flows in her veins, and only the finest will do her escort. What do you have in gold or silver, my good man?"

"It's not because I possess royal blood," she responded; and then, surprised at the shrillness she heard in her voice, she stopped and forced herself to relax. "The fashion is for closer-fitting clothes and less-subdued colors, that's all. You'll be attending functions in drawing rooms of the first stare. Surely you don't want to be a cause for comment and—and ridicule."

"No, of course not. Far be it from me to bring shame on the Cowalds."

She looked pointedly at the tailor, then turned warning eyes upon Mr. Turner. "I don't take your meaning, sir. I only wish to preserve your reputation."

"Oh, yes, ma'am, I *do* see. You're concerned only for *my* reputation. It's good of you to protect me. I am, after all, an ignorant provincial. In my country, we don't put so much significance in a man's outward appearance."

"Do you not?" she inquired in her most skeptical tones. "Do you not, indeed?"

His glance fell. After a moment, he glared at the tailor. "Very well, then. You've heard the lady; stitch me an entire wardrobe of your tightest work. Give me a suit in every color of the rainbow."

"I don't think you'll need that many, for surely it won't take so long to accomplish—" Constance caught herself in time and trailed off.

"Right. That's just as well, for I don't intend to spend a fortune for a cartload of clothes I'll never be able to use again in my life."

"Oh, but of course *I* mean to pay for your wardrobe," Constance said, without thinking.

The tailor's eyebrows flew toward his bare scalp, and his eyes widened with scandalized delight.

"No, ma'am, Lady Constance," said Mr. Turner, his ears flaming red, "that you will *not* do."

"As you wish, then," she mumbled, and, coughing discreetly, hurried from the room.

Thus it seemed nothing she did pleased him. She could not understand his prejudice against her. Hopefully it would not spoil his performance tonight.

Constance rose from her dressing table and draped a gossamer shawl around her shoulders, then eased from the room and down the stairs. She felt gratified to experience the full attention of her cousins and Mr. Turner as she descended. Her guest, himself compelling in black and tan, smiled at her in a flattering way that eased the knot of doubt in her throat. She was relieved to see the bruise had almost disappeared from his cheek. And then she saw, really *saw,* her cousins, and all thoughts of herself and this inexplicable man dissipated into astonishment.

"Why, cousins! You look . . ."

"Ravishing," supplied Mr. Turner, in a voice that carried warning.

She glanced at him in irritation. Did he think she meant to say *ridiculous?* Surely he didn't believe she could be so unfeeling, and besides, it would be untrue.

"You look lovely," she finished with a defiant glare.

Winifred, cheerful in a lavender-and-gray velvet gown, glanced down modestly. "I thought Clement wouldn't mind if I went into half-mourning."

"He *would* mind," said Beulah, still clad in black, though she wore a golden turban with spangles and a tassle that she continually tossed from her left eye, "even though he's been in the dirt for twenty years. That's why I'm glad you did it."

Constance eyed Beulah's headdress and forced the laughter from her voice as she complimented her oldest cousin. But the greatest surprise was Hermine, who stood a little apart from the others. Dressed in a claret-colored gown whose rounded neckline was not low, yet low enough to display her bounteous charms, her thick dark hair caught in curls that framed her round face and smooth, hairless skin (skin marred only by the slightest rash upon her chin), she stared fixedly at the ceiling, too fearful, perhaps, of seeing ridicule in their eyes.

"You're beautiful," Constance said sincerely, feeling her heart melt as Hermine beamed. Although the young lady tried mightily, she could not help staring at her cousin's chin. "How did you—" She recalled Mr. Turner's presence and stopped.

"A little trick with candlewax," Beulah droned. "More than that you don't want to know."

Having complimented one another sufficiently, the party-goers departed for the Hollingsworths'. In spite of traveling in Constance's largest coach, they avoided crushing one another's clothing only by sitting stiffly and scarcely breathing. Fortunately, the journey from King Street to Grosvenor Square was short.

Hollingsworth House was built on a palatial scale and possessed a flat facade decorated with a relief of gargoyles, incensed ravens, and other unknown, agonized beings. A canopy

covered the sidewalk for the protection of guests from a light
sprinkle of rain. Every window in the house blazed in welcome.

"I'll be glad to be done with chaperoning," Beulah grum-
bled as they walked toward the steps. "Make the most of tonight, Constance."

Constance, feeling a renewed wave of shame that she'd
become part of her cousins' plot, was careful not to look at
her escort. Within her a voice cried, *Is Vincent worth all this?*
But it was too late to turn back now.

"Well, *I* intend to enjoy myself," fluttered Winifred. "And
you know you don't have to come with us, Beulah. You only
do so because you're afraid you'll miss something."

"Miss something? You mean the backache I get from sitting
in those barbaric chairs they bring from the attics to torture
the chaperones? Don't make me laugh!"

Hermine pushed between her sisters and tapped Mr.
Turner's shoulder with her fan. "Don't forget, now. Constance's father met yours in America, and they've corre-
sponded ever since. You've come to visit in honor of that
friendship."

"Yes, ma'am, I remember," said Joshua, his eyes on Constance.

The younger lady found it hard to return his gaze, and
harder still to meet the curious glances that came their way
as she entered the hall. Nervously she introduced him to her
hosts and many of her friends and acquaintances. As she did,
she scanned the receiving rooms as unobtrusively as possible,
looking for Vincent. But it was not until they entered the ballroom that she saw him. He circled the room with his dancing
partner, a girl Constance didn't recognize but would hereafter,
for the child possessed abundant, red curls that frizzed like a
halo around her freckled face.

As usual, Vincent looked striking in black. He appeared
enchanted with his partner and failed to note their arrival.
Somewhat piqued, Constance saw that her cousins were com-

fortable in their corner, then submitted gracefully to the wave
of inferior beaux who came to sketch their names on her dance
card.

While the gentlemen passed her card from one to the other,
Mr. Turner stood slightly apart. Constance, feeling his eyes
upon her the entire time, felt on edge and could remain civil
to her admirers only with the greatest effort. When her card
was filled, she could no longer delay the role she had so stu-
pidly agreed to play. As the orchestra began another waltz,
she approached her guest.

"I have reserved my first and last dances for you," she said.

"Is that all? I thought you wanted us to be noticed."

"Two dances in one evening will be sufficient notice, I
assure you. More than that and I'd be ruined."

"Ya'll sure have some funny ideas over here, ma'am."

With reluctance she moved into his arms. "You needn't
shovel your accent so thickly with me. Unlike my cousins, I
don't find it impressive."

"If you want people to think I'm your suitor," he said
tersely, waltzing her onto the dance floor, "there ought to be
something about me that attracts such a fine, outstanding lady
as yourself."

Something about him? Didn't he realize *everything* about
him was attractive? She could not fail to see the envious eyes
of her contemporaries as she floated past. But only Vincent's
notice mattered, and where was he? Across the room twirling
another beauty—a *second* redhead, for pity's sake—around
the floor. He did not look their way, not once.

She sighed and returned her attention to her partner.
"You're an excellent dancer."

"You sound surprised. I'll bet you figured folks from Georgia only know how to stomp and clap to the fiddle in barns."

"I thought no such thing," she said indignantly. And then,
before she could prevent herself, she asked in plaintive tones,
"Why do you hate me so, Mr. Turner?"

His step faltered to a stop. The couple nearest them avoided a collision only by the fastest legwork on the part of the gentleman, who gave Mr. Turner a forbidding look. Constance felt her cheeks burn crimson as other couples swished past. Had Mr. Turner not held her so tightly, she'd have fled in shame.

"Hate you?" he asked. "What in the world makes you think I *hate* you?"

"Please, Mr. Turner," she begged, her gaze darting left and right. "We are like two rocks in a stream. People are looking."

"Hm?" His eyes were faraway and unreadable. "Oh." He moved them back into the flow of dancers. "I reckon—I mean, I *suppose* we don't want to attract *that* kind of notice."

"No, we do not," she said, forcing a bright smile and looking assured, as if stopping in the middle of a waltz was a thing she did all the time.

His gaze remained pinned to her face, making her fear his next action would be to stumble into one or more of the couples revolving around them, but he led her flawlessly. "You didn't answer my question. Why do you think I hate you?"

"Mr. Turner, I believe you're guilty of pretending ignorance. It's obvious that everything I do or say angers you."

"Is it?" He looked thoughtful. After a moment, he said, "I'm sorry if it seems that way to you, ma'am; I don't want to hurt your feelings. The fact is, I'm a little put off by your ways—oh, don't get in a tiff, I don't mean just *your* ways, but . . . the thinking over here is different, that's all."

"What do you mean?" She stared deeply into his eyes, really wanting to know. "Are you referring to the formality of our Society? I know you were vexed about the necessity for a new wardrobe; but if you look around, I think you'll see everyone conforms to a certain style."

He did not look around but kept his attention centered on her, a fact she couldn't help contrasting with Vincent's obliviousness. "No, ma'am, it's not that, or not exactly. You were right about the clothes; I would've been out of place here in my old things. I guess every culture has its customs and all. But when it comes down to marrying . . ." He shook his head.

"Yes? When it comes to marriage . . . ?"

"Well, ma'am, I just can't help believing that money and pride don't make good reasons for joining yourself to somebody."

She stiffened. "Is that what you think? Are you insinuating those are the reasons I await Lord Vincent?"

He studied her closely, making her uncomfortable. Were the other dancers beginning to notice the intensity of their conversation? She had caught more than one curious glance.

"Aren't they?" he asked.

"Of course not," she said angrily, then forced a pleasant nod at an acquaintance whirling past. "Wealth doesn't concern me in the least, for I have more than sufficient for my needs." She swallowed, embarrassed at speaking so frankly about financial matters. Quietly she added, "My father wanted me to wed Vincent; it was his greatest wish."

An inexplicably eager light came into Mr. Turner's eyes. "But that's not a good reason, either. I mean, it's to your credit you want to please your papa, but surely he wouldn't want you to be unhappy."

"Unhappy?" The thought startled her. "What makes you think Vincent would make me unhappy?"

As the gleam died from Mr. Turner's eyes, something within her stirred painfully. He looked wounded and lost. But why? He'd never even met the earl. Her union to Vincent was a long-awaited dream that could only bring bliss . . .

All this waltzing was making her dizzy. She tightened her hold on his hand. As if intuiting her need, he firmed his fingers over hers and strengthened his hold on her waist. Secure now, she gave him a grateful look, then quickly lowered her lashes. The probing, longing expression in his eyes drew the air from her lungs.

For the first time she began to visualize life *after* her wedding to Vincent. It was not a thing she'd contemplated to any extent, the task of getting him to the altar being of greater urgency. She recalled the half-hearted attention with which the earl listened to her conversation; the careless way he brushed past her when exiting a room; the restlessness of his eyes when he saw a lovely woman, and his ready gallantry until he grew tired of her; his manner of talking endlessly of prizefights and shooting and horseflesh with his male companions while she sat nearby, excluded and alone.

Previously she had thought all men, excepting Papas, vicars, and rakes intent on seduction behaved in that fashion. Now that she'd met Mr. Turner and learned at least one gentleman regarded women as interesting and worthy of respect, the prospect of a lifetime of Vincent's neglect loomed with the appeal of a lengthy sojourn in the Arctic Circle.

"I'm sorry," Mr. Turner said quietly, echoing her thoughts. "I didn't understand. You are—you have a real attachment for Lord Oakwood."

"Of course I do!" she declared, more to reassure herself than him. Seeing interest kindle in the eyes of several dancers passing by, she lowered her voice. "I've known Vincent all my life and have a great affection for him."

A blank look descended into his eyes. "I understand." He glanced around searchingly. "Well, then, if he's what you want, then he's what you shall have."

"Pardon?" she said, blinking.

He ignored her question. "Which one is he?"

Although her heart remained mysteriously heavy, she peered past the shoulders of the other dancers. "Vincent's the tall one across the room. There—he's just passed the orchestra and is dancing with that carrot-haired lady in green. Do you see him?"

To Constance's great alarm, Mr. Turner did not answer but began spinning her like a top past the other dancers until they reached Vincent. In positioning themselves next to him, the American bumped lightly against the earl's sleeve.

"Oh, I do beg pardon, sir," Mr. Turner said graciously.

A faintly annoyed expression drifted across Vincent's face as he looked at the offender, but it faded when he recognized Constance. "Quite all right. Hullo, Constance."

"Hello, Vincent," she replied, her heart beating rapidly. Close proximity to her old friend's regal good looks and imposing personality made her recent doubts diminish. This was her moment. Would Vincent become jealous of Mr. Turner and justify her cousins' plan? So far, he had not spared her guest more than a glance.

The waltz ground to a halt. While the crowd applauded the number, Vincent began leading his partner from the floor. With single-minded determination, Constance seized Mr. Turner's arm and stepped into Vincent's path.

She quickly introduced the gentlemen and was acquainted in turn with Vincent's flame-haired beauty. When it appeared the earl meant to pass by, now that introductions had been made, Constance again stepped in front of him. "Mr. Turner is staying with us," she said.

"Is he?" A mild interest stirred in Vincent's eye, and he glanced a second time at the other gentleman. "Why?"

"My father and his became acquainted during the rebellion," she recited quickly, conscious of how easy it was to lose his attention. "Mr. Turner visits us in honor of that old connection."

"Capital," said Vincent. " 'Tis important to keep the old ties." To her dismay, he again moved forward.

"Joshua has been studying steam engines," she said desperately.

Vincent remained motionless for a moment, his strong-looking back unreadable. Then, to the obvious annoyance of the girl clinging to his arm, the earl turned. "Has he now?" His heavily lidded eyes scanned Joshua from head to toe. "Ever do any shooting, *Joshua?* "

Constance held her breath as her escort stiffened. "A little," he said. "Now and then."

Couples began crowding past them onto the dance floor,

readying themselves for the quadrille. A young man claimed
Vincent's lady; she moved away with a decided lack of grace.
The short, pockmarked dandy who had signed to partner Constance for the set stood nearby, his face a study in anxiety as
he looked from one gentleman to the other.

"How long do you stay with the Cowalds, Joshua?" Vincent
asked pleasantly.

"Oh, I don't know . . . Vincent," Joshua answered, giving
Constance a caressing glance that accelerated her pulse into
dangerous ranges. "It all depends."

"I'd imagine a colonial like yourself would soon become
homesick for buffalo steaks and corn liquor," said the earl
with a smile.

Even as fire ignited in the depths of his eyes, Joshua's lips
curved upward. "Yes, sir, and a lot more besides. However,"
he added, breathing expansively while giving Constance another significant look, "your country has its own fine attractions. I feel right at home here and mean to stay awhile."

Vincent bowed. "How gracious of you to say so. Since you
feel that way, perhaps you'd do me the honor of visiting my
estate at Sevenoaks a fortnight from Saturday. Constance
naturally you and your family are invited."

Constance's thoughts teetered between fear and delight. I
seemed the plan *had* borne fruit, though Vincent did not outwardly regard her with more interest than before. Perhaps he
invited them in order to shoot Joshua, for seldom did even hi
closest friends dare speak so familiarly with the earl. She had
far rather stay home, neglected, than take a chance with he
guest's life.

Cringing to imagine her cousins' disappointment, she began, "Oh, thank you, Vincent—"

"We would be delighted to accept," finished Joshua.

"We would?" she asked, casting a frightened look at he
guest.

"Most assuredly. I want to see if you're as beautiful in th
country as you are in town, Lady Constance. And besides,

have a hankering to fish as well as shoot. What about it, Vincent? You have decent fishing nearby?"

Showing guarded interest, the earl said, "Several rivers, actually. The salmon run well."

The first notes of the quadrille lilted through the ballroom. With a discreet wink, Joshua handed Constance to her new partner, then walked companionably off the floor with Vincent. She stared after them in bafflement, straining to hear what they were saying. The last words she discerned were Joshua's—something about the outstanding fishing available in Georgia where, he declared with a laugh, the trout grew as large as small dogs.

The morning after the ball brought the first of a flood of visitors, many of them female. Ladies who had not called in years, if ever, pounded the front knocker hoping for admittance into the Cowald drawing room or, failing that, deposited their cards in the salver with messages for Joshua scrawled across them. *Hope you are enjoying your visit to England,* read several of them. *Call upon us,* beseeched others.

His debut had been a success beyond imagining. Constance's first emotion was one of relief, for she had had her doubts about the acceptability of an unknown American. Evidently the Cowald connection had been reference enough, and Vincent's grudging notice had not hurt, either.

"He's so handsome," effused Alicia Mercer for the third time behind her fan on the afternoon following the ball. Constance and her cousins were entertaining in the study; Joshua sat across the room with the older ladies, while Constance found herself increasingly forced to remain gracious to a foursome with whom she'd attended boarding school.

"I love his accent," added Davidda Wilson, gazing wishfully at Joshua while tossing back her golden ringlets. When he failed to notice this display, her lips turned downward in a pout.

"My mama thinks he's wonderful," whispered Margaret Jocher, her enormous, shy eyes looking no farther than her lap. "She said, 'Imagine his asking those old biddies to dance!'" The young lady's face flushed brilliantly. "Oh! That was my mama speaking, you understand, and she didn't mean anything, except that we all thought him sweet to ask chaperones to dance when everyone knows they are well past it, but of course, your cousins surprised us all by not fainting or dying but looking as if they enjoyed themselves, especially Lady Hermine, though mama said her red dress made her look like a ripe tomato or a lightskirt, but in her case it would be a heavy—oh! She did not mean anything, and after all, no one else thought badly, for then why would Sir Stanley Bricket ask her for a waltz, for he is quite respectable, even though mama says he has bandy legs and a hollow chest—*oh!*"

"Quite all right," said Constance absently, patting Margaret's hand as she had done throughout four years of school. Truly, how tired she was becoming of hearing Joshua's virtues extolled! "I take your meaning."

Alicia fluttered her fan. "Does he have a sweetheart?"

"Calm yourself, Alicia," said Becky van Meevern with a slow, wide smile. "Can you not see how often Mr. Turner gazes upon Constance? I'd say his heart is taken."

Four pairs of eyes turned upon Constance. "Your pardon?" she said, looking across the room in spite of herself. Joshua sat next to Alicia's aunt on the settle and appeared to be absorbed in her every word. Yet, as Constance watched, he lifted his gaze to hers.

The moment stretched between them; stretched and sizzled until a roaring noise sounded in her ears. After an eternity of this, Alicia's aunt gave her an inquiring, vexed look. Constance squirmed and turned her burning face toward her old schoolmates.

"You see I am right," Becky said.

Constance shook her head. "Oh no. You don't—you can't think—"

She could hardly say the American was only pretending to like her in order to make Vincent jealous. Saying such a thing would thwart her plans, for she had no false illusions about her friends' discretion. Besides, it would pain her to admit Joshua's regard was false.

And why is that? a little voice asked inside.

She did not know the answer. Surely it couldn't be she wanted his affection to be real. Such a desire would spell disaster, for it would mean—it would mean—

"Very eloquent, Constance," said Becky, amusement lighting her golden eyes. "It will serve Lord Oakwood well if Mr. Turner whisks you off to the American frontier."

"What nonsense you speak!" Constance refuted.

"Yes, and would it not be dangerous?" Margaret asked, so quietly they had to bend forward to hear. "Are there not savages and tornadoes and dust storms there, and don't the ladies have to walk in the dirt beside their carriages and live in tents and cook their own meals over campfires in the ground?"

Constance's eyes widened. "Not in Georgia," she asserted, though her heart quivered a little in doubt.

"Yes, where *is* Georgia?" Alicia questioned. "I had meant to find it on my globe, but I couldn't find the globe itself when I looked."

"It's in the Southeast," Becky informed her. "Plantations, cotton, tobacco, and slaves. Do you not remember anything from Miss Hadley's?"

"Only to hold my head erect at all times, as if I carried a plate of crystal upon it," Alicia said, and immediately straightened her shoulders and raised her chin, as did her companions.

"Does Mr. Turner live on a plantation?" asked Davidda, still appearing sulky at the American's lack of interest in her. "I shouldn't like to own slaves; it's not quite the thing, is it?"

Constance, whose attention had drifted toward Joshua again, suddenly became aware that her friends were watching her expectantly. "I beg pardon?"

"Plantations, slaves," condensed Becky. "Does Mr. Turner have them?"

The question surprised her. Why had she never thought to inquire beyond Joshua's expressed interest in steam engines? She really knew nothing about him or his family. Seeing his strong profile as he held out his teacup for Hermine to fill, she felt overwhelmed by the desire to learn everything about him. Would these people never go home?

"I don't know," she said thoughtlessly. Seeing the surprise on their faces, she added, "That is, no. Surely not."

"You don't *know?*" asked Davidda. "I thought his father was your father's friend. How can Mr. Turner's occupation be unknown to you?"

"Perhaps Mr. Turner is independently wealthy," commented Becky lazily.

Constance forced a laugh. "Oh, how foolish I am to forget for a moment. His interest lies in steam engines."

"Steam engines," Alicia repeated consideringly. The young ladies exchanged glances and, deciding as one the subject was unworthy of pursuit, began speaking of Becky's betrothal to a baron and other exciting topics.

Hours later, or so it seemed to Constance, Beulah began to snore. Unable to ignore this discreet hint, the ladies at last took their leave. Polite to the end, Constance stood in the hall while her guests swarmed around the butler collecting bonnets, gloves, reticules, and parasols.

Davidda, waiting impatiently for her mother, noticed the odd collection of flowers on the hall table. "These are the tokens from your admirers, I imagine," she said somewhat nastily, for she had ever been competitive with Constance in attaining masculine favor. "Are those posies from Lord Oakwood? He ought to send you *something,* for it's shameful how he never asks you to dance anymore."

"Davidda," censured Becky and Mrs. Wilson at the same moment.

"Actually, the rose is from him," Constance replied airily

"He sent it with a note of apology for being too late to reserve a space on my dance card last evening."

Even though she knew the earl's gesture could only have been prompted by Joshua's feigned interest in herself, Constance felt gratified when Davidda's expression fell flat. Becky's secret smile buoyed her further, and she bade her guests goodbye with unusually good spirits.

When the butler closed the door upon them, however, her mood lowered. All she could see was the back of Joshua's head as her cousins herded him toward the study. She never had the opportunity to speak with him alone except when they were dancing. There were many things she needed to know.

"Joshua!" she called, almost shouting.

He stopped instantly. Alarmed, Winifred clutched her hand to her chest; Hermine's features spelled puzzlement, and Beulah looked cross.

"Ex—excuse me, I did not mean to be so loud," Constance said. "I thought—I thought perhaps Joshua—Mr. Turner—might enjoy a turn around the square."

The willingness with which he acceded to this plan both pleased and frightened her. There was one deadening moment when Winifred volunteered to join them, but Hermine, watching Constance with unusual alertness, dissuaded her sister by prophesying the weather would wilt her curls. Constance, unwilling to risk further obstacles, quickly ran upstairs to fetch her bonnet.

"Why is it called *Golden Square?*" asked Joshua a half-hour later. He really wasn't interested, but thought someone ought to start the conversation. Except to point out a picturesque Georgian home within the square, the lovely lady at his side appeared to have lost the power of speech.

Something was bothering her, he could see that. He glanced at her again and saw little more than her downturned bonnet. It was a fetching little thing made of straw with a pink ribbon, but he wished he could sweep it off her head and expose her glorious, thick hair to the sunlight. He'd like to run his fingers through that honeyed hair, loosen her pinned curls, free them to flow across her shoulders and down her back. That was how her hair looked the first night he saw her, the night she rescued him.

That was how he'd always remember her.

A weight dragged at his chest and slowed his steps. He'd be leaving soon, leaving this chestnut-eyed beauty, whose heart and smile were not cold as a London rain as he'd first thought, but bright and boundless as a Georgia sky.

He was eight ways a fool, falling for another impossible dream. And this one worse than the other, for he should have been able to hold his emotions in check. He'd known his purpose in staying was to get her hitched to the aristocrat, but even that knowledge hadn't kept him from slipping down the road to ruin.

Every day he argued with himself, tried to persuade his heart she was too hoity-toity, too prideful, too interested in bloodlines and wealth for him. And every day her countless kindnesses to her cousins and servants proved him wrong. He even cherished their arguments, for her reasoning was as keen as anyone's he knew, and she didn't push aside her own thoughts just to please him. Except for her woeful fixation on the earl, he could find no fault in her at all.

The earl. Why had this warm, vital woman given her love to such a cold fish? There was no understanding the workings of the human heart.

He of all people should know that by now.

His thoughts were driving him deeper into gloom. Why wouldn't she talk to him, stir him from his downward spiral?

"Lady Constance?" he prodded.

She looked up, a startled expression in her eyes. "Yes, Mr. Turner?"

He forced a smile. "Now don't you go back to calling me 'Mr. Turner,' not when you said my name so easily last night.

A spot of color flared in each cheek. "Very well . . . Joshua."

"That's better. Now, tell me why they call this place 'Golden Square.' Is there buried treasure hidden here? Is this where the rainbow ends?"

She laughed lightly. "Nothing so romantic, I'm afraid. The square was once called 'Gelding,' after an inn of the same designation. The residents didn't find the name appealing and changed it."

"I don't blame them."

"Neither do I."

She fell silent again, but the parasol resting on her left shoulder began to twirl. Sensing her growing nervousness, he briefly touched the hand she rested on his arm. Her fingers stiffened, then relaxed.

"Mr. Turner—Joshua . . ."

"Yes, Lady Constance? If something's troubling you, don't be shy; you can say anything to me."

"I am *not* shy," she said, sounding irked. In a softer voice, she added, "It's merely that I've been thinking my cousins and I have been unfair to impose upon you for so long. You have business to attend, and your family will doubtless be wondering what delays you."

"That needn't concern you," he said with bitterness. "I'm sorry. I didn't mean to be rude. But you don't need to worry about that; my family isn't expecting me at any certain time."

Curiosity gleamed in her eyes. "Won't you tell me about your family? Or am I prying into another area that needn't concern me?"

He accepted her reproof with a shamed smile. "You haven't been spending much time with Lady Hermine lately. She's begun to question me like a judge about my background. If I didn't know better, I'd think she was afraid I was planning to make off with the family silver."

"Oh, I'm sorry, I didn't know. I'll speak with her."

"Don't you dare," he said, cursing himself for causing her

embarrassment. "Your cousins are delightful ladies who make me more homesick than cornbread would, if I could get any. Especially Hermine, who reminds me of a great-aunt of mine. Either one of them is sharp enough to rule the world, but since this is an unfair planet, each contents herself with directing the lives of everyone in her household."

"You have described Hermine precisely," she laughed. "And, like you, she is my favorite. But you must promise not to tell."

He placed a hand over his heart and pledged secrecy. Happy to see merriment restored to his companion's eyes, he slowed, drawing her near a high iron fence that bordered the sidewalk. Inside the railing, a generous lawn led to a brown-bricked house. In front of the manse, a small boy and girl tossed a ball back and forth while a nurse dozed on a bench. When the servant opened her eyes and frowned, Joshua tipped his hat and pulled Constance onward.

"Not very trusting, your people," he said.

"No less trusting than you," she returned. When he regarded her blankly she said, "I have asked about your family but you diverted me quite expertly. Are you always so secretive?"

He waited a moment before replying. "I guess it does seem that way, doesn't it? No, I haven't always been reluctant to talk about my family. It's a recent thing." An older couple impeccably dressed and silent, approached them from the opposite direction, and he waited until they passed to continue. "My folks and I didn't part on the best of terms."

"Oh, I see. I beg your pardon, Joshua. I never meant to stir painful memories."

"I know you didn't. And I do want to talk about it—at least I do with you. I think it'll be a relief." He tilted his face to the sun, scanned the gathering clouds, then returned his gaze to the walk in front of him. "There's nothing very scandalous to tell. My family has lived and farmed in Savannah for generations."

"Farmed," she said, frowning a little. "Are you speaking of a little farm with geese and chickens, or a big one with—with crops?"

He looked at her strangely. "I guess you'd have to call it a big one. Several thousand acres."

"I cannot believe it," she said, as if to herself. "We were just—" She turned an accusing glare upon him. "Joshua, do you own a plantation?"

"You could call it that, I suppose," he answered. "It's my father's, though."

"But it will be yours one day."

"Well, no. Southwinds passes to Luke, my older brother."

She stopped walking and withdrew her hand from his arm. "But in America you don't entail all the property to the eldest male, do you? There will be sufficient left over for you to build your own planation and raise tobacco, and—and cotton, and—"

"Cotton, yes, but no tobacco," he supplied helpfully. "Peanuts and peaches."

"Peanuts, peaches, and *slaves!*" she finished loudly, startling him. "I cannot understand how a human being can be so unfeeling as to buy, breed, and sell others! It's so monstrous a thing that—that, *oh!* I cannot bear to look at you!"

In demonstration of this sentiment, she turned her back to him and began to march homeward. When feeling returned to his limbs, he trotted after her, grabbed her shoulders, and turned her roughly around.

"Listen here, Lady Righteous," he seethed. "Don't go asking me to tell you about my family and then throw a hysterical fit when I do. You aren't the only one who knows slavery's wrong. When I was six years old, my parents gave me my first slave. Joby was only a couple of years older than I was. He was supposed to be my personal lackey, but he became my best friend. We grew up together, even fell in love at the same time: me with the daughter of our neighbor, Joby with one of the housemaids. It didn't work out for either of us, at least, not at first. Muriel dropped one plate too many in front of important guests, and my father decided she had to go. I begged him against it, said I'd buy her for Joby. But he wouldn't agree. He didn't approve of the strong friendship we had; said it was time I grew up and understood things. So I did the only thing I could."

"What was that?" she asked in a small voice.

Her pale face and remorseful eyes did little to stay his anger. "I helped them escape to Canada. It took about three months."

"But they arrived safely?"

"Yes," he said, growing a little calmer. "As far as I know, they're still all right."

"And . . . when you returned home?"

He dropped his hands from her shoulders. "Oh, my father disowned me for a little while, but my mother softened him up. There's still a few hundred acres waiting for me if I want them."

"And do you?"

"Oh, most certainly," he said, and saw that the answer surprised her. "Farming is in my blood, Constance. The land means everything. That's why I'm studying steam engines."

A breath of air teased loose a tendril of her hair, and she pushed it beneath her bonnet with an impatient gesture. "I'm afraid I don't understand."

"No, of course you don't." All anger gone, he walked a few paces, then turned in growing excitement, eager to make her comprehend. "Have you heard of Whitney's cotton gin? His machine separates cotton seed from the fiber. With one invention he freed hundreds of slaves from menial tasks. Can you imagine what labor-saving devices might eventually evolve from the steam engine? Think of tilling the fields, harvesting crops, hauling produce to market—all with the help of machines. You see what might result, don't you? At present, the South can't survive without slave labor. Everyone knows it, and few landowners are willing to risk financial ruin for conscience's sake. But if that labor could be provided by machines and as cheaply—then they *will* listen to reason; then they will understand that an economy bought at the price of human misery is bought at too dear a cost."

Tears glimmering in her eyes, Constance said, "You are a visionary. I beg your forgiveness for my outburst."

Half-embarrassed, he grinned and offered his arm. "That's all right, ma'am. I apologize, too, for blurting out my entire life story on the edge of the road. I guess once I got started, I just couldn't stop."

Smiling shakily, she replaced her fingers on his arm. They began the walk toward her house.

After a lengthy silence, she said, "I feel more guilty now than ever. You should be busy with your machines instead of squiring me to balls and parties, all of which must seem silly to you."

"Not at all. Don't think it's any different in Georgia. We have our society functions, too; it's the lifeblood of our ladies." Forcing cheerfulness, he added, "Besides, I don't think it will take much longer to bring your earl around."

Her gaze shifted from his. "You don't?"

"He said a lot of flattering things about you in the card room last night."

Joshua did not add that most of the comments were in response to his own loud praises. It was beyond his comprehension, but a cloud seemed to fog the earl's eyes concerning Constance. Only a fool could fail to love her.

"Did he?" she asked.

She sounded remarkably cool for a lady looking to snare a bridegroom. Puzzled, Joshua peered past the brim of her bonnet, hoping to see her expression; but she averted her head to watch a passing coach-and-four.

"Yes, ma'am, he truly did." Probably her little heart ached with the long wait for Lord Woodhead. Well, he'd talked with the earl sufficiently to have him pegged. Nothing was valuable unless someone else wanted it—then, *watch out*. Yes, he could handle Lord Blockhead. "No, Lady Constance, it won't be long now," he assured her again.

Several minutes passed before she spoke. "Joshua . . ."

The longing in her voice made his heart thump. "Yes, ma'am?"

"You mentioned that you and Joby fell in love with ladies at the same time, but it didn't work out for either of you, at least, not at first. I'm glad to know your friend found happiness, but . . . what about you?"

Joshua remained silent for the space of several heartbeats. "Her name is Charlene. I think I told you her family's estate bordered ours. We played together, her brothers and sisters and mine, all our lives. I always loved her and thought she loved me. We laughed together as much as we talked. But she was never able to understand my feelings about things, especially about Joby." He rubbed the back of his neck with his free hand. "When I returned from Canada, I discovered she and Luke were betrothed."

"Oh, no," Constance moaned. "I'm so sorry."

"Don't be," he said thinly. "I learned a great lesson from my experience. I decided only a fool makes the same mistake twice. That's why I'll never love another woman, not as long as I live."

The words sounded more full of conviction than he expected, especially in the light of his heart pounding *liar! liar!* with every breath. But it felt good to voice his old vow. Maybe with enough repetitions he'd come to believe it again.

"Oh, I see," Constance said in a whispery voice. "You have been hurt very badly. I—I can understand how you might feel that way."

Her bereft expression pained him. What a tender heart she possessed, to care for such as he.

"Don't trouble yourself about me, my dear," he said, and closed his fingers over hers. "I'm all right. It's *your* love life which concerns me, and I intend to do everything in my power to assure you'll have Lord Wood—I mean, Lord Oakwood's ring upon your finger before the month is gone."

He gave her a brave smile and was stunned to hear a sob in return.

"It—it is only that I'm so . . . happy," she explained.

The following days stretched into a week, then two. Lord Vincent's attentiveness toward Constance increased unmistakably. He brought her a cup of punch at the Smythesons' musicale; the afternoon following Lord Brasher's rout, he took her for a drive in Hyde Park; and at Almack's one Wednesday evening, he was first to sign her dance card. Whatever divinations Joshua had used to lead the earl onward, they appeared to be working.

Constance viewed Vincent's attentions as through murky waters. Only when Joshua came near did she trouble to appear animated. She couldn't let her guest think his efforts were wasted, for he was boyishly eager to please and shared every favorable comment the earl chanced to make about her, as if Vincent's words were priceless gems.

In her country estate in Sussex, Constance owned a cat that prided itself in catching mice, birds, and baby rabbits. The feline had an unfortunate way of sharing her victories with her human family and would often leave snatches of feathers and tragic carcasses at the back threshold.

Constance could no more present her true feelings to Joshua than she could punish the cat for following her nature. For the truth was, the young lady no longer had the slightest interest in Vincent. But she could hardly tell Joshua that, not when he toiled so valiantly for her.

It appeared the only solution was to bob along in this river of her own making until the earl made an offer or Joshua tired of playing the game and returned to his engines. He did, after all, have more important things to do. She tried repeatedly to persuade him not to stay for her, but he would have none of it.

How shocked he would be to know the reason she wanted him to leave was not only the one she told him—that his work was most urgent and vital—but that he'd caused her to see Vincent in a new light. Compared to Joshua, the earl appeared a hollow shell of a man, trivial and vain. His loftily spoken digs spun her nerves into spasms; his sardonic, private smiles made her scream inside.

She could not bear him.

Vincent himself was a paradox. The less interested she appeared in him, the more intrigued he became with her. Had she previously known the route to his heart lay in blank looks and impatient sighs, she could have been long wed, she supposed. But the knowledge came too late. Too late in more ways than one, for her heart belonged to another now.

So long as I live, I shall not love another woman, Joshua had said. If she'd entertained the slightest notion he cared for her, she'd have made an effort to prove him wrong. But Joshua only pretended to like her to entangle Vincent.

Thus, when the carriage she and Joshua and her cousins were traveling within pulled to a stop before the earl's house in Kent on the appointed Saturday morning, she felt dead inside . . . dead and resigned and directionless.

She struggled to cheer herself. Perhaps if she could make it through one more dreadful weekend of pulled emotions she could renew her persuasions upon Joshua to leave.

Failing that, she might try feigning madness. But then he would probably feel obligated to nurse her back to sanity. That was the kind of man he was.

Once inside the imposing, turreted house where Constance had spent many past holidays, the travelers were ushered into the library. Other guests had already gathered in the large, vaulted room, most of them having arrived the day before. Constance recognized two debutantes and their families; three gentlemen who claimed close friendship with Vincent; and several older individuals, all of them Vincent's relatives, excepting Sir Stanley Brickett.

Surprised to see the older gentleman who had twice called upon Hermine since asking her to waltz at the Hollingsworths' ball, Constance darted a look at her cousin. Hermine's breathing had quickened, and the indigo plume woven into her hair trembled dangerously.

Constance bent toward Hermine's ear. "It was thoughtful of the earl to invite Sir Brickett."

Hermine's hopeful expression hardened as she whispered back, "You can rest assured, he didn't do it for me. I saw the look in his eye when he noticed Stanley and me waltzing at the ball. He hopes to amuse himself at my expense. Well, it don't hurt me; let him gossip. I plan to enjoy myself."

Constance, feeling ire at another example of Vincent's nature, agreed she should.

Hermine's feather shook even more when the old man, his twinkling eyes rippling lines across his face, approached her. Without another glance toward her sisters or cousin, Hermine followed Sir Brickett to a distant sofa and settled beside him for a whispered coze. Winifred sniffed loudly and joined the group of the earl's elderly relatives lounging around the fire, and Beulah drifted after.

Constance and Joshua made their way to an empty pair of chairs near one of the debutante's families. She recalled the Addison name just in time to introduce young Lydia to him, as well as her parents, and they began to converse in the kind of generalities half-strangers employ. Within moments, Constance became uncomfortably aware of Lydia casting surreptitious, resentful looks in her direction. When their tardy host appeared and the young girl's demeanor became charged with animation, she understood the cause.

"Forgive my late arrival," said Vincent, after greeting everyone. Constance had to admit to herself he looked regal in leather breeches, tan jacket, and high boots. Lydia thought so, too, if her shining eyes were any indication. "I did mean to get an earlier start for I hoped to do some pheasant-shooting. What say you, gentlemen? Are we too late?"

The men's answers were favorable to this activity, much to the dismay of Miss Addison. "Oh, do you mean to leave us all day, then?" she cried, to the shame of her mother, who rapidly shushed her.

One noble eyebrow raised. "Ah, Miss—Miss—"

"Addison," she supplied, looking hurt that he'd forgotten. "Lydia."

"Oh, yes, of course. Not to worry; Cook has prepared an elegant picnic luncheon for the ladies to enjoy on the southmost lawn. A summerhouse and a pond are there; you will be able to feed the ducks."

"I had rather shoot pheasants," Lydia declared with a fetching look, causing her mother to cry out again.

The earl smiled faintly. "Another time, perhaps."

Before long, the men hurried off to change into suitable hunting attire and the ladies were left to entertain themselves. Constance endured the long, hazy day as cheerfully as she could. She ate cold chicken and pears on a bench near the pond. She fed the ducks and walked along the grounds. Later that afternoon, she stared at the high bedroom ceiling in her bedroom and failed to nap. And when the men returned with their trophies, she congratulated Joshua and Vincent for miraculously downing the same number of birds.

"It wasn't easy," Joshua explained, when he arrived at her bedroom door to escort her to dinner. "I matched him shot for shot, but he wouldn't stop; therefore I couldn't stop. I thought it important he realize I've as good an aim as he, for I don't believe he looks upon me too kindly. If poor Sir Brickett hadn't almost passed out from the heat and hunger, we might be there still."

Constance shivered at this reminder of Vincent's expertise with a gun. Was Joshua in danger? Surely even Vincent wouldn't shoot one of his guests, no matter how possessive he was. But the thought stole her appetite for the elegant dinner served in the dining hall, and she only pretended to eat as one course followed another.

The earl had made arrangements for an informal dance after dinner. A local chamber orchestra played waltz after waltz in the ballroom. After dancing first with Vincent, then with Joshua, then Vincent, then Joshua, she began to feel like a pheasant herself. At the indecently early hour of nine-thirty, she pled a headache and went to bed, much to the undisguised pleasure of Lydia Addison.

Joshua watched Constance leave with a heavy heart. While Vincent dawdled, she was pining away. He had to think of something to hurry things along. After dancing with each of Constance's cousins, he wandered down the hall and into the game room to plan. But the hard day of shooting in the hot sun had taken its toll. Instead of thinking, he sank into a deep leather chair and fell asleep.

He awoke in a befuddled state. The game room was dark as a cave. Some helpful servant must have seen him dozing and doused the lamps. For a moment he considered spending the remainder of the night in the chair; it would be easier than feeling his way upstairs and possibly walking into the wrong bedroom. But a sudden shooting pain in his neck convinced him otherwise, and he pushed to his feet with a deep sigh.

Extending his arms outward as one blind, he fumbled toward where he believed the door to be. As his eyes adjusted, the faint light from the windows brought the furniture into focus, and he began to walk more confidently. When he reached the hall, however, a discouraging darkness awaited him. Here there were no windows, and evidently Lord Blockhead did not instruct his servants to place helpful candles burning in the corridors throughout the night. It seemed a needless economy. With ceilings as lofty as these, the earl could leave pitch torches flaming in the sconces without causing a fire hazard. Was the man a miser as well as a fool?

Joshua returned to the game room, hoping to find a candle in one of the drawers. But as he approached a likely looking cabinet, furtive shadows passed outside the windows. Immediately he crouched. When he looked a second time, the figures had disappeared, disappeared so quickly he wondered if he'd imagined them. Perhaps his nerves were on edge, stimulated by the darkness of this house and the recent assault upon himself. Perhaps he was still asleep in the chair and this was only a dream.

No. He'd seen someone. He moved softly to one of the windows and opened it, flinching when the sash screeched. For a taut moment he waited without breathing. When no one jumped from the shrubs with a cudgel, he relaxed and threw his leg over the sill.

Keeping as close to the house as possible, he crept from bush to bush. After some time of this, his legs, already tired from a day of shooting, began to cramp. The building was larger than he thought. If he found nothing around the next corner, he'd return to the game room and sleep on the carpet with the fleas.

It was then he heard a noise. He stopped, listening as attentively as a hound sniffing game. The sounds were coming from the direction of the pond. He heard whispers, and if he was not mistaken, a feminine giggle. Feeling like a fool for imagining thieves, he straightened. And now he could see them: a man and woman scurrying across the lawn, heading for the summerhouse. A couple of the earl's guests, or perhaps a pair of servants, were having a midnight assignation, that was all. He turned back, then hesitated. Something about the height and build of the man . . .

A sudden, blinding rage washed through him. Without pausing for thought, Joshua dashed from the hedge and ran after the pair. The couple was too far away and too absorbed in one another to notice his pursuit. By the time he reached them, they had already entered the summerhouse and were half-reclined upon a wicker lounge when he burst through the door.

"You—you *cad!*" Joshua spat between gritted teeth. "You *bounder!*"

Lord Vincent looked up in mild surprise. Lydia Addison gasped and rolled from his arms to the floor.

"Good lord, man, you gave me quite a turn," said the earl.

"A turn, is it? I'll give you more than that! Get up, you stealer of innocent hearts!"

Vincent's smile did not reach his eyes. He remained motionless as he contemplated Joshua.

With amazing rapidity, Lydia struggled to her feet, smoothed her skirts, and patted her curls, all the while looking back and forth between the men. With a sudden dramatic movement, she seized Joshua's arm.

"Please, please do not fight over me," she begged, her eyes shining in delight. "If anything should happen to either of you, I would never forgive myself."

Joshua gave her a look of incomprehension and pulled his arm free. "Get up, Oakwood, or I swear I'll kick that smile off your face."

"No, no, please don't harm him on my account," Lydia cried loudly. "I love him."

"Be quiet, you silly goose," said Vincent, rising at last.

Joshua launched himself at the earl. Vincent sprawled backward with the American landing on top of him. The framed building shook as the men began rolling over and over, upsetting furniture and causing plaster to shower from the walls, while Lydia squealed and danced out of the way.

Using one another as props, the assailants climbed to their feet. Joshua, clutching Vincent's lapels and shaking him, panted, "Why have you done this? Does it give you pleasure to trounce upon a young lady's hopes and dreams? Does it make you feel like a man, you high-nosed lily?"

The earl brought his arms between Joshua's and struck outward, breaking the American's hold, then followed with a quick blow to his stomach. Joshua doubled over.

"How does the lily smell to you now?" barked Vincent,

following with an uppercut to Joshua's jaw. When Joshua sailed backward, the earl added, "I'm not obligated to any woman, you drum-brain. There's plenty of days for that."

Touching his jaw with careful fingers, Joshua glared at him from the floor. "But when you're ready, you expect her to be waiting, don't you?"

"I'll wait," Lydia called from the far side of the room. "I'll wait forever, if necessary."

Neither man looked at her. Vincent replied, "And why should she not? I have much to offer."

"You do," Lydia smiled. "You are worth the waiting, however long."

"In the meantime," Joshua growled, "she suffers. You think such a precious prize will wait endlessly for you?"

Vincent stood over him menacingly. "And what other choice does she have?"

"Oh, she has a choice. There's *always* a choice. In this instance, it's the offer of a man who really loves her."

"Meaning you, I suppose?" sneered the earl.

"Yes," Joshua said, stumbling to his feet with deliberate slowness, then punching the earl's nose with all his strength. "Meaning me."

"No!" screamed Lydia. "You are most appealing, sir, but I don't know anything about you! Don't hurt my dear earl, please! Have you broken his nose?"

"No one is talking about you!" cried Vincent through his hand, as blood spurted through his fingers. "We are speaking of Constance Cowald, you ninny!"

Lydia regarded them both in deep, astonished silence and then ran wailing into the night.

Constance awoke to the sound of rapid, furtive tapping upon her bedroom door. Bleary-eyed, she reached for the ormolu clock on her bedside table. It was a few minutes past two. She had only been able to fall asleep only an hour or s ago. What could be wrong at this time of the night? Was the house on fire?

The tappings continued as she struggled from the bed, lit the lamp, and fumbled into her dressing gown. Whoever was out there now whispered her name through the door.

"All right, all right, I'm coming," she said, too befuddled and depressed to disguise the annoyance in her voice. Thinking her caller was probably one of her cousins whose sleeplessness had devised another useless scheme with which to trick the earl, she reached for the latch and opened the door.

It was the earl. His hair stood in spikes on his head, his clothing hung in tatters, and a makeshift bandage crossed his nose.

"Bay I cub in?" he asked.

Too astonished to protest the lateness of the hour or the unseemliness of his request, she stood aside. He strolled across the threshold. She began to close the door, then hesitated, leaving it slightly ajar. Observing her caution, he chuckled grimly.

"I assure you, Constance, you have nudding to fear from be."

"What has happened to you, Vincent? Why are you here?"

"I've cub for the highest of reasons. I've cub to ask you to be by wife."

Constance felt her heart stop. *"What?"*

At that moment, the door swung open and bounced against the wall. "So there you are, you high-born jacksnipe," Joshua said bitterly. "What do you mean, breaking into Constance's bedroom like this?"

"Joshua!" she cried, rushing to him. His eye was blackening, he had a bruise on his chin, and he held one arm pressed to his stomach. When she touched him, he flinched. She pressed a hand to her mouth and backed away.

"It's too late, Turner," Vincent said. "I've just asked her to be by wife."

"Oh, no, you don't," Joshua said. "Not before I have *my*

say." He swung to face Constance. "I know how much you
care for this man, and I wouldn't hurt you for the world. I did
everything I could to make him want to marry you. In spite
of how I felt about you, I *thought* I could let you marry him.
But now that I've seen what he really is, I can't let you shackle
yourself to a scoundrel who's going to break your heart into
little pieces for the rest of your life. You deserve better."

"I'b no scoundrel," the earl protested. "I'b a ban with nor
bal appetites. I suppose you're going to say you're different.
He's not, Constance. He's a ban, just like be."

Joshua stepped closely to Constance. "Don't listen to him.
He knows I'm offering for you, and that's the only reason he's
declaring himself tonight. Otherwise, he'd wait until you both
have gray hair while *he* plays around. And now he expects to
wed you while he *continues* to play. Well, honey, I'm not saying I'm perfect; but I can promise you my undivided heart."

"Bosh," said the earl with a pained expression, as he tenderly felt his nose. "This ban is full of bealy-bouthed nonsense. Rebebber our fathers' wishes, Constance. Look around
you and see what can be yours and our children's. Don't trade
it for a busket and a bule."

"It *would* mean a different kind of life," Joshua admitted.
"Not so soft as this one, but certainly not what *he's* describing.
There'll be traveling and hotel living until I've finished my
research, of course. But then we can go home, home to Savannah. I'm not a poor man. We can build our own place, start
our own bloodline in the new country. And no slaves, I promise. What do you say, sweet Constance?"

"Don't fall for his pretty words," Vincent warned. "He will
bake a bockery of you—"

"Stop it!" Constance cried. "Stop it, both of you! Just—just
stop!"

She walked toward the window—a place where neither of
them stood—and pressed the heels of her hands against her
eyes, trying but not entirely able to shut away the sight of the
two men. For the past few moments she had been looking

back and forth between them in open-mouthed astonishment. Now they watched her as cautiously as they would a half-mad snake. She was further discommoded to realize an audience was gathering in the hall—an audience that consisted of her cousins Hermine and Beulah. And now old Sir Brickett, wrapped in a tartan robe, toddled to join them. Humiliation and embarrassment poured through her in a deluge.

"How—how can you do this to me?" she said in a thin, pitiable voice. "This is the most unfeeling jest that could ever be turned upon a woman."

A deep silence fell as Joshua and Vincent exchanged glances of surprise and consternation.

"Dear lady, look at us," Joshua said, appearing almost as hurt and defenseless as he had the first time she'd seen him. "Does this truly seem a jest to you?"

Constance timidly studied him, then the earl, who smiled with growing hope. Her spirits slowly but steadily began to rise.

"You are both . . . asking me to marry you?" she asked.

"Yes, ma'am," Joshua affirmed.

"Yes, ba'ab," Vincent echoed. "I bean, yes."

In the hall, Hermine and Beulah beamed at one another like suns. Unseen down the corridor, Winifred was heard to call, "What's afoot?" and within seconds had joined her sisters while still knotting the tie of her wrapper. Sir Brickett immediately shushed her into silence.

Constance was only dimly aware of them. Lowering her eyes, she said fishingly, "Neither one of you has mentioned the most important thing of all."

"I love you," Vincent said immediately.

Joshua's eyes grew round and hurt at being so quickly beaten. "Surely you can't doubt my feelings, Constance. He's more practiced at saying the right things, but I—I feel love for you right down to my bones."

Constance tried and failed to subdue her smile. She walked close to Vincent. His chin rose; his eyes glimmered in triumph.

"Thank you Vincent," she said quietly. "You have honored me greatly, but I must decline. I love another."

And so saying, she hurried to Joshua and threw her arms around his neck. After an initial yelp of pain, he returned her embrace and lowered his lips to hers.

"You've chosen well," said Vincent to anyone who might be listening as he exited, "for I *was* only jesting. I ab not a ban for barrying."

Hermine could not resist clapping her hands after he passed by. " 'Tis better than a play!"

"Young love," Winifred said fondly, wiping a tear from her eye as she watched the extended embrace between Constance and Joshua. "How well I remember it. Nothing in life is better and how unfortunate you never experienced it, my sisters."

"Um, don't know about that," said Sir Brickett, eyeing Hermine bawdily. "Mature love can be just as exciting."

"Blither and blather as long as you will," droned Beulah, shuffling toward her bedroom and yawning. "I'm going to bed."

About the Author

Marcy Stewart lives with her family in Dayton, Tennessee. She is the author of three Zebra regency romances: CHARITY'S GAMBIT, MY LORD FOOTMAN and LORD MERLYN'S MAGIC. Her next Zebra regency romance, DARBY'S ANGEL, will be published in July 1996. Marcy loves hearing from her readers and you may write to her c/o Zebra Books. Please include a self-addressed stamped envelope if you wish a response.

WATCH FOR THESE ZEBRA REGENCIES
NEXT MONTH!

LADY STEPHANIE   (0-8217-5341-X, $4.50)
by Jeanne Savery
Lady Stephanie Morris has only one true love: the family estate she has
managed ever since her mother died. But then Lord Anthony Rider
arrives on her estate, claiming he has plans for both the land and the
woman. Stephanie soon realizes she's fallen in love with a man whose
sensual caresses will plunge her into a world of peril and intrigue . . .
a man as dangerous as he is irresistible.

BRIGHTON BEAUTY   (0-8217-5340-1, $4.50)
by Marilyn Clay
Chelsea Grant, pretty and poor, naively takes school friend Alayna
Marchmont's place and spends a month in the country. The devastating
man had sailed from Honduras to claim his promised bride, Miss
Marchmont. An affair of the heart may lead to disaster . . . unless a
resourceful Brighton beauty finds a way to stop a masquerade and keep
a lord's love.

LORD DIABLO'S DEMISE   (0-8217-5338-X, $4.50)
by Meg-Lynn Roberts
The sinfully handsome Lord Harry Glendower was a gambler and the
black sheep of his family. About to be forced into a marriage of con-
venience, the devilish fellow engineered his own demise, never having
dreamed that faking his death would lead him to the heavenly refuge
of spirited heiress Gwyn Morgan, the daughter of a physician.

A PERILOUS ATTRACTION   (0-8217-5339-8, $4.50)
by Dawn Aldridge Poore
Alissa Morgan is stunned when a frantic passenger thrusts her baby into
Alissa's arms and flees, having heard rumors that a notorious highwayman posed a threat to their coach. Handsome stranger Hugh Sebastian
secretly possesses the treasured necklace the highwayman seeks and
volunteers to pose as Alissa's husband to save her reputation. With
lost baby and missing necklace in their care, the couple embarks on
journey into peril—and passion.

*Available wherever paperbacks are sold, or order direct from the
Publisher. Send cover price plus 50¢ per copy for mailing and
handling to Penguin USA, P.O. Box 999, c/o Dept. 17109, Bergenfield, NJ 07621. Residents of New York and Tennessee must
include sales tax. DO NOT SEND CASH.*